THE

ADVENTURES OF TOM SAWYER.

MARK TWAIN 100TH ANNIVERSARY COLLECTION

THE ADVENTURES

OF

TOM SAWYER

BY

MARK TWAIN

1876

ILLUSTRATED WORKS OF MARK TWAIN
PUBLISHED BY

SEAWOLF PRESS

THE ADVENTURES OF TOM SAWYER
Copyright ©2018 by SeaWolf Press

PUBLISHED BY SEAWOLF PRESS
All rights reserved. No part of this book may be duplicated in any manner what-
soever without the express written consent of the publisher, except in the form of
brief excerpts or quotations used for the purposes of review.
Printed in the U.S.A.

FIRST EDITION INFORMATION
The first edition was published by The American Publishing Company in 1876.
This book uses the original spellings and punctuation (or lack thereof)
from the first edition book.

SeaWolf Press
P.O. Box 961
Orinda, CA 94563
Email: support@seawolfpress.com
Web: http://www.SeaWolfPress.com

About *The Adventures of Tom Sawyer*
Mark Twain created the memorable characters Tom Sawyer and Huckleberry
Finn drawing from the characters of boys he grew up with in Missouri. Set by
the Mississippi River in the 1840's, it follows these boys as they get into predicament after predicament. Tom's classic whitewashing of the fence has become part
of American legend, and the book paints a nostalgic picture of life in the middle
of the nineteenth century. The boys run away from home to an island in the river,
chase Injun Joe and his treasure, and Tom gets trapped in a cave for days. The
book is one of Twain's most beloved books.

About Mark Twain
Born Samuel Langhorne Clemens in 1835, Mark Twain is one of America's most
beloved authors. Raised in Hannibal, Missouri he used the Mississippi River as
the setting for many of his stories. He was a riverboat pilot on this river where
he picked up his pen name 'Mark Twain' which was called out to indicate a river
depth of 2 fathoms. Twain went out west to Gold Rush country and used that
experience as the source of more stories, including his famous *The Celebrated
Jumping Frog of Calaveras County*. His travels abroad led to other books, including *The Innocents Abroad*, *A Tramp Abroad*, and *Following the Equator*. His most
well-known books are *The Adventures of Tom Sawyer* and *Adventures of Huckleberry
Finn*, making those two characters part of our American culture. Born during
Halley's comet 1835 visit, he predicted he would "go out with it" and died in 1910
during the comet's next visit. He has been called America's greatest humorist and
father of American literature.

About the Mark Twain 100th **Anniversary Collection**
SeaWolf Press is proud to release the works of Mark Twain to honor the 100th
anniversary of his death in 1910. During his career, he produced more than 50
books on a wide variety of subjects. Fonts common 100 years ago are used and
the format and illustrations from the first editions are reproduced--recreating
the feeling of reading the original book when it was published.

Books by Mark Twain

The Celebrated Jumping Frog of Calaveras County (1867)

The Innocents Abroad (1869)

Mark Twain's (Burlesque) Autobiography and First Romance (1871)

Roughing It (1872)

The Gilded Age: A Tale of Today (1873)

Sketches New and Old (1875)

Old Times on the Mississippi (1876)

The Adventures of Tom Sawyer (1876)

Ah Sin (with Bret Harte) (1876)

A True Story and the Recent Carnival of Crime (1877)

Punch, Brothers, Punch! and other Sketches (1878)

A Tramp Abroad (1880)

The Prince and the Pauper (1882)

The Stolen White Elephant(1882)

Life on the Mississippi (1883)

Adventures of Huckleberry Finn (1884)

A Connecticut Yankee in King Arthur's Court (1889)

Merry Tales (1892)

The American Claimant (1892)

The £1,000,000 Bank Note and Other New Stories (1893)

Pudd'nhead Wilson and Those Extraordinary Twins(1894)

Tom Sawyer Abroad (1894)

Personal Recollections of Joan of Arc (1896)

Tom Sawyer, Detective (1896)

Following the Equator (1897)

How to Tell a Story and other Essays (1897)

The Man That Corrupted Hadleyburg (1900)

A Double Barrelled Detective Story (1902)

My debut as a Literary Person(1903)

A Dog's Tale (1903)

Extracts from Adam's Diary (1904)

King Leopold's Soliloquy (1905)

Eve's Diary (1906)

The $30,000 Bequest and Other Stories (1906)

What Is Man? (1906)

A Horse's Tale (1907)

Christian Science (1907)

Is Shakespeare Dead? (1907)

Captain Stormfield's Visit to Heaven (1909)

Mark Twain's Speeches(1910)

The Mysterious Stranger (1916)

Europe and Elsewhere(1923)

Mark Twain's Autobiography (1924)

To
MY WIFE
THIS BOOK
IS
AFFECTIONATELY DEDICATED.

PREFACE

Most of the adventures recorded in this book really occurred; one or two were experiences of my own, the rest those of boys who were schoolmates of mine. Huck Finn is drawn from life; Tom Sawyer also, but not from an individual—he is a combination of the characteristics of three boys whom I knew, and therefore belongs to the composite order of architecture.

The odd superstitions touched upon were all prevalent among children and slaves in the West at the period of this story—that is to say, thirty or forty years ago.

Although my book is intended mainly for the entertainment of boys and girls, I hope it will not be shunned by men and women on that account, for part of my plan has been to try to pleasantly remind adults of what they once were themselves, and of how they felt and thought and talked, and what queer enterprises they sometimes engaged in.

THE AUTHOR

HARTFORD, 1876.

CONTENTS.

CHAPTER XXV.

CHAPTER XXVI.

CHAPTER XXVII.

CHAPTER XXVIII.

CHAPTER XXIX.

CHAPTER XXX.

CHAPTER XXXI.

CHAPTER XXXII.

CHAPTER XXXIII.

CHAPTER XXXIV.

CHAPTER XXXV.

ILLUSTRATIONS.

THE ADVENTURES OF TOM SAWYER.

CHAPTER I.

"TOM!"

No answer.

"TOM!"

No answer.

"What's gone with that boy, I wonder? You TOM!"

No answer.

The old lady pulled her spectacles down and looked over them about the room; then she put them up and looked out under them. She seldom or never looked *through* them for so small a thing as a boy; they were her state pair, the pride of her heart, and were built for "style," not service—she could have seen through a pair of stove lids just as well. She looked perplexed for a moment, and then said, not fiercely, but still loud enough for the furniture to hear:

"Well, I lay if I get hold of you I'll—"

She did not finish, for by this time she was bending down and punching under the bed with the broom, and so she needed breath to punctuate the punches with. She resurrected nothing but the cat.

"I never did see the beat of that boy!"

TOM AT HOME.

She went to the open door and stood in it and looked out among the tomato vines and "jimpson" weeds that constituted the garden. No Tom. So she lifted up her voice at an angle calculated for distance, and shouted:

"Y-o-u-u *Tom!*"

There was a slight noise behind her and she turned just in time to

seize a small boy by the slack of his roundabout and arrest his flight.

"There! I might 'a' thought of that closet. What you been doing in there?"

"Nothing."

"Nothing! Look at your hands. And look at your mouth. What *is* that truck?"

"*I* don't know, aunt."

"Well, *I* know. It's jam—that's what it is. Forty times I've said if you didn't let that jam alone I'd skin you. Hand me that switch."

The switch hovered in the air—the peril was desperate—

"My! Look behind you, aunt!"

The old lady whirled round, and snatched her skirts out of danger. The lad fled, on the instant, scrambled up the high board-fence, and disappeared over it.

AUNT POLLY BEGUILED.

His aunt Polly stood surprised a moment, and then broke into a gentle laugh.

"Hang the boy, can't I never learn anything? Ain't he played me tricks enough like that for me to be looking out for him by this time? But old fools is the biggest fools there is. Can't learn an old dog new tricks, as the saying is. But my goodness, he never plays them alike, two days, and how is a body to know what's coming? He 'pears to know just how long he can torment me before I get my dander up, and he knows if he can make out to put me off for a minute or make me laugh, it's all down again and I can't hit him a lick. I ain't doing my duty by that boy, and that's the Lord's truth, goodness knows.

Spare the rod and spile the child, as the Good Book says. I'm a lay-ing up sin and suffering for us both, *I* know. He's full of the Old Scratch, but laws-a-me! he's my own dead sister's boy, poor thing, and I ain't got the heart to lash him, somehow. Every time I let him off, my conscience does hurt me so, and every time I hit him my old heart most breaks. Well-a-well, man that is born of woman is of few days and full of trouble, as the Scripture says, and I reckon it's so. He'll play hookey this evening,[1] and I'll just be obleeged to make him work, tomorrow, to punish him. It's mighty hard to make him work Saturdays, when all the boys is having holiday, but he hates work more than he hates anything else, and I've *got* to do some of my duty by him, or I'll be the ruination of the child."

Tom did play hookey, and he had a very good time. He got back home barely in season to help Jim, the small colored boy, saw next-day's wood and split the kindlings before supper—at least he was there in time to tell his adventures to Jim while Jim did three-fourths of the work. Tom's younger brother (or rather, half-brother) Sid, was already through with his part of the work (picking up chips) for he was a quiet boy, and had no adventurous, troublesome ways.

While Tom was eating his supper, and stealing sugar as opportu-nity offered, Aunt Polly asked him questions that were full of guile,

A GOOD OPPORTUNITY

and very deep—for she wanted to trap him into damaging revealments. Like many other simple-hearted souls, it was her pet vanity to believe she was endowed with a tal-ent for dark and mysteri-ous diplomacy, and she loved to contemplate her most transparent devices as marvels of low cunning. Said she:

"Tom, it was middling warm in school, warn't it?"

"Yes'm."

"Powerful warm, warn't it?"

"Yes'm."

[1] South-western for "afternoon."

"Didn't you want to go in a-swimming, Tom?"

A bit of a scare shot through Tom—a touch of uncomfortable suspicion. He searched Aunt Polly's face, but it told him nothing. So he
said:

"No'm—well, not very much." The old lady reached out her hand
and felt Tom's shirt, and said:

"But you ain't too warm now, though." And it flattered her to reflect that she had discovered that the shirt was dry without anybody
knowing that that was what she had in her mind. But in spite of her,
Tom knew where the wind lay, now. So he forestalled what might be
the next move:

"Some of us pumped on our heads—mine's damp yet. See?"

Aunt Polly was vexed to think she had overlooked that bit of
circumstantial evidence, and missed a trick. Then she had a new
inspiration:

"Tom, you didn't have to undo your shirt collar where I sewed it,
to pump on your head, did you? Unbutton your jacket!"

The trouble vanished out of Tom's face. He opened his jacket. His
shirt collar was securely sewed.

"Bother! Well, go 'long with you. I'd made sure you'd played
hookey and been a-swimming. But I forgive ye, Tom. I reckon you're
a kind of a singed cat, as the saying is—better'n you look. *This* time."

She was half sorry her sagacity had miscarried, and half glad that
Tom had stumbled into obedient conduct for once.

But Sidney said:

"Well, now, if I didn't think you sewed his collar with white
thread, but it's black."

"Why, I did sew it with white! Tom!"

But Tom did not wait for the rest. As he went out at the door he said:

"Siddy, I'll lick you for that."

In a safe place Tom examined two large needles which were thrust
into the lappels of his jacket, and had thread bound about them—one
needle carried white thread and the other black. He said:

"She'd never noticed if it hadn't been for Sid. Confound it! sometimes she sews it with white, and sometimes she sews it with black. I

wish to geeminy she'd stick to one or t'other—*I* can't keep the run of 'em. But I bet you I'll lam Sid for that. I'll learn him!"

He was not the Model Boy of the village. He knew the model boy very well though—and loathed him.

Within two minutes, or even less, he had forgotten all his troubles. Not because his troubles were one whit less heavy and bitter to him than a man's are to a man, but because a new and powerful interest bore them down and drove them out of his mind for the time—just as men's misfortunes are forgotten in the excitement of new enterprises. This new interest was a valued novelty in whistling, which he had just acquired from a negro, and he was suffering to practice it undisturbed. It consisted in a peculiar bird-like turn, a sort of liquid warble, produced by touching the tongue to the roof of the mouth at short intervals in the midst of the music—the reader probably remembers how to do it, if he has ever been a boy. Diligence and attention soon gave him the knack of it, and he strode down the street with his mouth full of harmony and his soul full of gratitude. He felt much as an astronomer feels who has discovered a new planet—no doubt, as far as strong, deep, unalloyed pleasure is concerned, the advantage was with the boy, not the astronomer.

The summer evenings were long. It was not dark, yet. Presently Tom checked his whistle. A stranger was before him—a boy a shade larger than himself. A new comer of any age or either sex was an impressive curiosity in the poor little shabby village of St. Petersburgh. This boy was well-dressed, too—well-dressed on a week-day. This was simply astounding. His cap was a dainty thing, his close-buttoned blue cloth roundabout was new and natty, and so were his pantaloons. He had shoes on—and it was only Friday. He even wore a necktie, a bright bit of ribbon. He had a citified air about him that ate into Tom's vitals. The more Tom stared at the splendid marvel, the higher he turned up his nose at his finery and the shabbier and shabbier his own outfit seemed to him to grow. Neither boy spoke. If one moved, the other moved—but only sidewise, in a circle; they kept face to face and eye to eye all the time. Finally Tom said:

"I can lick you!"

"I'd like to see you try it."

"Well, I can do it."

"No you can't, either."

"Yes I can."

"No you can't."

"I can."

"You can't."

"Can!"

"Can't!"

An uncomfortable pause. Then Tom said:

"What's your name?"

"'Tisn't any of your business, maybe."

"Well I 'low I'll *make* it my business."

"Well why don't you?"

"If you say much I will."

"Much—much—*much*. There now."

"Oh, you think you're mighty smart, *don't* you? I could lick you with one hand tied behind me, if I wanted to."

"Well why don't you *do* it? You *say* you can do it."

"Well I *will*, if you fool with me."

"Oh yes—I've seen whole families in the same fix."

"Smarty! You think you're *some*, now, *don't* you? Oh what a hat!"

"You can lump that hat if you don't like it. I dare you to knock it off—and anybody that'll take a dare will suck eggs."

"You're a liar!"

"You're another."

"You're a fighting liar and dasn't take it up."

"Aw—take a walk!"

"Say—if you give me much more of your sass I'll take and bounce a rock off'n your head."

"Oh, of *course* you will."

"Well I *will*."

"Well why don't you *do* it then? What do you keep *saying* you will for? Why don't you *do* it? It's because you're afraid."

"I *ain't* afraid."

"You are."

"I ain't."

"You are."

Another pause, and more eyeing and sidling around each other. Presently they were shoulder to shoulder. Tom said:

"Get away from here!"

"Go away yourself!"

"I won't."

"*I* won't either."

So they stood, each with a foot placed at an angle as a brace, and

WHO'S AFRAID?

both shoving with might and main, and glowering at each other with hate. But neither could get an advantage. After struggling till both were hot and flushed, each relaxed his strain with watchful caution, and Tom said:

"You're a coward and a pup. I'll tell my big brother on you, and he can thrash you with his little finger, and I'll make him do it, too."

"What do I care for your big brother? I've got a brother that's bigger than he is—and what's more, he can throw him over that fence, too." [Both brothers were imaginary.]

"That's a lie."

"*Your* saying so don't make it so."

Tom drew a line in the dust with his big toe, and said:

"I dare you to step over that, and I'll lick you till you can't stand up. Anybody that'll take a dare will steal sheep."

The new boy stepped over promptly, and said:

"Now you said you'd do it, now let's see you do it."

"Don't you crowd me now; you better look out."

"Well, you *said* you'd do it—why don't you do it?"

"By jingo! for two cents I *will* do it."

The new boy took two broad coppers out of his pocket and held them out with derision. Tom struck them to the ground. In an instant both boys were rolling and tumbling in the dirt, gripped together like cats; and for the space of a minute they tugged and tore at each other's hair and clothes, punched and scratched each other's noses, and covered themselves with dust and glory. Presently the confusion took form and through the fog of battle Tom appeared, seated astride the new boy, and pounding him with his fists.

"Holler 'nuff!" said he.

The boy only struggled to free himself. He was crying,—mainly from rage.

"Holler 'nuff!"—and the pounding went on.

At last the stranger got out a smothered "'Nuff!" and Tom let him up and said:

"Now that'll learn you. Better look out who you're fooling with next time."

The new boy went off brushing the dust from his clothes, sobbing, snuffling, and occasionally looking back and shaking his head and threatening what he would do to Tom the "next time he caught him out." To which Tom responded with jeers, and started off in high feather, and as soon as his back was turned the new boy snatched up a stone, threw it and hit him between the shoulders and then turned tail and ran like an antelope. Tom chased the traitor home, and thus found out where he lived. He then held a position at the gate for some time, daring the enemy to come outside, but the enemy only made faces at him through the window and declined. At last the enemy's mother appeared, and called Tom a bad, vicious, vulgar child, and ordered him away. So he went away; but he said he "'lowed" to "lay" for that boy.

He got home pretty late, that night, and when he climbed cautiously in at the window, he uncovered an ambuscade, in the person of his aunt; and when she saw the state his clothes were in her resolution to turn his Saturday holiday into captivity at hard labor became adamantine in its firmness.

CHAPTER II.

JIM.

SATURDAY morning was come, and all the summer world was bright and fresh, and brimming with life. There was a song in every heart; and if the heart was young the music issued at the lips. There was cheer in every face and a spring in every step. The locust trees were in bloom and the fragrance of the blossoms filled the air. Cardiff Hill, beyond the village and above it, was green with vegetation, and it lay just far enough away to seem a Delectable Land, dreamy, reposeful, and inviting.

Tom appeared on the sidewalk with a bucket of whitewash and a long-handled brush. He surveyed the fence, and all gladness left him and a deep melancholy settled down upon his spirit. Thirty yards of board fence nine feet high. Life to him seemed hollow, and existence but a burden. Sighing he dipped his brush and passed it along the topmost plank; repeated the operation; did it again; compared the insignificant whitewashed streak with the far-reaching continent of unwhitewashed fence, and sat down on a tree-box discouraged. Jim came skipping out at the gate with a tin pail, and singing "Buffalo

Gals." Bringing water from the town pump had always been hateful work in Tom's eyes, before, but now it did not strike him so. He remembered that there was company at the pump. White, mulatto, and negro boys and girls were always there waiting their turns, resting, trading playthings, quarreling, fighting, skylarking. And he remembered that although the pump was only a hundred and fifty yards off, Jim never got back with a bucket of water under an hour—and even then somebody generally had to go after him. Tom said:

"Say, Jim, I'll fetch the water if you'll whitewash some."

Jim shook his head and said:

"Can't, Mars Tom. Ole missis, she tole me I got to go an' git dis water an' not stop foolin' roun' wid anybody. She say she spec' Mars Tom gwine to ax me to whitewash, an' so she tole me go 'long an' 'tend to my own business—she 'lowed *she'd* 'tend to de whitewashin'."

"Oh, never you mind what she said, Jim. That's the way she always talks. Gimme the bucket—I won't be gone only a minute. *She* won't ever know."

"Oh, I dasn't Mars Tom. Ole missis she'd take an' tar de head off'n me. 'Deed she would."

"*She!* She never licks anybody—whacks 'em over the head with her thimble—and who cares for that, I'd like to know. She talks awful, but talk don't hurt—anyways it don't if she don't cry. Jim, I'll give you a marvel. I'll give you a white alley!"

Jim began to waver.

"White alley, Jim! And it's a bully taw."

"My! Dat's a mighty gay marvel, *I* tell you! But Mars Tom I's powerful 'fraid ole missis—"

"And besides, if you will I'll show you my sore toe."

Jim was only human—this attraction was too much for him. He put down his pail, took the white alley, and bent over the toe with absorbing interest while the bandage was being unwound. In another moment he was flying down the street with his pail and a tingling rear, Tom was whitewashing with vigor, and Aunt Polly was retiring from the field with a slipper in her hand and triumph in her eye.

But Tom's energy did not last. He began to think of the fun he had planned for this day, and his sorrows multiplied. Soon the free boys would come tripping along on all sorts of delicious expeditions, and they would make a world of fun of him for having to work—the very thought of it burnt him like fire. He got out his worldly wealth and examined it—bits of toys, marbles, and trash; enough to buy an exchange of *work*, maybe, but not half enough to buy so much as half an hour of pure freedom. So he returned his straightened means to his pocket, and gave up the idea of trying to buy the boys. At this dark and hopeless moment an inspiration burst upon him! Nothing less than a great, magnificent inspiration.

TENDIN' TO BUSINESS.

He took up his brush and went tranquilly to work. Ben Rogers hove in sight presently—the very boy, of all boys, whose ridicule he had been dreading. Ben's gait was the hop-skip-and-jump—proof enough that his heart was light and his anticipations high. He was eating an apple, and giving a long, melodious whoop, at intervals, followed by a deep-toned ding-dong-dong, ding-dong-dong, for he was personating a steamboat. As he drew near, he slackened speed, took the middle of the street, leaned far over to starboard and rounded to ponderously and with laborious pomp and circumstance—for he was personating the "Big Missouri," and considered himself to be drawing nine feet of water. He was boat, and captain, and engine-bells combined, so he had to imagine himself standing on his own hurricane-deck giving the orders and executing them:

"Stop her, sir! Ting-a-ling-ling!" The headway ran almost out and he drew up slowly toward the side-walk.

"Ship up to back! Ting-a-ling-ling!" His arms straightened and stiffened down his sides.

"Set her back on the stabboard! Ting-a-ling-ling! Chow! ch-chow-wow! Chow!" His right hand, meantime, describing stately circles,—for it was representing a forty-foot wheel.

"Let her go back on the labboard! Ting-a-ling-ling! Chow-ch-chow-chow!" The left hand began to describe circles.

"Stop the stabboard! Ting-a-ling-ling! Stop the labbord! Come ahead on the stabboard! Stop her! Let your outside turn over slow! Ting-a-ling-ling! Chow-ow-ow! Get out that head-line! *Lively* now! Come—out with your spring-line—what're you about there! Take a turn round that stump with the bight of it! Stand by that stage, now—let her go! Done with the engines, sir! Ting-a-ling-ling! *Sh't! s'h't! sh't!*" (trying the gauge-cocks.)

Tom went on whitewashing—paid no attention to the steamboat. Ben stared a moment and then said:

"Hi-*yi*! *You're* up a stump, ain't you!"

No answer. Tom surveyed his last touch with the eye of an artist; then he gave his brush another gentle sweep and surveyed the result, as before. Ben ranged up alongside of him. Tom's mouth watered for the apple, but he stuck to his work. Ben said:

"Hello, old chap, you got to work, hey?"

Tom wheeled suddenly and said:

"Why it's you Ben! I warn't noticing."

"Say—*I'm* going in a swimming, *I* am. Don't you wish you could? But of course you'd druther *work*—wouldn't you? Course you would!"

Tom contemplated the boy a bit, and said:

"What do you call work?"

"Why ain't *that* work?"

Tom resumed his whitewashing, and answered carelessly:

"Well, maybe it is, and maybe it aint. All I know, is, it suits Tom Sawyer."

"Oh come, now, you don't mean to let on that you *like* it?"

The brush continued to move.

"Like it? Well I don't see why I oughtn't to like it. Does a boy get a chance to whitewash a fence every day?"

That put the thing in a new light. Ben stopped nibbling his apple. Tom swept his brush daintily back and forth—stepped back to note the effect—added a touch here and there—criticised the effect again—Ben watching every move and getting more and more interested, more and more absorbed. Presently he said:

"Say, Tom, let *me* whitewash a little."

Tom considered, was about to consent; but he altered his mind:

'AIN'T THAT WORK?

"No—no—I reckon it wouldn't hardly do, Ben. You see, Aunt Polly's awful particular about this fence—right here on the street, you know—but if it was the back fence I wouldn't mind and *she* wouldn't. Yes, she's awful particular about this fence; it's got to be done very careful; I reckon there ain't one boy in a thousand, maybe two thousand, that can do it the way it's got to be done.

"No—is that so? Oh come, now—lemme just try. Only just a little—I'd let *you*, if you was me, Tom."

"Ben, I'd like to, honest injun; but Aunt Polly—well Jim wanted to do it, but she wouldn't let him; Sid wanted to do it, and she wouldn't let Sid. Now don't you see how I'm fixed? If you was to tackle this fence and anything was to happen to it—"

"Oh, shucks, I'll be just as careful. Now lemme try. Say—I'll give you the core of my apple."

"Well, here—No, Ben, now don't. I'm afeard—"

"I'll give you *all* of it!"

Tom gave up the brush with reluctance in his face but alacrity in his heart. And while the late steamer "Big Missouri" worked and sweated in the sun, the retired artist sat on a barrel in the shade close by, dangled his legs, munched his apple, and planned the slaughter of more innocents. There was no lack of material; boys happened along every little while; they came to jeer, but remained to white-wash. By the time Ben was fagged out, Tom had traded the next chance to Billy Fisher for a kite, in good repair; and when *he* played out, Johnny Miller bought in for a dead rat and a string to swing it with—and so on, and so on, hour after hour. And when the middle of the afternoon came, from being a poor poverty, stricken boy in the morning, Tom was literally rolling in wealth. He had beside the things before mentioned, twelve marbles, part of a jews-harp, a piece of blue bottle-glass to look through, a spool cannon, a key that wouldn't unlock anything, a fragment of chalk, a glass stopper of a decanter, a tin soldier, a couple of tadpoles, six firecrackers, a kitten with only one eye, a brass doorknob, a dog-collar—but no dog—the handle of a knife, four pieces of orange-peel, and a dilapidated old window-sash.

He had had a nice, good, idle time all the while—plenty of company—and the fence had three coats of whitewash on it! If he hadn't run out of whitewash, he would have bankrupted every boy in the village.

Tom said to himself that it was not such a hollow world, after all. He had discovered a great law of human action, without knowing it—namely, that in order to make a man or a boy covet a thing, it is only necessary to make the thing difficult to attain. If he had been a great and wise philosopher, like the writer of this book, he would now have comprehended that Work consists of whatever a body is *obliged* to do, and that Play consists of whatever a body is not obliged to do. And this would help him to understand why constructing artificial flowers or performing on a treadmill is work, while rolling ten-pins or climbing Mont Blanc is only amusement. There are wealthy gentlemen in England who drive four-horse passenger-coaches twenty

AMUSEMENT.

or thirty miles on a daily line, in the summer, because the privilege costs them considerable money; but if they were offered wages for the service, that would turn it into work and then they would resign.

The boy mused a while over the substantial change which had taken place in his worldly circumstances, and then wended toward headquarters to report.

CHAPTER III

BECKY THATCHER

TOM presented himself before Aunt Polly, who was sitting by an open window in a pleasant rearward apartment, which was bedroom, breakfast-room, dining-room, and library, combined. The balmy, summer air, the restful quiet, the odor of the flowers, and the drowsing murmur of the bees had had their effect, and she was nodding over her knitting— for she had no company but the cat, and it was asleep in her lap. Her spectacles were propped up on her gray head for safety. She had thought that of course Tom had deserted long ago, and she wondered at seeing him place himself in her power again in this intrepid way. He said: "Mayn't I go and play now, aunt?"

"What, a'ready? How much have you done?"

"It's all done, aunt."

"Tom, don't lie to me—I can't bear it."

"I ain't, aunt; it *is* all done."

Aunt Polly placed small trust in such evidence. She went out to see for herself; and she would have been content to find twenty per cent of Tom's statement true. When she found the entire fence whitewashed, and not only whitewashed but elaborately coated and recoated, and even a streak added to the ground, her astonishment was almost unspeakable. She said:

"Well, I never! There's no getting round it, you *can* work when your'e a mind to, Tom." And then she diluted the compliment by adding, "But it's powerful seldom you're a mind to, I'm bound to say. Well, go 'long and play; but mind you get back sometime in a week, or I'll tan you."

She was so overcome by the splendor of his achievement that she took him into the closet and selected a choice apple and delivered it

PAYING OFF.

to him, along with an improving lecture upon the added value and flavor a treat took to itself when it came without sin through virtuous effort. And while she closed with a happy-scriptural flourish, he "hooked" a doughnut.

Then he skipped out, and saw Sid just starting up the outside stairway that led to the back rooms on the second floor. Clods were handy and the air was full of them in a twinkling. They raged around Sid like a hail-storm; and before Aunt Polly could collect her surprised faculties and sally to the rescue, six or seven clods had taken personal effect, and Tom was over the fence and gone. There was a gate, but as a general thing he was too crowded for time to make use of it. His soul was at peace, now that he had settled with Sid for calling attention to his black thread and getting him into trouble.

Tom skirted the block, and came round into a muddy alley that led by the back of his aunt's cow-stable. He presently got safely beyond the reach of capture and punishment, and hasted toward the public square of the village, where two "military" companies of boys had met for conflict, according to previous appointment. Tom was General of one of these armies, Joe Harper (a bosom friend,) General of the other. These two great commanders did not condescend to fight in person— that being better suited to the still smaller fry but sat together on an eminence and conducted the field operations by orders delivered through aides-de-camp. Tom's army won a great victory, after a long and hard-fought battle. Then the dead were counted, prisoners exchanged, the terms of the next disagreement agreed upon and the day for the necessary battle appointed; after which the armies fell into line and marched away, and Tom turned homeward alone.

AFTER THE BATTLE.

As he was passing by the house where Jeff Thatcher lived, he saw a new girl in the garden—a lovely little blue-eyed creature with yellow hair plaited into two long tails, white summer frock and embroidered pantalettes. The fresh-crowned hero fell without firing a shot. A certain Amy Lawrence vanished out of his heart and left not even a memory of herself behind. He had thought he loved her to distraction, he had regarded his passion as adoration; and behold it was only a poor little evanescent partiality. He had been months winning her; she had confessed hardly a week ago; he had been the happiest and the proudest boy in the world only seven short days, and here in one instant of time she had gone out of his heart like a casual stranger whose visit is done.

He worshiped this new angel with furtive eye, till he saw that she had discovered him; then he pretended he did not know she was present, and began to "show off" in all sorts of absurd boyish ways, in order to win her admiration. He kept up this grotesque foolishness for some time; but by and by, while he was in the midst of some dangerous gymnastic performances, he glanced aside and saw that the little girl was wending her way toward the house. Tom came up to the fence and leaned on it, grieving, and hoping she would tarry yet a while longer. She halted a moment on the steps and then moved toward the door. Tom heaved a great sigh as she put her foot on the threshold. But his face lit up, right away, for she tossed a pansy over the fence a moment before she disappeared.

The boy ran around and stopped within a foot or two of the flower,

"SHOWING OFF"

and then shaded his eyes with his hand and began to look down street as if he had discovered something of interest going on in that direction. Presently he picked up a straw and began trying to balance it on his nose, with his head tilted far back; and as he moved from side to side, in his efforts, he edged nearer and nearer toward the pansy; finally his bare foot rested upon it, his pliant toes closed upon it, and he hopped away with the treasure and disappeared round the corner. But only for a minute—only while he could button the flower inside his jacket, next his heart—or next his stomach, possibly, for he was not much posted in anatomy, and not hypercritical, anyway.

He returned, now, and hung about the fence till nightfall, "showing off," as before; but the girl never exhibited herself again, though Tom comforted himself a little with the hope that she had been near some window, meantime, and been aware of his attentions. Finally he rode home reluctantly, with his poor head full of visions.

All through supper his spirits were so high that his aunt wondered "what had got into the child." He took a good scolding about clodding Sid, and did not seem to mind it in the least. He tried to steal sugar under his aunt's very nose, and got his knuckles rapped for it. He said:

"Aunt, you don't whack Sid when he takes it."

"Well, Sid don't torment a body the way you do. You'd be always into that sugar if I warn't watching you."

Presently she stepped into the kitchen, and Sid, happy in his im-munity, reached for the sugar-bowl—a sort of glorying over Tom which was well-nigh unbearable. But Sid's fingers slipped and the bowl dropped and broke. Tom was in ecstasies. In such ecstasies that he even controlled his tongue and was silent. He said to himself that he would not speak a word, even when his aunt came in, but would sit perfectly still till she asked who did

NOT AMISS.

the mischief; and then he would tell, and there would be nothing so good in the world as to see that pet model "catch it." He was so brimfull of exultation that he could hardly hold himself when the old lady came back and stood above the wreck discharging lightnings of wrath from over her spectacles. He said to himself, "Now it's coming!" And the next instant he was sprawling on the floor! The potent palm was uplifted to strike again when Tom cried out:

"Hold on, now, what 'er you belting *me* for?—Sid broke it!"

Aunt Polly paused, perplexed, and Tom looked for healing pity. But when she got her tongue again, she only said:

"Umf! Well, you didn't get a lick amiss, I reckon. You been into some other audacious mischief when I wasn't around, like enough."

Then her conscience reproached her, and she yearned to say something kind and loving; but she judged that this would be construed into a confession that she had been in the wrong, and discipline forbade that. So she kept silence, and went about her affairs with a troubled heart. Tom sulked in a corner and exalted his woes. He knew that in her heart his aunt was on her knees to him, and he was morosely gratified by the consciousness of it. He would hang out no signals, he would take notice of none. He knew that a yearning glance fell upon

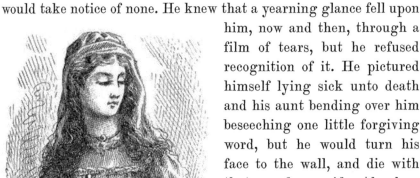

him, now and then, through a film of tears, but he refused recognition of it. He pictured himself lying sick unto death and his aunt bending over him beseeching one little forgiving word, but he would turn his face to the wall, and die with that word unsaid. Ah, how would she feel then? And he pictured himself brought home from the river, dead, with his curls all wet, and his sore heart at rest. How she would throw herself upon him, and how her

MARY.

tears would fall like rain, and her lips pray God to give her back her boy and she would never, never abuse him any more! But he would lie there cold and white and make no sign—a poor little sufferer, whose griefs were at an end. He so worked upon his feelings with the pathos of these dreams, that he had to keep swallowing, he was

so like to choke; and his eyes swam in a blur of water, which overflowed when he winked, and ran down and trickled from the end of his nose. And such a luxury to him was this petting of his sorrows, that he could not bear to have any worldly cheeriness or any grating delight intrude upon it; it was too sacred for such contact; and so, presently, when his cousin Mary danced in, all alive with the joy of seeing home again after an age-long visit of one week to the country, he got up and moved in

clouds and darkness out at one door as she brought song and sunshine in at the other.

He wandered far from the accustomed haunts of boys, and sought

desolate places that were in harmony with his spirit. A log raft in the river invited him, and he seated himself on its outer edge and contemplated the dreary vastness of the stream, wishing, the while, that he could only be drowned, all at once and unconsciously, without undergoing the uncomfortable routine devised by nature. Then he thought of his flower. He got it out, rumpled and wilted, and it mightily increased his dismal felicity. He wondered if *she* would pity him if she knew? Would she cry, and wish that she had a right to put her arms around his neck and comfort him? Or would she turn coldly away like all the hollow world? This picture brought such an agony of pleasureable suffering that he worked it over and over again in his mind and set it up in new and varied lights, till he wore it threadbare. At last he rose up sighing and departed in the darkness.

About half past nine or ten o'clock he came along the deserted street to where the Adored Unknown lived; he paused a moment; no sound fell upon his listening' ear; a candle was casting a dull glow upon the curtain of a second-story window. Was the sacred presence there? He climbed the fence, threaded his stealthy way through the plants, till he stood under that window; he looked up at it long, and with emotion; then he laid him down on the ground under it, disposing himself upon his back, with his hands clasped upon his breast and holding his poor wilted flower. And thus he would die—out in the cold world, with no shelter over his homeless head, no friendly hand to wipe the death-damps from his brow, no loving face to bend pityingly over him when the great agony came. And thus *she* would see him when she looked out upon the glad morning, and oh! would she drop one little tear upon his poor, lifeless form, would she heave one little sigh to see a bright young life so rudely blighted, so untimely cut down?

The window went up, a maid-servant's discordant voice profaned the holy calm, and a deluge of water drenched the prone martyr's remains!

The strangling hero sprang up with a relieving snort. There was a whiz as of a missile in the air, mingled with the murmur of a curse, a sound as of shivering glass followed, and a small, vague form went over the fence and shot away in the gloom.

Not long after, as Tom, all undressed for bed, was surveying his drenched garments by the light of a tallow dip, Sid woke up; but if he had any dim idea of making any "references to allusions," he thought better of it and held his peace, for there was danger in Tom's eye.

Tom turned in without the added vexation of prayers, and Sid made mental note of the omission.

CHAPTER IV.

THE sun rose upon a tranquil world, and beamed down upon the peaceful village like a benediction. Breakfast over, Aunt Polly had family worship; it began with a prayer built from the ground up of solid courses of Scriptural quotations, welded together with a thin mortar of originality; and from the summit of this she delivered a grim chapter of the Mosaic Law, as from Sinai.

Then Tom girded up his loins, so to speak, and went to work to "get his verses." Sid had learned his lesson days before. Tom bent all his energies to the memorizing of five verses, and he chose part of the Sermon on the Mount, because he could find no verses that were shorter. At the end of half an hour Tom had a vague general idea of his lesson, but no more, for his mind was traversing the whole field of human thought, and his hands were busy with distracting recreations. Mary took his book to hear him recite, and he tried to find his way through the fog:

"Blessed are the—a—a—"

"Poor"—

"Yes—poor; blessed are the poor—a—a—"

"In spirit—"

"In spirit; blessed are the poor in spirit, for they—they—"

"*Theirs*—"

"For *theirs*. Blessed are the poor in spirit, for *theirs* is the kingdom of heaven. Blessed are they that mourn, for they—they—"

"Sh—"

"For they—a—"

"S, H, A—"

"For they S, H—Oh I don't know what it is!"

"*Shall!*"

"Oh, *shall!* for they shall—for they shall—a—a—shall mourn—a—a—blessed are they that shall—they that—a—they that shall mourn, for they shall—a—shall *what?* Why don't you tell me Mary?—what do you want to be so mean for?"

"Oh, Tom, you poor thick-headed thing, I'm not teasing you. I wouldn't do that. You must go and learn it again. Don't you be discouraged, Tom, you'll manage it—and if you do, I'll give you something ever so nice. There, now, that's a good boy."

"All right! What is it, Mary, tell me what it is."

"Never you mind, Tom. You know if I say it's nice, it *is* nice."

"You bet'you that's so, Mary. All right, I'll tackle it again."

And he did "tackle it again"—and under the double pressure of curiosity and prospective gain, he did it with such spirit that he accomplished a shining success. Mary gave him a bran-new "Barlow" knife worth twelve and a half cents; and the convulsion of delight that swept his system shook him to his foundations. True, the knife would not cut anything, but it was a "sure-enough" Barlow, and there was inconceivable grandeur in that—though where the western boys ever got the idea that such a weapon could possibly be counterfeited to its injury, is an imposing mystery and will always remain so, perhaps. Tom contrived to scarify the cupboard with it, and was arranging to begin on the bureau, when he was called off to dress for Sunday-School.

Mary gave him a tin basin of water and a piece of soap, and he went outside the door and set the basin on a little bench there; then he dipped the soap in the water and laid it down; turned up his sleeves; poured out the water on the ground, gently, and then entered the kitchen and began to wipe his face diligently on the towel behind the door. But Mary removed the towel and said:

"Now ain't you ashamed, Tom. You mustn't be so bad. Water won't hurt you."

Tom was a trifle disconcerted. The basin was refilled, and this time he stood over it a little while, gathering resolution; took in a big breath and began. When he entered the kitchen presently, with

USING THE "BARLOW."

both eyes shut and groping for the towel with his hands, an honorable testimony of suds and water was dripping from his face. But when he emerged from the towel, he was not yet satisfactory, for the clean territory stopped short at his chin and his jaws, like a mask; below and beyond this line there was a dark expanse of unirrigated soil that spread downward in front and backward around his neck. Mary took him in hand, and when she was done with him he was a man and a brother, without distinction of color, and his saturated hair was neatly brushed, and its short curls wrought into a dainty and symmetrical general effect. [He privately smoothed out the curls, with labor and difficulty, and plastered his hair close down to his head; for he held curls to be effeminate, and his own filled his life with bitterness.] Then Mary got out a suit of his clothing that had been used only on Sundays during two years—they were simply called his "other clothes"—and so by that we know the size of his wardrobe. The girl "put him to rights" after he had dressed himself; she buttoned his neat roundabout up to his chin, turned his vast shirt collar down over his shoulders, brushed him off and crowned him with his speckled straw hat. He now looked exceedingly improved and uncomfortable. He was fully as uncomfortable as he looked; for there was a restraint about whole clothes and cleanliness that galled him. He hoped that Mary would forget his shoes, but the hope was blighted; she coated them thoroughly with tallow, as was the custom, and brought them out. He lost his temper and said he was always being made to do everything he didn't want to do. But Mary said, persuasively:

"Please, Tom—that's a good boy."

So he got into the shoes snarling. Mary was soon ready, and the three children set out for Sunday-school—a place that Tom hated with his whole heart; but Sid and Mary were fond of it.

Sabbath-school hours were from nine to half past ten; and then

church service. Two of of the children always remained for the sermon voluntarily, and the other always remained too—for stronger reasons. The church's high-backed, uncushioned pews would seat about three hundred persons; the edifice was but a small, plain affair, with a sort of pine board tree-box on top of it for a steeple. At the door Tom dropped back a step and accosted a Sunday-dressed comrade:

"Say, Billy, got a yaller ticket?"

"Yes."

THE CHURCH.

"What'll you take for her?"

"What'll you give?"

"Piece of lickrish and a fish-hook."

"Less see 'em."

Tom exhibited. They were satisfactory, and the property changed hands. Then Tom traded a couple of white alleys for three red tickets, and some small trifle or other for a couple of blue ones. He waylaid other boys as they came, and went on buying tickets of various colors ten or fifteen minutes longer. He entered the church, now, with a swarm of clean and noisy boys and girls, proceeded to his seat and started a quarrel with the first boy that came handy. The teacher, a grave, elderly man, interfered; then turned his back a moment and Tom pulled a boy's hair in the next bench, and was absorbed in his book when the boy turned around; stuck a pin in another boy, presently, in order to hear him say "Ouch!" and got a new reprimand from his teacher. Tom's whole class were of a pattern—restless, noisy, and troublesome. When they came to recite their lessons, not one of them knew his verses perfectly, but had to be prompted all along. However, they worried through, and each got his reward—in small blue tickets, each with a passage of Scripture on it; each blue ticket was pay for two verses of the recitation. Ten blue tickets equalled a red one, and could be exchanged for it; ten red tickets equalled a yellow one: for ten yellow tickets the Superintendant gave a very plainly bound Bible, (worth forty cents in those easy times,) to the pupil. How many of my readers would have the industry and application to memorize two thousand verses, even for a Doré Bible? And yet Mary had acquired two Bibles in this way—it was the patient work of two years—and a boy of German parentage had won four or five. He once recited three thousand verses without stopping; but the strain upon his mental faculties was too great, and he was little better than an idiot from that day forth—a grievous misfortune for the school, for on great occasions, before company, the Superintendent (as Tom expressed it) had always made this boy come out and "spread himself." Only the older pupils managed to keep their tickets and stick to their tedious work long enough to get a Bible, and so the delivery of one of these prizes was a rare and noteworthy circumstance; the successful pupil was so great and conspicuous for that day that on the spot every scholar's heart was fired with a fresh ambition that often lasted a couple of weeks. It is possible that Tom's mental stomach had never really hungered for one of those prizes, but unquestionably his entire being had for many a day longed for the glory and the eclat that came with it.

In due course the Superintendent stood up in front of the pulpit, with a closed hymn book in his hand and his forefinger inserted between its leaves, and commanded attention. When a Sunday-school Superintendent makes his customary little speech, a hymn-book in the hand is as necessary as is the inevitable sheet of music in the hand of a singer who stands forward on the platform and sings a solo

at a concert—though why, is a mystery: for neither the hymn-book
nor the sheet of music is ever referred to by the sufferer. This Superintendent was a slim creature of thirty-five, with a sandy goatee
and short sandy hair; he wore a stiff standing-collar whose upper

NECESSITIES.

edge almost reached his ears and whose sharp points curved forward
abreast the corners of his mouth—a fence that compelled a straight
lookout ahead, and a turning of the whole body when a side view was
required; his chin was propped on a spreading cravat which was as
broad and as long as a bank note, and had fringed ends; his boot toes
were turned sharply up, in the fashion of the day, like sleigh-run-
ners—an effect patiently and laboriously produced by the young men
by sitting with their toes pressed against a wall for hours together.
Mr. Walters was very earnest of mein, and very sincere and honest at
heart; and he held sacred things and places in such reverence, and so
separated them from worldly matters, that unconsciously to himself
his Sunday-school voice had acquired a peculiar intonation which was
wholly absent on weekdays. He began after this fashion:

"Now children, I want you all to sit up just as straight and pretty as you can and give me all your attention for a minute or two.
There—that is it. That is the way good little boys and girls should
do. I see one little girl who is looking out of the window—I am afraid
she thinks I am out there somewhere—perhaps up in one of the trees

making a speech to the little birds. [Applausive titter.] I want to tell you how good it makes me feel to see so many bright, clean little faces assembled in a place like this, learning to do right and be good." And so forth and so on. It is not necessary to set down the rest of the oration. It was of a pattern which does not vary, and so it is familiar to us all.

The latter third of the speech was marred by the resumption of fights and other recreations among certain of the bad boys, and by fidgetings and whisperings that extended far and wide, washing even to the bases of isolated and incorruptible rocks like Sid and Mary. But now every sound ceased suddenly, with the subsidence of Mr. Walters' voice, and the conclusion of the speech was received with a burst of silent gratitude.

A good part of the whispering had been occasioned by an event which was more or less rare—the entrance of visitors; lawyer Thatcher, accompanied by a very feeble and aged man; a fine, portly, middle-aged gentleman with iron-gray hair; and a dignified lady who was doubtless the latter's wife. The lady was leading a child. Tom had been restless and full of chafings and repinings; conscience-smitten, too—he could not meet Amy Lawrence's eye, he could not brook her loving gaze. But when he saw this small newcomer his soul was all ablaze with bliss in a moment. The next moment he was "showing off" with all his might—cuffing boys, pulling hair, making faces— in a word, using every art that seemed likely to fascinate a girl and win her applause. His exaltation had but one alloy—the memory of his humiliation in this angel's garden—and that record in sand was fast washing out, under the waves of happiness that were sweeping over it now.

The visitors were given the highest seat of honor, and as soon as Mr. Walters' speech was finished, he introduced them to the school. The middle-aged man turned out to be a prodigious personage—no less a one than the county judge—altogether the most august creation these children had ever looked upon—and they wondered what kind of material he was made of—and they half wanted to hear him roar, and were half afraid he might, too. He was from Constantinople, twelve miles away—so he had traveled, and seen the world—these

very eyes had looked upon the county court house—which was said to
have a tin roof. The awe which these reflections inspired was attested
by the impressive silence and the ranks of staring eyes. This was the
great Judge Thatcher, brother of their own lawyer. Jeff Thatcher
immediately went forward, to be familiar with the great man and be
envied by the school. It would have been music to his soul to hear the
whisperings:

"Look at him, Jim! He's a going up there. Say—look! he's a going
to shake hands with him—he *is* shaking hands with him! By jings,
don't you wish you was Jeff?"

Mr. Walters fell to "showing off," with all sorts of official bus-
tlings and activities giving orders, delivering judgments, discharging directions here, there, everywhere that he could find a target. The
librarian "showed off"—running hither and thither with his arms
full of books and making a deal of the splutter and fuss that insect
authority delights in. The young lady teachers "showed off"—bending sweetly over pupils that were lately being boxed, lifting pretty
warning fingers at bad little boys and patting good ones lovingly.
The young gentlemen teachers "showed off" with small scoldings and
other little displays of authority and fine attention to discipline—and
most of the teachers, of both sexes, found business up at the library,
by the pulpit; and it was business that frequently had to be done over
again two or three times, (with much seeming vexation.) The little
girls "showed off" in various ways, and the little boys "showed off"
with such diligence that the air was thick with paper wads and the
murmur of scufflings. And above it all the great man sat and beamed
a majestic judicial smile upon all the house, and warmed himself in
the sun of his own grandeur—for he was "showing off," too.

There was only one thing wanting, to make Mr. Walters' ecstacy
complete, and that was a chance to deliver a Bible-prize and exhib-
it a prodigy. Several pupils had a few yellow tickets, but none had
enough—he had been around among the star pupils inquiring. He
would have given worlds, now, to have that German lad back again
with a sound mind.

And now at this moment, when hope was dead, Tom Sawyer came
forward with nine yellow tickets, nine red tickets, and ten blue ones,

and demanded a Bible. This was a thunderbolt out of a clear sky. Walters was not expecting an application from this source for the next ten years. But there was no getting around it—here were the certified checks, and they were good for their face. Tom was therefore elevated to a place with the Judge and the other elect, and the great news was announced from headquarters. It was the most stunning surprise of the decade, and so profound was the sensation that it lifted the new hero up to the judicial one's altitude, and the school had two marvels to gaze upon in place of one. The boys were all eaten up with envy—but those that suffered the bitterest pangs were those who perceived too late that they themselves had contributed to this hated splendor by trading tickets to Tom for the wealth he had amassed in selling whitewashing privileges. These despised themselves, as being the dupes of a wily fraud, a guileful snake in the grass.

The prize was delivered to Tom with as much effusion as the Superintendent could pump up under the circumstances; but it lacked somewhat of the true gush, for the poor fellow's instinct taught him that there was a mystery here that could not well bear the light, perhaps; it was simply preposterous that *this* boy had warehoused two thousand sheaves of Scriptural wisdom on his premises—a dozen would strain his capacity, without a doubt.

Amy Lawrence was proud and glad, and she tried to make Tom see it in her face—but he wouldn't look. She wondered; then she was just a grain troubled; next a dim suspicion came and went—came again; she watched; a furtive glance told her worlds—and then her heart broke, and she was jealous, and angry, and the tears came and she hated everybody. Tom most of all, (she thought.)

Tom was introduced to the Judge; but his tongue was tied, his breath would hardly come, his heart quaked—partly because of the awful greatness of the man, but mainly because he was *her* parent. He would have liked to fall down and worship him, if it were in the dark. The Judge put his hand on Tom's head and called him a fine little man, and asked him what his name was. The boy stammered, gasped, and got it out:

"Tom."

"Oh, no, not Tom—it is—"

"Thomas."

"Ah, that's it. I thought there was more to it, maybe. That's very well. But you've another one I daresay, and you'll tell it to me, won't you?"

"Tell the gentleman your other name, Thomas," said Walters, "and say *sir.*—You mustn't forget your manners."

"Thomas Sawyer—sir."

"That's it! That's a good boy. Fine boy. Fine, manly little fellow. Two thousand verses is a great many—very, very great many.

TOM AS A SUNDAY-SCHOOL HERO.

And you never can be sorry for the trouble you took to learn them; for knowledge is worth more than anything there is in the world; it's what makes great men and good men; you'll be a great man and a good man yourself, some day, Thomas, and then you'll look back and say, It's all owing to the precious Sunday-school privileges of my boyhood—it's all owing to my dear teachers that taught me to learn—it's all owing to the good Superintendent, who encouraged me, and watched over me, and gave me a beautiful Bible—a splendid elegant Bible, to keep and have it all for my own, always—it's all owing to right bringing up! That is what you will say, Thomas—and you wouldn't take any money for those two thousand verses—no indeed you wouldn't. And now you wouldn't mind telling me and this lady some of the things you've learned—no, I know you wouldn't—for we are proud of little boys that learn. Now no doubt you know the names of all the twelve disciples. Won't you tell us the names of the first two that were appointed?"

Tom was tugging at a button hole and looking sheepish. He blushed, now, and his eyes fell. Mr. Walters' heart sank within him.

He said to himself, it is not possible that the boy can answer the simplest question—why *did* the Judge ask him? Yet he felt obliged to speak up and say;

"Answer the gentleman, Thomas—don't be afraid."

Tom still hung fire.

"Now I know you'll tell *me*" said the lady. "The names of the first two disciples were—"

"DAVID AND GOLIAH!"

Let us draw the curtain of charity over the rest of the scene.

Chapter V.

ABOUT half-past ten the cracked bell of the small church began to ring, and presently the people began to gather for the morning sermon. The Sunday school children distributed themselves about the house and occupied pews with their parents, so as to be under supervision. Aunt Polly came, and Tom and Sid and Mary sat with her—Tom being placed next the aisle, in order that he might be as far away from the open window and the seductive outside summer scenes as possible. The crowd filed up the aisles: the aged and needy postmaster, who had seen better days; the mayor and his wife—for they had a mayor there, among other unnecessaries; the justice of the peace; the widow Douglass, fair, smart and forty, a generous, good-hearted soul and well-to-do, her hill mansion the only palace in the town, and the most hospitable and much the most lavish in the matter of festivities that St. Petersburg could boast; the bent and venerable Major and Mrs. Ward; lawyer Riverson, the new notable from a distance; next the belle of the village, followed by a troop of lawn-clad and ribbon-decked young heart-breakers; then all the young clerks in town in a body—for they

Tom's bosom friend sat next him, suffering just as Tom had been, and now he was deeply and gratefully interested in this entertainment in an instant. This bosom friend was Joe Harper. The two boys were sworn friends all the week, and embattled enemies on Saturdays. Joe took a pin out of his lappel and began to assist in exercising the prisoner. The sport grew in interest momently. Soon Tom said that they were interfering with each other, and neither getting the fullest benefit of the tick. So he put Joe's slate on the desk and drew a line down the middle of it from top to bottom.

"Now," said he, "as long as he is on your side you can stir him up and I'll let him alone; but if you let him get away and get on my side, you're to leave him alone as long as I can keep him from crossing over."

"All right, go ahead; start him up."

The tick escaped from Tom, presently, and crossed the equator. Joe harassed him a while, and then he got away and crossed back again. This change of base occurred often. While one boy was worrying the tick with absorbing interest, the other would look on with interest as strong, the two heads bowed together over the slate, and the two souls dead to all things else. At last luck seemed to settle and abide with Joe. The tick tried this, that, and the other course, and got as excited and as anxious as the boys themselves, but time and again just as he would have victory in his very grasp, so to speak, and Tom's fingers would be twitching to begin, Joe's pin would deftly head him off, and keep possession. At last Tom could stand it no longer. The temptation was too strong. So he reached out and lent a hand with his pin. Joe was angry in a moment. Said he:

"Tom, you let him alone."

"I only just want to stir him up a little, Joe."

"No, sir, it ain't fair; you just let him alone."

"Blame it, I ain't going to stir him much."

"Let him alone, I tell you!"

"I won't!"

"You shall—he's on my side of the line."

"Look here, Joe Harper, whose is that tick?"

"*I* don't care whose tick he is—he's on my side of the line, and you shan't touch him."

"Well I'll just bet I will, though. He's my tick and I'll do what I blame please with him, or die!"

A tremendous whack came down on Tom's shoulders, and its duplicate on Joe's; and for the space of two minutes the dust continued to fly from the two jackets and the whole school to enjoy it. The boys had been too absorbed to notice the hush that had stolen upon the school a while before when the master came tip-toeing down the room and stood over them. He had contemplated a good part of the performance before he contributed his bit of variety to it.

When school broke up at noon, Tom flew to Becky Thatcher, and whispered in her ear:

"Put on your bonnet and let on you're going home; and when you get to the corner, give the rest of 'em the slip, and turn down through the lane and come back. I'll go the other way and come it over 'em the same way."

So the one went off with one group of scholars, and the other with another. In a little while the two met at the bottom of the lane, and when they reached the school they had it all to themselves. Then they sat together, with a slate before them, and Tom gave Becky the pencil and held her hand in his, guiding it, and so created another surprising house. When the interest in art began to wane, the two fell to talking. Tom was swimming in bliss. He said:

"Do you love rats?"

"No! I hate them!"

"Well, I do too—*live* ones. But I mean dead ones, to swing round your head with a string."

"No, I don't care for rats much, anyway. What *I* like is chewing-gum."

"O, I should say so! I wish I had some now."

"Do you? I've got some. I'll let you chew it awhile, but you must give it back to me."

That was agreeable, so they chewed it turn about, and dangled their legs against the bench in excess of contentment.

"Was you ever at a circus?" said Tom.

"Yes, and my pa's going to take me again some time, if I'm good."

"I been to the circus three or four times—lots of times. Church ain't shucks to a circus. There's things going on at a circus all the time. I'm going to be a clown in a circus when I grow up."

"O, are you! That will be nice. They're so lovely, all spotted up."

"Yes, that's so. And they get slathers of money—most a dollar a day, Ben Rogers says. Say, Becky, was you ever engaged?"

"What's that?"

"Why, engaged to be married."

"No."

"Would you like to?"

"I reckon so. I don't know. What is it like?"

"Like?" Why it ain't like anything. You only just tell a boy you won't ever have any body but him, ever ever *ever*, and then you kiss and that's all. Anybody can do it."

"Kiss? What do you kiss for?"

"Why that, you know, is to—well, they always do that."

"Everybody?"

"Why yes, everybody that's in love with each other. Do you remember what I wrote on the slate?"

"Ye—yes."

"What was it?"

"I shant tell you."

"Shall I tell *you*?"

"Ye—yes—but some other time."

"No, now."

"No, not now—to-morrow."

"O, no, *now*. Please Becky—I'll whisper it, I'll whisper it ever so easy."

Becky hesitating, Tom took silence for consent, and passed his arm about her waist and whispered the tale ever so softly, with his mouth close to her ear. And then he added:

"Now you whisper it to me—just the same."

She resisted, for a while, and then said:

"You turn your face away so you can't see, and then I will. But you mustn't ever tell anybody—*will* you, Tom? Now you won't, *will* you?"

"No, indeed indeed I won't. Now Becky."

He turned his face away. She bent timidly around till her breath stirred his curls and whispered, "I—love—you!"

Then she sprang away and ran around and around the desks and benches, with Tom after her, and took refuge in a corner at last, with her little white apron to her face. Tom clasped her about her neck and pleaded:

"Now Becky, it's all done—all over but the kiss. Don't you be afraid of that—it aint anything at all. Please, Becky."—And he tugged at her apron and the hands.

By and by she gave up, and let her hands drop; her face, all glowing with the struggle, came up and submitted. Tom kissed the red lips and said:

"Now it's all done, Becky. And always after this, you know, you ain't ever to love anybody but me, and you ain't ever to marry anybody but me, never never and forever. Will you?"

"No, I'll never love anybody but you, Tom, and I'll never marry anybody but you—and you ain't to ever marry anybody but me, either."

"Certainly. Of course. That's *part* of it. And always coming to school or when we're going home, you're to walk with me, when there ain't anybody looking—and you choose me and I choose you at parties, because that's the way you do when you're engaged."

"It's so nice. I never heard of it before."

"Oh it's ever so gay! Why me and Amy Lawrence"—

The big eyes told Tom his blunder and he stopped, confused.

"O, Tom! Then I ain't the first you've ever been engaged to!"

The child began to cry. Tom said:

"O don't cry, Becky, I don't care for her any more."

"Yes you do, Tom,—you know you do."

Tom tried to put his arm about her neck, but she pushed him away, and turned her face to the wall, and went on crying. Tom tried again, with soothing words in his mouth, and was repulsed again. Then his pride was up, and he strode away and went outside. He

stood about, restless and uneasy, for a while, glancing at the door, every now and then, hoping she would repent and come to find him. But she did not. Then he began to feel badly and fear that he was in the wrong. It was a hard struggle with him to make new advances, now, but he nerved himself to it and entered. She was still standing back there in the corner, sobbing, with her face to the wall. Tom's heart smote him. He went to her and stood a moment, not knowing exactly how to proceed. Then he said hesitatingly:

VAIN PLEADING.

"Becky, I—I don't care for anybody but you."

No reply—but sobs.

"Becky,"—pleadingly. "Becky, won't you say something?"

More sobs.

Tom got out his chiefest jewel, a brass knob from the top of an andiron, and passed it around her so that she could see it, and said:

"Please, Becky, won't you take it?"

She struck it to the floor. Then Tom marched out of the house and over the hills and far away, to return to school no more that day. Presently Becky began to suspect. She ran to the door; he was not in sight; she flew around to the play-yard; he was not there. Then she called:

"Tom! Come back Tom!"

She listened intently, but there was no answer. She had no companions but silence and loneliness. So she sat down to cry again and upbraid herself; and by this time the scholars began to gather again, and she had to hide her griefs and still her broken heart and take up the cross of a long, dreary, aching afternoon, with none among the strangers about her to exchange sorrows with.

CHAPTER VIII.

TOM dodged hither and thither through lanes until he was well out of the track of returning scholars, and then fell into a moody jog. He crossed a small "branch" two or three times, because of a prevailing juvenile superstition that to cross water baffled pursuit. Half an hour later he was disappearing behind the Douglas mansion on the summit of Cardiff Hill, and the schoolhouse was hardly distinguishable away off in the valley behind him. He entered a dense wood, picked his pathless way to the centre of it, and sat down on a mossy spot under a spreading oak. There was not even a zephyr stirring; the dead noonday heat had even stilled the songs of the birds; nature lay in a trance that was broken by no sound but the occasional far-off hammering of a woodpecker, and this seemed to render the pervading silence and sense of loneliness the more profound. The boy's soul was steeped in melancholy; his feelings were in happy accord with his surroundings. He sat long with his elbows on his knees and his chin in his hands, meditating. It seemed to him that life was but a trouble, at best, and he more than half envied Jimmy Hodges, so lately released; it must be very peaceful, he thought, to lie and slumber and dream forever and ever, with the wind whispering through the trees and caressing the grass and the flowers over the grave, and nothing to bother and grieve about, ever any more. If he only had a clean Sunday-school record he could be willing to go, and be done with it all. Now as to this girl. What had he done? Nothing. He had meant the best in the world, and been treated like a dog—like a very dog. She would be sorry some day—maybe when it was too late. Ah, if he could only die *temporarily*!

But the elastic heart of youth cannot be compressed into one con-strained shape long at a time. Tom presently began to drift insensi-bly back into the concerns of this life again. What if he turned his back, now, and disappeared mysteriously? What if he went away— ever so far away, into unknown countries beyond the seas—and nev-er come back any more! How would she feel then! The idea of being a clown recurred to him now, only to fill him with disgust. For frivolity and jokes and spotted tights were an offense, when they intruded themselves upon a spirit that was exalted into the vague august realm of the romantic. No, he would be a soldier, and return after long years, all war-worn and illustrious. No—better still, he would join the Indians, and hunt buffaloes and go on the war-path in the mountain ranges and the trackless great plains of the Far West, and away in the future come back a great chief, bristling with feathers, hideous with paint, and prance into Sunday-school, some drowsy summer morning, with a blood-curdling war-whoop, and sear the eyeballs of all his companions with unappeasable envy. But no, there was something gaudier even than this. He would be a pirate! That was it! *Now* his future lay plain before him, and glowing with unimaginable splendor. How his name would fill the world, and make people shudder! How gloriously he would go plowing the dancing seas, in his long, low, black-hulled racer, the "Spirit of the Storm," with his grisly flag flying at the fore! And at the zenith of his fame, how he would suddenly appear at the old vil-lage and stalk into church, brown and weather-beaten, in his black velvet doublet and trunks, his great jack-boots, his crimson sash, his belt bristling with horse-pistols, his crime-rusted cutlass at his side, his slouch hat with waving plumes, his black flag unfurled, with the skull and crossbones on it, and hear with swelling ecstasy the whisperings, "It's Tom Sawyer the Pirate—the Black Avenger of the Spanish Main!"

Yes, it was settled; his career was determined. He would run away from home and enter upon it. He would start the very next morning. Therefore he must now begin to get ready. He would collect his resources together. He went to a rotten log near at hand and began to dig under one end of it with his Barlow knife. He soon struck wood that sounded hollow. He put his hand there and uttered this incantation impressively:

"What hasn't come here, *come*! What's here, *stay* here!"

Then he scraped away the dirt, and exposed a pine shingle. He took it up and disclosed a shapely little treasure-house whose bottom and sides were of shingles. In it lay a marble. Tom's astonishment was boundless! He scratched his head with a perplexed air, and said:

"Well, that beats anything?"

Then he tossed the marble away pettishly, and stood cogitating. The truth was, that a superstition of his had failed, here, which he and all his comrades had always looked upon as infallible. If you buried a marble with certain necessary incantations, and left it alone a fortnight, and then opened the place with the incantation he had just used, you would find that

TOM MEDITATES..

all the marbles you had ever lost had gathered themselves together there, meantime, no matter how widely they had been separated. But now, this thing had actually and unquestionably failed. Tom's whole structure of faith was shaken to its foundations. He had many a time heard of this thing succeeding, but never of its failing before. It did not occur to him that he had tried it several times before, himself, but could never find the hiding places afterwards. He puzzled over the matter some time, and finally decided that some witch had interfered and broken the charm. He thought he would satisfy himself on that point; so he searched around till he found a small sandy spot with a little funnel-shaped depression in it. He laid himself down and put his mouth close to this depression and called:

"Doodle-bug, doodle-bug, tell me what I want to know! Doodle-bug, doodle-bug tell me what I want to know!"

The sand began to work, and presently a small black bug appeared for a second and then darted under again in a fright.

"He dasn't tell! So it *was* a witch that done it. I just knowed it."

He well knew the futility of trying to contend against witches, so he gave up discouraged. But it occurred to him that he might as well have the marble he had just thrown away, and therefore he went and made a patient search for it. But he could not find it. Now he went back to his treasure-house and carefully placed himself just as he had been standing when he tossed the marble away; then he took another marble from his pocket and tossed it in the same way, saying:

"Brother go find your brother!"

He watched where it stopped, and went there and looked. But it must have fallen short or gone too far; so he tried twice more. The last repetition was successful. The two marbles lay within a foot of each other.

Just here the blast of a toy tin trumpet came faintly down the green aisles of the forest. Tom flung off his jacket and trousers, turned a suspender into a belt, raked away some brush behind the rotten log, disclosing a rude bow and arrow, a lath sword and a tin trumpet, and in a moment had seized these things and bounded away, bare legged, with fluttering shirt. He presently halted under a great elm, blew an answering blast, and then began to tip-toe and look warily out, this way and that. He said cautiously—to an imaginary company:

"Hold, my merry men! Keep hid till I blow."

Now appeared Joe Harper, as airily clad and elaborately armed as Tom. Tom called:

"Hold! Who comes here into Sherwood Forest without my pass?"

"Guy of Guisborne wants no man's pass. Who art thou that—that—"

"Dares to hold such language," said Tom, prompting—for they talked "by the book," from memory.

"Who art thou that dares to hold such language?"

"I, indeed! I am Robin Hood, as thy caitiff carcase soon shall know."

"Then art thou indeed that famous outlaw? Right gladly will I dispute with thee the passes of the merry wood. Have at thee!"

They took their lath swords, dumped their other traps on the ground, struck a fencing attitude, foot to foot, and began a grave, careful combat, "two up and two down." Presently Tom said:

"Now if you've got the hang, go it lively!"

So they "went it lively," panting and perspiring with the work. By and by Tom shouted:

"Fall! fall! Why don't you fall?"

"I shan't! Why don't you fall yourself? You're getting the worst of it."

ROBIN HOOD AND HIS FOE.

"Why that ain't anything. *I* can't fall; that ain't the way it is in the book. The book says 'Then with one back-handed stroke he slew poor Guy of Guisborne.' You're to turn around and let me hit you in the back."

There was no getting around the authorities, so Joe turned, received the whack and fell.

"Now," said Joe, getting up, "You got to let me kill *you*. That's fair."

"Why I can't do that, it ain't in the book."

"Well it's blamed mean,—that's all."

"Well, say, Joe, you can be Friar Tuck or Much the miller's son and lam me with a quarter-staff; or I'll be the Sheriff of Nottingham and you be Robin Hood a little while and kill me."

This was satisfactory, and so these adventures were carried out.

DEATH OF ROBIN HOOD.

Then Tom became Robin Hood again, and was allowed by the treacherous nun to bleed his strength away through his neglected wound. And at last Joe, representing a whole tribe of weeping outlaws, dragged him sadly forth, gave his bow into his feeble hands, and Tom said, "Where this arrow falls, there bury poor Robin Hood under the greenwood tree." Then he shot the arrow and fell back and would have died but he lit on a nettle and sprang up too gaily for a corpse.

The boys dressed themselves, hid their accoutrements, and went off grieving that there were no outlaws any more, and wondering what modern civilization could claim to have done to compensate for their loss. They said they would rather be outlaws a year in Sherwood Forest than President of the United States forever.

CHAPTER IX.

At half past nine, that night, Tom and Sid were sent to bed, as usual. They said their prayers, and Sid was soon asleep. Tom lay awake and waited, in restless impatience. When it seemed to him that it must be nearly daylight, he heard the clock strike ten! This was despair. He would have tossed and fidgeted, as his nerves demanded, but he was afraid he might wake Sid. So he lay still, and stared up into the dark. Everything was dismally still. By and by, out of the stillness, little, scarcely preceptible noises began to emphasize themselves. The ticking of the clock began to bring itself into notice. Old beams began to crack mysteriously. The stairs creaked faintly. Evidently spirits were abroad. A measured, muffled snore issued from Aunt Polly's chamber. And now the tiresome chirping of a cricket that no human ingenuity could locate, began. Next the ghastly ticking of a death-watch in the wall at the bed's head made Tom shudder—it meant that somebody's days were numbered. Then the howl of a far-off dog rose on the night air, and was answered by a fainter howl from a remoter distance. Tom was in an agony. At last he was satisfied that time had ceased and eternity begun; he began to doze, in spite of himself; the

clock chimed eleven but he did not hear it. And then there came min-
gling with his half-formed dreams, a most melancholy caterwauling.
The raising of a neighboring window disturbed him. A cry of "Scat!
you devil!" and the crash of an empty bottle against the back of his
aunt's woodshed brought him wide awake, and a single minute later
he was dressed and out of the window and creeping along the roof of
the "ell" on all fours. He "meow'd" with caution once or twice, as

he went; then jumped to the roof of
the wood-shed and thence to the
ground. Huckleberry Finn was
there, with his dead cat. The boys
moved off and disappeared in the
gloom. At the end of half an hour
they were wading through the tall
grass of the graveyard.

It was a graveyard of the old-
fashioned western kind. It was on a
hill, about a mile and a half from the
village. It had a crazy board fence
around it, which leaned inward in
places, and outward the rest of the
time, but stood upright nowhere.

TOM'S MODE OF EGRESS.

Grass and weeds grew rank over the
whole cemetery. All the old graves were sunken in, there was not a
tombstone on the place; round-topped, worm-eaten boards staggered
over the graves, leaning for support and finding none. "Sacred to the
memory of" So-and-So had been painted on them once, but it could
no longer have been read, on the most of them, now, even if there had
been light.

A faint wind moaned through the trees, and Tom feared it might
be the spirits of the dead, complaining at being disturbed. The boys
talked little, and only under their breath, for the time and the place
and the pervading solemnity and silence oppressed their spirits.
They found the sharp new heap they were seeking, and ensconced
themselves within the protection of three great elms that grew in a
bunch within a few feet of the grave.

Then they waited in silence for what seemed a long time. The hooting of a distant owl was all the sound that troubled the dead stillness. Tom's reflections grew oppressive. He must force some talk. So he said in a whisper:

"Hucky, do you believe the dead people like it for us to be here?"

Huckleberry whispered:

"I wisht I knowed. It's awful solemn like, *ain't* it?"

"I bet it is."

There was a considerable pause, while the boys canvassed this matter inwardly. Then Tom whispered:

"Say, Hucky—do you reckon Hoss Williams hears us talking?"

"O' course he does. Least his sperrit does."

Tom, after a pause:

"I wish I'd said *Mister* Williams. But I never meant any harm. Everybody calls him Hoss."

"A body can't be too partic'lar how they talk 'bout theseyer dead people, Tom."

This was a damper, and conversation died again. Presently Tom seized his comrade's arm and said:

"Sh!"

"What is it, Tom?" And the two clung together with beating hearts.

"Sh! There 'tis again! Didn't you hear it?"

"I—"

"There! Now you hear it."

"Lord, Tom they're coming! They're coming, sure. What'll we do?"

"I dono. Think they'll see us?"

"O, Tom, they can see in the dark, same as cats. I wisht I hadn't come."

"O, don't be afeard. *I* don't believe they'll bother us. We ain't doing any harm. If we keep perfectly still, maybe they won't notice us at all."

"I'll try to, Tom, but Lord I'm all of a shiver."

"Listen!"

The boys bent their heads together and scarcely breathed. A muffled sound of voices floated up from the far end of the graveyard.

"Look! See there!" whispered Tom. "What is it?"

"It's devil-fire. O, Tom, this is awful."

Some vague figures approached through the gloom, swinging an old-fashioned tin lantern that freckled the ground with innumerable little spangles of light. Presently Huckleberry whispered with a shudder:

"It's the devils sure enough. Three of 'em! Lordy, Tom, we're goners! Can you pray?"

"I'll try, but don't you be afeard. They ain't going to hurt us. Now I lay me down to sleep, I—"

"Sh!"

"What is it, Huck?"

"They're *humans!* One of 'em is, anyway. One of 'em's old Muff Potter's voice."

"No—tain't so, is it?"

"I bet I know it. Don't you stir nor budge. *He* ain't sharp enough to notice us. Drunk, same as usual, likely— blamed old rip!"

"All right, I'll keep still. Now they're stuck. Can't find it. Here they come again. Now they're hot. Cold again. Hot again. Red hot! They're

TOM'S EFFORT AT PRAYER.

p'inted right, this time. Say Huck, I know another o' them voices; it's Injun Joe."

"That's so—that murderin' half-breed! I'd druther they was devils a dern sight. What kin they be up to?"

The whispers died wholly out, now, for the three men had reached the grave and stood within a few feet of the boys' hiding-place.

"Here it is," said the third voice; and the owner of it held the lantern up and revealed the face of young Dr. Robinson.

Potter and Injun Joe were carrying a handbarrow with a rope and a couple of shovels on it. They cast down their load and began to open the grave. The doctor put the lantern at the head of the grave and came and sat down with his back against one of the elm trees. He was so close the boys could have touched him.

"Hurry, men!" he said in a low voice; "the moon might come out at any moment."

They growled a response and went on digging. For some time there was no noise but the grating sound of the spades discharging their freight of mould and gravel. It was very monotonous. Finally a spade struck upon the coffin with a dull woody accent, and within another minute or two the men had hoisted it out on the ground. They pried off the lid with their shovels, got out the body and dumped it rudely on the ground. The moon drifted from behind the clouds and exposed the pallid face. The barrow was got ready and the corpse placed on it, covered with a blanket, and bound to its place with the rope. Potter took out a large spring-knife and cut off the dangling end of the rope and then said:

"Now the cussed thing's ready, Sawbones, and you'll just out with another five, or here she stays."

"That's the talk!" said Injun Joe.

"Look here, what does this mean?" said the doctor. "You required your pay in advance, and I've paid you."

"Yes, and you done more than that," said Injun Joe, approaching the doctor, who was now standing. "Five years ago you drove me away from your father's kitchen one night, when I come to ask for something to eat, and you said I warn't there for any good; and when I swore I'd get even with you if it took a hundred years, your father had me jailed for a vagrant. Did you think I'd forget? The Injun blood ain't in me for nothing. And now I've *got* you, and you got to *settle*, you know!"

He was threatening the doctor, with his fist in his face, by this time. The doctor struck out suddenly and stretched the ruffian on the ground. Potter dropped his knife, and exclaimed:

"Here, now, don't you hit my pard!" and the next moment he had grappled with the doctor and the two were struggling with might and main, trampling the grass and tearing the ground with their heels. Injun Joe sprang to his feet, his eyes flaming with passion, snatched up Potter's knife, and went creeping, catlike and stooping, round and round about the combatants, seeking an opportunity. All at once the doctor flung himself free, seized the heavy head board of Williams' grave and felled Potter to the earth with it—and in the same instant the half-breed saw his chance and drove the knife to the hilt in the young man's breast. He reeled and fell partly upon Potter, flooding him with his blood, and in the same moment the clouds blotted out the dreadful spectacle and the two frightened boys went speeding away in the dark.

Presently, when the moon emerged again, Injun Joe was standing over the two forms, contemplating them. The doctor murmured inarticulately, gave a long gasp or two and was still. The half-breed muttered:

"*That* score is settled damn you."

Then he robbed the body. After which he put the fatal knife in Potter's open right hand, and sat down on the dismantled coffin. Three—four—five minutes passed, and then Potter began to stir and moan. His hand closed upon the knife; he raised it, glanced at it, and let it fall, with a shudder. Then he sat up, pushing the body from him, and gazed at it, and then around him, confusedly. His eyes met Joe's.

"Lord, how is this, Joe?" he said.

"It's a dirty business," said Joe, without moving. "What did you do it for?"

"I! I never done it!"

"Look here! That kind of talk won't wash."

Potter trembled and grew white.

"I thought I'd got sober, I'd no business to drink to-night. But it's in my head yet—worse'n when we started here. I'm all in a muddle; can't recollect anything of it hardly. Tell me, Joe—*honest*, now, old feller—did I do it? Joe, I never meant to—'pon my soul and honor I never meant to, Joe. Tell me how it was Joe. O, it's awful—and him so young and promising."

"Why you two was scuffling, and he fetched you one with the head-board and you fell flat; and then up you come, all reeling and staggering, like, and snatched the knife and jammed it into him, just as he fetched you another awful clip—and here you've laid, as dead as a wedge till now."

"O, I didn't know what I was a doing. I wish I may die this minute if I did. It was all on account of the whisky; and the excitement, I reckon. I never used a weepon in my life before, Joe. I've fought, but never with weepons. They'll all say that. Joe, don't tell! Say you won't tell, Joe—that's a good feller. I always liked you Joe, and stood up for you, too. Don't you remember? You *won't* tell, *will* you Joe?" And the poor creature dropped on his knees before the stolid murderer, and clasped his appealing hands.

MUFF POTTER OUTWITTED.

"No, you've always been fair and square with me, Muff Potter, and I won't go back on you.—There, now, that's as fair as a man can say."

"O, Joe, you're an angel. I'll bless you for this the longest day I live." And Potter began to cry.

"Come, now, that's enough of that. This ain't any time for blubbering. You be off yonder way and I'll go this. Move, now, and don't leave any tracks behind you."

Potter started on a trot that quickly increased to a run. The half-breed stood looking after him. He muttered:

"If he's as much stunned with the lick and fuddled with the rum as he had the look of being, he won't think of the knife till he's gone so far he'll be afraid to come back after it to such a place by himself—chicken-heart!"

Two or three minutes later the murdered man, the blanketed corpse, the lid-less coffin and the open grave were under no inspection but the moon's. The stillness was complete again, too.

CHAPTER X.

 two boys flew on and on, toward the village, speechless with horror. They glanced backward over their shoulders from time to time, apprehensively, as if they feared they might be followed. Every stump that started up in their path seemed a man and an enemy, and made them catch their breath; and as they sped by some outlying cottages that lay near the village, the barking of the aroused watch-dogs seemed to give wings to their feet.

"If we can only get to the old tannery, before we break down!" whispered Tom, in short catches between breaths, "I can't stand it much longer."

Huckleberry's hard pantings were his only reply, and the boys fixed their eyes on the goal of their hopes and bent to their work to win it. They gained steadily on it, and at last, breast to breast they burst through the open door and fell grateful and exhausted in the sheltering shadows beyond. By and by their pulses slowed down, and Tom whispered:

"Huckleberry, what do you reckon 'll come of this?"

"If Dr. Robinson dies, I reckon hanging 'll come of it."

"Do you though?"

"Why I *know* it, Tom."

Tom thought a while, then he said:

"Who'll tell? We?"

"What are you talking about? S'pose something happened and Injun Joe *didn't* hang? Why he'd kill us some time or other, just as dead sure as we're a laying here."

"That's just what I was thinking to myself, Huck."

"If anybody tells, let Muff Potter do it, if he's fool enough. He's generally drunk enough."

Tom said nothing—went on thinking. Presently he whispered:

"Huck, Muff Potter don't *know* it. How can he tell?"

"What's the reason he don't know it?"

"Because he'd just got that whack when Injun Joe done it. D' you reckon he could see anything? D' you reckon he knowed anything?"

"By hokey, that's so Tom!"

"And besides, look-a-here—maybe that whack done for *him!*"

"No, 'taint likely Tom. He had liquor in him; I could see that; and besides, he always has. Well when pap's full, you might take and belt him over the head with a church and you couldn't phase him. He says so, his own self. So it's the same with Muff Potter, of course. But if a man was dead sober, I reckon maybe that whack might fetch him; I dono."

After another reflective silence, Tom said:

"Hucky, you sure you can keep mum?"

"Tom, we *got* to keep mum. *You* know that. That Injun devil would'nt make any more of drownding us than a couple of cats, if we was to squeak 'bout this and they didn't hang him. Now look-a-here, Tom, less take and swear to one another—that's what we got to do—swear to keep mum."

"I'm agreed. It's the best thing. Would you just hold hands and swear that we—"

"O, no, that wouldn't do for this. That's good enough for little rubbishy common things—specially with gals, cuz *they* go back on you anyway, and blab if they get in a huff—but there orter be writing 'bout a big thing like this. And blood."

Tom's whole being applauded this idea. It was deep, and dark, and awful; the hour, the circumstances, the surroundings, were in keeping with it. He picked up a clean pine shingle that lay in the moonlight, took a little fragment of "red keel" out of his pocket, got the moon on his work, and painfully scrawled these lines, emphasizing each slow down-stroke by clamping his tongue between his teeth, and letting up the pressure on the up-strokes:

> "Huck Finn and Tom Sawyer swears they will keep mum about this and they wish they may drop down dead in their tracks if they ever tell and Rot."

Huckleberry was filled with admiration of Tom's facility in writing, and the sublimity of his language. He at once took a pin from his lappel and was going to prick his flesh, but Tom said:

"Hold on! Don't do that. A pin's brass. It might have verdigrease on it."

"What's verdigrease?"

"It's p'ison. That's what it is. You just swaller some of it once— you'll see."

So Tom unwound the thread from one of his needles, and each boy pricked the ball of his thumb and squeezed out a drop of blood. In time, after many squeezes, Tom managed to sign his initials, using the ball of his little finger for a pen. Then he showed Huckleberry how to make an H and an F, and the oath was complete. They buried the shingle close to the wall, with some dismal ceremonies and incantations, and the fetters that bound their tongues were considered to be locked and the key thrown away.

A figure crept stealthily through a break in the other end of the ruined building, now, but they did not notice it.

"Tom," whispered Huckleberry, "does this keep us from *ever* telling—*always*?"

"Of course it does. It don't make any difference *what* happens, we got to keep mum. We'd drop down dead—don't *you* know that?"

"Yes, I reckon that's so."

They continued to whisper for some little time. Presently a dog set up a long, lugubrious howl just outside—within ten feet of them. The boys clasped each other suddenly, in an agony of fright.

"Which of us does he mean?" gasped Huckleberry.

"I dono—peep through the crack. Quick!"

"No, *you*, Tom!"

"I can't—I can't *do* it, Huck!"

"Please, Tom. There 'tis again!"

"O, lordy, I'm thankful!" whispered Tom. "I know his voice. It's Bull Harbison."[1]

"O, that's good—I tell you, Tom, I was most scared to death; I'd a bet anything it was a *stray* dog."

The dog howled again. The boys' hearts sank once more.

"O, my! that ain't no Bull Harbison!" whispered Huckleberry. "*Do*, Tom!"

Tom, quaking with fear, yielded, and put his eye to the crack. His whisper was hardly audible when he said:

"O, Huck, IT'S A STRAY DOG!"

"Quick, Tom, quick! Who does he mean?"

---

[1] If Mr. Harbison had owned a slave named Bull, Tom would have spoken of him as "Harbison's Bull," but a son or a dog of that name was "Bull Harbison."

"Huck, he must mean us both—we're right together."

"O, Tom, I reckon we're goners. I reckon there ain't no mistake 'bout where *I'll* go to. I been so wicked."

"Dad fetch it! This comes of playing hookey and doing everything a feller's told *not* to do. I might a been good, like Sid, if I'd a tried—but no, I wouldn't, of course. But if ever I get off this time, I lay I'll just *waller* in Sunday-schools!" And Tom began to snuffle a little.

"*You* bad!" and Huckleberry began to snuffle too. "Consound it, Tom Sawyer, you're just old pie, 'longside o'what I am. O, *lordy*, lordy, lordy, I wisht I only had half your chance."

Tom choked off and whispered:

"Look, Hucky, look! He's got his *back* to us!"

Hucky looked, with joy in his heart.

"Well he has, by jingoes! Did he before?"

"Yes, he did. But I, like a fool, never thought. O, this is bully, you know, *Now* who can he mean?"

The howling stopped. Tom pricked up his ears.

"Sh! What's that?" he whispered.

"Sounds like—like hogs grunting. No—it's somebody snoring, Tom."

"That *is* it? Where 'bouts is it, Huck?"

"I bleeve it's down at 'tother end. Sounds so, anyway. Pap used to sleep there, sometimes, 'long with the hogs, but laws bless you, he just lifts things when *he* snores. Besides, I reckon he ain't ever coming back to this town any more."

The spirit of adventure rose in the boys' souls once more.

"Hucky, do you das't to go if I lead?"

"I don't like to, much. Tom, s'pose it's Injun Joe!"

Tom quailed. But presently the temptation rose up strong again and the boys agreed to try, with the understanding that they would take to their heels if the snoring stopped. So they went tip-toeing stealthily down, the one behind the other. When they had got to within five steps of the snorer, Tom stepped on a stick, and it broke with a sharp snap. The man moaned, writhed a little, and his face came into the moonlight. It was Muff Potter. The boys' hearts had stood still, and their hopes too, when the man moved, but their fears passed away now. They tip-toed out, through the broken weather-boarding, and stopped at a little distance to exchange a parting word. That long, lugubrious howl rose on the night air again! They turned and saw the strange dog standing within a few feet of where Potter was lying, and *facing* Potter, with his nose pointing heavenward.

DISTURBING MUFF'S SLEEP.

"O, geeminy it's *him!*" exclaimed both boys, in a breath.

"Say, Tom—they say a stray dog come howling around Johnny Miller's house, 'bout midnight, as much as two weeks ago; and a whippoorwill come in and lit on the bannisters and sung, the very same evening; and there ain't anybody dead there yet."

"Well I know that. And suppose there ain't. Didn't Gracie Miller fall in the kitchen fire and burn herself terrible the very next Saturday?"

"Yes, but she ain't *dead*. And what's more, she's getting better, too."

"All right, you wait and see. She's a goner, just as dead sure as Muff Potter's a goner. That's what the niggers say, and they know all about these kind of things, Huck."

Then they separated, cogitating. When Tom crept in at his bedroom window, the night was almost spent. He undressed with excessive caution, and fell asleep congratulating himself that nobody knew of his escapade. He was not aware that the gently-snoring Sid was awake, and had been so for an hour.

When Tom awoke, Sid was dressed and gone. There was a late look in the light, a late sense in the atmosphere. He was startled. Why had he not been called—persecuted till he was up, as usual? The thought filled him with bodings. Within five minutes he was dressed and down stairs, feeling sore and drowsy. The family were still at table, but they had finished breakfast. There was no voice of rebuke; but there were averted eyes; there was a silence and an air of solemnity that struck a chill to the culprit's heart. He sat down and tried to seem gay, but it was uphill work; it roused no smile, no response, and he lapsed into silence and let his heart sink down to the depths.

After breakfast his aunt took him aside, and Tom almost brightened in the hope that he was going to be flogged; but it was not so. His aunt wept over him and asked him how he could go and break her old heart so; and finally told him to go on, and ruin himself and bring her grey hairs with sorrow to the grave, for it was no use for her to try any more. This was worse than a thousand whippings, and Tom's heart was sorer now than his body. He cried, he pleaded for forgiveness, promised reform over and over again and then received his dismissal, feeling that he had won but an imperfect forgiveness and established but a feeble confidence.

He left the presence too miserable to even feel revengeful toward Sid; and so the latter's prompt retreat through the back gate was unnecessary. He moped to school gloomy and sad, and took his flogging, along with Joe Harper, for playing hooky the day before, with the air of one whose heart was busy with heavier woes and wholly dead to trifles. Then he betook himself to his seat, rested his elbows on his desk and his jaws in his hands and stared at the wall with the stony stare of suffering that has reached the limit and can no further go. His elbow was pressing against some hard substance. After a long time he slowly and sadly changed his position, and took up this object with a sigh. It was in a paper. He unrolled it. A long, lingering, colossal sigh followed, and his heart broke. It was his brass andiron knob!

This final feather broke the camel's back.

CHAPTER XI.

MUFF POTTER.

CLOSE upon the hour of noon the whole village was suddenly electrified with the ghastly news. No need of the as yet undreamed-of telegraph; the tale flew from man to man, from group to group, from house to house, with little less than telegraphic speed. Of course the schoolmaster gave holiday for that afternoon; the town would have thought strangely of him if he had not.

A gory knife had been found close to the murdered man, and it had been recognized by somebody as belonging to Muff Potter—so the story ran. And it was said that a belated citizen had come upon Potter washing himself in the "branch" about one or two o'clock in the morning, and that Potter had at once sneaked off—suspicious circumstances, especially the washing, which was not a habit with Potter. It was also said that the town had been ransacked for this "murderer," (the public are not slow in the matter of sifting evidence and arriving at a verdict), but that he could not be found. Horsemen had departed down all the roads in every direction, and the Sheriff "was confident" that he would be captured before night.

All the town was drifting toward the graveyard. Tom's heartbreak vanished and he joined the procession, not because he would not a thousand times rather go any where else, but because an awful, unac-

A SUSPICIOUS INCIDENT.

countable fascination drew him on. Arrived at the dreadful place, he wormed his small body through the crowd and saw the dismal spectacle. It seemed to him an age since he was there before. Somebody pinched his arm. He turned, and his eyes met Huckleberry's. Then both looked elsewhere at once, and wondered if anybody had noticed anything in their mutual glance. But everybody was talking, and intent upon the grisly spectacle before them.

"Poor fellow!" "Poor young fellow!" "This ought to be a lesson to grave-robbers!" "Muff Potter'll hang for this if they catch him!" This was the drift of remark; and the minister said, "It was a judgment; His hand is here."

Now Tom shivered from head to heel; for his eye fell upon the stolid face of Injun Joe. At this moment the crowd began to sway and struggle, and voices shouted, "It's him! it's him! he's coming himself!"

"Who? Who?" from twenty voices.

"Muff Potter!"

"Hallo, he's stopped!—Look out, he's turning! Don't let him get away!"

People in the branches of the trees over Tom's head, said he wasn't trying to get away—he only looked doubtful and perplexed.

"Infernal impudence!" said a bystander; "wanted to come and take a quiet look at his work, I reckon—didn't expect any company."

The crowd fell apart, now, and the Sheriff came through, ostentatiously leading Potter by the arm. The poor fellow's face was haggard, and his eyes showed the fear that was upon him. When he stood before the murdered man, he shook as with a palsy, and he put his face in his hands and burst into tears.

"I didn't do it, friends," he sobbed; "'pon my word and honor I never done it."

"Who's accused you?" shouted a voice.

INJUN JOE'S TWO VICTIMS.

This shot seemed to carry home. Potter lifted his face and looked around him with a pathetic hopelessness in his eyes. He saw Injun Joe, and exclaimed:

"O, Injun Joe, you promised me you'd never—"

"Is that your knife?" and it was thrust before him by the Sheriff.

Potter would have fallen if they had not caught him and eased him to the ground. Then he said:

"Something told me 't if I didn't come back and get—" He shuddered; then waved his nerveless hand with a vanquished gesture and said, "Tell 'em, Joe, tell 'em—it ain't any use any more."

Then Huckleberry and Tom stood dumb and staring, and heard the stony-hearted liar reel off his serene statement, they expecting every moment that the clear sky would deliver God's lightnings upon his head, and wondering to see how long the stroke was delayed. And when he had finished and still stood alive and whole, their wavering impulse to break their oath and save the poor betrayed prisoner's life faded and vanished away, for plainly this miscreant had sold himself to Satan and it would be fatal to meddle with the property of such a power as that.

"Why didn't you leave? What did you want to come here for?" somebody said.

"I couldn't help it—I couldn't help it," Potter moaned. "I wanted to run away, but I couldn't seem to come anywhere but here." And he fell to sobbing again.

Injun Joe repeated his statement, just as calmly, a few minutes afterward on the inquest, under oath; and the boys, seeing that the lightnings were still withheld, were confirmed in their belief that Joe had sold himself to the devil. He was now become, to them, the most balefully interesting object they had ever looked upon, and they could not take their fascinated eyes from his face.

They inwardly resolved to watch him, nights, when opportunity should offer, in the hope of getting a glimpse of his dread master.

Injun Joe helped to raise the body of the murdered man and put it in a wagon for removal; and it was whispered through the shuddering crowd that the wound bled a little! The boys thought that this happy circumstance would turn suspicion in the right direction; but they were disappointed, for more than one villager remarked:

"It was within three feet of Muff Potter when it done it."

Tom's fearful secret and gnawing conscience disturbed his sleep for as much as a week after this; and at breakfast one morning Sid said:

"Tom, you pitch around and talk in your sleep so much that you keep me awake about half the time."

Tom blanched and dropped his eyes.

"It's a bad sign," said Aunt Polly, gravely. "What you got on your mind, Tom?"

"Nothing. Nothing 't I know of." But the boy's hand shook so that he spilled his coffee.

"And you do talk such stuff," Sid said. "Last night you said 'it's blood, it's blood, that's what it is!' You said that over and over. And you said, 'Don't torment me so—I'll tell!' Tell *what*? What is it you'll tell?"

Everything was swimming before Tom. There is no telling what might have happened, now, but luckily the concern passed out of Aunt Polly's face and she came to Tom's relief without knowing it. She said:

"Sho! It's that dreadful murder. I dream about it most every night myself. Sometimes I dream it's me that done it."

Mary said she had been affected much the same way. Sid seemed satisfied. Tom got out of the presence as quick as he plausibly could, and after that he complained of toothache for a week, and tied up his jaws every night. He never knew that Sid lay nightly watching, and frequently slipped the bandage free and then leaned on his elbow listening a good while at a time, and afterward slipped the bandage back to its place again. Tom's distress of mind wore off gradually and the toothache grew irksome and was discarded. If Sid really managed to make anything out of Tom's disjointed mutterings, he kept it to himself.

It seemed to Tom that his schoolmates never would get done holding inquests on dead cats, and thus keeping his trouble present to his mind. Sid noticed that Tom never was coroner at one of these inquiries, though it had been his habit to take the lead in all new enterprises; he noticed, too, that Tom never acted as a witness,—and that was strange; and Sid did not overlook the fact that Tom even showed a marked aversion to these inquests, and always avoided them when he could. Sid marveled, but said nothing. However, even inquests went out of vogue at last, and ceased to torture Tom's conscience.

Every day or two, during this time of sorrow, Tom watched his opportunity and went to the little grated jail-window and smuggled such small comforts through to the "murderer" as he could get hold of. The jail was a trifling little brick den that stood in a marsh at the edge of the village, and no guards were afforded for it; indeed it was seldom occupied. These offerings greatly helped to ease Tom's conscience.

The villagers had a strong desire to tar-and-feather Injun Joe and ride him on a rail, for body-snatching, but so formidable was his character that nobody could be found who was willing to take the lead in the matter, so it was dropped. He had been careful to begin both of his inquest-statements with the fight, without confessing the grave-robbery that preceded it; therefore it was deemed wisest not to try the case in the courts at present.

CHAPTER XII.

PETER.

ONE of the reasons why Tom's mind had drifted away from its secret troubles was, that it had found a new and weighty matter to interest itself about. Becky Thatcher had stopped coming to school. Tom had struggled with his pride a few days, and tried to "whistle her down the wind," but failed. He began to find himself hanging around her father's house, nights, and feeling very miserable. She was ill. What if she should die! There was distraction in the thought. He no longer took an interest in war, nor even in piracy. The charm of life was gone; there was nothing but dreariness left. He put his hoop away, and his bat; there was no joy in them any more. His aunt was concerned. She began to try all manner of remedies on him. She was one of those people who are infatuated with patent medicines and all new-fangled methods of producing health or mending it. She was an inveterate experimenter in these things. When something fresh in this line came out she was in a fever, right away, to try it; not on herself, for she was never ailing, but on anybody else that came handy. She was a subscriber for all the "Health" periodicals and phreneological frauds; and the solemn ignorance they were inflated with was breath to her nostrils. All the "rot" they contained about ventilation, and how to go to bed, and how to get up, and what to eat, and what to drink, and how much exercise to take, and what frame of mind to keep one's self in, and what sort of clothing to wear, was all gospel to her, and she never observed that her health-journals of the current month customarily upset everything they had recommended the month before. She was as simple-hearted and honest as the day was long, and so she was an easy victim. She gathered together her quack periodicals and her quack medicines, and thus armed with death, went about on her pale horse, metaphorically speaking, with "hell following after." But she never suspected that she was not an angel of healing and the balm of Gilead in disguise, to the suffering neighbors.

The water treatment was new, now, and Tom's low condition was

a windfall to her. She had him out at daylight every morning, stood him up in the woodshed and drowned him with a deluge of cold water; then she scrubbed him down with a towel like a file, and so brought him to; then she rolled him up in a wet sheet and put him away under blankets till she sweated his soul clean and "the yellow stains of it came through his pores" as Tom said.

AUNT POLLY SEEKS INFORMATION.

Yet notwithstanding all this, the boy grew more and more melancholy and pale and dejected. She added hot baths, sitz baths, shower baths and plunges. The boy remained as dismal as a hearse. She began to assist the water with a slim oatmeal diet and blister plasters. She calculated his capacity as she would a jug's and filled him up every day with quack cure-alls.

Tom had become indifferent to persecution by this time. This phase filled the old lady's heart with consternation. This indifference must be broken up at any cost. Now she heard of Pain-killer for the first time. She ordered a lot at once. She tasted it and was filled with gratitude. It was simply fire in a liquid form. She dropped the water treatment and everything else, and pinned her faith to Pain-killer. She gave Tom a tea-spoonful and watched with the deepest anxiety for the result. Her troubles were instantly at rest, her soul at peace again; for the "indifference" was broken up. The boy could not have shown a wilder, heartier interest, if she had built a fire under him.

Tom felt that it was time to wake up; this sort of life might be romantic enough, in his blighted condition, but it was getting to have too little sentiment and too much distracting variety about it. So he thought over various plans for relief, and finally hit upon that of professing to be fond of Pain-killer. He asked for it so often that he became a nuisance, and his aunt ended by telling him to help himself and quit bothering her. If it had been Sid, she would have had no misgivings to alloy her delight; but since it was Tom, she watched the bottle clandestinely. She found that the medicine did really diminish, but it did not occur to her that the boy was mending the health of a crack in the sitting-room floor with it.

One day Tom was in the act of dosing the crack when his aunt's yellow cat came along, purring, eyeing the teaspoon avariciously, and begging for a taste. Tom said:

"Don't ask for it unless you want it, Peter."

But Peter signified that he did want it.

"You better make sure."

Peter was sure.

"Now you've asked for it, and I'll give it to you, because there ain't anything mean about *me*; but if you find you don't like it, you musn't blame anybody but your own self."

Peter was agreeable. So Tom pried his mouth open and poured down the Pain-killer. Peter sprang a couple of yards in the air, and then delivered a war-whoop and set off round and round the room, banging against furniture, upsetting flower pots and making general havoc. Next he rose on his hind feet and pranced around, in a frenzy of enjoyment, with his head over his shoulder and his voice proclaiming his unappeasable happiness. Then he went tearing around the house again spreading chaos and destruction in his path. Aunt Polly entered in time to see him throw a few double summersets, deliver a final mighty hurrah, and sail through the open window, carrying the rest of the flower-pots with him. The old lady stood petrified with astonishment, peering over her glasses; Tom lay on the floor expiring with laughter.

A GENERAL GOOD TIME.

"Tom, what on earth ails that cat?"

"*I* don't know, aunt," gasped the boy.

"Why I never see anything like it. What *did* make him act so?"

"Deed I don't know Aunt Polly; cats always act so when they're having a good time."

"They do, do they?" There was something in the tone that made Tom apprehensive.

"Yes'm. That is, I believe they do."

"You *do*?"

"Yes'm."

The old lady was bending down, Tom watching, with interest emphasized by anxiety. Too late he divined her "drift." The handle of the tell-tale tea-spoon was visible under the bed-valance. Aunt Polly took it, held it up. Tom winced, and dropped his eyes. Aunt Polly raised him by the usual handle—his ear—and cracked his head soundly with her thimble.

"Now, sir, what did you want to treat that poor dumb beast so, for?"

"I done it out of pity for him—because he hadn't any aunt."

"Hadn't any aunt!—you numscull. What has that got to do with it?"

"Heaps. Because if he'd a had one she'd a burnt him out herself! She'd a roasted his bowels out of him 'thout any more feeling than if he was a human!"

Aunt Polly felt a sudden pang of remorse. This was putting the thing in a new light; what was cruelty to a cat *might* be cruelty to a boy, too. She began to soften; she felt sorry. Her eyes watered a little, and she put her hand on Tom's head and said gently:

"I was meaning for the best, Tom. And Tom, it *did* do you good."

Tom looked up in her face with just a preceptible twinkle peeping through his gravity:

"I know you was meaning for the best, aunty, and so was I with Peter. It done *him* good, too. I never see him get around so since—"

"O, go 'long with you, Tom, before you aggravate me again. And you try and see if you can't be a good boy, for once, and you needn't take any more medicine."

Tom reached school ahead of time. It was noticed that this strange thing had been occurring every day latterly. And now, as usual of late, he hung about the gate of the school-yard instead of playing with his comrades. He was sick, he said, and he looked it. He tried to seem to be looking everywhere but whither he really was looking—down the road. Presently Jeff Thatcher hove in sight, and Tom's face lighted; he gazed a moment, and then turned sorrowfully away. When Jeff arrived, Tom accosted him, and "led up" warily to opportunities for remark about Becky, but the giddy lad never could see the bait. Tom watched and watched, hoping whenever a frisking frock came in sight, and hating the owner of it as soon as he saw she was not the right one. At last frocks ceased to appear, and he dropped hopelessly into the dumps; he entered the empty school house and sat down to surfer. Then one more frock passed in at the gate, and Tom's heart gave a great bound. The next instant he was out, and "going on" like an Indian; yelling, laughing, chasing boys, jumping over the fence at risk of life and limb, throwing hand-springs, standing on his head—doing all the heroic things he could conceive of, and keeping a furtive eye out, all the while, to see if Becky Thatcher was noticing. But she seemed to be unconscious of it all; she never looked. Could it be posssble that she was not aware that he was there? He carried his exploits to her immediate vicinity; came war-whooping around, snatched a boy's cap, hurled it to the roof of the schoolhouse, broke through a group of boys, tumbling them in every direction, and fell sprawling, himself, under Becky's nose, almost upsetting her—and she turned, with her nose in the air, and he heard her say. "Mf! some people think they're mighty smart—always showing off!"

Tom's cheeks burned. He gathered himself up and sneaked off, crushed and crestfallen.

JOE HARPER

CHAPTER XIII.

Tom's mind was made up now. He was gloomy and desperate. He was a forsaken, friendless boy, he said; nobody loved him; when they found out what they had driven him to, perhaps they would be sorry; he had tried to do right and get along, but they would not let him; since nothing would do them but to be rid of him, let it be so; and let them blame *him* for the consequences— why shouldn't they? What right had the friendless to complain?

Yes, they had forced him to it at last: he would lead a life of crime. There was no choice.

By this time he was far down Meadow Lane, and the bell for school to "take up" tinkled faintly upon his ear. He sobbed, now, to think he should never, never hear that old familiar sound any more—it was very hard, but it was forced on him; since he was driven out into the cold world, he must submit—but he forgave them. Then the sobs came thick and fast.

Just at this point he met his soul's sworn comrade, Joe Harper—hard-eyed, and with evidently a great and dismal purpose in his heart. Plainly here were "two souls with but a single thought." Tom, wiping his eyes with his sleeve, began to blubber out something about a resolution to escape from hard usage and lack of sympathy at home by roaming abroad into the great world never to return; and ended by hoping that Joe would not forget him.

But it transpired that this was a request which Joe had just been going to make of Tom, and had come to hunt him up for that purpose. His mother had whipped him for drinking some cream which he had never tasted and knew nothing about; it was plain that she was tired of him and wished him to go; if she felt that way, there was nothing for him to do but succumb; he hoped she would be happy, and never regret having driven her poor boy out into the unfeeling world to suffer and die.

As the two boys walked sorrowing along, they made a new compact to stand by each other and be brothers and never separate till death relieved them of their troubles. Then they began to lay their plans. Joe was for being a hermit, and living on crusts in a remote cave, and dying, some time, of cold, and want, and grief; but after listening to Tom, he conceded that there were some conspicuous advantages about a life of crime, and so he consented to be a pirate.

Three miles below St. Petersburg, at a point where the Mississippi river was a trifle over a mile wide, there was a long, narrow, wooded island, with a shallow bar at the head of it, and this offered well as a rendezvous. It was not inhabited; it lay far over toward the further shore, abreast a dense and almost wholly unpeopled forest. So Jackson's Island was chosen. Who were to be the subjects of their piracies, was a matter that did not occur to them. Then they hunted up Huckleberry Finn, and he joined them promptly, for all careers were one to him; he was indifferent. They presently separated to meet at a lonely spot on the river bank two miles above the village at the favorite hour—which was midnight. There was a small log raft there which they meant to capture. Each would bring hooks and lines, and such provision as he could steal in the most dark and mysterious way—as became outlaws. And before the afternoon was done, they had all managed to enjoy the sweet glory of spreading the fact that pretty soon the town would "hear something." All who got this vague hint were cautioned to "be mum and wait."

About midnight Tom arrived with a boiled ham and a few trifles, and stopped in a dense undergrowth on a small bluff overlooking the meeting-place. It was starlight, and very still. The mighty river lay like an ocean at rest. Tom listened a moment, but no sound disturbed the quiet. Then he gave a low, distinct whistle. It was answered from under the bluff. Tom whistled twice more; these signals were answered in the same way. Then a guarded voice said:

"Who goes there?"

"Tom Sawyer, the Black Avenger of the Spanish Main. Name your names."

"Huck Finn the Red-Handed, and Joe Harper the Terror of the Seas." Tom had furnished these titles, from his favorite literature.

"Tis well. Give the countersign."

Two hoarse whispers delivered the same awful word simultaneously to the brooding night:

"BLOOD!"

Then Tom tumbled his ham over the bluff and let himself down after it, tearing both skin and clothes to some extent in the effort. There was an easy, comfortable path along the shore under the bluff, but it lacked the advantages of difficulty and danger so valued by a pirate.

The Terror of the Seas had brought a side of bacon, and had about worn himself out with getting it there. Finn the Red-Handed had stolen a skillet and a quantity of half-cured leaf tobacco, and had also brought a few corn-cobs to make pipes with. But none of the pirates smoked or "chewed" but himself. The Black Avenger of the Spanish Main said it would never do to start without some fire. That was a wise thought; matches were hardly known there in that day. They saw a fire smouldering upon a great raft a hundred yards above, and they went stealthily thither and helped themselves to a chunk. They made an imposing adventure of it, saying "Hist!" every now and then, and suddenly halting with finger on lip; moving with hands on imaginary dagger-hilts; and giving orders in dismal whispers that if "the foe" stirred, to "let him have it to the hilt," because "dead men tell no tales." They knew well enough that the raftsmen were all down at the village laying in stores or having a spree, but still that was no excuse for their conducting this thing in an unpiratical way.

They shoved off, presently, Tom in command, Huck at the after oar and Joe at the forward. Tom stood amidships, gloomy-browed, and with folded arms, and gave his orders in a low, stern whisper:

"Luff, and bring her to the wind!"

"Aye-aye, sir!"

"Steady, stead-y-y-y!"

"Steady it is, sir!"

"Let her go off a point!"

"Point it is, sir!"

As the boys steadily and monotonously drove the raft toward midstream it was no doubt understood that these orders were given only for style," and were not intended to mean anything in particular.

"What sail's she carrying?"

"Courses, tops'ls and flying-jib, sir."

"Send the r'yals up! Lay out aloft, there, half a dozen of ye,— foretopmast-stuns'l! Lively, now!"

"Aye-aye, sir!"

"Shake out that maintogalans'l! Sheets and braces! Now, my hearties!"

"Aye-aye, sir!"

"Hellum'-a-lee—hard a port! Stand by to meet her when she comes! Port, port! *Now*, men! With a will! Stead-y-y-y!"

"Steady it is, sir!"

The raft drew beyond the middle of the river; the boys pointed her head right, and then lay on their oars. The river was not high, so there was not more than a two or three-mile current. Hardly a word was said during the next three-quarters of an hour. Now the raft was passing before the distant town. Two or three glimmering lights showed where it lay, peacefully sleeping, beyond the vague vast sweep of star-gemmed water, unconscious of the tremendous event that was happening. The Black Avenger stood still with folded arms, "looking his last" upon the scene of his former joys and his later sufferings, and wishing "she" could see him now, abroad on the wild sea, facing peril and death with dauntless heart, going to his doom with a grim smile on his lips. It was but a small strain on his imagination to remove Jackson's Island beyond eye-shot of the village, and so he "looked his last" with a broken and satisfied heart. The other pirates were looking their last, too; and they all looked so long that they came near letting the current drift them out of the range of the island. But they discovered the danger in time, and made shift to avert it. About two o'clock in the morning the raft grounded on the bar two hundred yards above the head of the island, and they waded back and forth until they had landed their freight. Part of the little raft's belongings consisted of an old sail, and this they spread over a nook in the bushes for a tent to shelter their provisions; but they themselves would sleep in the open air in good weather, as became outlaws.

ON BOARD THEIR FIRST PRIZE.

They built a fire against the side of a great log twenty or thirty steps within the sombre depths of the forest, and then cooked some bacon in the frying-pan for supper, and used up half of the corn "pone" stock they had brought. It seemed glorious sport to be feasting in that wild free way in the virgin forest of an unexplored and uninhabited island, far from the haunts of men, and they said they never would return to civilization. The climbing fire lit up their faces and threw its ruddy glare upon the pillared tree trunks of their forest temple, and upon the varnished foliage and festooning vines.

When the last crisp slice of bacon was gone, and the last allowance of corn pone devoured, the boys stretched themselves out on the grass, filled with contentment. They could have found a cooler place, but they would not deny themselves such a romantic feature as the roasting campfire.

"*Ain't* it gay?" said Joe.

"It's *nuts!*" said Tom. "What would the boys say if they could see us?"

"Say? Well they'd just die to be here—hey Hucky!"

"I reckon so," said Huckleberry; "anyways *I'*m suited. I don't

want nothing better'n this. I don't ever get enough to eat, gen'ally— and here they can't come and pick at a feller and bullyrag him so."

"It's just the life for me," said Tom. "You don't have to get up, mornings, and you don't have to go to school, and wash, and all that blame foolishness. You see a pirate don't have to do *anything*, Joe, when he's ashore, but a hermit *he* has to be praying considerable, and then he don't have any fun, anyway, all by himself that way."

THE PIRATES ASHORE.

"O yes, that's so," said Joe, "but I hadn't thought much about it, you know. I'd a good deal rather be a pirate, now that I've tried it."

"You see," said Tom, "people don't go much on hermits, now-a-days, like they used to in old times, but a pirate's always respected. And a hermit's got to sleep on the hardest place he can find, and put sack-cloth and ashes on his head, and stand out in the rain, and—"

"What does he put sack-cloth and ashes on his head for?" inquired Huck.

"*I* dono. But they've *got* to do it. Hermits always do. You'd have to do that if you was a hermit."

"Dern'd if I would," said Huck.

"Well what would you do?"

"I dono. But I wouldn't do that."

"Why Huck, you'd *have* to. How'd you get around it?"

"Why I just wouldn't stand it. I'd run away."

"Run away! Well you *would* be a nice old slouch of a hermit. You'd be a disgrace."

The Red-Handed made no response, being better employed. He had finished gouging out a cob, and now he fitted a weed stem to it, loaded it with tobacco, and was pressing a coal to the charge and blowing a cloud of fragrant smoke—he was in the full bloom of luxurious contentment. The other pirates envied him this majestic vice, and secretly resolved to acquire it shortly. Presently Huck said:

"What does pirates have to do?"

Tom said:

"Oh they have just a bully time—take ships, and burn them, and get the money and bury it in awful places in their island where there's ghosts and things to watch it, and kill everybody in the ships—make 'em walk a plank."

"And they carry the women to the island," said Joe; "they don't kill the women."

"No," assented Tom, "they don't kill the women—they're too noble. And the women's always beautiful, too."

"And don't they wear the bulliest clothes! Oh, no! All gold and silver and di'monds," said Joe, with enthusiasm.

"Who?" said Huck.

"Why the pirates."

Huck scanned his own clothing forlornly.

"I reckon I ain't dressed fitten for a pirate," said he, with a regretful pathos in his voice; "but I ain't got none but these."

But the other boys told him the fine clothes would come fast enough, after they should have begun their adventures. They made him understand that his poor rags would do to begin with, though it was customary for wealthy pirates to start with a proper wardrobe.

Gradually their talk died out and drowsiness began to steal upon the eyelids of the little waifs. The pipe dropped from the fingers of the Red-Handed, and he slept the sleep of the conscience-free and the weary. The Terror of the Seas and the Black Avenger of the Spanish Main had more difficulty in getting to sleep. They said their prayers inwardly, and lying down, since there was nobody there with authority to make them kneel and recite aloud; in truth they had a mind not to say them at all, but they were afraid to proceed to such lengths as that, lest they might call down a sudden and special thunderbolt from Heaven. Then at once they reached and hovered upon the imminent verge of sleep—but an intruder came, now, that would not "down." It was conscience. They began to feel a vague fear that they had been doing wrong to run away; and next they thought of the stolen meat, and then the real torture came. They tried to argue it away by reminding conscience that they had purloined sweetmeats and apples scores of times; but conscience was not to be appeased by such thin plausibilities; it seemed to them, in the end, that there was no getting around the stubborn fact that taking sweetmeats was only "hooking," while taking bacon and hams and such valuables was plain simple *stealing*—and there was a command against that in the Bible. So they inwardly resolved that so long as they remained in the business, their piracies should not again be sullied with the crime of stealing. Then conscience granted a truce, and these curiously inconsistent pirates fell peacefully to sleep.

CHAPTER XIV.

WHEN Tom awoke in the morning, he wondered where he was. He sat up and rubbed his eyes and looked around. Then he comprehended. It was the cool gray dawn, and there was a delicious sense of repose and peace in the deep pervading calm and silence of the woods. Not a leaf stirred; not a sound obtruded upon great Nature's meditation. Beaded dew-drops stood upon the leaves and grasses. A white layer of ashes covered the fire, and a thin blue breath of smoke rose straight into the air. Joe and Huck still slept.

Now, far away in the woods a bird called; another answered; presently the hammering of a woodpecker was heard. Gradually the cool dim gray of the morning whitened, and as gradually sounds multiplied and life manifested itself. The marvel of Nature shaking off sleep and going to work unfolded itself to the musing boy. A little green worm came crawling over a dewy leaf, lifting two-thirds of his body into the air from time to time and "sniffing around," then proceeding again—for he was measuring, Tom said; and when the worm approached him, of its own accord, he sat as still as a stone, with his hopes rising and falling, by turns, as the creature still came toward him or seemed inclined to go elsewhere; and when at last it considered a painful moment with its curved body in the air and then came decisively down upon Tom's leg and began a journey over him, his whole heart was glad—for that meant that he was going to have a new suit of clothes—without the shadow of a doubt a gaudy piratical uniform. Now a procession of ants appeared, from nowhere in particular, and went about their labors; one struggled manfully by with a dead spider five times as big as itself in its arms, and lugged it straight up a tree-trunk. A brown spotted lady-bug climbed the dizzy height of a grass blade, and Tom bent down close to it and said, "Lady-bug, lady-bug, fly away home, your house is on fire, your children's alone," and she took wing and went off to see about it—which did not surprise the boy, for he knew of old that this insect was credulous about conflagrations and he had practiced upon its simplicity more than once. A tumble-bug came next, heaving sturdily at its ball, and Tom touched the creature, to see it shut its legs against its body and pretend to be dead. The birds were fairly rioting by this time. A cat-bird, the northern mocker, lit in a tree over Tom's head, and trilled out her imitations of her neighbors in a rapture of enjoyment; then a shrill jay swept down, a flash of blue flame, and stopped on a twig almost within the boy's reach, cocked his head to one side and eyed the strangers with a consuming curiosity; a gray squirrel and a big fellow of the "fox" kind came skurrying along, sitting up at intervals to inspect and chatter at the boys, for the wild things had probably never seen a human being before and scarcely knew whether to be afraid or not. All Nature was wide awake and stirring, now; long lances of sunlight pierced down through the dense foliage far and near, and a few butterflies came fluttering upon the scene.

Tom stirred up the other pirates and they all clattered away with a shout, and in a minute or two were stripped and chasing after and tumbling over each other in the shallow limpid water of the white sandbar. They felt no longing for the little village sleeping in the distance beyond the majestic waste of water. A vagrant current or a slight rise in the river had carried off their raft, but this only gratified them, since its going was something like burning the bridge between them and civilization.

They came back to camp wonderfully refreshed, glad-hearted, and ravenous; and they soon had the campfire blazing up again. Huck found a spring of clear cold water close by, and the boys made cups of broad oak or hickory leaves, and felt that water, sweetened with such a wild-wood charm as that, would be a good enough substitute for coffee. While Joe was slicing bacon for breakfast, Tom and Huck asked him to hold on a minute; they stepped to a promising nook in the river bank and threw in their lines; almost immediately they had reward. Joe had not had time to get impatient before they were back again with some handsome bass, a couple of sun-perch and a small cat-fish—provisions enough for quite a family. They fried the fish with the bacon and were astonished; for no fish had ever seemed so delicious before. They did not know that the quicker a fresh water fish is on the fire after he is caught the better he

THE PIRATES' BATH.

is; and they reflected little upon what a sauce open air sleeping, open air exercise, bathing, and a large ingredient of hunger makes, too.

They lay around in the shade, after breakfast, while Huck had a smoke, and then went off through the woods on an exploring expedition. They tramped gaily along, over decaying logs, through tangled underbrush, among solemn monarchs of the forest, hung from their crowns to the ground with a drooping regalia of grape-vines. Now and then they came upon snug nooks carpeted with grass and jeweled with flowers.

They found plenty of things to be delighted with but nothing to be astonished at. They discovered that the island was about three miles long and a quarter of a mile wide, and that the shore it lay closest to was only separated from it by a narrow channel hardly two hundred yards wide. They took a swim about every hour, so it was close upon the middle of the afternoon when they got back to camp. They were too hungry to stop to fish, but they fared sumptuously upon cold ham, and then threw themselves down in the shade to talk. But the talk soon began to drag, and then died. The stillness, the solemnity that brooded in the woods, and the sense of loneliness, began to tell upon the spirits of the boys. They fell to thinking. A sort of undefined longing crept upon them. This took dim shape, presently—it was budding home-sickness. Even Finn the Red-Handed was dreaming of his door-steps and empty hogsheads. But they were all ashamed of their weakness, and none was brave enough to speak his thought.

For some time, now, the boys had been dully conscious of a peculiar sound in the distance, just as one sometimes is of the ticking of a clock which he takes no distinct note of. But now this mysterious sound became more pronounced, and forced a recognition. The boys started, glanced at each other, and then each assumed a listening attitude. There was a long silence, profound and unbroken; then a deep, sullen boom came floating down out of the distance.

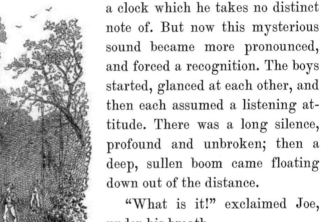

THE PLEASANT STROLL.

"What is it!" exclaimed Joe, under his breath.

"I wonder," said Tom in a whisper.

"Tain't thunder," said Huckleberry, in an awed tone, "becuz thunder—"

"Hark!" said Tom. "Listen—don't talk."

They waited a time that seemed an age, and then the same muffled boom troubled the solemn hush.

"Let's go and see."

They sprang to their feet and hurried to the shore toward the town. They parted the bushes on the bank and peered out over the water. The little steam ferry boat was about a mile below the village, drifting with the current. Her broad deck seemed crowded with people. There were a great many skiffs rowing about or floating with the stream in the neighborhood of the ferry boat, but the boys could not determine what the men in them were doing. Presently a great jet of white smoke burst from the ferry boat's side, and as it expanded and rose in a lazy cloud, that same dull throb of sound was borne to the listeners again.

"I know now!" exclaimed Tom; "somebody's drownded!"

THE SEARCH FOR THE DROWNED.

"That's it!" said Huck; "they done that last summer, when Bill Turner got drownded; they shoot a cannon over the water, and that makes him come up to the top. Yes, and they take loaves of bread and put quicksilver in 'em and set 'em afloat, and wherever there's anybody that's drownded, they'll float right there and stop."

"Yes, I've heard about that," said Joe. "I wonder what makes the bread do that."

"Oh it ain't the bread, so much," said Tom; "I reckon it's mostly what they *say* over it before they start it out."

"But they don't say anything over it," said Huck. "I've seen 'em and they don't."

"Well that's funny," said Tom. "But maybe they say it to themselves. Of *course* they do. Anybody might know that."

The other boys agreed that there was reason in what Tom said, because an ignorant lump of bread, uninstructed by an incantation, could not be expected to act very intelligently when sent upon an errand of such gravity.

"By jings I wish I was over there, now," said Joe.

"I do too," said Huck. "I'd give heaps to know who it is."

The boys still listened and watched. Presently a revealing thought flashed through Tom's mind, and he exclaimed:

"Boys, I know who's drownded—it's us!"

They felt like heroes in an instant. Here was a gorgeous triumph; they were missed; they were mourned; hearts were breaking on their account; tears were being shed; accusing memories of unkindnesses to these poor lost lads were rising up, and unavailing regrets and remorse were being indulged; and best of all, the departed were the talk of the whole town, and the envy of all the boys, as far as this dazzling notoriety was concerned. This was fine. It was worth while to be a pirate, after all.

As twilight drew on, the ferry boat went back to her accustomed business and the skiffs disappeared. The pirates returned to camp. They were jubilant with vanity over their new grandeur and the illustrious trouble they were making. They caught fish, cooked supper and ate it, and then fell to guessing at what the village was thinking and saying about them; and the pictures they drew of the public distress on their account were gratifying to look upon—from their point of view. But when the shadows of night closed them in, they gradually ceased to talk, and sat gazing into the fire, with their minds evidently wandering elsewhere. The excitement was gone, now, and Tom and Joe could not keep back thoughts of certain persons at home who were not enjoying this fine frolic as much as they were. Misgivings came; they grew troubled and unhappy; a sigh or two escaped, unawares. By and by Joe timidly ventured upon a round-about "feeler" as to how the others might look upon a return to civilization—not right now, but—

Tom withered him with derision! Huck, being uncommitted, as yet, joined in with Tom, and the waverer quickly "explained," and was glad to get out of the scrape with as little taint of chicken-hearted home-sickness clinging to his garments as he could. Mutiny was effectually laid to rest for the moment.

As the night deepened, Huck began to nod, and presently to snore. Joe followed next. Tom lay upon his elbow motionless, for some time, watching the two intently. At last he got up cautiously, on his knees, and went searching among the grass and the flickering reflections flung by the campfire. He picked up and inspected several large semi-cylinders of the thin white bark of a sycamore, and finally chose two which seemed to suit him. Then he knelt by the fire and painfully wrote something upon each of these with his "red keel;" one he rolled up and put in his jacket pocket, and the other he put in Joe's hat and removed it to a little distance from the owner. And he also put into the hat certain schoolboy treasures of almost inestimable value—among them a lump of chalk, an India rubber ball, three fishhooks, and one of that kind of mar-

TOM'S MYSTERIOUS WRITING.

bles known as a "sure 'nough crystal." Then he tip-toed his way cautiously among the trees till he felt that he was out of hearing, and straightway broke into a keen run in the direction of the sandbar.

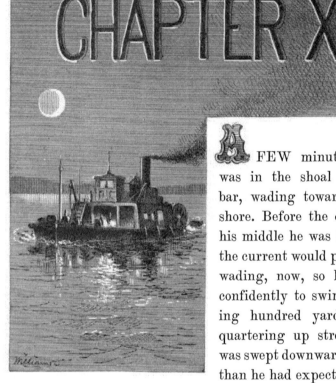

CHAPTER XV.

A FEW minutes later Tom was in the shoal water of the bar, wading toward the Illinois shore. Before the depth reached his middle he was half way over; the current would permit no more wading, now, so he struck out confidently to swim the remaining hundred yards. He swam quartering up stream, but still was swept downward rather faster than he had expected. However, he reached the shore finally, and drifted along till he found a low place and drew himself out. He put his hand on his jacket pocket, found his piece of bark safe, and then struck through the woods, following the shore, with streaming garments. Shortly before ten o'clock he came out into an open place opposite the village, and saw the ferry boat lying in the shadow of the trees and the high bank. Everything was quiet under the blinking stars. He crept down the bank, watching with all his eyes, slipped into the water, swam three or four strokes and climbed into the skiff that did "yawl" duty at the boat's stern. He laid himself down under the thwarts and waited, panting.

Presently the cracked bell tapped and a voice gave the order to "cast off." A minute or two later the skiff's head was standing high up, against the boat's swell, and the voyage was begun. Tom felt happy in his success, for he knew it was the boat's last trip for the night. At the end of a long twelve or fifteen minutes the wheels stopped, and Tom slipped overboard and swam ashore in the dusk, landing fifty yards down stream, out of danger of possible stragglers.

He flew along unfrequented alleys, and shortly found himself at his aunt's back fence. He climbed over, approached the "ell" and looked in at the sitting-room window, for a light was burning there. There sat Aunt Polly, Sid, Mary, and Joe Harper's mother, grouped together, talking. They were by the bed, and the bed was between them and the door. Tom went to the door and began to softly lift the latch; then he pressed gently and the door yielded a crack; he continued pushing cautiously, and quaking every time it creaked, till he judged he might squeeze through on his knees; and so he put his head through and began, warily.

"What makes the candle blow so?" said Aunt Polly. Tom hurried up. "Why that door's open, I believe. Why of course it is. No end of strange things now. Go 'long and shut it, Sid."

Tom disappeared under the bed just in time. He lay and "breathed" himself for a time, and then crept to where he could almost touch his aunt's foot.

"But as I was saying," said Aunt Polly, "he warn't *bad*, so to say only mischievous. Only just giddy, and harum-scarum, you know. He warn't any more responsible than a colt. *He* never meant any harm, and he was the best-hearted boy that ever was"—and she began to cry.

"It was just so with my Joe—always full of his devilment, and up to every kind of mischief, but he was just as unselfish and kind as he could be—and laws bless me, to think I went and whipped him for taking that cream, never once recollecting that I throwed it out myself because it was sour, and I never to see him again in this world, never, never, never, poor abused boy!" And Mrs Harper sobbed as if her heart would break.

"I hope Tom's better off where he is," said Sid, "but if he'd been better in some ways—"

"*Sid!*" Tom felt the glare of the old lady's eye, though he could not see it. "Not a word against my Tom, now that he's gone! God'll take care of *him*—never you trouble *your*self, sir! Oh, Mrs. Harper, I don't know how to give him up! I don't know how to give him up! He was such a comfort to me, although he tormented my old heart out of me, 'most."

WHAT TOM SAW.

"The Lord giveth and the Lord hath taken away.—Blessed be the name of the Lord! But it's *so* hard—Oh, it's so hard! Only last Saturday my Joe busted a firecracker right under my nose and I knocked him sprawling. Little did I know then, how soon—O, if it was to do over again I'd hug him and bless him for it."

"Yes, yes, yes, I know just how you feel, Mrs. Harper, I know just exactly how you feel. No longer ago than yesterday noon, my Tom took and filled the cat full of Pain-Killer, and I did think the cretur would tear the house down. And God forgave me, I cracked Tom's head with my thimble, poor boy, poor dead boy. But he's out of all his troubles now. And the last words I ever heard him say was to reproach—"

But this memory was too much for the old lady, and she broke entirely down. Tom was snuffling, now, himself—and more in pity of himself than anybody else. He could hear Mary crying, and putting in a kindly word for him from time to time. He began to have a nobler opinion of himself than ever before. Still he was sufficiently touched by his aunt's grief to long to rush out from under the bed and overwhelm her with joy—and the theatrical gorgeousness of the thing appealed strongly to his nature, too, but he resisted and lay still.

He went on listening, and gathered by odds and ends that it was conjectured at first that the boys had got drowned while taking a swim; then the small raft had been missed; next, certain boys said the missing lads had promised that the village should "hear something" soon; the wise-heads had "put this and that together" and decided that the lads had gone off on that raft and would turn up at the next town below, presently; but toward noon the raft had been found, lodged against the Missouri shore some five or six miles below the village,—and then hope perished; they must be drowned, else hunger would have driven them home by nightfall if not sooner. It was believed that the search for the bodies had been a fruitless effort merely because the drowning must have occurred in mid-channel, since the boys, being good swimmers, would otherwise have escaped to shore. This was Wednesday night. If the bodies continued missing until Sunday, all hope would be given over, and the funerals would be preached on that morning. Tom shuddered.

Mrs. Harper gave a sobbing good-night and turned to go. Then with a mutual impulse the two bereaved women flung themselves into each other's arms and had a good, consoling cry, and then parted. Aunt Polly was tender far beyond her wont, in her good-night to Sid and Mary. Sid snuffled a bit and Mary went off crying with all her heart.

Aunt Polly knelt down and prayed for Tom so touchingly, so appealingly, and with such measureless love in her words and her old trembling voice, that he was weltering in tears again, long before she was through.

He had to keep still long after she went to bed, for she kept making broken-hearted ejaculations from time to time, tossing unrestfully, and turning over. But at last she was still, only moaning a little in her sleep. Now the boy stole out, rose gradually by the bedside, shaded the candlelight with his hand, and stood regarding her. His heart was full of pity for her. He took out his sycamore scroll and placed it by the candle. But something occurred to him, and he lingered considering. His face lighted with a happy solution of his thought; he put the bark hastily in his pocket. Then he bent over and kissed the faded lips, and straightway made his stealthy exit, latching the door behind him.

He threaded his way back to the ferry landing, found nobody at large there, and walked boldly on board the boat, for he knew she was tenantless except that there was a watchman, who always turned in and slept like a graven image. He untied the skiff at the stern, slipped into it, and was soon rowing cautiously up stream. When he had pulled a mile above the village, he started quartering across and bent himself stoutly to his work. He hit the landing on the other side neatly, for this was a familiar bit of work to him. He was moved to capture the skiff, arguing that it might be considered a ship and therefore legitimate prey for a pirate, but he knew a thorough search would be made for it and that might end in revelations. So he stepped ashore and entered the wood.

He sat down and took a long rest, torturing himself meantime to keep awake, and then started wearily down the home-stretch. The night was far spent. It was broad daylight before he found himself fairly abreast the island bar. He rested again until the sun was well up and gilding the great river with its splendor, and then he plunged into the stream. A little later he paused, dripping, upon the threshold of the camp, and heard Joe say:

"No, Tom's true-blue, Huck, and he'll come back. He won't desert. He knows that would be a disgrace to a pirate, and Tom's too proud for that sort of thing. He's up to something or other. Now I wonder what?"

"Well, the things is ours, anyway, ain't they?"

"Pretty near, but not yet, Huck. The writing says they are if he ain't back here to breakfast."

"Which he is!" exclaimed Tom, with fine dramatic effect, stepping grandly into camp.

A sumptuous breakfast of bacon and fish was shortly provided, and as the boys set to work upon it, Tom recounted (and adorned) his adventures. They were a vain and boastful company of heroes when the tale was done. Then Tom hid himself away in a shady nook to sleep till noon, and the other pirates got ready to fish and explore.

CHAPTER XVI.

AFTER dinner all the gang turned out to hunt for turtle eggs on the bar. They went about poking sticks into the sand, and when they found a soft place they went down on their knees and dug with their hands. Sometimes they would take fifty or sixty eggs out of one hole. They were perfectly round white things a trifle smaller than an English walnut. They had a famous fried-egg feast that night, and another on Friday morning.

After breakfast they went whooping and prancing out on the bar, and chased each other round and round, shedding clothes as they went, until they were naked, and then continued the frolic far away up the shoal water of the bar, against the stiff current, which latter tripped their legs from under them from time to time and greatly increased the fun. And now and then they stooped in a group and splashed water in each other's faces with their palms, gradually approaching each other, with averted faces to avoid the strangling sprays and finally gripping and struggling till the best man ducked his neighbor, and then they all went under in a tangle of white legs and arms and came up blowing, sputtering, laughing and gasping for breath at one and the same time.

When they were well exhausted, they would run out and sprawl on the dry, hot sand, and lie there and cover themselves up with it, and by and by break for the water again and go through the original performance once more. Finally it occurred to them that their naked skin represented flesh-colored "tights" very fairly; so they drew a ring in the sand and had a circus—with three clowns in it, for none would yield this proudest post to his neighbor.

Next they got their marbles and played "knucks" and "ring-taw" and "keeps" till that amusement grew stale. Then Joe and Huck had another swim, but Tom would not venture, because he found that in kicking oft his trousers he had kicked his string of rattlesnake rat-

THE PIRATES' EGG MARKET.

tles off his ankle, and he wondered how he had escaped cramp so long without the protection of this mysterious charm. He did not venture again until he had found it, and by that time the other boys were tired and ready to rest. They gradually wandered apart, dropped into the "dumps," and fell to gazing longingly across the wide river to where the village lay drowsing in the sun. Tom found himself writing "BECKY" in the sand with his big toe; he scratched it out, and was angry with himself for his weakness. But he wrote it again, nevertheless; he could not help it. He erased it once more and then took himself out of temptation by driving the other boys together and joining them.

But Joe's spirits had gone down almost beyond resurrection. He was so home-sick that he could hardly endure the misery of it. The tears lay very near the surface. Huck was melancholy, too. Tom was down-hearted, but tried hard not to show it. He had a secret which he was not ready to tell, yet, but if this mutinous depression was not broken up soon, he would have to bring it out. He said, with a great show of cheerfulness:

"I bet there's been pirates on this island before, boys. We'll explore it again. They've hid treasures here somewhere. How'd you feel to light on a rotten chest full of gold and silver—hey?"

But it roused only a faint enthusiasm, which faded out, with no reply. Tom tried one or two other seductions; but they failed, too. It was discouraging work. Joe sat poking up the sand with a stick and looking very gloomy. Finally he said:

"O, boys, let's give it up. I want to go home. It's so lonesome."

"Oh, no, Joe, you'll feel better by and by," said Tom. "Just think of the fishing that's here."

"I don't care for fishing. I want to go home."

"But Joe, there ain't such another swimming place anywhere."

"Swimming's no good. I don't seem to care for it, somehow, when there ain't anybody to say I shan't go in. I mean to go home."

"O, shucks! Baby! You want to see your mother, I reckon."

"Yes, I *do* want to see my mother—and you would too, if you had one. I ain't any more baby than you are." And Joe snuffled a little.

"Well, we'll let the cry-baby go home to his mother, *won't* we Huck? Poor thing—does it want to see its mother? And so it shall. *You* like it here, *don't* you Huck? We'll stay, won't we?"

Huck said "Y-e-s"—without any heart in it.

"I'll never speak to you again as long as I live," said Joe, rising. "There now!" And he moved moodily away and began to dress himself.

"Who cares!" said Tom. "Nobody wants you to. Go 'long home and get laughed at. O, you're a nice pirate. Huck and me ain't cry-babies. We'll stay, won't we Huck? Let him go if he wants to. I reckon we can get along without him, per'aps."

But Tom was uneasy, nevertheless, and was alarmed to see Joe go sullenly on with his dressing. And then it was discomforting to see Huck eyeing Joe's preparations so wistfully, and keeping up such an ominous silence. Presently, without a parting word, Joe began to wade off toward the Illinois shore. Tom's heart began to sink. He glanced at Huck. Huck could not bear the look, and dropped his eyes. Then he said:

"I want to go, too, Tom. It was getting so lonesome anyway, and now it'll be worse. Let's us go too, Tom."

"I won't! You can all go, if you want to. I mean to stay."

"Tom, I better go."

"Well go 'long—who's hendering you.'

Huck began to pick up his scattered clothes. He said:

"Tom, I wisht you'd come too. Now you think it over. We'll wait for you when we get to shore."

"Well you'll wait a blame long time, that's all."

Huck started sorrowfully away, and Tom stood looking after him, with a strong desire tugging at his heart to yield his pride and go along too. He hoped the boys would stop, but they still waded slowly on. It suddenly dawned on Tom that it was become very lonely and still. He made one final struggle with his pride, and then darted after his comrades, yelling:

"Wait! Wait! I want to tell you something!"

They presently stopped and turned around. When he got to where they were, he began unfolding his secret, and they listened moodily till at last they saw the "point" he was driving at, and then they set up a war-whoop of applause and said it was "splendid!" and said if he had told them at first, they wouldn't have started away. He made a plausible excuse; but his real reason had been the fear that not even the secret would keep them with him any very great length of time, and so he had meant to hold it in reserve as a last seduction.

The lads came gaily back and went at their sports again with a will, chattering all the time about Tom's stupendous plan and admiring the genius of it. After a dainty egg and fish dinner, Tom said he wanted to learn to smoke, now. Joe caught at the idea and said he would like to try, too. So Huck made pipes and filled them. These novices had never smoked anything before but cigars made of grape-vine and they "bit" the tongue and were not considered manly, anyway.

Now they stretched themselves out on their elbows and began to puff, charily, and with slender confidence. The smoke had an unpleasant taste, and they gagged a little, but Tom said:

"Why it's just as easy! If I'd a knowed *this* was all, I'd a learnt long ago."

"So would I," said Joe. "It's just nothing."

"Why many a time I've looked at people smoking, and thought well I wish I could do that; but I never thought I could," said Tom.

"That's just the way with me, hain't it Huck? You've heard me talk just that way—haven't you Huck? I'll leave it to Huck if I haven't."

"Yes—heaps of times," said Huck.

"Well I have too," said Tom; "O, hundreds of times. Once down by the slaughterhouse. Don't you remember, Huck? Bob Tanner was there, and Johnny Miller, and Jeff Thatcher, when I said it. Don't you remember Huck, 'bout me saying that?"

"Yes, that's so," said Huck. "That was the day after I lost a white alley. No, 'twas the day before."

"There—I told you so," said Tom. "Huck recollects it."

"I bleeve I could smoke this pipe all day," said Joe. "*I* don't feel sick.'

"Neither do I," said Tom. "*I* could smoke it all day. But I bet you Jeff Thatcher couldn't."

"Jeff Thatcher! Why he'd keel over just with two draws. Just let him try it once. *He'd* see!"

"I bet he would. And Johnny Miller—I wish I could see Johnny Miller tackle it once."

"O, dont *I*!" said Joe, "Why I bet you Johnny Miller couldn't any more do this than nothing. Just one little snifter would fetch *him*."

"'Deed it would, Joe. Say I wish the boys could see us now."

"So do I."

"Say—boys, don't say anything about it, and some time when they're around, I'll come up to you and say 'Joe, got a pipe? I want a smoke.' And you'll say, kind of careless like, as if it warn't anything, you'll say, 'Yes, I got my *old* pipe, and another one, but my tobacker ain't very good.' And I'll say, 'Oh, that's all right, if it's *strong* enough.' And then you'll out with the pipes, and we'll light up just as ca'm, and then just see 'em look!"

"By jings that'll be gay, Tom! I wish it was *now!*"

"So do I! And when we tell 'em we learned when we was off pirat-ing, won't they wish they'd been along?"

"O, I reckon not! I'll just *bet* they will!"

So the talk ran on. But presently it began to flag a trifle, and grow disjointed. The silences widened; the expectoration marvelously increased. Every pore inside the boys' cheeks became a spouting fountain; they could scarcely bail out the cellars under their tongues fast enough to prevent an inundation; little overflowings down their throats occurred in spite of all they could do, and sudden retchings followed every time. Both boys were looking very pale and miserable, now. Joe's pipe dropped from his nerveless fingers. Tom's followed. Both fountains were going furiously and both pumps bailing with might and main. Joe said feebly:

"I've lost my knife. I reckon I better go and find it."

Tom said, with quivering lips and halting utterance:

"I'll help you. You go over that way and I'll hunt around by the spring. No, you needn't come, Huck—we can find it."

So Huck sat down again, and waited an hour. Then he found it lonesome, and went to find his comrades. They were wide apart in the woods, both very pale, both fast asleep. But something informed

TOM LOOKING FOR JOE'S KNIFE.

him that if they had had any trouble they had got rid of it.

They were not talkative at supper that night. They had a humble look, and when Huck prepared his pipe after the meal and was go-ing to prepare theirs, they said no, they were not feeling very well— something they ate at dinner had disagreed with them.

About midnight Joe awoke, and called the boys. There was a brooding oppressiveness in the air that seemed to bode something. The boys huddled themselves together and sought the friendly companionship of the fire, though the dull dead heat of the breathless atmosphere was stifling. They sat still, intent and waiting. The solemn hush continued. Beyond the light of the fire everything was swallowed up in the blackness of darkness. Presently there came a quivering glow that vaguely revealed the foliage for a moment and then vanished. By and by another came, a little stronger. Then another. Then a faint moan came sighing through the branches of the forest and the boys felt a fleeting breath upon their cheeks, and shuddered with the fancy that the Spirit of the Night had gone by. There was a pause. Now a wierd flash turned night into day and showed every little grass-blade, separate and distinct, that grew about their feet. And it showed three white, startled faces, too. A deep peal of thunder went rolling and tumbling down the heavens and lost itself in sullen rumblings in the distance. A sweep of chilly air passed by, rustling all the leaves and snowing the flaky ashes broadcast about the fire. Another fierce glare lit up the forest and an instant crash followed that seemed to rend the tree-tops right over the boys' heads. They clung together in terror, in the thick gloom that followed. A few big rain-drops fell pattering upon the leaves.

"Quick! boys, go for the tent!" exclaimed Tom.

They sprang away, stumbling over roots and among vines in the dark, no two plunging in the same direction. A furious blast roared through the trees, making everything sing as it went. One blinding flash after another came, and peal on peal of deafening thunder. And now a drenching rain poured down and the rising hurricane drove it in sheets along the ground. The boys cried out to each other, but the roaring wind and the booming thunder-blasts drowned their voices utterly. However one by one they straggled in at last and took shelter under the tent, cold, scared, and streaming with water; but to have company in misery seemed something to be grateful for. They could not talk, the old sail flapped so furiously, even if the other noises would have allowed them. The tempest rose higher and higher, and presently the sail tore loose from its fastenings and went winging away on the blast. The boys seized each others' hands and fled, with many tumblings and bruises, to the shelter of a great oak that stood upon the river bank. Now the battle was at its highest. Under the ceaseless conflagration of lightning that flamed in the skies, everything below stood out in clean-cut and shadowless distinctness: the bending trees, the billowy river, white with foam, the driving spray of spume-flakes, the dim outlines of the high bluffs on the other side, glimpsed through the drifting cloud-rack and the slanting veil of rain. Every little while some giant tree yielded the fight and fell

crashing through the younger growth; and the unflagging thunder-peals came now in ear-splitting explosive bursts, keen and sharp, and unspeakably appalling. The storm culminated in one matchless effort that seemed likely to tear the island to pieces, burn it up, drown it to the tree tops, blow it away, and deafen every creature in it, all at one and the same moment. It was a wild night for homeless young heads to be out in.

But at last the battle was done, and the forces retired with weaker and weaker threatenings and grumblings, and peace resumed her sway. The boys went back to camp, a good deal awed; but they found there was still something to be thankful for, because the great sycamore, the shelter of their beds, was a ruin, now, blasted by the lightnings, and they were not under it when the catastrophe happened.

Everything in camp was drenched, the campfire as well; for they were but heedless lads, like their generation, and had made no provision against rain. Here was matter for dismay, for they were soaked through and chilled. They were eloquent in their distress; but they presently discovered that the fire had eaten so far up under the great log it had been built against, (where it curved upward and separated itself from the ground,) that a hand-breadth or so of it had escaped wetting; so they patiently wrought until, with shreds and bark gathered from the under sides of sheltered logs, they coaxed the fire to burn again. Then they piled on great dead boughs till they had a roaring furnace and were glad-hearted once more. They dried their boiled ham and had a feast, and after that they sat by the fire and expanded and glorified their midnight adventure until morning, for there was not a dry spot to sleep on, anywhere around.

As the sun began to steal in upon the boys, drowsiness came over them and they went out on the sandbar and lay down to sleep. They got scorched out by and by, and drearily set about getting breakfast. After the meal they felt rusty, and stiff-jointed, and a little homesick once more. Tom saw the signs, and fell to cheering up the pirates as well as he could. But they cared nothing for marbles, or circus, or swimming, or anything. He reminded them of the imposing secret, and raised a ray of cheer. While it lasted, he got them interested in a new device. This was to knock off being pirates, for a while, and be Indians for a change. They were attracted by this idea; so it was not long before they were stripped, and striped from head to heel with black mud, like so many zebras,—all of them chiefs, of course— and then they went tearing through the woods to attack an English settlement.

By and by they separated into three hostile tribes, and darted upon each other from ambush with dreadful war-whoops, and killed and scalped each other by thousands. It was a gory day. Consequently it was an extremely satisfactory one.

They assembled in camp toward supper time, hungry and happy; but now a difficulty arose—hostile Indians could not break the bread of hospitality together without first making peace, and this was a simple impossibility without smoking a pipe of peace. There was no other process that ever they had heard of. Two of the savages almost wished they had remained pirates. However, there was no other way; so with such show of cheerfulness as they could muster they called for the pipe and took their whiff as it passed, in due form.

And behold they were glad they had gone into savagery, for they had gained something; they found that they could now smoke a little without having to go and hunt for a lost knife; they did not get sick enough to be seriously uncomfortable. They were not likely to fool away this high promise for lack of effort. No, they practiced cautiously, after supper, with right fair success, and so they spent a jubilant evening. They were prouder and happier in their new acquirement than they would have been in the scalping and skinning of the Six Nations. We will leave them to smoke and chatter and brag, since we have no further use for them at present.

TERRIBLE SLAUGHTER.

CHAPTER XVII.

BUT there was no hilarity in the little town that same tranquil Saturday afternoon. The Harpers, and Aunt Polly's family, were being put into mourning, with great grief and many tears. An unusual quiet possessed the village, although it was ordinarily quiet enough, in all conscience. The villagers conducted their concerns with an absent air, and talked little; but they sighed often. The Saturday holiday seemed a burden to the children. They had no heart in their sports, and gradually gave them up.

In the afternoon Becky Thatcher found herself moping about the deserted school-house yard, and feeling very melancholy. But she found nothing there to comfort her. She soliloquised:

"Oh, if I only had his brass andiron-knob again! But I haven't got anything now to remember him by." And she choked back a little sob.

Presently she stopped, and said to herself:

"It was right here. O, if it was to do over again, I wouldn't say that—I wouldn't say it for the whole world. But he's gone now; I'll never never never see him any more."

This thought broke her down and she wandered away, with the tears rolling down her cheeks. Then quite a group of boys and girls,—

playmates of Tom's and Joe's—came by, and stood looking over the paling fence and talking in reverent tones of how Tom did so-and-so, the last time they saw him, and how Joe said this and that small trifle (pregnant with awful prophecy, as they could easily see now!)—and each speaker pointed out the exact spot where the lost lads stood at the time, and then added something like "and I was a standing just so—just as I am now, and as if you was him—I was as close as that—and he smiled, just this way—and then something seemed to go all over me, like,—awful you know—and I never thought what it meant, of course, but I can see now!"

Then there was a dispute about who saw the dead boys last in life, and many claimed that dismal distinction, and offered evidences, more or less tampered with by the witness; and when it was ultimately decided who *did* see the departed last, and exchanged the last words with them, the lucky parties took upon themselves a sort of sacred importance, and were gaped at and envied by all the rest. One poor chap, who had no other grandeur to offer, said with tolerably manifest pride in the remembrance:

"Well, Tom Sawyer he licked me once."

But that bid for glory was a failure. Most of the boys could say that, and so that cheapened the distinction too much. The group loitered away, still recalling memories of the lost heroes, in awed voices.

When the Sunday-school hour was finished, the next morning, the bell began to toll, instead of ringing in the usual way. It was a very still Sabbath, and the mournful sound seemed in keeping with the musing hush that lay upon nature. The villagers began to gather, loitering a moment in the vestibule to converse in whispers about the sad event. But there was no whispering in the house; only the funereal rustling of dresses as the women gathered to their seats, disturbed the silence there. None could remember when the little church had been so full before. There was finally a waiting pause, an expectant dumbness, and then Aunt Polly entered, followed by Sid and Mary, and they by the Harper family, all in deep black, and the whole congregation, the old minister as well, rose reverently and stood, until the mourners were seated in the front pew. There was another communing silence, broken at intervals by muffled sobs, and then the minister spread his hands abroad and prayed. A moving hymn was sung, and the text followed: "I am the Resurrection and the Life."

As the service proceeded, the clergyman drew such pictures of the graces, the winning ways and the rare promise of the lost lads, that every soul there, thinking he recognized these pictures, felt a pang in remembering that he had persistently blinded himself to them, always before, and had as persistently seen only faults and flaws in the poor boys. The minister related many a touching incident in the lives of the departed, too, which illustrated their sweet, generous natures, and the people could easily see, now, how noble and beautiful those episodes were, and remembered with grief that at the time they occurred they had seemed rank rascalities, well deserving of the cowhide. The congregation became more and more moved, as the pathetic tale went on, till at last the whole company broke down and joined the weeping mourners in a chorus of anguished sobs, the preacher himself giving way to his feelings, and crying in the pulpit.

There was a rustle in the gallery, which nobody noticed; a moment later the church door creaked; the minister raised his streaming eyes above his handkerchief, and stood transfixed! First one and then another pair of eyes followed the minister's, and then almost with one impulse the congregation rose and stared while the three dead boys came marching up the aisle, Tom in the lead, Joe next, and Huck, a ruin of drooping rags, sneaking sheepishly in the rear! They had been hid in the unused gallery listening to their own funeral sermon!

Aunt Polly, Mary and the Harpers threw themselves upon their restored ones, smothered them with kisses and poured out thanksgivings, while poor Huck stood abashed and uncomfortable, not knowing exactly what to do or where to hide from so many unwelcoming eyes. He wavered, and started to slink away, but Tom seized him and said:

"Aunt Polly, it ain't fair. Somebody's got to be glad to see Huck."

"And so they shall. *I'm* glad to see him, poor motherless thing!" And the loving attentions Aunt Polly lavished upon him were the one thing capable of making him more uncomfortable than he was before.

Suddenly the minister shouted at the top of his voice: "Praise God from whom all blessings flow—SING!—and put your hearts in it!"

And they did. Old Hundred swelled up with a triumphant burst, and while it shook the rafters Tom Sawyer the Pirate looked around upon the envying juveniles about him and confessed in his heart that this was the proudest moment of his life.

TOM'S PROUDEST MOMENT.

As the "sold" congregation trooped out they said they would almost be willing to be made ridiculous again to hear Old Hundred sung like that once more.

Tom got more cuffs and kisses that day—according to Aunt Polly's varying moods—than he had earned before in a year; and he hardly knew which expressed the most gratefulness to God and affection for himself.

CHAPTER XVIII.

AMY LAWRENCE.

THAT was Tom's great secret—the scheme to return home with his brother pirates and attend their own funerals. They had paddled over to the Missouri shore on a log, at dusk on Saturday, landing five or six miles below the village; they had slept in the woods at the edge of the town till nearly day-light, and had then crept through back lanes and alleys and fin-ished their sleep in the gallery of the church among a chaos of invalided benches.

At breakfast, Monday morning, Aunt Polly and Mary were very loving to Tom, and very attentive to his wants. There was an unusual amount of talk. In the course of it Aunt Polly said:

"Well, I don't say it wasn't a fine joke, Tom, to keep everybody suffering 'most a week so you boys had a good time, but it is a pity you could be so hard-hearted as to let *me* suffer so. If you could come over on a log to go to your funeral, you could have come over and give me a hint some way that you warn't *dead*, but only run off."

"Yes, you could have done that, Tom," said Mary; "and I believe you would if you had thought of it."

"Would you Tom?" said Aunt Polly, her face lighting wistfully. "Say, now, would you, if you'd thought of it?"

"I—well I don't know. 'Twould a spoiled everything."

"Tom, I hoped you loved me that much," said Aunt Polly, with a grieved tone that discomforted the boy. "It would been something if you'd cared enough to *think* of it, even if you didn't *do* it."

"Now auntie, that ain't any harm," pleaded Mary; "it's only Tom's giddy way—he is always in such a rush that he never thinks of anything."

"More's the pity. Sid would have thought. And Sid would have come and *done* it, too. Tom, you'll look back, some day, when it's too late, and wish you'd cared a little more for me when it would have cost you so little."

"Now auntie, you know I do care for you," said Tom.

"I'd know it better if you acted more like it."

"I wish now I'd thought," said Tom, with a repentant tone; "but I dreamed about you, anyway. That's something, ain't it?"

"It ain't much—a cat does that much—but it's better than nothing. What did you dream?"

"Why Wednesday night I dreamt that you was sitting over there by the bed, and Sid was sitting by the wood-box, and Mary next to him."

"Well, so we did. So we always do. I'm glad your dreams could take even that much trouble about us."

"And I dreamt that Joe Harper's mother was here."

"Why, she *was* here! Did you dream any more?"

"O, lots. But it's so dim, now."

"Well, *try* to recollect—can't you?"

"Some how it seems to me that the wind—the wind blowed the—the—"

"Try harder, Tom! The wind did blow something. Come!"

Tom pressed his fingers on his forehead an anxious minute, and then said:

"I've got it now! I've got it now! It blowed the candle!"

"Mercy on us! Go on, Tom—go on!"

"And it seems to me that you said, 'Why I believe that that door—'"

"Go *on*, Tom!"

"Just let me study a moment—just a moment. Oh, yes—you said you believed the door was open."

"As I'm a sitting here, I did! Didn't I, Mary! Go on!"

TOM TRIES TO REMEMBER.

"And then—and then—well I won't be certain, but it seems like as if you made Sid go and—and—"

"Well? Well? What did I make him do, Tom? What did I make him do?"

"You made him—you—O, you made him shut it."

"Well for the land's sake! I never heard the beat of that in all my days! Don't tell *me* there ain't anything in dreams, any more. Sereny Harper shall know of this before I'm an hour older. I'd like to see her get around *this* with her rubbage 'bout superstition. Go on, Tom!"

"Oh, it's all getting just as bright as day, now. Next you said I warn't *bad* only mischeevous and harum-scarum, and not any more responsible than—than—I think it was a colt, or something."

"And so it was! Well, goodness gracious! Go on, Tom!"

"And then you began to cry."

"So I did. So I did. Not the first time, neither. And then—"

"Then Mrs. Harper she began to cry, and said Joe was just the same and she wished she hadn't whipped him for taking cream when she'd throwed it out her own self—"

"Tom! The sperrit was upon you! You was a prophecying—that's what you was doing! Land alive, go on, Tom!"

"Then Sid he said—he said—"

"I don't think I said anything," said Sid.

"Yes you did, Sid," said Mary.

"Shut your heads and let Tom go on! What did he say, Tom?"

"He said—I *think* he said he hoped I was better off where I was gone to, but if I'd been better sometimes—"

"*There*, d'you hear that! It was his very words!"

"And you shut him up sharp."

"I lay I did! There must a been an angel there. There was an angel there, somewheres!"

"And Mrs. Harper told about Joe scaring her with a firecracker, and you told about Peter and the Pain-killer—"

"Just as true as I live!"

"And then there was a whole lot of talk 'bout dragging the river for us, and 'bout having the funeral Sunday, and then you and old Miss Harper hugged and cried, and she went."

"It happened just so! It happened just so, as sure as I'm a sitting in these very tracks. Tom you couldn't told it more like, if you'd a seen it! And *then* what? Go on, Tom?"

"Then I thought you prayed for me—and I could see you and hear every word you said. And you went to bed, and I was so sorry, that I took and wrote on a piece of sycamore bark, '*We ain't dead—we are only off being pirates,*' and put it on the table by the candle; and then you looked so good, laying there asleep, that I thought I went and leaned over and kissed you on the lips."

"Did you, Tom, *did* you! I just forgive you everything for that!" And she siezed the boy in a crushing embrace that made him feel like the guiltiest of villains.

"It was very kind, even though it was only a—dream," Sid soliloquised just audibly.

"Shut up Sid! A body does just the same in a dream as he'd do if he was awake. Here's a big Milum apple I've been saving for you Tom, if you was ever found again—now go 'long to school. I'm thankful to the good God and Father of us all I've got you back, that's long-suffering and merciful to them that believe on Him and keep His word, though goodness knows I'm unworthy of it, but if only the worthy ones got His blessings and had His hand to help them over the rough places, there's few enough would smile here or ever enter into His rest when the long night comes. Go 'long Sid, Mary, Tom—take yourselves off—you've hendered me long enough."

The children left for school, and the old lady to call on Mrs. Harper and vanquish her realism with Tom's marvelous dream. Sid had better judgment than to utter the thought that was in his mind as he left the house. It was this: "Pretty thin—as long a dream as that, without any mistakes in it!"

THE HERO.

What a hero Tom was become, now! He did not go skipping and prancing, but moved with a dignified swagger as became a pirate who felt that the public eye was on him. And indeed it was; he tried not to seem to see the looks or hear the remarks as he passed along, but they were food and drink to him. Smaller boys than himself flocked at his heels, as proud to be seen with him, and tolerated by him, as if he had been the drummer at the head of a procession or the elephant leading a menagerie into town. Boys of his own size pretended not to know he had been away at all; but they were consuming with envy, nevertheless. They would have given anything to have that swarthy sun-tanned skin of his, and his glittering notoriety; and Tom would not have parted with either for a circus.

At school the children made so much of him and of Joe, and delivered such eloquent admiration from their eyes, that the two heroes were not long in becoming insufferably "stuck-up." They began to tell their adventures to hungry listeners—but they only began; it was not a thing likely to have an end, with imaginations like theirs to furnish material. And finally, when they got out their pipes and went serenely puffing around, the very summit of glory was reached.

Tom decided that he could be independent of Becky Thatcher now. Glory was sufficient. He would live for glory. Now that he was distinguished, maybe she would be wanting to "make up." Well, let her—she should see that he could be as indifferent as some other people. Presently she arrived. Tom pretended not to see her. He moved away and joined a group of boys and girls and began to talk. Soon he observed that she was tripping gayly back and forth with flushed face and dancing eyes, pretending to be busy chasing schoolmates, and screaming with laughter when she made a capture; but he noticed that she always made her captures in his vicinity, and that she seemed to cast a conscious eye in his direction at such times, too. It gratified all the vicious vanity that was in him; and so, instead of winning him it only "set him up" the more and made him the more diligent to avoid betraying that he knew she was about. Presently she gave over skylarking, and moved irresolutely about, sighing once or twice and glancing furtively and wistfully toward Tom. Then she observed that now Tom was talking more particularly to Amy Lawrence than to any one else. She felt a sharp pang and grew disturbed and uneasy at once. She tried to go away, but her feet were treacherous, and carried her to the group instead. She said to a girl almost at Tom's elbow—with sham vivacity:

"Why Mary Austin! you bad girl, why didn't you come to Sunday-school?"

"I did come—didn't you see me?"

"Why no! Did you? Where did you sit?

"I was in Miss Peter's class, where I always go. I saw *you*."

"Did you? Why it's funny I didn't see you. I wanted to tell you about the pic-nic."

"O, that's jolly. Who's going to give it?"

"My ma's going to let me have one."

"O, goody; I hope she'll let *me* come."

"Well she will. The pic-nic's for me. She'll let anybody come that I want, and I want you."

"That's ever so nice. When is it going to be?"

"By and by. Maybe about vacation."

"O, won't it be fun! You going to have all the girls and boys?"

"Yes, every one that's friends to me—or wants to be;" and she glanced ever so furtively at Tom, but he talked right along to Amy Lawrence about the terrible storm on the island, and how the lightning tore the great sycamore tree "all to flinders" while he was "standing within three feet of it."

"O, may I come?" said Grade Miller.

"Yes."

"And me?" said Sally Rogers.

"Yes."

"And me, too?" said Susy Harper. "And Joe?"

"Yes."

And so on, with clapping of joyful hands till all the group had

begged for invitations but Tom and Amy. Then Tom turned coolly away, still talking, and took Amy with him. Becky's lips trembled and the tears came to her eyes; she hid these signs with a forced gayety and went on chattering, but the life had gone out of the pic-nic, now, and out of everything else; she got away as soon as she could and hid herself and had what her sex call "a good cry." Then she sat moody, with wounded pride till the bell rang. She roused up, now, with a vindictive cast in her eye, and gave

A FLIRTATION.

her plaited tails a shake and said she knew what *she'd* do.

At recess Tom continued his flirtation with Amy with jubilant self-satisfaction. And he kept drifting about to find Becky and lacerate her with the performance. At last he spied her, but there was a sudden falling of his mercury. She was sitting cosily on a little bench behind the schoolhouse looking at a picture book with Alfred Temple—and so absorbed were they, and their heads so close together over the book that they did not seem to be conscious of anything in the world besides. Jealousy ran red hot through Tom's veins. He began to hate himself for throwing away the chance Becky had offered for a reconciliation. He called himself a fool, and all the hard names he could think of. He wanted to cry with vexation. Amy chatted happily along, as they walked, for her heart was singing, but Tom's tongue had lost its function. He did not hear what Amy was saying, and whenever she paused expectantly he could only stammer an awkward assent, which was as often misplaced as otherwise. He kept drifting to the rear of the school-house, again and again, to sear his eye-balls with the hateful spectacle there. He could not help it. And it maddened him to see, as he thought he saw, that Becky Thatcher never once suspected that he was even in the land of the living. But she did see, nevertheless; and she knew she was winning her fight, too, and was glad to see him suffer as she had suffered.

BECKY RETALIATES.

Amy's happy prattle became intolerable. Tom hinted at things he had to attend to; things that must be done; and time was fleeting. But in vain—the girl chirped on. Tom thought, "O hang her, ain't I ever going to get rid of her?" At last he *must* be attending to those things—and she said artlessly that she would be "around" when school let out. And he hastened away, hating her for it.

"Any other boy!" Tom thought, grating his teeth. "Any boy in the whole town but that Saint Louis smarty that thinks he dresses so fine and is aristocracy! O, all right, I licked you the first day you ever saw this town, mister, and I'll lick you again! You just wait till I catch you out! I'll just take and—"

And he went through the motions of thrashing an imaginary boy—pummeling the air, and kicking and gouging. "Oh, you do, do you? You holler 'nough, do you? Now, then, let that learn you!" And so the imaginary flogging was finished to his satisfaction.

Tom fled home at noon. His conscience could not endure any more of Amy's grateful happiness, and his jealousy could bear no more of the other distress. Becky resumed her picture-inspections with Alfred, but as the minutes dragged along and no Tom came to suffer,

A SUDDEN FROST.

her triumph began to cloud and she lost interest; gravity and absentmindedness followed, and then melancholy; two or three times she pricked up her ear at a footstep, but it was a false hope; no Tom came. At last she grew entirely miserable and wished she hadn't carried it so far. When poor Alfred, seeing that he was losing her, he did not know how, and kept exclaiming: "O here's a jolly one! look at this!" she lost patience at last, and said, "Oh, don't bother me! I don't care for them!" and burst into tears, and got up and walked away.

Alfred dropped alongside and was going to try to comfort her, but she said:

"Go away and leave me alone, can't you! I hate you!"

So the boy halted, wondering what he could have done—for she had said she would look at pictures all through the nooning—and she walked on, crying. Then Alfred went musing into the deserted schoolhouse. He was humiliated and angry. He easily guessed his way to the truth—the girl had simply made a convenience of him to vent her spite upon Tom Sawyer. He was far from hating Tom the less when this thought occurred to him. He wished there was some way to get that boy into trouble without much risk to himself. Tom's spelling book fell under his eye. Here was his opportunity. He gratefully opened to the lesson for the afternoon and poured ink upon the page.

Becky, glancing in at a window behind him at the moment, saw the act, and moved on, without discovering herself. She started homeward, now, intending to find Tom and tell him; Tom would be thankful and their troubles would be healed. Before she was half way home, however, she had changed her mind. The thought of Tom's treatment of her when she was talking about her pic-nic came scorching back and filled her with shame. She resolved to let him get whipped on the damaged spelling-book's account, and to hate him forever, into the bargain.

COUNTER-IRRITATION.

AUNT POLLY.

TOM arrived at home in a dreary mood, and the first thing his aunt said to him showed him that he had brought his sorrows to an unpromising market:

"Tom, I've a notion to skin you alive!"

"Auntie, what have I done?"

"Well, you've done enough. Here I go over to Sereny Harper, like an old softy, expecting I'm going to make her believe all that rubbage about that dream, when lo and behold you she'd found out from Joe that you was over here and heard all the talk we had that night. Tom I don't know what is to become of a boy that will act like that. It makes me feel so bad to think you could let me go to Sereny Harper and make such a fool of myself and never say a word."

This was a new aspect of the thing. His smartness of the morning had seemed to Tom a good joke before, and very ingenious. It merely looked mean and shabby now. He hung his head and could not think of anything to say for a moment. Then he said:

"Auntie, I wish I hadn't done it—but I didn't think."

"O, child you never think. You never think of anything but your own selfishness. You could think to come all the way over here from Jackson's Island in the night to laugh at our troubles, and you could think to fool me with a lie about a dream; but you couldn't ever think to pity us and save us from sorrow."

"Auntie, I know now it was mean, but I didn't mean to be mean. I didn't, honest. And besides I didn't come over here to laugh at you that night."

"What did you come for, then?"

"It was to tell you not to be uneasy about us, because we hadn't got drowned."

"Tom, Tom, I would be the thankfullest soul in this world if I could believe you ever had as good a thought as that, but you know you never did—and *I* know it, Tom."

"Indeed and 'deed I did, auntie—I wish I may never stir if I didn't."

"O, Tom, don't lie—don't do it. It only makes things a hundred times worse."

"It ain't a lie, auntie, it's the truth. I wanted to keep you from grieving—that was all that made me come."

"I'd give the whole world to believe that—it would cover up a power of sins Tom. I'd 'most be glad you'd run off and acted so bad. But it aint reasonable; because, why didn't you tell me, child?"

"Why, you see, auntie, when you got to talking about the funeral, I just got all full of the idea of our coming and hiding in the church, and I couldn't somehow bear to spoil it. So I just put the bark back in my pocket and kept mum."

"What bark?"

"The bark I had wrote on to tell you we'd gone pirating. I wish, now, you'd waked up when I kissed you—I do, honest."

The hard lines in his aunt's face relaxed and a sudden tenderness dawned in her eyes.

"*Did* you kiss me, Tom?"

"Why yes I did."

"Are you sure you did, Tom?"

"Why yes I did, auntie—certain sure."

"What did you kiss me for, Tom?"

"Because I loved you so, and you laid there moaning and I was so sorry."

The words sounded like truth. The old lady could not hide a tremor in her voice when she said:

"Kiss me again, Tom!—and be off with you to school, now, and don't bother me any more."

The moment he was gone, she ran to a closet and got out the ruin  of a jacket which Tom had gone pirating in. Then she stopped, with it in her hand, and said to herself:

"No, I don't dare. Poor boy, I reckon he's lied about it—but it's a blessed, blessed lie, there's such comfort come from it. I hope the Lord—I *know* the Lord will forgive him, because it was such goodheartedness in him to tell it. But I don't want to find out it's a lie. I won't look."

She put the jacket away, and stood by musing a minute. Twice she put out her hand to take the

TOM JUSTIFIED.

garment again, and twice she refrained. Once more she ventured, and this time she fortified herself with the thought: "It's a good lie—it's a good lie—I won't let it grieve me." So she sought the jacket pocket. A moment later she was reading Tom's piece of bark through flowing tears and saying: "I could forgive the boy, now, if he'd committed a million sins!"

"Wait—wait a moment. Never mind mentioning your companion's name. We will produce him at the proper time. Did you carry anything there with you."

Tom hesitated and looked confused.

"Speak out my boy—don't be diffident. The truth is always respectable. What did you take there?"

"Only a—a—dead cat."

There was a ripple of mirth, which the court checked.

"We will produce the skeleton of that cat. Now my boy, tell us everything that occurred—tell it in your own way—don't skip anything, and don't be afraid."

Tom began—hesitatingly at first, but as he warmed to his subject his words flowed more and more easily; in a little while every sound ceased but his own voice; every eye fixed itself upon him; with parted lips and bated breath the audience hung upon his words, taking no note of time, rapt in the ghastly fascinations of the tale. The strain upon pent emotion reached its climax when the boy said—

"—and as the doctor fetched the board around and Muff Potter fell, Injun Joe jumped with the knife and—"

Crash! Quick as lightning the half-breed sprang for a window, tore his way through all opposers, and was gone!

CHAPTER XXIV.

TOM was a glittering hero once more—the pet of the old, the envy of the young. His name even went into immortal print, for the village paper magnified him. There were some that believed he would be President, yet, if he escaped hanging.

As usual, the fickle, unreasoning world took Muff Potter to its bosom and fondled him as lavishly as it had abused him before. But that sort of conduct is to the world's credit; therefore it is not well to find fault with it.

THE DETECTIVE.

Tom's days were days of splendor and exultation to him, but his nights were seasons of horror. Injun Joe infested all his dreams, and always with doom in his eye. Hardly any temptation could persuade the boy to stir abroad after nightfall. Poor Huck was in the same state of wretchedness and terror, for Tom had told the whole story to the lawyer the night before the great day of the trial, and Huck was sore afraid that his share in the business might leak out, yet, notwithstanding Injun Joe's flight had saved him the suffering of testifying in court. The poor fellow had got the attorney to promise secrecy, but what of that? Since Tom's harrassed conscience had managed to drive him to the lawyer's house by night and wring a dread tale from lips that had been sealed with the dismalest and most formidable of oaths, Huck's confidence in the human race was well nigh obliterated.

Daily Muff Potter's gratitude made Tom glad he had spoken; but nightly he wished he had sealed up his tongue.

Half the time Tom was afraid Injun Joe would never be captured;

TOM DREAMS.

the other half he was afraid he would be. He felt sure he never could draw a safe breath again until that man was dead and he had seen the corpse.

Rewards had been offered, the country had been scoured, but no Injun Joe was found. One of those omniscient and awe-inspiring marvels, a detective, came up from St Louis, moused around, shook his head, looked wise, and made that sort of astounding success which members of that craft usually achieve. That is to say he "found a clew." But you can't hang a "clew" for murder and so after that detective had got through and gone home, Tom felt just as insecure as he was before.

The slow days drifted on, and each left behind it a slightly lightened weight of apprehension.

TREASURE

CHAPTER XXV

THERE comes a time in every rightly constructed boy's life when he has a raging desire to go somewhere and dig for hidden treasure. This desire suddenly came upon Tom one day. He sallied out to find Joe Harper, but failed of success. Next he sought Ben Rogers; he had gone fishing. Presently he stumbled upon Huck Finn the Red-Handed. Huck would answer. Tom took him to a private place and opened the matter to him confidentially. Huck was willing. Huck was always willing to take a hand in any enterprise that offered entertainment and required no capital, for he had a troublesome superabundance of that sort of time which is *not* money. "Where'll we dig?" said Huck.

"O, most anywhere."

"Why, is it hid all around?"

"No indeed it ain't. It's hid in mighty particular places, Huck— sometimes on islands, sometimes in rotten chests under the end of a limb of an old dead tree, just where the shadow falls at midnight; but mostly under the floor in ha'nted houses."

"Who hides it?"

"Why robbers, of course—who'd you reckon? Sunday-school sup'rintendents?"

"I don't know. If 'twas mine I wouldn't hide it; I'd spend it and have a good time."

"So would I. But robbers don't do that way. They always hide it and leave it there."

"Don't they come after it any more?"

"No, they think they will, but they generally forget the marks, or else they die. Anyway it lays there a long time and gets rusty; and by and by somebody finds an old yellow paper that tells how to find the marks—a paper that's got to be ciphered over about a week because it's mostly signs and hy'roglyphics."

"Hyro—which?"

"Hy'rogliphics—pictures and things, you know, that don't seem to mean anything."

"Have you got one of them papers, Tom?"

"No."

"Well then, how you going to find the marks?"

"I don't want any marks. They always bury it under a ha'nted house or on an island, or under a

THE PRIVATE CONFERENCE.

dead tree that's got one limb sticking out. Well, we've tried Jackson's Island a little, and we can try it again some time; and there's the old ha'nted house up the Still-House branch, and there's lots of dead-limb trees—dead loads of 'em."

"Is it under all of them?"

"How you talk! No!"

"Then how you going to know which one to go for?"

"Go for all of 'em!"

"Why Tom, it'll take all summer."

"Well, what of that? Suppose you find a brass pot with a hundred dollars in it, all rusty and gay, or a rotten chest full of di'monds. How's that?"

Huck's eyes glowed.

"That's bully. Plenty bully enough for me. Just you gimme the hundred dollars and I don't want no di'monds."

"All right. But I bet you *I* ain't going to throw off on di'monds. Some of 'em's worth twenty dollars apiece—there ain't any, hardly, but's worth six bits or a dollar."

"No! Is that so?"

"Cert'nly—anybody'll tell you so. Hain't you ever seen one, Huck?"

"Not as I remember."

"O, kings have slathers of them."

"Well, I don't know no kings, Tom."

"I reckon you don't. But if you was to go to Europe you'd see a raft of 'em hopping around."

A KING, POOR FELLOW!

"Do they hop?"

"Hop?—your granny! No!"

"Well what did you say they did, for?"

"Shucks, I only meant you'd *see* 'em—not hopping, of course—what do they want to hop for?—but I mean you'd just see 'em—scattered around, you know, in a kind of a general way. Like that old hump-backed Richard."

"Richard? What's his other name?"

"He didn't have any other name. Kings don't have any but a given name."

"No?"

"But they don't."

"Well, if they like it, Tom, all right; but I don't want to be a king and have only just a given name like a nigger. But say—where you going to dig first?"

"Well, I don't know. S'pose we tackle that old dead-limb tree on the hill t'other side of Still-House branch?"

"I'm agreed."

So they got a crippled pick and a shovel, and set out on their three-mile tramp. They arrived hot and panting, and threw themselves down in the shade of a neighboring elm to rest and have a smoke.

"I like this," said Tom.

"So do I."

"Say, Huck, if we find a treasure here, what you going to do with your share?"

"Well I'll have pie and a glass of soda every day, and I'll go to every circus that comes along. I bet I'll have a gay time."

"Well ain't you going to save any of it?"

"Save it? What for?"

"Why so as to have something to live on, by and by."

"O, that ain't any use. Pap would come back to thish-yer town some day and get his claws on it if I didn't hurry up, and I tell you he'd clean it out pretty quick. What you going to do with yourn, Tom?"

"I'm going to buy a new drum, and a sure-'nough sword, and a red necktie and a bull pup, and get married."

"Married!"

"That's it."

"Tom, you—why you ain't in your right mind."

"Wait—you'll see."

"Well that's the foolishest thing you could do. Look at pap and my mother. Fight! Why they used to fight all the time. I remember, mighty well."

"That ain't anything. The girl I'm going to marry won't fight."

"Tom, I reckon they're all alike. They'll all comb a body. Now you better think 'bout this a while. I tell you you better. What's the name of the gal?"

"It ain't a gal at all—it's a girl."

"It's all the same, I reckon; some says gal, some says girl—both's right, like enough. Anyway, what's her name, Tom?"

"I'll tell you some time—not now."

"All right—that'll do. Only if you get married I'll be more lonesomer than ever."

"No you won't. You'll come and live with me. Now stir out of this and we'll go to digging."

They worked and sweated for half an hour. No result. They toiled another half hour. Still no result. Huck said:

"Do they always bury it as deep as this?"

"Sometimes—not always. Not generally. I reckon we haven't got the right place."

So they chose a new spot and began again. The labor dragged a little but still they made progress. They pegged away in silence for some time. Finally Huck leaned on his shovel, swabbed the beaded drops from his brow with his sleeve, and said:

"Where you going to dig next, after we get this one?"

"I reckon maybe we'll tackle the old tree that's over yonder on Cardiff Hill back of the widow's."

"I reckon that'll be a good one. But won't the widow take it away from us Tom? It's on her land."

"*She* take it away! Maybe she'd

BUSINESS.

like to try it once. Whoever finds one of these hid treasures, it belongs to him. It don't make any difference whose land it's on."

That was satisfactory. The work went on. By and by Huck said:—

"Blame it, we must be in the wrong place again. What do you think?"

"It *is* mighty curious Huck. I don't understand it. Sometimes witches interfere. I reckon maybe that's what's the trouble now."

"Shucks, witches ain't got no power in the daytime."

"Well, that's so. I didn't think of that. Oh, *I* know what the matter is! What a blamed lot of fools we are! You got to find out where the shadow of the limb falls at midnight, and that's where you dig!"

"Then consound it, we've fooled away all this work for nothing. Now hang it all, we got to come back in the night. It's an awful long way. Can you get out?"

"I bet I will. We've got to do it to night, too, because if some body sees these holes they'll know in a minute what's here and they'll go for it."

"Well, I'll come around and maow to night."

"All right. Let's hide the tools in the bushes."

The boys were there that night, about the appointed time. They sat in the shadow waiting. It was a lonely place, and an hour made solemn by old traditions. Spirits whispered in the rustling leaves, ghosts lurked in the murky nooks, the deep baying of a hound floated up out of the distance, an owl answered with his sepulchral note. The boys were subdued by these solemnities, and talked little. By and by they judged that twelve had come; they marked where the shadow fell, and began to dig. Their hopes commenced to rise. Their interest grew stronger, and their industry kept pace with it. The hole deepened and still deepened, but every time their hearts jumped to hear the pick strike upon something, they only suffered a new disappointment. It was only a stone or a chunk. At last Tom said:—

"It ain't any use, Huck, we're wrong again."

"Well but we *can't* be wrong. We spotted the shadder to a dot."

"I know it, but then there's another thing."

"What's that?"

"Why we only guessed at the time. Like enough it was too late or too early."

Huck dropped his shovel.

"That's it," said he. "That's the very trouble. We got to give this one up. We can't ever tell the right time, and besides this kind of thing's too awful, here this time of night with witches and ghosts a fluttering around so. I feel as if something's behind me all the time; and I'm afeard to turn around, becuz maybe there's others in front a-waiting for a chance. I been creeping all over, ever since I got here."

"Well, I've been pretty much so, too, Huck. They most always put in a dead man when they bury a treasure under a tree, to look out for it."

"Lordy!"

"Yes, they do. I've always heard that."

"Tom I don't like to fool around much where there's dead people. A body's bound to get into trouble with 'em, sure."

"I don't like to stir 'em up, either. S'pose this one here was to stick his skull out and say something!"

"Don't, Tom! It's awful."

"Well it just is. Huck, I don't feel comfortable a bit."

"Say, Tom, let's give this place up, and try somewheres else."

"All right, I reckon we better."

"What'll it be?"

Tom considered a while; and then said—

"The ha'nted house. That's it!"

"Blame it, I don't like ha'nted houses Tom. Why they're a dern sight worse'n dead people. Dead people might talk, maybe, but they don't come sliding around in a shroud, when you ain't noticing, and peep over your shoulder all of a sudden and grit their teeth, the way a ghost does. I couldn't stand such a thing as that, Tom—nobody could."

"Yes, but Huck, ghosts don't travel around only at night. They won't hender us from digging there in the day time."

"Well that's so. But you know mighty well people don't go about that ha'nted house in the day nor the night."

"Well, that's mostly because they don't like to go where a man's been murdered, anyway—but nothing's ever been seen around that house except in the night—just some blue lights slipping by the windows—no regular ghosts."

"Well where you see one of them blue lights flickering around, Tom, you can bet there's a ghost mighty close behind it. It stands to reason. Becuz *you* know that they don't anybody but ghosts use 'em."

"Yes, that's so. But anyway they don't come around in the daytime, so what's the use of our being afeared?"

"Well, all right. We'll tackle the ha'nted house if you say so—but I reckon it's taking chances."

They had started down the hill by this time. There in the middle of the moon-lit valley below them stood the "ha'nted" house, utterly

THE HA'NTED HOUSE.

isolated, its fences gone long ago, rank weeds smothering the very doorsteps, the chimney crumbled to ruin, the window-sashes vacant, a corner of the roof caved in. The boys gazed a while, half expecting to see a blue light flit past a window; then talking in a low tone, as befitted the time and the circumstances, they struck far off to the right, to give the haunted house a wide berth, and took their way homeward through the woods that adorned the rearward side of Cardiff Hill.

CHAPTER XXVI.

INJUN JOE.

ABOUT noon the next day the boys arrived at the dead tree; they had come for their tools. Tom was impatient to go to the haunted house; Huck was measurably so, also—but suddenly said—

"Lookyhere, Tom, do you know what day it is?"

Tom mentally ran over the days of the week, and then quickly lifted his eyes with a startled look in them—

"My! I never once thought. of it, Huck!"

"Well I didn't neither, but all at once it popped onto me that it was Friday."

"Blame it, a body can't be too careful, Huck. We might a got into an awful scrape, tackling such a thing on a Friday."

"*Might*! Better say we *would*! There's some lucky days, maybe, but Friday ain't."

"Any fool knows that. I don't reckon *you* was the first that found it out, Huck."

"Well, I never said I was, did I? And Friday ain't all, neither. I had a rotten bad dream last night—dreampt about rats."

"No! Sure sign of trouble. Did they fight?"

"No."

"Well that's good, Huck. When they don't fight it's only a sign that there's trouble around, you know. All we got to do is to look mighty sharp and keep out of it. We'll drop this thing for today, and play. Do you know Robin Hood, Huck?"

"No. Who's Robin Hood?"

"Why he was one of the greatest men that was ever in England—and the best. He was a robber."

"Cracky, I wisht I was. Who did he rob?"

"Only sheriffs and bishops and rich people and kings, and such like. But he never bothered the poor. He loved 'em. He always divided up with 'em perfectly square."

THE GREATEST AND BEST.

"Well, he must 'a' been a brick."

"I bet you he was, Huck. Oh, he was the noblest man that ever was. They ain't any such men now, I can tell you. He could lick any man in England, with one hand tied behind him; and he could take his yew bow and plug a ten cent piece every time, a mile and a half."

"What's a *yew* bow?"

"*I* don't know. It's some kind of a bow, of course. And if he hit that dime only on the edge he would set down and cry—and curse. But we'll play Robin Hood—it's noble fun. I'll learn you."

"I'm agreed."

So they played Robin Hood all the afternoon, now and then casting a yearning eye down upon the haunted house and passing a remark about the morrow's prospects and possibilities there. As the sun began to sink into the west they took their way homeward athwart the long shadows of the trees and soon were buried from sight in the forests of Cardiff Hill.

On Saturday, shortly after noon, the boys were at the dead tree again. They had a smoke and a chat in the shade, and then dug a little in their last hole, not with great hope, but merely because Tom said there were so many cases where people had given up a treasure after getting down within six inches of it, and then somebody else had come along and turned it up with a single thrust of a shovel. The thing failed this time, however, so the boys shouldered their tools and went away feeling that they had not trifled with fortune but had fulfilled all the requirements that belong to the business of treasure-hunting.

When they reached the haunted house there was something so wierd and grisly about the dead silence that reigned there under the baking sun, and something so depressing about the loneliness and desolation of the place, that they were afraid, for a moment, to venture in. Then they crept to the door and took a trembling peep. They saw a weed-grown, floorless room, unplastered, an ancient fireplace, vacant windows, a ruinous staircase; and here, there, and everywhere, hung ragged and abandoned cobwebs. They presently entered, softly, with quickened pulses, talking in whispers, ears alert to catch the slightest sound, and muscles tense and ready for instant retreat.

In a little while familiarity modified their fears and they gave the place a critical and interested examination, rather admiring their own boldness, and wondering at it, too. Next they wanted to look up stairs. This was something like cutting off retreat, but they got to daring each other, and of course there could be but one result—they threw their tools into a corner and made the ascent. Up there were the same signs of decay. In one corner they found a closet that promised mystery, but the promise was a fraud—there was nothing in it. Their courage was up now and well in hand. They were about to go down and begin work when—

"Sh!" said Tom.

"What is it?" whispered Huck, blanching with fright.

"Sh! . . . There! . . . Hear it?"

"Yes! . . . O, my! Let's run!"

"Keep still! Don't you budge! They're coming right toward the door."

The boys stretched themselves upon the floor with their eyes to knot holes in the planking, and lay waiting, in a misery of fear.

"They've stopped . . . No—coming . . . Here they are. Don't whisper another word, Huck. My goodness, I wish I was out of this!"

Two men entered. Each boy said to himself: "There's the old deaf and dumb Spaniard that's been about town once or twice lately—never saw t'other man before."

"T'other" was a ragged, unkempt creature, with nothing very pleasant in his face. The Spaniard was wrapped in a *serapè*; he had bushy white whiskers; long white hair flowed from under his sombrero, and he wore green goggles. When they came in, "t'other" was talking in a low voice; they sat down on the ground, facing the door, with their backs to the wall, and the speaker continued his remarks. His manner became less guarded and his words more distinct as he proceeded:

"No," said he, "I've thought it all over, and I don't like it. It's dangerous."

"Dangerous!" grunted the "deaf and dumb" Spaniard,—to the vast surprise of the boys. "Milksop!"

This voice made the boys gasp and quake. It was Injun Joe's! There was silence for some time. Then Joe said:

"What's any more dangerous than that job up yonder—but nothing's come of it."

"That's different. Away up the river so, and not another house about. 'Twon't ever be known that we tried, anyway, long as we didn't succeed."

"Well, what's more dangerous than coming here in the day time!—anybody would suspicion us that saw us."

"*I* know that. But there warn't any other place as handy after that fool of a job. I want to quit this shanty. I wanted to yesterday, only it warn't any use trying to stir out of here, with those infernal boys playing over there on the hill right in full view."

"Those infernal boys," quaked again under the inspiration of this remark, and thought how lucky it was that they had remembered it was Friday and concluded to wait a day. They wished in their hearts they had waited a year.

The two men got out some food and made a luncheon. After a long and thoughtful silence, Injun Joe said:

"Look here, lad—you go back up the river where you belong. Wait there till you hear from me. I'll take the chances on dropping into this town just once more, for a look. We'll do that 'dangerous' job after I've spied around a little and think things look well for it. Then for Texas! We'll leg it together!"

This was satisfactory. Both men presently fell to yawning, and Injun Joe said:

"I'm dead for sleep! It's your turn to watch."

He curled down in the weeds and soon began to snore. His comrade stirred him once or twice and he became quiet. Presently the watcher began to nod; his head drooped lower and lower, both men began to snore now.

The boys drew a long, grateful breath. Tom whispered—

"Now's our chance—come!"

Huck said:

"I can't—I'd die if they was to wake."

Tom urged—Huck held back. At last Tom rose slowly and softly, and started alone. But the first step he made wrung such a hideous creak from the crazy floor that he sank down almost dead with fright. He never made a second attempt. The boys lay there counting the dragging moments till it seemed to them that time must be done and eternity growing gray; and then they were grateful to note that at last the sun was setting.

Now one snore ceased. Injun Joe sat up, stared around—smiled grimly upon his comrade, whose head was drooping upon his knees—stirred him up with his foot and said—

"Here! *You're* a watchman, ain't you! All right, though—nothing's happened."

"My! have I been asleep?"

"Oh, partly, partly. Nearly time for us to be moving, pard. What'll we do with what little swag we've got left?"

"I don't know—leave it here as we've always done, I reckon. No use to take it away till we start south. Six hundred and fifty in silver's something to carry."

"Well—all right—it won't matter to come here once more."

"No—but I'd say come in the night as we used to do—it's better."

"Yes; but look here; it may be a good while before I get the right chance at that job; accidents might happen; 'tain't in such a very good place; we'll just regularly bury it—and bury it deep."

"Good idea," said the comrade, who walked across the room, knelt down, raised one of the rearward hearthstones and took out a bag that jingled pleasantly. He subtracted from it twenty or thirty dollars for himself and as much for Injun Joe and passed the bag to the latter, who was on his knees in the corner, now, digging with his bowie knife.

The boys forgot all their fears, all their miseries in an instant. With gloating eyes they watched every movement. Luck!—the splendor of it was beyond all imagination! Six hundred dollars was money enough to make half a dozen boys rich! Here was treasure-hunting under the happiest auspices—there would not be any bothersome uncertainty as to where to dig. They nudged each other every moment—eloquent nudges and easily understood, for they simply meant—"O, but ain't you glad *now* we're here!"

Joe's knife struck upon something.

"Hello!" said he.

"What is it?" said his comrade.

"Half-rotten plank—no it's a box, I believe. Here—bear a hand and we'll see what it's here for. Never mind, I've broke a hole."

He reached his hand in and drew it out—

"Man, it's money!"

The two men examined the handful of coins. They were gold. The boys above were as excited as themselves, and as delighted.

Joe's comrade said—

"We'll make quick work of this. There's an old rusty pick over amongst the weeds in the corner the other side of the fireplace—I saw it a minute ago."

He ran and brought the boys' pick and shovel. Injun Joe took the pick, looked it over critically, shook his head, muttered something to himself, and then began to use it. The box was soon unearthed. It was not very large; it was iron bound and had been very strong before the slow years had injured it. The men contemplated the treasure a while in blissful silence.

"Pard, there's thousands of dollars here," said Injun Joe.

"'Twas always said that Murrel's gang used around here one summer," the stranger observed.

HIDDEN TREASURES UNEARTHED.

"I know it," said Injun Joe; "and this looks like it, I should say."

"*Now* you won't need to do that job."

The half-breed frowned. Said he—

"You don't know me. Least you don't know all about that thing. Tain't robbery altogether—it's *revenge!*" and a wicked light flamed in his eyes. "I'll need your help in it. When it's finished—then Texas. Go home to your Nance and your kids, and stand by till you hear from me."

"Well—if you say so, what'll we do with this—bury it again?"

"Yes. [Ravishing delight overhead.] *No!* by the great Sachem, no! [Profound distress overhead.] I'd nearly forgot. That pick had fresh earth on it! [The boys were sick with terror in a moment.] What business has a pick and a shovel here? What business with fresh earth on them? Who brought them here—and where are they gone? Have you heard anybody?—seen anybody? What! bury it again and leave them to come and see the ground disturbed? Not exactly—not exactly. We'll take it to my den."

"Why of course! Might have thought of that before. You mean Number One?"

"No—Number Two—under the cross. The other place is bad—too common."

"All right. It's nearly dark enough to start."

Injun Joe got up and went about from window to window cautiously peeping out. Presently he said:

"Who could have brought those tools here? Do you reckon they can be up stairs?"

The boys' breath forsook them. Injun Joe put his hand on his knife, halted a moment, undecided, and then turned toward the stairway. The boys thought of the closet, but their strength was gone. The steps came creaking up the stairs—the intolerable distress of the situation woke the stricken resolution of the lads—they were about to spring for the closet, when there was a crash of rotten timbers and Injun Joe landed on the ground amid the *debris* of the ruined stairway. He gathered himself up cursing, and his comrade said:

"Now what's the use of all that? If it's anybody, and they're up there, let them *stay* there—who cares? If they want to jump down, now, and get into trouble, who objects? It will be dark in fifteen minutes—and then let them follow us if they want to. I'm willing. In my opinion, whoever hove those things in here caught a sight of us and took us for ghosts or devils or something. I'll bet they're running yet."

Joe grumbled a while; then he agreed with his friend that what daylight was left ought to be economized in getting things ready for leaving. Shortly afterward they slipped out of the house in the deepening twilight, and moved toward the river with their precious box.

Tom and Huck rose up, weak but vastly relieved, and stared after them through the chinks between the logs of the house. Follow? Not they. They were content to reach ground again without broken necks, and take the townward track over the hill. They did not talk much. They were too much absorbed in hating themselves—hating the ill luck that made them take the spade and the pick there. But for that, Injun Joe never would have suspected. He would have hidden the silver with the gold to wait there till his "revenge" was satisfied, and then he would have had the misfortune to find that money turn up missing. Bitter, bitter luck that the tools were ever brought there!

They resolved to keep a lookout for that Spaniard when he should come to town spying out for chances to do his revengeful job, and follow him to "Number Two," wherever that might be. Then a ghastly thought occurred to Tom:

"Revenge?" What if he means *us*, Huck!"

"O, don't!" said Huck, nearly fainting.

They talked it all over, and as they entered town they agreed to believe that he might possibly mean somebody else—at least that

THE BOYS' SALVATION

he might at least mean nobody but Tom, since only Tom had testified.

Very, very small comfort it was to Tom to be alone in danger! Company would be a palpable improvement, he thought.

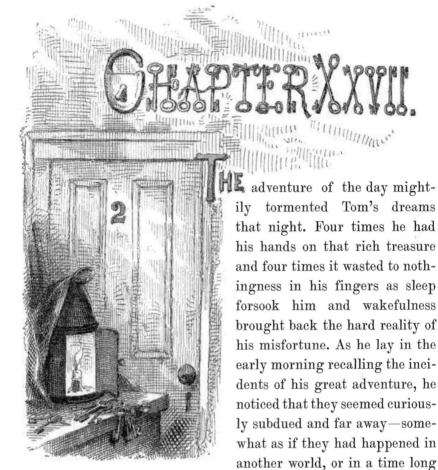

CHAPTER XXVII.

THE adventure of the day mightily tormented Tom's dreams that night. Four times he had his hands on that rich treasure and four times it wasted to nothingness in his fingers as sleep forsook him and wakefulness brought back the hard reality of his misfortune. As he lay in the early morning recalling the incidents of his great adventure, he noticed that they seemed curiously subdued and far away—somewhat as if they had happened in another world, or in a time long gone by. Then it occurred to him that the great adventure itself must be a dream! There was one very strong argument in favor of this idea—namely, that the quantity of coin he had seen was too vast to be real. He had never seen as much as fifty dollars in one mass before, and he was like all boys of his age and station in life, in that he imagined that all references to "hundreds" and "thousands" were mere fanciful forms of speech, and that no such sums really existed in the world. He never had supposed for a moment that so large a sum as a hundred dollars was to be found in actual money in any one's possession. If his notions of hidden treasure had been analyzed, they would have been found to consist of a handful of real dimes and a bushel of vague, splendid, ungraspable dollars.

But the incidents of his adventure grew sensibly sharper and clearer under the attrition of thinking them over, and so he presently found himself leaning to the impression that the thing might not

have been a dream, after all. This uncertainty must be swept away. He would snatch a hurried breakfast and go and find Huck.

Huck was sitting on the gunwale of a flatboat, listlessly dangling his feet in the water and looking very melancholy. Tom concluded to let Huck lead up to the subject. If he did not do it, then the adventure would be proved to have been only a dream.

"Hello, Huck!"

"Hello, yourself." Silence, for a minute.

THE NEXT DAY'S CONFERENCE.

"Tom, if we'd a left the blame tools at the dead tree, we'd 'a' got the money. O, ain't it awful!"

"'Tain't a dream, then, 'tain't a dream! Somehow I most wish it was. Dog'd if I don't, Huck."

"What ain't a dream?"

"Oh, that thing yesterday. I been half thinking it was."

"Dream! If them stairs hadn't broke down you'd 'a' seen how much dream it was! I've had dreams enough all night—with that patch-eyed Spanish devil going for me all through 'em—rot him!"

"No, not rot him. *Find* him! Track the money!"

"Tom, we'll never find him. A feller don't have only once chance for such a pile—and that one's lost. I'd feel mighty shaky if I was to see him, anyway."

"Well, so'd I; but I'd like to see him, anyway—and track him out—to his Number Two."

"Number Two—yes, that's it. I ben thinking 'bout that. But I can't make nothing out of it. What do you reckon it is?"

"I dono. It's too deep. Say, Huck—maybe it's the number of a house!"

"Goody! . . . No, Tom, that ain't it. If it is, it ain't in this one-horse town. They ain't no numbers here."

"Well, that's so. Lemme think a minute. Here—it's the number of a room—in a tavern, you know!"

"O, that's the trick! They ain't only two taverns. We can find out quick."

"You stay here, Huck, till I come."

Tom was off at once. He did not care to have Huck's company in public places. He was gone half an hour. He found that in the best tavern, No. 2 had long been occupied by a young lawyer, and was still so occupied. In the less ostentatious house No. 2 was a mystery. The tavern-keeper's young son said it was kept locked all the time, and he never saw anybody go into it or come out of it except at night; he did not know any particular reason for this state of things; had had some little curiosity, but it was rather feeble; had made the most of the mystery by entertaining himself with the idea that that room was "ha'nted;" had noticed that there was a light in there the night before.

"That's what I've found out, Huck. I reckon that's the very No. 2 we're after."

"I reckon it is, Tom. Now what you going to do?"

"Lemme think."

Tom thought a long time. Then he said:

"I'll tell you. The back door of that No. 2 is the door that comes out into that little close alley between the tavern and the old rattle-trap of a brick store. Now you get hold of all the door-keys you can find, and I'll nip all of Auntie's and the first dark night we'll go there and try 'em. And mind you keep a lookout for Injun Joe, because he said he was going to drop into town and spy around once more for a chance to get his revenge. If you see him, you just follow him; and if he don't go to that No. 2, that ain't the place."

"Lordy I don't want to foller him by myself!"

"Why it'll be night, sure. He mightn't ever see you—and if he did, maybe he'd never think anything."

"Well, if it's pretty dark I reckon I'll track him. I dono—I dono. I'll try."

"You bet *I*'ll follow him, if it's dark, Huck. Why he might 'a' found out he couldn't get his revenge, and be going right after that money."

"It's so, Tom, it's so. I'll foller him; I will, by jingoes!"

"Now you're *talking*! Don't you ever weaken, Huck, and I won't."

CHAPTER XXVIII.

UNCLE JAKE

That night Tom and Huck were ready for their adventure. They hung about the neighborhood of the tavern until after nine, one watching the alley at a distance and the other the tavern door. Nobody entered the alley or left it; nobody resembling the Spaniard entered or left the tavern door. The night promised to be a fair one; so Tom went home with the understanding that if a considerable degree of darkness came on, Huck was to come and "maow," whereupon he would slip out and try the keys. But the night remained clear, and Huck closed his watch and retired to bed in an empty sugar hogshead about twelve.

Tuesday the boys had the same ill luck. Also Wednesday. But Thursday night promised better. Tom slipped out in good season with his aunt's old tin lantern, and a large towel to blindfold it with. He hid the lantern in Huck's sugar hogshead and the watch began. An hour before midnight the tavern closed up and its lights (the only ones thereabouts) were put out. No Spaniard had been seen. Nobody had entered or left the alley. Everything was auspicious. The blackness of darkness reigned, the perfect stillness was interrupted only by occasional mutterings of distant thunder.

Tom got his lantern, lit it in the hogs-head, wrapped it closely in the towel, and the two adventurers crept in the gloom toward the tavern. Huck stood sentry and Tom felt his way into the alley. Then

HUCK AT HOME.

there was a season of waiting anxiety that weighed upon Huck's spirits like a mountain. He began to wish he could see a flash from the lantern—it would frighten him, but it would at least tell him that Tom was alive yet. It seemed hours since Tom had disappeared. Surely he must have fainted; maybe he was dead; maybe his heart had burst under terror and excitement. In his uneasiness Huck found himself drawing closer and closer to the alley; fearing all sorts of dreadful things, and momentarily expecting some catastrophe to happen that would take away his breath. There was not much to take away, for he seemed only able to inhale it by thimblefuls, and his heart would soon wear itself out, the way it was beating. Suddenly there was a flash of light and Tom came tearing by him:

"Run!" said he; "run, for your life!"

He needn't have repeated it; once was enough; Huck was making thirty or forty miles an hour before the repetition was uttered. The boys never stopped till they reached the shed of a deserted slaughter-house at the lower end of the village. Just as they got within its shelter the storm burst and the rain poured down. As soon as Tom got his breath he said:

"Huck, it was awful! I tried two of the keys, just as soft as I could; but they seemed to make such a power of racket that I couldn't hardly get my breath I was so scared. They wouldn't turn in the lock, either. Well, without noticing what I was doing, I took hold of the knob, and open comes the door! It warn't locked! I hopped in, and shook off the towel, and, *great Caesar's ghost!*"

"What!—what 'd you see, Tom!"

"Huck, I most stepped onto Injun Joe's hand!"

"No!"

"Yes! He was laying there, sound asleep on the floor, with his old patch on his eye and his arms spread out."

THE HAUNTED ROOM.

"Lordy, what did you do? Did he wake up?"

"No, never budged. Drunk, I reckon. I just grabbed that towel and started!"

"I'd never 'a' thought of the towel, I bet!"

"Well, *I* would. My aunt would make me mighty sick if I lost it."

"Say, Tom, did you see that box?"

"Huck I didn't wait to look around. I didn't see the box, I didn't see the cross. I didn't see anything but a bottle and a tin cup on the floor by Injun Joe; yes, and I saw two barrels and lots more bottles in the room. Don't you see, now, what's the matter with that ha'nted room?"

"How?"

"Why it's ha'nted with whisky! Maybe *all* the Temperance Taverns have got a ha'nted room, hey Huck?"

"Well I reckon maybe that's so. Who'd 'a' thought such a thing? But say, Tom, now's a mighty good time to get that box, if Injun Joe's drunk."

"It is, that! You try it!"

Huck shuddered.

"Well, no—I reckon not."

"And *I* reckon not, Huck. Only one bottle alongside of Injun Joe ain't enough. If there'd been three, he'd be drunk enough and I'd do it."

There was a long pause for reflection, and then Tom said:

"Lookyhere, Huck, less not try that thing any more till we know Injun Joe's not in there. It's too scary. Now if we watch every night, we'll be dead sure to see him go out, some time or other, and then we'll snatch that box quicker'n lightning."

"Well, I'm agreed. I'll watch the whole night long, and I'll do it every night, too, if you'll do the other part of the job."

"All right, I will. All you got to do is to trot up Hooper street a block and maow—and if I'm asleep, you throw some gravel at the window and that'll fetch me."

"Agreed, and good as wheat!"

"Now Huck, the storm's over, and I'll go home. It'll begin to be daylight in a couple of hours. You go back and watch that long, will you?"

"I said I would, Tom, and I will. I'll ha'nt that tavern every night for a year! I'll sleep all day and I'll stand watch all night."

"That's all right. Now where you going to sleep?"

"In Ben Rogers's hayloft. He let's me, and so does his pap's nigger man, Uncle Jake. I tote water for Uncle Jake whenever he wants me to, and any time I ask him he gives me a little something to eat if he can spare it. That's a mighty good nigger, Tom. He likes me, becuz I don't ever act as if I was above him. Sometimes I've set right down and eat *with* him. But you needn't tell that. A body's got to do things when he's awful hungry he wouldn't want to do as a steady thing."

"Well, if I don't want you in the day time, I'll let you sleep. I won't come bothering around. Any time you see something's up, in the night, just skip right around and maow."

M⁰DOUGAL'S CAVE

CHAPTER XXIX.

THE first thing Tom heard on Friday morning was a glad piece of news—Judge Thatcher's family had come back to town the night before. Both Injun Joe and the treasure sunk into secondary importance for a moment, and Becky took the chief place in the boy's interest. He saw her and they had an exhausting good time playing "hi-spy" and "gully-keeper" with a crowd of their schoolmates. The day was completed and crowned in a peculiarly satisfactory way: Becky teased her mother to appoint the next day for the long-promised and long-delayed picnic, and she consented. The child's delight was boundless; and Tom's not more moderate. The invitations were sent out before sunset, and straightway the young folks of the village were thrown into a fever of preparation and pleasurable anticipation. Tom's excitement enabled him to keep awake until a pretty late hour, and he had good hopes of hearing Huck's "maow," and of having his treasure to astonish Becky and the pic-nickers with, next day; but he was disappointed. No signal came that night.

Morning came, eventually, and by ten or eleven o'clock a giddy and rollicking company were gathered at Judge Thatcher's, and ev-

erything was ready for a start. It was not the custom for elderly people to mar pic-nics with their presence. The children were considered
safe enough under the wings of a few young ladies of eighteen and a
few young gentlemen of twenty-three or thereabouts. The old steam
ferry-boat was chartered for the occasion; presently the gay throng
filed up the main street laden with provision baskets. Sid was sick
and had to miss the fun; Mary remained at home to entertain him.
The last thing Mrs. Thatcher said to Becky, was—

"You'll not get back till late. Perhaps you'd better stay all night
with some of the girls that live near the ferry landing, child."

"Then I'll stay with Susy Harper, mamma."

"Very well. And mind and behave yourself and don't be any
trouble."

Presently, as they tripped along, Tom said to Becky:

"Say—I'll tell you what we'll do. 'Stead of going to Joe Harper's
we'll climb right up the hill and stop at the Widow Douglas's. She'll
have ice cream! She has it most every day—dead loads of it. And
she'll be awful glad to have us."

"O, that will be fun!"

Then Becky reflected a moment and said:

"But what will mamma say?"

"How'll she ever know?"

The girl turned the idea over in her mind, and said reluctantly:

"I reckon it's wrong—but—"

"But shucks! Your mother won't know, and so what's the harm?
All she wants is that you'll be safe; and I bet you she'd 'a' said go
there if she'd 'a' thought of it. I know she would!"

The widow Douglas's splendid hospitality was a tempting bait. It
and Tom's persuasions presently carried the day. So it was decided
to say nothing to anybody about the night's programme. Presently
it occurred to Tom that maybe Huck might come this very night
and give the signal. The thought took a deal of the spirit out of his
anticipations. Still he could not bear to give up the fun at Widow
Douglas's. And why should he give it up, he reasoned—the signal
did not come the night before, so why should it be any more likely to
come to-night? The sure fun of the evening outweighed the uncertain

treasure; and boy like, he determined to yield to the stronger inclination and not allow himself to think of the box of money another time that day.

Three miles below town the ferry-boat stopped at the mouth of a woody hollow and tied up. The crowd swarmed ashore and soon the forest distances and craggy heights echoed far and near with shoutings and laughter. All the different ways of getting hot and tired were gone through with, and by and by the rovers straggled back to camp fortified with responsible appetites, and then the destruction of the good things began. After the feast there was a refreshing season of rest and chat in the shade of spreading oaks. By and by somebody shouted—

"Who's ready for the cave?"

Everybody was. Bundles of candles were procured, and straightway there was a general scamper up the hill. The mouth of the cave was up the hillside—an opening shaped like a letter A. It's massive oaken door stood unbarred. Within was a small chamber, chilly as an ice-house, and walled by Nature with solid limestone that was dewy with a cold sweat. It was romantic and mysterious to stand here in the deep gloom and look out upon the green valley shining in the sun. But the impressiveness of the situation quickly wore off, and the romping began again. The moment a candle was lighted there was a general rush upon the owner of it; a struggle and a gallant defense followed, but the candle was soon knocked down or blown out, and then there was a glad clamor of laughter and a new chase. But all things have an end. By and by the procession went filing down the steep descent of the main avenue, the flickering rank of lights dimly revealing the lofty walls of rock almost to their point of junction sixty feet overhead. This main avenue was not more than eight or ten feet wide. Every few steps other lofty and still narrower crevices branched from it on either hand—for McDougal's cave was but a vast labyrinth of crooked isles that ran into each other and out again and led nowhere. It was said that one might wander days and nights together through its intricate tangle of rifts and chasms, and never find the end of the cave; and that he might go down, and down, and still down, into the earth, and it was just the same—labyrinth underneath labyrinth, and no end to any of them. No man "knew" the cave. That was an impossible thing. Most of the young men knew a portion of it, and it was not customary to venture much beyond this known portion. Tom Sawyer knew as much of the cave as any one.

The procession moved along the main avenue some three-quarters of a mile, and then groups and couples began to slip aside into branch avenues, fly along the dismal corridors, and take each other by surprise at points where the corridors joined again. Parties were able to elude each other for the space of half an hour without going beyond the "known" ground.

By and by, one group after another came straggling back to the mouth of the cave, panting, hilarious, smeared from head to foot with tallow drippings, daubed with clay, and entirely delighted with the success of the day. Then they were astonished to find that they had been taking no note of time and that night was about at hand. The clanging bell had been calling for half an hour. However, this sort of close to the day's adventures was romantic and therefore satisfactory. When the ferry-boat with her wild freight pushed into the stream, nobody cared sixpence for the wasted time but the captain of the craft.

Huck was already upon his watch when the ferry-boat's lights went glinting past the wharf. He heard no noise on board, for the young people were as subdued and still as people usually are who are

nearly tired to death. He wondered what boat it was, and why she did
not stop at the wharf—and then he dropped her out of his mind and
put his attention upon his business. The night was growing cloudy
and dark. Ten o'clock came, and the noise of vehicles ceased, scattered lights began to wink out, all straggling foot passengers disappeared, the village betook itself to its slumbers and left the small
watcher alone with the silence and the ghosts. Eleven o'clock came,
and the tavern lights were put out; darkness everywhere, now. Huck
waited what seemed a weary long time, but nothing happened. His
faith was weakening. Was there any use? Was there really any use?
Why not give it up and turn in?

A noise fell upon his ear. He was all attention in an instant. The
alley door closed softly. He sprang to the corner of the brick store.
The next moment two men brushed by him, and one seemed to have
something under his arm. It must be that box! So they were going to
remove the treasure. Why call Tom now? It would be absurd—the

HUCK ON DUTY.

men would get away with the box
and never be found again. No, he
would stick to their wake and follow them; he would trust to the
darkness for security from discovery. So communing with himself,
Huck stepped out and glided
along behind the men, cat-like,
with bare feet, allowing them to
keep just far enough ahead not to
be invisible.

They moved up the river street
three blocks, then turned to the
left up a cross street. They went
straight ahead, then, until they
came to the path that led up Cardiff Hill; this they took. They passed
by the old Welchman's house, half way up the hill without hesitating, and still climbed upward. Good, thought Huck, they will bury it
in the old quarry. But they never stopped at the quarry. They passed
on, up the summit. They plunged into the narrow path between the

tall sumach bushes, and were at once hidden in the gloom. Huck closed up and shortened his distance, now, for they would never be able to see him. He trotted along a while; then slackened his pace, fearing he was gaining too fast; moved on a piece, then stopped altogether; listened; no sound; none, save that he seemed to hear the beating of his own heart. The hooting of an owl came from over the hill—ominous sound! But no footsteps. Heavens, was everything lost! He was about to spring with winged feet, when a man cleared his throat not four feet from him! Huck's heart shot into his throat, but he swallowed it again; and then he stood there shaking as if a dozen agues had taken charge of him at once, and so weak that he thought he must surely fall to the ground. He knew where he was. He knew he was within five steps of the stile leading into Widow Douglas's grounds. Very well, he thought, let them bury it there; it won't be hard to find.

Now there was a voice—a very low voice—Injun Joe's:

"Damn her, maybe she's got company—there's lights, late as it is."

"I can't see any."

This was that stranger's voice—the stranger of the haunted house. A deadly chill went to Huck's heart—this, then, was the "revenge" job! His thought was, to fly. Then he remembered that the Widow Douglas had been kind to him more than once, and maybe these men were going to murder her. He wished he dared venture to warn her; but he knew he didn't dare—they might come and catch him. He thought all this and more in the moment that elapsed between the stranger's remark and Injun Joe's next—which was—

"Because the bush is in your way. Now—this way—now you see, don't you?"

"Yes. Well there *is* company there, I reckon. Better give it up."

"Give it up, and I just leaving this country forever! Give it up and maybe never have another chance. I tell you again, as I've told you before, I don't care for her swag—you may have it. But her husband was rough on me—many times he was rough on me— and mainly he was the justice of the peace that jugged me for a vagrant. And that ain't all. It ain't a millionth part of it! He had me *horsewhipped*!—horsewhipped in front of the jail, like a nigger!—with all the town looking on! HORSEWHIPPED!—do you understand? He took advantage of me and died. But I'll take it out of *her*."

"Oh, don't kill her! Don't do that!"

"Kill? Who said anything about killing? I would kill *him* if he was here; but not her. When you want to get revenge on a woman you don't kill her—bosh! you go for her looks. You slit her nostrils—you notch her ears like a sow!"

"By God, that's—"

"Keep your opinion to yourself! It will be safest for you. I'll tie her to the bed. If she bleeds to death, is that my fault? I'll not cry, if she does. My friend, you'll help in this thing—for *my* sake—that's why you're here—I mightn't be able alone. If you flinch, I'll kill you. Do you understand that? And if I have to kill you, I'll kill her—and then I reckon nobody'll ever know much about who done this business."

"Well, if it's got to be done, let's get at it. The quicker the better— I'm all in a shiver."

"Do it *now*? And company there? Look here—I'll get suspicious of you, first thing you know. No—we'll wait till the lights are out— there's no hurry."

Huck felt that a silence was going to ensue—a thing still more awful than any amount of murderous talk; so he held his breath and stepped gingerly back; planted his foot carefully and firmly, after balancing, one-legged, in a precarious way and almost toppling over, first on one side and then on the other. He took another step back, with the same elaboration and the same risks; then another and another, and—a twig snapped under his foot! His breath stopped and he listened. There was no sound—the stillness was perfect. His gratitude was measureless. Now he turned in his tracks, between the walls of sumach bushes—turned himself as carefully as if he were a ship—and then stepped quickly but cautiously along. When he emerged at the quarry he felt secure, and so he picked up his nimble heels and flew. Down, down he sped, till he reached the Welchman's. He banged at the door, and presently the heads of the old man and his two stalwart sons were thrust from windows.

"What's the row there? Who's banging? What do you want?"

A ROUSING ACT.

"Let me in—quick! I'll tell everything."

"Why who are you?"

"Huckleberry Finn—quick, let me in!"

"Huckleberry Finn, indeed! It ain't a name to open many doors, I judge! But let him in, lads, and let's see what's the trouble."

"Please don't ever tell *I* told you," were Huck's first words when he got in. "Please don't—I'd be killed, sure—but the Widow's been good friends to me sometimes, and I want to tell—I *will* tell if you'll promise you won't ever say it was me."

"By George he *has* got something to tell, or he wouldn't act so!" exclaimed the old man; "out with it and nobody here'll ever tell, lad."

Three minutes later the old man and his sons, well armed, were up the hill, and just entering the sumach path on tip-toe, their weapons in their hands. Huck accompanied them no further. He hid behind a great bowlder and fell to listening. There was a lagging, anxious silence, and then all of a sudden there was an explosion of firearms and a cry.

Huck waited for no particulars. He sprang away and sped down the hill as fast as his legs could carry him.

CHAPTER XXX.

THE WELSHMAN.

As the earliest suspicion of dawn appeared on Sunday morning, Huck came groping up the hill and rapped gently at the old Welchman's door. The inmates were asleep but it was a sleep that was set on a hair-trigger, on account of the exciting episode of the night. A call came from a window—

"Who's there!"

Huck's scared voice answered in a low tone:

"Please let me in! It's only Huck Finn!"

"It's a name that can open this door night or day, lad!—and welcome!"

These were strange words to the vagabond boy's ears, and the pleasantest he had ever heard. He could not recollect that the closing word had ever been applied in his case before. The door was quickly unlocked, and he entered. Huck was given a seat and the old man and his brace of tall sons speedily dressed themselves.

"Now my boy I hope you're good and hungry, because breakfast will be ready as soon as the sun's up, and we'll have a piping hot one, too—make yourself easy about that! I and the boys hoped you'd turn up and stop here last night."

"I was awful scared," said Huck, "and I run. I took out when the pistols went off, and I didn't stop for three mile. I've come now becuz I wanted to know about it, you know; and I come before daylight becuz I didn't want to run acrost them devils, even if they was dead."

"Well, poor chap, you do look as if you'd had a hard night of it— but there's a bed here for you when you've had your breakfast. No, they ain't dead, lad—we are sorry enough for that. You see we knew right where to put our hands on them, by your description; so we crept along on tip-toe till we got within fifteen feet of them—dark as a cellar that sumach path was—and just then I found I was going to sneeze. It was the meanest kind of luck! I tried to keep it back, but no use— 'twas bound to come, and it did come! I was in the lead with my pistol raised, and when the sneeze started those scoundrels a-rustling to get out of the path, I sung out, 'Fire, boys!' and blazed away at the place where the rustling was. So did the boys. But they were off in a jiffy, those villains, and we after

RESULT OF A SNEEZE.

them, down through the woods. I judge we never touched them. They fired a shot apiece as they started, but their bullets whizzed by and didn't do us any harm. As soon as we lost the sound of their feet we quit chasing, and went down and stirred up the constables. They got a posse together, and went off to guard the river bank, and as soon as it is light the sheriff and a gang are going to beat up the woods. My boys will be with them presently. I wish we had some sort of description of those rascals—'twould help a good deal. But you could'nt see what they were like, in the dark, lad, I suppose?"

"O, yes, I saw them down town and follered them."

"Splendid! Describe them—describe them, my boy!"

"One's the old deaf and dumb Spaniard that's ben around here once or twice, and t'other's a mean looking ragged—"

"That's enough, lad, we know the men! Happened on them in the woods back of the widow's one day, and they slunk away. Off with you, boys, and tell the sheriff—get your breakfast tomorrow morning!"

The Welchman's sons departed at once. As they were leaving the room Huck sprang up and exclaimed:

"Oh, please don't tell *any*body it was me that blowed on them! Oh, please!"

"All right if you say it, Huck, but you ought to have the credit of what you did."

"Oh, no, no! Please don't tell!"

When the young men were gone, the old Welchman said—

"They won't tell—and I won't. But why don't you want it known?"

Huck would not explain, further than to say that he already knew too much about one of those men and would not have the man know that he knew anything against him for the whole world—he would be killed for knowing it, sure.

The old man promised secrecy once more, and said:

"How did you come to follow these fellows, lad? Were they looking suspicious?"

Huck was silent while he framed a duly cautious reply. Then he said:

"Well, you see, I'm a kind of a hard lot,—least everybody says so, and I don't see nothing agin it—and sometimes I can't sleep much, on accounts of thinking about it and sort of trying to strike out a new way of doing. That was the way of it last night. I couldn't sleep, and so I come along up street 'bout midnight, a-turning it all over, and when I got to that old shackly brick store by the Temperance Tavern, I backed up agin the wall to have another think. Well, just then along comes these two chaps slipping along close by me, with something under their arm and I reckoned they'd stole it. One was a-smoking, and t'other one wanted a light; so they stopped right before me and the cigars lit up their faces and I see that the big one was the deaf and dumb Spaniard, by his white whiskers and the patch on his eye, and t'other one was a rusty, ragged looking devil."

"Could you see the rags by the light of the cigars?"

This staggered Huck for a moment. Then he said:

"Well, I don't know—but somehow it seems as if I did."

"Then they went on, and you—"

"Follered 'em—yes. That was it. I wanted to see what was up—they sneaked along so. I dogged 'em to the widder's stile, and stood in the dark and heard the ragged one beg for the widder, and the Spaniard swear he'd spile her looks just as I told you and your two—"

"What! The *deaf and dumb* man said all that!"

Huck had made another terrible mistake! He was trying his best to keep the old man from getting the faintest hint of who the Spaniard might be, and yet his tongue seemed determined to get him into trouble in spite of all he could do. He made several efforts to creep out of his scrape, but the old man's eye was upon him and he made blunder after blunder. Presently the Welchman said:

"My boy, don't be afraid of me. I wouldn't hurt a hair of your head for all the world. No—I'd protect you—I'd protect you. This Spaniard is not deaf and dumb; you've let that slip without intending it; you can't cover that up now. You know something about that Spaniard that you want to keep dark. Now trust me—tell me what it is, and trust me—I won't betray you."

CORNERED.

Huck looked into the old man's honest eyes a moment, then bent over and whispered in his ear—

"'Tain't a Spaniard—it's Injun Joe!"

The Welchman almost jumped out of his chair. In a moment he said:

"It's all plain enough, now. When you talked about notching ears and slitting noses I judged that that was your own embellishment, because white men don't take that sort of revenge. But an Injun! That's a different matter altogether."

During breakfast the talk went on, and in the course of it the old man said that the last thing which he and his sons had done, before going to bed, was to get a lantern and examine the stile and its vicinity for marks of blood. They found none, but captured a bulky bundle of—

"Of WHAT?"

If the words had been lightning they could not have leaped with a more stunning suddenness from Huck's blanched lips. His eyes were staring wide, now, and his breath suspended—waiting for the answer. The Welchman started—stared in return—three seconds—five seconds—ten—then replied—

"Of burglar's tools. Why what's the *matter* with you?"

Huck sank back, panting gently, but deeply, unutterably grateful. The Welchman eyed him gravely, curiously—and presently said—

"Yes, burglar's tools. That appears to relieve you a good deal. But what did give you that turn? What were *you* expecting we'd found?"

Huck was in a close place—the inquiring eye was upon him—he would have given anything for material for a plausible answer—nothing suggested itself—the inquiring eye was boring deeper and deeper—a senseless reply offered—there was no time to weigh it, so at a venture he uttered it—feebly:

"Sunday-school books, maybe."

Poor Huck was too distressed to smile, but the old man laughed loud and joyously, shook up the details of his anatomy from head to foot, and ended by saying that such a laugh was money in a man's pocket, because it cut down the doctor's bills like everything. Then he added:

"Poor old chap, you're white and jaded—you ain't well a bit—no wonder you're a little flighty and off your balance. But you'll come out of it. Rest and sleep will fetch you out all right, I hope."

Huck was irritated to think he had been such a goose and betrayed such a suspicious excitement, for he had dropped the idea that the parcel brought from the tavern was the treasure, as soon as he had heard the talk at the widow's stile. He had only *thought* it was not the treasure, however—he had not known that it wasn't—and so the suggestion of a captured bundle was too much for his self-possession. But on the whole he felt glad the little episode had happened, for now he knew beyond all question that that bundle was not *the* bundle, and so his mind was at rest and exceedingly comfortable. In fact everything seemed to be drifting just in the right direction, now; the treasure must be still in No. 2, the men would be captured and jailed that day, and he and Tom could seize the gold that night without any trouble or any fear of interruption.

Just as breakfast was completed there was a knock at the door. Huck jumped for a hiding place, for he had no mind to be connected even remotely with the late event. The Welchman admitted several ladies and gentlemen, among them the widow Douglas, and noticed that groups of citzens were climbing up the hill—to stare at the stile. So the news had spread.

The Welchman had to tell the story of the night to the visitors. The widow's gratitude for her preservation was outspoken.

"Don't say a word about it madam. There's another that you're more beholden to than you are to me and my boys, maybe, but he don't allow me to tell his name. We wouldn't have been there but for him."

Of course this excited a curiosity so vast that it almost belittled the main matter—but the Welchman allowed it to eat into the vitals of his visitors, and through them be transmitted to the whole town, for he refused to part with his secret. When all else had been learned, the widow said:

"I went to sleep reading in bed and slept straight through all that noise. Why didn't you come and wake me?"

"We judged it warn't worth while. Those fellows warn't likely to come again—they hadn't any tools left to work with, and what was the use of waking you up and scaring you to death? My three negro men stood guard at your house all the rest of the night. They've just come back."

More visitors came, and the story had to be told and re-told for a couple of hours more.

There was no Sabbath-school during day-school vacation, but everybody was early at church. The stirring event was well canvassed.

News came that not a sign of the two villains had been yet discovered. When the sermon was finished, Judge Thatcher's wife dropped alongside of Mrs. Harper as she moved down the aisle with the crowd and said:

"Is my Becky going to sleep all day? I just expected she would be tired to death."

"Your Becky?"

"Yes," with a startled look,—"didn't she stay with you last night?"

"Why, no."

Mrs. Thatcher turned pale, and sank into a pew, just as Aunt

ALARMING DISCOVERIES.

Polly, talking briskly with a friend, passed by. Aunt Polly said:

"Good morning, Mrs. Thatcher. Good morning Mrs. Harper. I've got a boy that's turned up missing. I reckon my Tom staid at your house last night—one of you. And now he's afraid to come to church. I've got to settle with him."

Mrs. Thatcher shook her head feebly and turned paler than ever.

"He didn't stay with us," said Mrs. Harper, beginning to look uneasy. A marked anxiety came into Aunt Polly's face.

"Joe Harper, have you seen my Tom this morning?"

"No'm."

"When did you see him last?"

Joe tried to remember, but was not sure he could say. The people had stopped moving out of church. Whispers passed along, and a boding uneasiness took possession of every countenance. Children were anxiously questioned, and young teachers. They all said they had not noticed whether Tom and Becky were on board the ferry-boat on the homeward trip; it was dark; no one thought of inquiring if any one was missing. One young man finally blurted out his fear that they were still in the cave! Mrs. Thatcher swooned away. Aunt Polly fell to crying and wringing her hands.

The alarm swept from lip to lip, from group to group, from street to street, and within five minutes the bells were wildly clanging and the whole town was up! The Cardiff Hill episode sank into instant insignificance, the burglars were forgotten, horses were saddled, skiffs were manned, the ferry-boat ordered out, and before the horror was half an hour old, two hundred men were pouring down high-road and river toward the cave.

TOM AND BECKY STIR UP THE TOWN.

All the long afternoon the village seemed empty and dead. Many women visited Aunt Polly and Mrs. Thatcher and tried to comfort them. They cried with them, too, and that was still better than words. All the tedious night the town waited for news; but when the morning dawned at last, all the word that came was, "Send more candles— and send food." Mrs. Thatcher was almost crazed; and Aunt Polly also. Judge Thatcher sent messages of hope and encouragement from the cave, but they conveyed no real cheer.

The old Welchman came home toward daylight, spattered with candle grease, smeared with clay, and almost worn out. He found Huck still in the bed that had been provided for him, and delirious with fever. The physicians were all at the cave, so the Widow Douglas came and took charge of the patient. She said she would do her best by him, because, whether he was good, bad, or indifferent, he was the Lord's, and nothing that was the Lord's was a thing to be neglected. The Welchman said Huck had good spots in him, and the widow said—

"You can depend on it. That's the Lord's mark. He don't leave it off. He never does. Puts it somewhere on every creature that comes from his hands."

Early in the forenoon parties of jaded men began to straggle into the village, but the strongest of the citizens continued searching. All the news that could be gained was that remotenesses of the cavern were being ransacked that had never been visited before; that

TOM'S MARK.

every corner and crevice was going to be thoroughly searched; that wherever one wandered through the maze of passages, lights were to be seen flitting hither and thither in the distance, and shoutings and pistol shots sent their hollow reverberations to the ear down the sombre aisles. In one place, far from the section usually traversed by tourists, the names "BECKY & TOM" had been found traced upon the rocky wall with candle smoke, and near at hand a grease-soiled bit of ribbon. Mrs. Thatcher recognized the ribbon and cried over it. She said it was the last relic she should ever have of her child; and that no other memorial of her could ever be so precious, because this one parted latest from the living body before the awful death came. Some said that now and then, in the cave, a faraway speck of light would glimmer, and then a glorious shout would burst forth and a score of men go trooping down the echoing aisle—and then a sickening disappointment always followed; the children were not there; it was only a searcher's light.

Three dreadful days and nights dragged their tedious hours along, and the village sank into a hopeless stupor. No one had heart for anything. The accidental discovery, just made, that the proprietor of the Temperance Tavern kept liquor on his premises, scarcely fluttered the public pulse, tremendous as the fact was. In a lucid interval, Huck feebly led up to the subject of taverns, and finally asked—dimly dreading the worst—if anything had been discovered at the Temperance Tavern since he had been ill?

"Yes," said the widow.

Huck started up in bed, wild-eyed:

"What! What was it?"

"Liquor!—and the place has been shut up. Lie down, child—what a turn you did give me!"

"Only tell me just one thing—only just one—please! Was it Tom Sawyer that found it?"

The widow burst into tears. "Hush, hush, child, hush! I've told you before, you must *not* talk. You are very, very sick!"

HUCK QUESTIONS THE WIDOW.

Then nothing but liquor had been found; there would have been a great pow-wow if it had been the gold. So the treasure was gone forever—gone forever! But what could she be crying about? Curious that she should cry.

These thoughts worked their dim way through Huck's mind, and under the weariness they gave him he fell asleep. The widow said to herself:

"There he's asleep, poor wreck. Tom Sawyer find it! Pity but somebody could find Tom Sawyer! Ah, there ain't many left, now, that's got hope enough, or strength enough, either, to go on searching."

CHAPTER XXXI.

NOW to return to Tom and Becky's share in the pic-nic. They tripped along the murky aisles with the rest of the company, visiting the familiar wonders of the cave—wonders dubbed with rather over-descriptive names, such as "The Drawing-Room," "The Cathedral," "Aladdin's Palace," and so on. Presently the hide-and-seek frolicking began, and Tom and Becky engaged in it with zeal until the exertion began to grow a trifle wearisome; then they wandered down a sinuous avenue holding their candles aloft and reading the tangled webwork of names, dates, post-office addresses and mottoes with which the rocky walls had been frescoed (in candle smoke.) Still drifting along and talking, they scarcely noticed that they were now in a part of the cave whose walls were not frescoed. They smoked their own names under an overhanging shelf and moved on. Presently they came to a place where a little stream of water, trickling over a ledge and carrying a limestone sediment with it, had, in the slow-dragging ages, formed a laced and ruffled Niagara in gleaming and imperishable stone. Tom squeezed his small body behind it in order to illuminate it for Becky's gratification. He found that it curtained a sort of steep natural stairway which was enclosed between narrow walls, and

at once the ambition to be a discoverer seized him. Becky responded
to his call, and they made a smoke-mark for future guidance, and
started upon their quest. They wound this way and that, far down
into the secret depths of the cave, made another mark, and branched
off in search of novelties to tell the upper world about. In one place
they found a spacious cavern, from whose ceiling depended a multi-
tude of shining stalactites of the length and circumference of a
man's leg; they walked all about it, wondering and admiring, and
presently left it by one of the numerous passages that opened into it.
This shortly brought them to a be-
witching spring, whose basin was
encrusted with a frost work of
glittering crystals; it was in the
midst of a cavern whose walls were
supported by many fantastic pil-
lars which had been formed by the
joining of great stalactites and
stalagmites together, the result of
the ceaseless water-drip of centuries. Under the roof vast knots of
bats had packed themselves together, thousands in a bunch; the
lights disturbed the creatures and
they came flocking down by hundreds, squeaking and darting furiously at the candles. Tom knew
their ways and the danger of this
sort of conduct. He siezed Becky's
hand and hurried her into the first

WONDERS OF THE CAVE.

corridor that offered; and none too soon, for a bat struck Becky's
light out with its wing while she was passing out of the cavern. The
bats chased the children a good distance; but the fugitives plunged
into every new passage that offered, and at last got rid of the peril-
ous things. Tom found a subterranean lake, shortly, which stretched
its dim length away until its shape was lost in the shadows. He
wanted to explore its borders, but concluded that it would be best to
sit down and rest a while, first. Now, for the first time, the deep

stillness of the place laid a clammy hand upon the spirits of the children. Becky said—

"Why, I didn't notice, but it seems ever so long since I heard any of the others."

ATTACKED BY NATIVES.

"Come to think, Becky, we are away down below them—and I don't know how far away north, or south, or east, or whichever it is. We couldn't hear them here."

Becky grew apprehensive.

"I wonder how long we've been down here, Tom. We better start back."

"Yes, I reckon we better. P'raps we better."

"Can you find the way, Tom? It's all a mixed-up crookedness to me."

"I reckon I could find it—but then the bats. If they put both our candles out it will be an awful fix. Let's try some other way, so as not to go through there."

"Well. But I hope we won't get lost. It would be so awful!" and the girl shuddered at the thought of the dreadful possibilities.

They started through a corridor, and traversed it in silence a long way, glancing at each new opening, to see if there was anything familiar about the look of it; but they were all strange. Every time Tom made an examination, Becky would watch his face for an encouraging sign, and he would say cheerily—

"Oh, it's all right. This ain't the one, but we'll come to it right away!"

But he felt less and less hopeful with each failure, and presently began to turn off into diverging avenues at sheer random, in desperate hope of finding the one that was wanted! He still said it was "all right," but there was such a leaden dread at his heart, that the words had lost their ring and sounded just as if he had said, "All is lost!" Becky clung to his side in an anguish of fear, and tried hard to keep back the tears, but they would come. At last she said:

"O, Tom, never mind the bats, let's go back that way! We seem to get worse and worse off all the time."

Tom stopped.

"Listen!" said he.

Profound silence; silence so deep that even their breathings were conspicuous in the hush. Tom shouted. The call went echoing down the empty aisles and died out in the distance in a faint sound that resembled a ripple of mocking laughter.

"Oh, don't do it again, Tom, it is too horrid," said Becky.

"It is horrid, but I better, Becky; they *might* hear us, you know" and he shouted again.

The "might" was even a chillier horror than the ghostly laughter, it so confessed a perishing hope. The children stood still and listened; but there was no result. Tom turned upon the back track at once, and hurried his steps. It was but a little while before a certain indecision in his manner revealed another fearful fact to Becky—he could not find his way back!

"O, Tom, you didn't make any marks!"

"Becky I was such a fool! Such a fool! I never thought we might want to come back! No—I can't find the way. It's all mixed up."

"Tom, Tom, we're lost! we're lost! We never can get out of this awful place! O, why *did* we ever leave the others!"

She sank to the ground and burst into such a frenzy of crying

DESPAIR.

that Tom was appalled with the idea that she might die, or lose her reason. He sat down by her and put his arms around her; she buried her face in his bosom, she clung to him, she poured out her terrors, her unavailing regrets, and the far echoes turned them all to jeering laughter. Tom begged her to pluck up hope again, and she said she could not. He fell to blaming and abusing himself for getting her into this miserable situation; this had a better effect. She said she would try to hope again, she would get up and follow wherever he might lead if only he would not talk like that any more. For he was no more to blame than she, she said.

So they moved on, again—aimlessly—simply at random—all they could do was to move, keep moving. For a little while, hope made a show of reviving—not with any reason to back it, but only because it is its nature to revive when the spring has not been taken out of it by age and familiarity with failure.

By and by Tom took Becky's candle and blew it out. This economy meant so much! Words were not needed. Becky understood, and her hope died again. She knew that Tom had a whole candle and three or four pieces in his pockets—yet he must economise.

By and by, fatigue began to assert its claims; the children tried to pay no attention, for it was dreadful to think of sitting down when time was grown to be so precious; moving, in some direction, in any direction, was at least progress and might bear fruit; but to sit down was to invite death and shorten its pursuit.

At last Becky's frail limbs refused to carry her farther. She sat down. Tom rested with her, and they talked of home, and the friends there, and the comfortable beds and above all, the light! Becky cried, and Tom tried to think of some way of comforting her, but all his encouragements were grown thread-bare with use, and sounded like sarcasms. Fatigue bore so heavily upon Becky that she drowsed off to sleep. Tom was grateful. He sat looking into her drawn face and saw it grow smooth and natural under the influence of pleasant dreams; and by and by a smile dawned and rested there. The peaceful face reflected somewhat of peace and healing into his own spirit, and his thoughts wandered away to by-gone times and dreamy memories. While he was deep in his musings, Becky woke up with a breezy little laugh—but it was stricken dead upon her lips, and a groan followed it.

"Oh, how *could* I sleep! I wish I never, never had waked! No! No, I don't, Tom! Don't look so! I won't say it again."

"I'm glad you've slept, Becky; you'll feel rested, now, and we'll find the way out."

"We can try, Tom; but I've seen such a beautiful country in my dream. I reckon we are going there."

"Maybe not, maybe not. Cheer up, Becky, and let's go on trying."

They rose up and wandered along, hand in hand and hopeless. They tried to estimate how long they had been in the cave, but all they knew was that it seemed days and weeks, and yet it was plain that this could not be, for their candles were not gone yet. A long time after this—they could not tell how long—Tom said they must go softly and listen for dripping water—they must find a spring. They found one presently, and Tom said it was time to rest again. Both were cruelly tired, yet Becky said she thought she could go on a little farther. She was surprised to hear Tom dissent. She could not understand it. They sat down, and Tom fastened his candle to the wall in front of them with some clay. Thought was soon busy; nothing was said for some time. Then Becky broke the silence:

"Tom, I am so hungry!"

Tom took something out of his pocket.

"Do you remember this?" said he.

Becky almost smiled.

"It's our wedding cake, Tom."

"Yes I wish it was as big as a barrel, for it's all we've got."

"I saved it from the pic-nic for us to dream on, Tom, the way grown-up people do with wedding cake—but it'll be our—"

She dropped the sentence where it was. Tom divided the cake

THE WEDDING CAKE.

and Becky ate with good appetite, while Tom nibbled at his moiety. There was abundance of cold water to finish the feast with. By and by Becky suggested that they move on again. Tom was silent a moment. Then he said:

"Becky, can you bear it if I tell you something?"

Becky's face paled, but she thought she could.

"Well then, Becky, we must stay here, where there's water to drink. That little piece is our last candle!"

Becky gave loose to tears and wailings. Tom did what he could to comfort her but with little effect. At length Becky said:

"Tom!"

"Well, Becky?"

"They'll miss us and hunt for us!"

"Yes, they will! Certainly they will!"

"Maybe they're hunting for us now, Tom."

"Why I reckon maybe they are. I hope they are."

"When would they miss us, Tom?"

"When they get back to the boat, I reckon."

"Tom, it might be dark, then—would they notice we hadn't come?"

"I don't know. But anyway, your mother would miss you as soon as they got home."

A frightened look in Becky's face brought Tom to his senses and he saw that he had made a blunder. Becky was not to have gone home that night! The children became silent and thoughtful. In a moment a new burst of grief from Becky showed Tom that the thing in his mind had struck hers also that the Sabbath morning might be half spent before Mrs. Thatcher discovered that Becky was not at Mrs. Harper's.

The children fastened their eyes upon their bit of candle and watched it melt slowly and pitilessly away; saw the half inch of wick stand alone at last; saw the feeble flame rise and fall, climb the thin column of smoke, linger at its top a moment, and then—the horror of utter darkness reigned!

How long afterward it was that Becky came to a slow consciousness that she was crying in Tom's arms, neither could tell. All that they knew was, that after what seemed a mighty stretch of time, both awoke out of a dead stupor of sleep and resumed their miseries once more. Tom said it might be Sunday, now—maybe Monday. He tried to get Becky to talk, but her sorrows were too oppressive, all her hopes were gone. Tom said that they must have been missed long ago, and no doubt the search was going on. He would shout and maybe some one would come. He tried it; but in the darkness the distant echoes sounded so hideously that he tried it no more.

The hours wasted away, and hunger came to torment the captives again. A portion of Tom's half of the cake was left; they divided and ate it. But they seemed hungrier than before. The poor morsel of food only whetted desire.

By and by Tom said:

"*Sh*! Did you hear that?"

Both held their breath and listened. There was a sound like the faintest, far-off shout. Instantly Tom answered it, and leading Becky by the hand, started groping down the corridor in its direction. Presently he listened again; again the sound was heard, and apparently a little nearer.

"It's them!" said Tom; "they're coming! Come along Becky—we're all right now!"

The joy of the prisoners was almost overwhelming. Their speed was slow, however, because pitfalls were somewhat common, and had to be guarded against. They shortly came to one and had to stop. It might be three feet deep, it might be a hundred—there was no passing it at any rate. Tom got down on his breast and reached as far down as he could. No bottom. They must stay there and wait until the searchers came. They listened; evidently the distant shoutings were growing more distant! a moment or two more and they had gone altogether. The heart-sinking misery of it! Tom whooped until he was hoarse, but it was of no use. He talked hopefully to Becky; but an age of anxious waiting passed and no sounds came again.

The children groped their way back to the spring. The weary time dragged on; they slept again, and awoke famished and woe-stricken. Tom believed it must be Tuesday by this time.

Now an idea struck him. There were some side passages near at hand. It would be better to explore some of these than bear the weight of the heavy time in idleness. He took a kite-line from his pocket, tied it to a projection, and he and Becky started, Tom in the

A NEW TERROR.

lead, unwinding the line as he groped along. At the end of twenty steps the corridor ended in a "jumping-off place." Tom got down on his knees and felt below, and then as far around the corner as he could reach with his hands conveniently; he made an effort to stretch yet a little further to the right, and at that moment, not twenty yards away, a human hand, holding a candle, appeared from behind a rock! Tom lifted up a glorious shout, and instantly that hand was followed by the body it belonged to—Injun Joe's! Tom was paralyzed; he could not move. He was vastly gratified the next moment, to see the "Spaniard" take to his heels and get himself out of sight. Tom wondered that Joe had not recognized his voice and come over and killed him for testifying in court. But the echoes must have disguised the voice. Without doubt, that was it, he reasoned. Tom's fright weakened every muscle in his body. He said to himself that if he had strength enough to get back to the spring he would stay there, and nothing should tempt him to run the risk of meeting Injun Joe again. He was careful to keep from Becky what it was he had seen. He told her he had only shouted "for luck."

But hunger and wretchedness rise superior to fears in the long run. Another tedious wait at the spring and another long sleep brought changes. The children awoke tortured with a raging hunger. Tom believed that it must be Wednesday or Thursday or even Friday or Saturday, now, and that the search had been given over. He proposed to explore another passage. He felt willing to risk Injun Joe and all other terrors. But Becky was very weak. She had sunk into a dreary apathy and would not be roused. She said she would wait, now, where she was, and die—it would not be long. She told Tom to go with the kite-line and explore if he chose; but she implored him to come back every little while and speak to her; and she made him promise that when the awful time came, he would stay by her and hold her hand until all was over.

Tom kissed her, with a choking sensation in his throat, and made a show of being confident of finding the searchers or an escape from the cave; then he took the kite-line in his hand and went groping down one of the passages on his hands and knees, distressed with hunger and sick with bodings of coming doom.

CHAPTER XXXII.

DAYLIGHT.

TUESDAY afternoon came, and waned to the twilight. The village of St. Petersburg still mourned. The lost children had not been found. Public prayers had been offered up for them, and many and many a private prayer that had the petitioner's whole heart in it; but still no good news came from the cave. The majority of the searchers had given up the quest and gone back to their daily avocations, saying that it was plain the children could never be found. Mrs. Thatcher was very ill, and a great part of the time delirious. People said it was heart-breaking to hear her call her child, and raise her head and listen a whole minute at a time, then lay it wearily down again with a moan. Aunt Polly had drooped into a settled melancholy, and her gray hair had grown almost white. The village went to its rest on Tuesday night, sad and forlorn.

Away in the middle of the night a wild peal burst from the village bells, and in a moment the streets were swarming with frantic half-clad people, who shouted, "Turn out! turn out! they're found! they're found!" Tin pans and horns were added to the din, the population

massed itself and moved toward the river, met the children coming
in an open carriage drawn by shouting citizens, thronged around it,
joined its homeward march, and swept magnificently up the main
street roaring huzzah after huzzah!

THE "TURN OUT" TO RECEIVE TOM AND BECKY.

The village was illuminated; nobody went to bed again; it was the
greatest night the little town had ever seen. During the first half
hour a procession of villagers filed through Judge Thatcher's house,
siezed the saved ones and kissed them, squeezed Mrs. Thatcher's
hand, tried to speak but couldn't—and drifted out raining tears all
over the place.

Aunt Polly's happiness was complete, and Mrs. Thatcher's nearly so. It would be complete, however, as soon as the messenger dis-
patched with the great news to the cave should get the word to her
husband. Tom lay upon a sofa with an eager auditory about him and
told the history of the wonderful adventure, putting in many striking additions to adorn it withal; and closed with a description of how
he left Becky and went on an exploring expedition; how he followed
two avenues as far as his kite-line would reach; how he followed a
third to the fullest stretch of the kite-line, and was about to turn back
when he glimpsed a far-off speck that looked like daylight; dropped
the line and groped toward it, pushed his head and shoulders through
a small hole and saw the broad Mississippi rolling by! And if it had

only happened to be night he would not have seen that speck of day-light and would not have explored that passage any more! He told how he went back for Becky and broke the good news and she told him not to fret her with such stuff, for she was tired, and knew she

THE ESCAPE FROM THE CAVE.

was going to die, and wanted to. He described how he labored with her and convinced her; and how she almost died for joy when she had groped to where she actually saw the blue speck of daylight; how he pushed his way out at the hole and then helped her out; how they sat there and cried for gladness; how some men came along in a skiff and Tom hailed them and told them their situation and their famished condition; how the men didn't believe the wild tale at first, "because," said they, "you are five miles down the river below the valley the cave is in"—then took them aboard, rowed to a house, gave them supper, made them rest till two or three hours after dark and then brought them home.

Before day-dawn, Judge Thatcher and the handful of searchers with him were tracked out, in the cave, by the twine clews they had strung behind them, and informed of the great news.

Three days and nights of toil and hunger in the cave were not to be shaken off at once, as Tom and Becky soon discovered. They were bedridden all of Wednesday and Thursday, and seemed to grow more and more tired and worn, all the time. Tom got about, a little, on

Thursday, was down town Friday, and nearly as whole as ever Saturday; but Becky did not leave her room until Sunday, and then she looked as if she had passed through a wasting illness.

Tom learned of Huck's sickness and went to see him on Friday, but could not be admitted to the bedroom; neither could he on Saturday or Sunday. He was admitted daily after that, but was warned to keep still about his adventure and introduce no exciting topic. The widow Douglas staid by to see that he obeyed. At home Tom learned of the Cardiff Hill event; also that the "ragged man's" body had eventually been found in the river near the ferry landing; he had been drowned while trying to escape, perhaps.

About a fortnight after Tom's rescue from the cave, he started off to visit Huck, who had grown plenty strong enough, now, to hear exciting talk, and Tom had some that would interest him, he thought. Judge Thatcher's house was on Tom's way, and he stopped to see Becky. The Judge and some friends set Tom to talking, and some one asked him ironically if he wouldn't like to go to the cave again. Tom said he thought he wouldn't mind it. The Judge said:

"Well, there are others just like you, Tom, I've not the least doubt. But we have taken care of that. Nobody will get lost in that cave any more."

"Why?"

"Because I had its big door sheathed with boiler iron two weeks ago, and triple-locked—and I've got the keys".

Tom turned as white as a sheet.

"What's the matter, boy! Here, run, somebody! Fetch a glass of water!"

The water was brought and thrown into Tom's face.

"Ah, now you're all right. What was the matter with you, Tom?"

"Oh, Judge, Injun Joe's in the cave!"

CHAPTER XXXIII.

WITHIN a few minutes the news had spread, and a dozen skiff-loads of men were on their way to McDougal's cave, and the ferry-boat, well filled with passengers, soon followed. Tom Sawyer was in the skiff that bore Judge Thatcher.

When the cave door was unlocked, a sorrowful sight presented itself in the dim twilight of the place. Injun Joe lay stretched upon the ground, dead, with his face close to the crack of the door, as if his longing eyes had been fixed, to the latest moment, upon the light and the cheer of the free world outside. Tom was touched, for he knew by his own experience how this wretch had suffered. His pity was moved, but nevertheless he felt an abounding sense of relief and security, now, which revealed to him in a degree which he had not fully appreciated before how vast a weight of dread had been lying upon him since the day he lifted his voice against this bloody-minded outcast.

Injun Joe's bowie knife lay close by, its blade broken in two. The great foundation-beam of the door had been chipped and hacked through, with tedious labor; useless labor, too, it was, for the native rock formed a sill outside it, and upon that stubborn material

the knife had wrought no effect; the only damage done was to the
knife itself. But if there had been no stony obstruction there the labor would have been useless still, for if the beam had been wholly cut
away Injun Joe could not have squeezed his body under the door,

CAUGHT AT LAST.

and he knew it. So he had only hacked that place in order to be doing
something—in order to pass the weary time—in order to employ his
tortured faculties. Ordinarily one could find half a dozen bits of candle stuck around in the crevices of this vestibule, left there by tourists; but there were none now. The prisoner had searched them out
and eaten them. He had also contrived to catch a few bats, and these,
also, he had eaten, leaving only their claws. The poor unfortunate
had starved to death. In one place near at hand, a stalagmite had
been slowly growing up from the ground for ages, builded by the
water-drip from a stalactite overhead. The captive had broken off the
stalagmite, and upon the stump had placed a stone, wherein he had
scooped a shallow hollow to catch the precious drop that fell once in
every three minutes with the dreary regularity of a clock-tick—a
dessert spoonful once in four and twenty hours. That drop was falling
when the Pyramids were new; when Troy fell; when the foundations
of Rome were laid; when Christ was crucified; when the Conqueror
created the British empire; when Columbus sailed; when the massa-
cre at Lexington was "news." It is falling now; it will still be falling

when all these things shall have sunk down the afternoon of history, and the twilight of tradition, and been swallowed up in the thick night of oblivion. Has everything a purpose and a mission?

DROP AFTER DROP.

Did this drop fall patiently during five thousand years to be ready for this flitting human insect's need? and has it another important object to accomplish ten thousand years to come? No matter. It is many and many a year since the hapless half-breed scooped out the stone to catch the priceless drops, but to this day the tourist stares longest at that pathetic stone and that slow dropping water when he comes to see the wonders of McDougal's cave. Injun Joe's cup stands first in the list of the cavern's marvels; even "Aladdin's Palace" cannot rival it.

Injun Joe was buried near the mouth of the cave; and people flocked there in boats and wagons from the towns and from all the farms and hamlets for seven miles around; they brought their children, and all sorts of provisions, and confessed that they had had almost as satisfactory a time at the funeral as they could have had at the hanging.

This funeral stopped the further growth of one thing—the petition to the Governor for Injun Joe's pardon. The petition had been largely signed; many tearful and eloquent meetings had been held, and a committee of sappy women been appointed to go in deep mourning and wail around the governor, and implore him to be a merciful ass and trample his duty under foot. Injun Joe was believed to have killed five citizens of the village, but what of that? If he had been Satan himself there would have been plenty of weaklings ready to scribble their names to a pardon-petition, and drip a tear on it from their permanently impaired and leaky water-works.

The morning after the funeral Tom took Huck to a private place to have an important talk. Huck had learned all about Tom's adventure from the Welchman and the widow Douglas, by this time, but

Tom said he reckoned there was one thing they had not told him; that thing was what he wanted to talk about now. Huck's face saddened. He said:

HAVING A GOOD TIME.

"I know what it is. You got into No. 2 and never found anything but whisky. Nobody told me it was you; but I just knowed it must 'a' ben you, soon as I heard 'bout that whisky business; and I knowed you hadn't got the money becuz you'd 'a' got at me some way or other and told me even if you was mum to everybody else. Tom, something's always told me we'd never get holt of that swag."

"Why Huck, *I* never told on that tavern-keeper. *You* know his tavern was all right the Saturday I went to the pic-nic. Don't you remember you was to watch there that night?"

"Oh, yes! Why it seems 'bout a year ago. It was that very night that I follered Injun Joe to the widder's."

"*You* followed him?"

"Yes—but you keep mum. I reckon Injun Joe's left friends behind him, and I don't want 'em souring on me and doing me mean tricks. If it hadn't ben for me he'd be down in Texas now, all right."

Then Huck told his entire adventure in confidence to Tom, who had only heard of the Welchmen's part of it before.

"Well," said Huck, presently, coming back to the main question, "whoever nipped the whisky in No. 2, nipped the money too, I reckon—anyways it's a goner for us, Tom."

"Huck, that money wasn't ever in No. 2!"

"What!" Huck searched his comrade's face keenly. "Tom, have you got on the track of that money again?"

"Huck, it's in the cave!"

Huck's eyes blazed.

"Say it again, Tom!"

"The money's in the cave!"

"Tom,—honest injun, now—is it fun, or earnest?"

"Earnest, Huck—just as earnest as ever I was in my life. Will you go in there with me and help get it out?"

"I bet I will! I will if it's where we can blaze our way to it and not get lost."

"Huck, we can do that without the least little bit of trouble in the world."

"Good as wheat! What makes you think the money's—"

"Huck, you just wait till we get in there. If we don't find it I'll agree to give you my drum and everything I've got in the world. I will, by jings."

"All right—it's a whiz. When do you say?"

"Right now, if you say it. Are you strong enough?"

"Is it far in the cave? I ben on my pins a little, three or four days, now, but I can't walk more'n a mile, Tom—least I don't think I could."

"It's about five mile into there the way anybody but me would go, Huck, but there's a mighty short cut that they don't anybody but me know about. Huck, I'll take you right to it in a skiff. I'll float the skiff down there, and I'll pull it back again all by myself. You needn't ever turn your hand over."

"Less start right off, Tom."

"All right. We want some bread and meat, and our pipes, and a little bag or two, and two or three kite-strings, and some of these new fangled things they call lucifer matches. I tell you many's the time I wished I had some when I was in there before."

A trifle after noon the boys borrowed a small skiff from a citizen who was absent, and got under way at once. When they were several miles below "Cave Hollow," Tom said:

"Now you see this bluff here looks all alike all the way down from the cave hollow—no houses, no wood-yards, bushes all alike. But do

you see that white place up yonder where there's been a landslide?
Well that's one of my marks. We'll get ashore, now."

They landed.

"Now Huck, where we're a-standing you could touch that hole I
got out of with a fishing-pole. See if you can find it."

Huck searched all the place about, and found nothing. Tom
proudly marched into a thick clump
of sumach bushes and said—

A BUSINESS TRIP.

"Here you are! Look at it, Huck;
it's the snuggest hole in this country. You just keep mum about it.
All along I've been wanting to be a
robber, but I knew I'd got to have
a thing like this, and where to run
across it was the bother. We've got
it now, and we'll keep it quiet, only
we'll let Joe Harper and Ben Rogers in—because of course there's got
to be a Gang, or else there wouldn't
be any style about it. Tom Sawyer's
Gang—it sounds splendid, don't it,
Huck?"

"Well, it just does, Tom. And
who'll we rob?"

"Oh, most anybody. Waylay people—that's mostly the way."

"And kill them?"

"No—not always. Hive them in
the cave till they raise a ransom."

"What's a ransom?"

"Money. You make them raise
all they can, off'n their friends;
and after you've kept them a year,
if it ain't raised then you kill them.
That's the general way. Only you don't kill the women. You shut up
the women, but you don't kill them. They're always beautiful and

rich, and awfully scared. You take their watches and things, but you always take your hat off and talk polite. They ain't anybody as polite as robbers—you'll see that in any book. Well the women get to loving you, and after they've been in the cave a week or two weeks they stop crying and after that you couldn't get them to leave. If you drove them out they'd turn right around and come back. It's so in all the books."

"Why it's real bully, Tom. I b'lieve it's better'n to be a pirate."

"Yes, it's better in some ways, because it's close to home and circuses and all that."

By this time everything was ready and the boys entered the hole, Tom in the lead. They toiled their way to the farther end of the tunnel, then made their spliced kite-strings fast and moved on. A few steps brought them to the spring and Tom felt a shudder quiver all through him. He showed Huck the fragment of candle-wick perched on a lump of clay against the wall, and described how he and Becky had watched the flame struggle and expire.

The boys began to quiet down to whispers, now, for the stillness and gloom of the place oppressed their spirits. They went on, and presently entered and followed Tom's other corridor until they reached the "jumping-off place." The candles revealed the fact that it was not really a precipice, but only a steep clay hill twenty or thirty feet high. Tom whispered—

"Now I'll show you something, Huck."

He held his candle aloft and said—

"Look as far around the corner as you can. Do you see that? There—on the big rock over yonder—done with candle smoke."

"Tom, its a *cross!*"

"*Now* where's your Number Two? '*Under the cross,*' hey? Right yonder's where I saw Injun Joe poke up his candle, Huck!"

Huck stared at the mystic sign a while, and then said with a shaky voice—

"Tom, less git out of here!"

"What! and leave the treasure?"

"Yes—leave it. Injun Joe's ghost is round about there, certain."

"No it ain't, Huck, no it ain't. It would ha'nt the place where he died—away out at the mouth of the cave—five mile from here."

"No, Tom, it wouldn't. It would hang round the money. I know the ways of ghosts, and so do you."

Tom began to fear that Huck was right. Misgivings gathered in his mind. But presently an idea occurred to him—

"Looky here, Huck, what fools we're making of ourselves! Injun Joe's ghost ain't a going to come around where there's a cross!"

The point was well taken. It had its effect.

"Tom I didn't think of that. But that's so. It's luck for us, that cross is. I reckon we'll climb down there and have a hunt for that box."

Tom went first, cutting rude steps in the clay hill as he descended. Huck followed. Four avenues opened out of the small cavern which the great rock stood in. The boys examined three of them with no result. They found a small recess in the one nearest the base of the rock, with a pallet of blankets spread down in it; also an old suspender, some bacon rhind, and the well gnawed bones of two or three fowls. But there was no money box. The lads searched and researched this place, but in vain. Tom said:

"He said *under* the cross. Well, this comes nearest to being under the cross. It can't be under the rock itself, because that sets solid on the ground."

They searched everywhere once more, and then sat down discouraged. Huck could suggest nothing. By and by Tom said:

"Looky here, Huck, there's footprints and some candle grease on the clay about one side of this rock, but not on the other sides. Now what's that for? I bet you the money *is* under the rock. I'm going to dig in the clay."

"That ain't no bad notion, Tom!" said Huck with animation.

Tom's "real Barlow" was out at once, and he had not dug four inches before he struck wood.

"Hey, Huck!—you hear that?"

Huck began to dig and scratch now. Some boards were soon uncovered and removed. They had concealed a natural chasm which led under the rock. Tom got into this and held his candle as far under the rock as he could, but said he could not see to the end of the rift He proposed to explore. He stooped and passed under; the narrow way descended gradually. He followed its winding course, first to the right, then to the left, Huck at his heels. Tom turned a short curve, by and by, and exclaimed—

"My goodness, Huck, looky here!"

It was the treasure box, sure enough, occupying a snug little cavern, along with an empty powder keg, a couple of guns in leather cases, two or three pairs of old moccasins, a leather belt, and some other rubbish well soaked with the water-drip.

"Got it at last!" said Huck, plowing among the tarnished coins with his hand. "My, but we're rich, Tom!"

"Huck, I always reckoned we'd get it. It's just too good to believe, but we *have* got it, sure! Say—let's not fool around here. Let's snake it out. Lemme see if I can lift the box."

It weighed about fifty pounds. Tom could lift it, after an awkward fashion, but could not carry it conveniently.

"I thought so," he said; "*they* carried it like it was heavy, that day at the ha'nted house. I noticed that. I reckon I was right to think of fetching the little bags along."

The money was soon in the bags and the boys took it up to the cross-rock.

"Now less fetch the guns and things," said Huck.

"No, Huck—leave them there. They're just the tricks to have when we go to robbing. We'll keep them there all the time, and we'll hold our orgies there, too. It's an awful snug place for orgies."

"What's orgies?"

"*I* dono. But robbers always have orgies, and of course we've got to have them, too. Come along, Huck, we've been in here a long time. It's getting late, I reckon. I'm hungry, too. We'll eat and smoke when we get to the skiff."

They presently emerged into the clump of sumach bushes, looked warily out, found the coast clear, and were soon lunching and smoking in the skiff. As the sun dipped toward the horizon they pushed out and got under way. Tom skimmed up the shore through the long twilight, chatting cheerily with Huck, and landed shortly after dark.

"Now Huck," said Tom, "we'll hide the money in the loft of the widow's woodshed, and I'll come up in the morning and we'll count it and divide, and then we'll hunt up a place out in the woods for it where it will be safe. Just you lay quiet here and watch the stuff till I run and hook Benny Taylor's little wagon; I won't be gone a minute."

"GOT IT AT LAST!"

He disappeared, and presently returned with the wagon, put the two small sacks into it, threw some old rags on top of them, and started off, dragging his cargo behind him. When the boys reached the Welchman's house, they stopped to rest. Just as they were about to move on, the Welchman stepped out and said:

"Hallo, who's that?"

"Huck and Tom Sawyer."

"Good! Come along with me, boys, you are keeping everybody waiting. Here—hurry up, trot ahead—I'll haul the wagon for you. Why, it's not as light as it might be. Got bricks in it?—or old metal?"

"Old metal," said Tom.

"I judged so; the boys in this town will take more trouble and fool away more time, hunting up six bit's worth of old iron to sell to the foundry than they would to make twice the money at regular work. But that's human nature—hurry along, hurry along!"

The boys wanted to know what the hurry was about.

"Never mind; you'll see, when we get to the Widow Douglas's."

Huck said with some apprehension—for he was long used to being falsely accused—

"Mr. Jones, we haven't been doing nothing."

The Welchman laughed.

"Well, I don't know, Huck, my boy. I don't know about that. Ain't you and the widow good friends?"

"Yes. Well, she's ben good friends to me, any ways."

"All right, then. What do you want to be afraid for?"

This question was not entirely answered in Huck' s slow mind before he found himself pushed, along with Tom, into Mrs. Douglas's drawing-room. Mr. Jones left the wagon near the door and followed.

The place was grandly lighted, and everybody that was of any consequence in the village was there. The Thatchers were there, the Harpers, the Rogerses, Aunt Polly, Sid, Mary, the minister, the editor, and a great many more, and all dressed in their best. The widow received the boys as heartily as any one could well receive two such looking beings. They were covered with clay and candle grease. Aunt Polly blushed crimson with humiliation, and frowned and shook her head at Tom. Nobody suffered half as much as the two boys did, however. Mr. Jones said:

"Tom wasn't at home, yet, so I gave him up; but I stumbled on him and Huck right at my door, and so I just brought them along in a hurry."

"And you did just right," said the widow:—
"Come with me, boys."

She took them to a bed chamber and said:

"Now wash and dress yourselves. Here are two new suits of clothes—shirts, socks, everything complete. They're Huck's—no, no thanks, Huck—Mr. Jones bought one and I the other. But they'll fit both of you. Get into them. We'll wait—come down when you are slicked up enough".

Then she left.

Chapter XXXIV.

WIDOW DOUGLAS.

HUCK said: "Tom, we can slope, if we can find a rope. The window ain't high from the ground."

"Shucks, what do you want to slope for?"

"Well I ain't used to that kind of a crowd. I can't stand it. I ain't going down there, Tom."

"O, bother! It ain't anything. I don't mind it a bit. I'll take care of you."

Sid appeared.

"Tom," said he, "Auntie has been waiting for you all the afternoon. Mary got your Sunday clothes ready, and everybody's been fretting about you. Say—ain't this grease and clay, on your clothes?"

"Now Mr. Siddy, you jist 'tend to your own business. What's all this blow-out about, anyway?"

"It's one of the widow's parties that she's always having. This time its for the Welchman and his sons, on account of that scrape they helped her out of the other night. And say—I can tell you something, if you want to know."

"Well, what?"

"Why old Mr. Jones is going to try to spring something on the people here to-night, but I overheard him tell auntie to-day about it, as a secret, but I reckon it's not much of a secret *now*. Everybody knows—the widow, too, for all she tries to let on she don't. Mr. Jones was bound Huck should be here—couldn't get along with his grand secret without Huck, you know!"

"Secret about what, Sid?"

"About Huck tracking the robbers to the widow's. I reckon Mr. Jones was going to make a grand time over his surprise, but I bet you it will drop pretty flat."

Sid chuckled in a very contented and satisfied way.

"Sid, was it you that told?"

"O, never mind who it was. *Somebody* told—that's enough."

"Sid, there's only one person in this town mean enough to do that, and that's you. If you had been in Huck's place you'd 'a' sneaked down the hill and never told anybody on the robbers. You can't do any but mean things, and you can't bear to see anybody praised for doing good ones. There—no thanks, as the widow says"—and Tom cuffed Sid's ears and helped him to the door with several kicks. "Now go and tell auntie if you dare—and to-morrow you'll catch it!"

Some minutes later the widow's guests were at the supper table, and a dozen children were propped up at little side tables in the same room, after the fashion of that country and that day. At the proper time Mr. Jones made his little speech, in which he thanked the widow for the honor she was doing himself and his sons, but said that there was another person whose modesty—

And so forth and so on. He sprung his secret about Huck's share in the adventure in the finest dramatic manner he was master of, but the surprise it occasioned was largely counterfeit and not as clamorous and effusive as it might have been under happier circumstances. However, the widow made a pretty fair show of astonishment, and heaped so many compliments and so much gratitude upon Huck that he almost forgot the nearly intolerable discomfort of his new clothes in the entirely intolerable discomfort of being set up as a target for everybody's gaze and everybody's laudations.

The widow said she meant to give Huck a home under her roof and have him educated; and that when she could spare the money she would start him in business in a modest way. Tom's chance was come. He said:

"Huck don't need it. Huck's rich!"

Nothing but a heavy strain upon the good manners of the company kept back the due and proper complimentary laugh at this pleasant joke. But the silence was a little awkward. Tom broke it—

TOM BACKS HIS STATEMENT.

"Huck's got money. Maybe you don't believe it, but he's got lots of it. Oh, you needn't smile—I reckon I can show you. You just wait a minute."

Tom ran out of doors. The company looked at each other with a perplexed interest—and inquiringly at Huck, who was tongue-tied.

"Sid, what ails Tom?" said Aunt Polly. "He—well, there ain't ever any making of that boy out. I never—"

Tom entered, struggling with the weight of his sacks, and Aunt Polly did not finish her sentence. Tom poured the mass of yellow coin upon the table and said—

"There—what did I tell you? Half of it's Huck's and half of it's mine!"

The spectacle took the general breath away. All gazed, nobody spoke for a moment. Then there was a unanimous call for an explanation. Tom said he could furnish it, and he did. The tale was long, but brim full of interest. There was scarcely an interruption from anyone to break the charm of its flow. When he had finished, Mr. Jones said—

"I thought I had fixed up a little surprise for this occasion, but it don't amount to anything now. This one makes it sing mighty small, I'm willing to allow".

The money was counted. The sum amounted to a little over twelve thousand dollars. It was more than any one present had ever seen at one time before, though several persons were there who were worth considerably more than that in property.

CHAPTER XXXV.

HUCK TRANSFORMED.

THE reader may rest satisfied that Tom's and Huck's windfall made a mighty stir in the poor little village of St. Petersburg. So vast a sum, all in actual cash, seemed next to incredible. It was talked about, gloated over, glorified, until the reason of many of the citizens tottered under the strain of the unhealthy excitement. Every "haunted" house in St. Petersburg and the neighboring villages was dissected, plank by plank, and its foundations dug up and ransacked for hidden treasure—and not by boys, but men—pretty grave, unromantic men, too, some of them. Wherever Tom and Huck appeared they were courted, admired, stared at. The boys were not able to remember that their remarks had possessed weight before; but now their sayings were treasured and repeated; everything they did seemed somehow to be regarded as remarkable; they had evidently lost the power of doing and saying commonplace things; moreover, their past history was raked up and discovered to bear marks of conspicuous originality. The village paper published biographical sketches of the boys.

Seattle, Washington, which has provided the primary religious resources to prevent male violence. Many students have also helped me over the years. Through the support and encouragement of many others, I began to believe that I could defect from the male patriarchy and work in solidarity with women to end violence against women. I have worked in accountability to the network of activists and intellectuals working to prevent male violence and have submitted my writing on a regular basis to women who could challenge the accuracy and helpfulness of what I wrote.

My first article about male violence appeared in 1988, "Child Sexual Abuse: A Rich Context for Thinking about God, Community, and Ministry," *Journal of Pastoral Care* 42, no. 1 (Spring 1988): 58–61. My initial thinking was based on my work in a child sexual abuse treatment agency. Since that time, I have published twenty academic articles and five books in which male violence has been a central theme. Preventing male violence has become a dominant theme of my ministry and writing career.

Because male violence continues as a serious social and religious problem in U.S. society, I have in this volume collected my seminal articles from the last fourteen years to serve as a resource for religious and secular professionals who want to think more carefully about the role of religion in preventing male violence. I am convinced that male violence will continue to be a serious problem until there is a concerted social movement to change the attitudes and behaviors of individual men and women and to change the ethos of society. I am also convinced that preventing male violence requires organized efforts by the religious communities. Patriarchy is a religious worldview that must be challenged so that women and men can live together in equality and justice. Religious communities provide the key ingredient in making this change.

Chapter 1 is an overview of the issues of male violence: definitions, statistics, the psychological and social context, pastoral care principles, and theological issues. It is a comprehensive overview for someone who is just beginning to think about male violence as a social and religious problem.

Chapter 2 is one of the earlier articles I wrote and shows my original concern with child sexual abuse, an issue that continues to trouble me greatly. My experience of teaching verifies that one-third of all women have been victims of child sexual abuse, and women in my seminary classes often choose this as a topic of study and reflection. Many men are also victims, although they are less likely to focus on their own journey of healing. In this article I share my own awakening to this problem and give an orientation to the basic social, ethical, and pastoral care issues that need our attention.

Chapter 3 is another of the earlier articles that draws on the resources of theological ethics for tools to understand male violence. Even though this academic discipline has not focused on male violence as a problem, their forms of reflection and analysis have been useful for me in my own journey to understanding. Why is male violence wrong? Is it wrong because it is a violation of God's laws, a pattern that leads to destructive consequences, or a violation of community character and narrative? These three types of ethical thinking are all helpful as we try to unravel the complexities of male violence.

Chapter 4 is the result of ten years of collaboration with Dr. Toinette Eugene, a womanist scholar who encouraged me to reflect more carefully on issues of race and culture. The burgeoning literature by African American women identified male violence as a critical problem. White slaveholders and overseers regularly raped women in slavery, and men in slavery were humiliated as being less than men. Twenty-first-century white racism continues to project unresolved sexual and violent images onto the African American community. The result is that U.S. society reproduces destructive stereotypes of the African American community that lead to economic and social deprivation. Male violence against and within the African American community is a complex problem that requires careful analysis, especially for white scholars. In this chapter, Dr. Eugene and I struggle to understand and present important issues that can help prevent male violence within the black community.[1]

Chapter 5 is my initial attempt to understand male violence within the Latin American culture and society, specifically in Nicaragua. With the help of Brenda Ruiz, pastoral counselor, I

---

[1]For more information about male violence in the African American context, see James Newton Poling and Toinette Eugene, *Balm for Gilead: Pastoral Care for African American Families Experiencing Abuse* (Nashville: Abingdon Press, 1998); and Poling, *Deliver Us from Evil: Resisting Racial and Gender Oppression* (Minneapolis: Fortress Press, 1996).

have talked with dozens of women and men in Nicaragua during eight trips in eleven years. The openness of the people to share their stories has been quite moving. Extreme poverty, war, natural disasters, and governmental corruption create very difficult circumstances for families. On the one hand, I was shocked and saddened by the levels of everyday violence I heard about during my interviews. On the other hand, I was inspired by the resilient love of the people for one another and their hopes for the future. This chapter is a journal from one of my trips that gives insight into the cultural reality of male violence in one Latino context.[2]

Chapters 6 and 7 are attempts to understand male perpetrators based on thirteen years of counseling with child molesters, rapists, and batterers. Chapter 6 focuses on the stories of several brave men who entered into therapy and tried to cope with the tragic issues of their lives. I summarize the pastoral counseling issues as I see them, including the powerful countertransference that occurs in the counselor. Chapter 7 summarizes some of the debates of feminist scholars with the writings of Freud, especially in the famous case study he wrote about Dora. Freud was insightful about gender dynamics and thematized sexuality and sexual identity for the U.S. culture. But Freud was at the same time the example *par excellence* of the male patriarch who believed that women enjoyed being dominated and sexualized by men. This deep structure of patriarchy is basic to understanding why male violence is so persistent and difficult to prevent.

Chapters 8 through 12 deal with issues of worship and preaching in light of the problem of male violence. Chapter 8 listens respectfully to the voices of female survivors as they write, especially in poetic form, about their experiences of trauma and healing. I believe that these voices represent a new religious witness about the action of God at our time in history. Survivors of violence often understand God's love at a deeper level, and their witness can lead to a renewal in the church.

Chapter 9 moves from the story of Karen, a survivor, into a more systematic theological reflection on the issues she raises about the love and justice of God. What is the nature of reality

---

[2]For more information on Nicaragua and male violence, see James Newton Poling, *Render Unto God: Economic Vulnerability, Family Violence, and Pastoral Theology* (St. Louis: Chalice Press, 2002).

based on the witness from Karen, and how can we begin to revise our theological confessions in light of these new insights?

Chapter 10 tackles some of the theoretical issues of worship and preaching in local congregations in light of the problem of male violence. If the church has ignored male violence for most of its history, then the themes of worship and preaching have been deficient. Feminist scholars have discovered resources in the biblical and historical traditions that can transform the worship and proclamation of God's love. In this chapter, I try to bring some of these insights into the discussion about male violence.

Chapter 11 is an attempt to write a sermon on one of the most difficult issues in this area–forgiveness. Many Christians argue that love and forgiveness of enemies is the central mark of the Christian gospel and that the Christian faith cannot be adequately understood without this doctrine. However, the church often batters survivors of sexual and domestic violence by demanding that they forgive and reconcile with their perpetrators. For many survivors, this doctrine has meant continued trauma as faithful Christian women and girls returned to their homes to endure additional violence from unrepentant male fathers, husbands, and partners. For other survivors, the demand to forgive and reconcile has meant years of self-blame and ostracism from the church community and denial of resources for healing. There must be another way to understand forgiveness that does not jeopardize the most vulnerable members of the church community. This sermon is one attempt to deal with this issue.

Chapter 12 has been written by a United Methodist pastor and former student, Hahnshik Min. Through all our work together, this young man became convicted that he should change his attitudes and behaviors as a man and a pastor. This chapter is his initial attempt to struggle with the issue of worship for recovering perpetrators. What would Christian worship look like if a pastor wanted to provide resources for men who were sincerely trying to change their violent patterns? What balance of accountability and grace would such a service contain? His valiant struggle ends this volume on a note of hope that men can be transformed and work as worthy allies with women to end male violence.

I pray that this book will empower the church to be more faithful to the God of love and justice revealed in Jesus Christ and to act courageously to deal with the sin of male violence within the covenant community and in the world.

1

Male Violence against Women and Children[1]

Introduction

Robert, a European American working-class man, sought pastoral counseling after he was arrested for child sexual abuse of his fourteen-year-old daughter. He wanted to stay out of prison, keep his marriage and family intact, and maintain his active membership in the Mormon Church. He committed himself to providing whatever resources she needed for her healing. He considered his sexual abuse of his daughter to be a sin that he must face, and he hoped that God and the church would forgive him over time and restore him to full membership.

Todd, an African American professional man, joined a psychoeducational group for men who batter after he was arrested for hitting his girlfriend. He wanted to avoid further legal difficulties and maintain his intimate relationship if possible. He also wanted to control his abuse of alcohol and stop the intergenerational cycle of physical and sexual abuse because he was becoming "just like my father." He recently returned to the Baptist Church

---

[1]Original version published as "Male Violence against Women and Children," *The Care of Men,* ed. James Poling and Christie Neuger (Nashville: Abingdon Press, 1997).

his mother attends because they have a program for recovering addicts.

These are two of the hopeful stories I have heard over the last ten years in my work as a pastoral counselor with men who have been convicted of violent offenses. Robert and Todd feel ashamed and guilty for their violence, and they are willing to do what is necessary to give themselves a future instead of committing more violence and facing the threat of imprisonment. However, they face many internal and external obstacles as they try to understand their history of physical, sexual, and emotional violence toward women and children. Their cultural, racial, and class locations influence how they perceive themselves as men and how they define the choices they have before them.

Robert and Todd are typical of some violent men who feel remorse and seek to avoid the consequences of their behaviors. They don't want to lose their marriages, their families, their jobs, or their freedom. Although most violent men are encouraged by the lack of response of churches and the courts to continue their violence, a few violent men are learning from the legal system and from other family members that their violence is not acceptable behavior. Although most men seek to avoid responsibility for their violence, a few are turning to pastors, pastoral counselors, and other professionals for help. It is imperative that the church become competent to provide assessment, referral, and care for men who genuinely want to overcome their violence and dominance over women and children.

How can violent men, many of whom are Christians, engage in violence against women and children and not seek help from pastors and other caregivers? They can do it because the churches have not identified male violence as a pressing ethical and religious issue. Why do many churches refuse to see male violence as a major threat to health of women, children, and families, and instead call for a return to "family values" (the male-dominated, heterosexual nuclear family) as a solution to society's ills? They do it because of the church's patriarchal theology, which gives priority to the rights of men over women and children.

This chapter primarily identifies male violence as an ethical and theological concern for the church and suggests ways that pastoral care can respond to the needs of men who are violent. A secondary goal is to help the church become aware of the cultural, class, and racial contexts in which male violence against women and children occurs.[2]

Review of the Literature on Male Violence against Women and Children

Male violence against women and children has many names: "wife abuse, marital assault, woman battery, spouse abuse, wife beating, conjugal violence, intimate violence, battering, partner abuse,"[3] child sexual abuse, child abuse, physical abuse, rape, emotional abuse. In this chapter I will rely on the following definitions of male violence that focus on behaviors of perpetrators and consequences for victims/survivors. These definitions emphasize the presence of male power and control in intimate relationships as well as the discrete acts of behavior.

Definitions of Male Violence

Male violence toward women encompasses physical, visual, verbal, or sexual acts that are experienced by a woman or girl as a threat, invasion, or assault and that have the effect of hurting her or degrading her and/or taking away her ability to control contact (intimate and otherwise) with another individual.[4]

Domestic violence is a pattern of assaultive and coercive behaviors, including physical, sexual, and psychological attacks, as well as economic coercion, that adults or adolescents use against their intimate partners. Such behaviors include physical assault, sexual assaults, psychological assaults, threats of violence and harm, attacks against property or pets and other acts of

---

[2]For a more complete discussion of many of the issues in this chapter, see James Poling, *The Abuse of Power: A Theological Problem* (Nashville: Abingdon Press, 1991); and Poling, *Deliver Us From Evil: Resisting Racial and Gender Oppression* (Minneapolis: Fortress Press, 1996).

[3]Carole Warshaw and Anne L. Ganley, *Improving the Health Care Response to Domestic Violence: A Resource Manual for Health Care Providers* (San Francisco: Family Violence Prevention Fund, 1995), 16.

[4]Mary P. Koss, Lisa A. Goodman, Angela Browne, Louise F. Fitzgerald, Gwendolyn Puryear Keita, and Nancy Filipe Russo, *Male Violence against Women at Home, at Work, and in the Community* (Washington, D.C.: American Psychological Association, 1994), xvi.

intimidation, emotional abuse, isolation, use of children, and use of economics.[5]

How Much Interpersonal Violence Is Male Violence?

In a book on men and their issues, the focus on the moral and theological aspects of male violence is understandable. But the preponderance of research shows that it is male violence against women and children that makes up the vast majority of interpersonal violence. The most conservative figure I have seen comes from police reports, which indicate that seventy percent of domestic violence calls come from women.[6] However, these figures are unreliable because men are learning to call the police to bring charges against their female partners in order to gain the advantage in court. Other studies suggest that 35 to 50 percent of women have experienced acts of violence from their male partners in their lifetime and that 95 percent of domestic violence calls to police are from women.

Based on the last seventeen years of empirical inquiry, experts now estimate that as many as 4 million women experience severe or life-threatening assault from a male partner in an average twelve-month period in the United States, and that one in every three women will experience at least one physical assault by an intimate partner during adulthood.[7] Some researchers suggest that as many as 50 percent of women will experience a violent assault from an intimate partner in their lifetime. These statistics mean that women are in great danger of violence from men and that the violence toward women is far more prevalent and severe than that against men. Men commit the bulk of the serious cases of physical violence toward women and children, and they are largely responsible for sexual aggression.[8]

What About Female Violence?

Some researchers believe that the violence of men and women is equal, and they argue for the existence of "sexual symmetry in

[5]Warshaw and Ganley, 16–24. See also John Archer, ed., *Male Violence* (London: Routledge, 1994), 2, 7; and R. Emerson Dobash and Russell P. Dobash, *Women, Violence and Social Change* (London: Routledge, 1992).

[6]Charlotte Krause Prozan, *Feminist Psychoanalytic Psychotherapy* (Northvale, N.J.: Jason Aronson, 1992), 213.

[7]Koss et al., 44.

[8]Archer, 6.

marital violence." Support for this position has been derived from studies that show "that equal numbers of men and women commit acts of physical aggression to their partners" and that "spousal homicides statistics...show equivalent numbers of male and female victims."[9]

Counter to this argument about sexual symmetry are crime statistics that show a ratio of 3:1 or more between male and female violent crimes.[10] Most research shows that men are more physically aggressive than women on minor scales, such as having hostile feelings or engaging in verbal abuse. Furthermore, when the consequences of violence are taken into account, "most acts of aggression which result in injury or death (and fear of these) are carried out by males, and in particular young males."[11]

At least two basic differences between female and male violence must be understood by us in the church:

• Women are more frequently injured or killed by male partners than men. "Over half (52 percent) of murdered women are killed by their male partners, compared to only 12 percent of murdered men who are killed by their female partners."[12] Also, "20–35% of women who present to hospital emergency rooms or community-based practices are there because of symptoms related to assaults by a husband or other intimate partner."[13] Injury from battering is the leading cause of emergency room visits for younger women.

• When women use violence, it is almost always a form of self-defense against male violence. Women use physical violence to protect themselves from battering, whereas most men use violence for power and control of their partner.[14]

There are also serious problems of interpersonal violence within gay and lesbian relationships, which need to be acknowledged and addressed with forms of analysis and intervention appropriate to the dynamics. Male violence against

---

[9]Ibid., 4.
[10]Ibid., 3.
[11]Ibid., 4.
[12]Lloyd Ohlin and Michael Tonry, *Family Violence: Crime and Justice: A Review of Research* (Chicago: University of Chicago Press, 1989), 204.
[13]Koss et al., 70.
[14]Warshaw and Ganley, 25.

women in heterosexual relationships is a paradigm for intimate violence in gay and lesbian relationships: One partner is intimidating and controlling the other through the use of or threat of physical violence.[15] More research needs to be done on gay and lesbian relationships to discern the particular patterns that need to be challenged.

Issues of Race and Class

Male violence against women and children occurs in every social class and all cultural groups in the United States, including European American, African American, Latino, Asian American, and Native American. Inadequate research methods, such as "the use of clinical samples, data from official police and agency reports, and the failure to control for social class,"[16] make it nearly impossible to evaluate racial and class differences on domestic violence. We do know that, in most cultures in the world, severe male violence against women and children is more common and more often tolerated and rationalized than female violence against men. We also know that male perpetrators use all kinds of rationalizations for their destructive behaviors, including cultural differences, to justify their violence, and that economic vulnerability contributes to the difficulty of protecting oneself against violence. However, neither cultural rationalizations nor the prejudices of the dominant culture should be used to justify the use of violence to coerce and terrorize those who are vulnerable. Methods of intervention to prevent male violence must be culturally sensitive to the needs of the victims. For example, the police and courts must be trained to be fair to ethnic and class differences so that interventions are effective.[17]

Prevalence of Male Violence

If we define male violence as physical or sexual behaviors that cause, or could cause, physical and psychological injury or death

---

[15]Ibid., 26.

[16]Koss et al., 51.

[17]Warshaw and Ganley, 26–27. See also Robert L. Hampton, ed., *Violence in the Black Family: Correlates and Consequences* (Lexington, Mass.: Lexington Books, 1987), 21–22; Evelyn C. White, ed., *The Black Women's Health Book: Speaking for Ourselves* (Seattle: Seal Press, 1994); Pearl Cleague, *Mad at Miles: A Blackwoman's Guide to Truth* (Southfield, Mich.: Cleague Group, 1989); Evelyn C. White, *Chain, Chain, Change: For Black Women Dealing with Physical and Emotional Abuse* (Seattle: Seal Press, 1985).

to someone else, how big a problem are we discussing? How many victims of male violence are there, and how many violent men are there? The common public assumption is that such violence is rare, especially within one's own social group. Whereas the public is afraid of being mugged, robbed, burglarized, or killed by strangers from other groups, it is commonly assumed that people are unlikely to face violence within their own social group. Actually, the prevalence of violence is highest within social groups and within the family.

I have never seen a study that tries to estimate the number of men who have committed violent acts. The social denial of the problem, and the refusal to face the vulnerability of women and children to male violence, means that reliable statistics cannot be collected. Scientists have made some progress recently in studying the number of victims of male violence, especially the number of women and children who have experienced some form of male violence in their lifetime. The results of this research show that society is facing a monumental problem that has been denied.

Prevalence of Rape

Using conservative definitions of rape and using conservative methods of collecting and interpreting data, Mary P. Koss reviews twenty empirical studies and estimates that at least 14 percent of all women have experienced a completed rape as adults. Results of the studies range from 8 percent to more than 20 percent.[18] This is an astounding percent of the female population. Adding attempted rapes doubles the number of victims in most studies.

Prevalence of Child Abuse

Estimates of physical abuse of children range from 200,000 to 4 million cases per year. The National Committee for the Prevention of Child Abuse estimates that more than 1 million children are seriously abused per year, including 2,000 to 5,000 murders of children.[19] Women are significantly involved in the physical abuse of young children where they are the primary

---

[18]Mary P. Koss, "Detecting the Scope of Rape: A Review of Prevalence Research Methods," *Journal of Interpersonal Violence* 8, no. 2 (June 1993): 198–222.

[19]Dante Cicchetti and Vicki Carlson, eds., *Child Maltreatment: Theory and Research on the Causes and Consequences of Child Abuse and Neglect* (Cambridge: Cambridge University Press, 1989), 48.

caregivers. However, men often abuse young children and are responsible for the majority of abuse of older children and adolescents. Estimates of child sexual abuse range from 12 percent to 28 percent of girls and 3 percent to 9 percent of boys. This means 210,000 cases per year, of which only 44,700 per year come to the attention of some professional person such as a teacher, pastor, physician, or social worker.[20] Most experts believe that a majority of physical and sexual abuse of children is never reported to authorities.

Prevalence of Battering

"We found that someone getting married runs greater than a one in four chance of being involved in marital violence at some time in the relationship."[21] In addition, live-in and dating relationships are also dangerous places because the rates of violence are almost as high.[22]

The credible research on male violence indicates that at least 25 percent of women and children will be victims of physical or sexual violence by men, with substantial physical and psychological injuries in their lifetime, either as children facing physical, sexual, or emotional abuse or as adults facing assault, battering, rape, or psychological control. These statistics do not diminish with social class, race, religion, or faithful church attendance, although they do correlate with gender (women are more frequently victims than men). This means that 25 percent or more of the members of the typical congregation have experienced male violence, either as survivors of child abuse or as adult survivors of rape, battering, and psychological abuse. If this is true, then the silence of the church about interpersonal violence and its consequences is one of the most disturbing realities that must be faced. The additional problems of sexual harassment and exploitation at work and in professional relationships extend the forms of male abuse of women even further.

---

[20]Ibid., 98–99.
[21]Richard J. Gelles and Murray A. Straus, *Intimate Violence* (New York: Simon and Schuster, 1988), 104.
[22]Prozan, 213.

Causes of Male Violence

Competing Social Science Theories

There are several competing, but not necessarily incompatible, theories among scientists who accept the reality of male violence: genetic and hormonal theories, evolutionary theories, socialization theories, and womanist and feminist theories of power and control.[23] Those who prefer genetic and biochemical explanations study the influence of chromosomes and testosterone on human aggression and predict that a certain percentage of men will act out their imbalances in violent behaviors. Those who prefer historical explanations go back to prehistoric experiences of hunting and gathering societies and the survival of the fittest, which produced species of human beings that are not adaptable to the technological information age of postindustrial democracies. Others favor sociological explanations about the construction of masculinity within the culture of violence in news, film, television, pornography, sports, guns, cars, military training, and preparation for war.

I prefer womanist and feminist theories of male violence, which emphasize themes of power, control, and dominance of men over women, children, and nature, and the competition of men for dominance over one another, which leads to racism, war, and economic oppression. This theory is not in competition with the other theories, which are true in their own ways. However, theories of power and control provide the active motive for individual men to continue their violence. In their book *Intimate Violence*, when Gelles and Straus ask why men use violence against women and children, they answer: "Because they can."[24] What they mean is this: Men are violent because they can get by with it, because there are usually no serious consequences for being violent, because they are encouraged to be violent, and because it works as a method of power and control. Violence works if a man wants to control others, and it will continue to work until society decides that the use of violence by men to maintain dominance over women and children is unacceptable and must be changed.

---

[23]Archer, 233–389. See also A. Bandura, *Aggression: A Social Learning Analysis* (Englewood Cliffs, N.J.: Prentice-Hall, 1973).

[24]Gelles and Straus, 17.

Religious Interpretations of Male Violence

Our society, including the church, has not decided that male violence is a moral problem serious enough to be challenged and changed. There are at least three conflicting religious interpretations of male violence in our society: (1) Male violence is a sign of the breakdown of God's natural hierarchy of the headship of men over women and children; (2) male violence is a problem of the sinfulness of human nature; (3) male violence is the use of force to enforce male dominance over women and children and to maintain other forms of oppression such as racism, classism, and heterosexism.

Some groups believe that male headship is a part of God's natural order and that God's hierarchy moves from men to women to children. This traditional conservative position promotes male dominance and hopes to limit the need for violence by educating women and men to adopt certain family values. Violence occurs, in this view, when the natural hierarchy of men over women and children is threatened and needs to be reestablished. Male violence is unfortunate because some men are too immature to know how to assume their rightful place at the head of the family without resorting to violence, and because many women have been led by womanism and feminism into rebellion against the leadership of men, which makes violence inevitable as men rightfully enforce their dominance.[25]

Some groups believe in abstract human rights, including the right to be free from violence, but despair of changing human nature. This traditional liberal position is that violence against women and children is an unfortunate consequence of the fact that people who get attached to one another act out their individual pathologies and inflict all kinds of damage on one another. We need to maintain our educational programs and provide support and resources for people so they can grow out of their need to be violent toward one another, but this process will be agonizingly slow. In the meantime we should not be punitive toward the poor souls who mistreat one another, but we must be compassionate

---

[25]For further discussion of evangelical Christianity on issues of gender, see Andy Smith, "Born Again, Free from Sin? Sexual Violence in Evangelical Communities," in *Violence against Women and Children: A Christian Theological Sourcebook,* ed. Carol J. Adams and Marie M. Fortune (New York: Continuum, 1995), 339–50. See also Susan D. Rose, *Keeping Them Out of the Hands of Satan: Evangelical Schooling in America* (New York: Routledge, 1988).

and help them to see that there are better ways to be partners, parents, and lovers. This view is especially susceptible to the assumption that women and men are equally violent. It is too bad that men are so much stronger and inflict the most injuries on others. But it considers the real problem to be individual sin and immaturity, which can only be solved through the slow process of education.[26]

By contrast, the womanist and feminist view of male violence is that gender inequality is socially constructed as a hierarchy, that most men base their personal identities on being members of the dominant class, and that the purpose of male violence is to enforce male dominance over women and children like other forms of oppression such as racism, classism, and heterosexism. As women have become conscious of themselves as an oppressed class, although experiencing different kinds of oppression from one another depending on race, economic status, sexual orientation, religion, and nationality, they have challenged both the liberal and conservative views. They reject the conservative view that gender inequality is God-ordained and that restoration of male dominance will decrease male violence. They also reject the liberal view that violence is caused by individual sinfulness. Violence is not evenly distributed within society as it would be if its basis were a fallen human nature. Rather, women and children, especially girl-children, experience violence out of proportion to their numbers.

Womanists and feminists have developed complex theories of gender power relations that unmask the purpose of male violence: to maintain male dominance. Therefore, male violence will not be stopped until gender equality is written into the laws and social practices of our society and until there are adequate consequences for violence against women and children as there must be against other violent crimes. This requires a massive social change along all fronts, from religion to law, education, and economics.[27]

---

[26]For a good summary of this debate within the liberal churches, see Tracy Trothen, "Prophetic or Followers? The United Church of Canada, Gender, Sexuality, and Violence against Women," in Adams and Fortune, 287–313.

[27]For a fuller discussion of the feminist alternative to conservative and liberal theologies, see Carol Adams, "Toward a Feminist Theology of Religion and the State," in Adams and Fortune, 15–35. See also Catherine MacKinnon, *Feminism Unmodified: Discourses on Life and Law* (Cambridge: Harvard University Press, 1987); and MacKinnon, *Toward a Feminist Theory of State* (Cambridge: Harvard University Press, 1989).

Guidelines for Assessment, Referral, and Pastoral Care of Men Who Are Violent[28]

The consequences of conservative/evangelical and progressive/liberal views of male violence have been tragic for many women and children. The litany of inappropriate pastoral responses is legion: *What kind of wife are you to make him so mad? You should have more faith and God will restore your marriage. What are you doing to create this kind of conflict? I think you need some marriage counseling to work out your problems.*

In these and similar ways, many churches advocate the unity of the family, the sanctity of the marriage, and the privacy of what happens in a Christian home. As a result, many survivors who talked to their pastors say that they have stayed in violent marriages and other relationships for decades, blaming themselves and taking responsibility for the behaviors of the men. Some pastors have tried couple counseling to mediate the conflict between them so the violence would stop, without analyzing the vulnerability and jeopardy of the women and children in the family. In most cases, Christian congregations have taken the side of the violent man because he is the head of the family, or because they don't want to get involved in a "domestic dispute." One female pastor discovered that the congregation in which she was newly installed had witnessed three murders among their members and extended families without understanding the dynamics of male violence.

Male violence has not been a designated area of research and training in the field of pastoral care and counseling, so we are unprepared to deal with the issues of male violence. Given the current state of ignorance about issues of male violence and gender injustice, pastors and pastoral counselors should not attempt to do care and counseling with men who are violent without specialized training and changed attitudes. In this section, I will suggest some guidelines for pastoral response to women who are victims and to men who are violent, and I will present some

---

[28]For further discussion of these issues, see Marie Fortune and James Poling, "Calling to Accountability: The Church's Response to Abusers," in Adams and Fortune, 451–63.

issues that require a revision of traditional pastoral care and counseling methods.[29]

The Priority of Safety and Pastoral Care for Victims of Abuse

I believe it is unethical to engage in pastoral care or counseling with a man who is violent without due consideration of the safety and pastoral care needs of his victims. Whenever a pastor or pastoral counselor identifies male violence as a potential problem in a relationship or family, past or present, she or he should begin an assessment of the safety of women and children around that man. For example, if the man has a history of abusing children, one must assume that any children he has access to are in potential danger, especially if no one else knows his history. If a man has a history of battering in previous relationships, one must assume that the current intimate partner is in jeopardy. As I will discuss later, I believe that the normal constraints of confidentiality do not apply when issues of violence are concerned. Men who have a history of engaging in violence should not be trusted to assess their own danger to others because they have a history of minimizing and rationalizing their behaviors and the consequences to others.

Ensuring the safety of potential victims requires contact with other professionals who have direct contact with the victims. In the case of child abuse, this may be the county Department of Social Services or private agencies who specialize in child abuse. In the case of battering, this may be the local shelter, rape crisis services, or other agencies that provide support and services for battered women. Anyone who works regularly with men who are violent must have ongoing consultative relationships with community agencies that work with victims.[30]

Use Wider Community Structures of Accountability

One of the most dangerous things a pastor or pastoral counselor can do is to work in isolation with a man who has

---

[29]For further perspective on the assessment, referral, and care of men who are violent, I suggest the following: Carol J. Adams, *Woman-Battering* (Minneapolis: Fortress Press, 1994); Carolyn Holderread Heggen, *Sexual Abuse in Christian Homes and Churches* (Scottdale, Pa.: Herald Press, 1993); Judith Lewis Herman, *Trauma and Recovery* (New York: Basic Books, 1992); Carrie Doehring, *Taking Care: Monitoring Power Dynamics and Relational Boundaries in Pastoral Care and Counseling* (Nashville: Abingdon Press, 1995).

[30]See the strong emphasis on issues of safety in Adams, *Woman-Battering,* 69–86, and Herman, 155–74.

violent symptoms. This perpetuates the very structure of secrecy and deception that fosters violence. Acts of physical or sexual violence against a woman or child, within or outside the family, are crimes and violations of law. Most likely, a pastor or pastoral counselor will find out about domestic violence through the woman or child who is harmed or through their advocate. In a case of incest, I heard about the abuse from the aunt of the adolescent victim and was able to initiate an intervention in the family with supervision by the director of clinical services at the local mental health center.

In situations of child abuse, professional leaders such as teachers, social workers, and mental health workers have a legal mandate to report the suspicion to the authorities, either the local police or a city, county, or state hotline. Some states require religious leaders to report child abuse, whereas other states exempt clergy from this requirement. However, I believe pastors and pastoral counselors have an ethical mandate to report because it is the only way to protect endangered children.[31] Learning how to follow up on such reports during the family crisis usually requires special training and supervision.

Through several decades of this dangerous work, the leaders of the domestic violence network have learned how to assess a variety of situations. Knowing how to support women when they are in danger is very difficult, and pastors should always have supervision from community experts in each situation.

It is important to reiterate that most pastors and pastoral counselors are ill-equipped to deal with situations of domestic violence. We need to see ourselves as *part* of the response team of the larger community: directors of women's shelters, hotline organizers, police and courts, and advocates for women and children. Unless we work as members of the team, it is likely that our interventions will endanger those who are vulnerable.

Combat Secrecy and Deception of Abusers

One of the skills pastoral counselors need is compassionate confrontation, that is, the ability to form a therapeutic alliance with the healthy aspects of the man's personality by requiring

---

[31]Marie Fortune, *Violence in the Family: A Workshop Curriculum for Clergy and Other Helpers* (Cleveland: Pilgrim Press, 1991), 227. See also Carol Adams' chapter "Accountability" in *Woman-Battering*, 87–102.

accountability, but without being abusive or punitive in the process. This is necessary because of the internal structure of violence itself. The purpose of violent behavior is coercion of another's behavior to one's own will without consequences for one's own violent behavior. Violent men hide the true character of their violent interpersonal behavior and deceive those in authority about what is actually going on. In earlier patriarchal societies where men had the explicit right to beat their wives according to the "rule of thumb,"[32] such deception was not required. In the United States we must work for a time when physical and sexual violence against women and children is no longer tolerated, either by law or by accepted practice.

Men's defensive rationalizations of violence are legion: *I hardly touched her. She bruises easily. I was trying to grab her and she fell. I was acting in self-defense. My daughter came into my bedroom when my wife was gone. She was only my stepdaughter.*

Pastoral counseling techniques that depend on ambivalence and guilt for destructive behaviors are totally inadequate for working with male abusers who have spent a lifetime rationalizing and justifying their violent behaviors and avoiding the consequences. For them it is a way of thinking and feeling that is ego-syntonic and not easily changed. This is why a pastoral counselor must have a larger context besides the intrapsychic world of the man in which to work. Unfortunately, most of our intrapsychic and family theories are also rife with male dominance and collude with male aggressive disorders. Thus, contact with outside agencies and professionals with womanist and feminist orientations are absolutely crucial in order to counteract the secrecy and deception of abusers and create the means for accountability.[33]

Work Cooperatively with Other Professionals

I hope that pastoral counselors will eventually have adequate theories, attitudes, and skills to work with men with violent symptoms. Until then, we must work in consultation and with

---

[32]"Many people do not know the origin of the expression 'the rule of thumb,' which dates to medieval times when English law declared that a man could not beat his wife with a stick wider than his thumb," Prozan, 211.

[33]For a detailed curriculum on issues of denial and deception, see the materials of the Domestic Abuse Intervention Project, Minnesota Program Development, 206 West Fourth Street, Duluth, MN, 55806.

accountability to community professionals who do have these skills. Through individual and group supervision, didactic sessions, and participation in regular networks of professionals who work with victims and abusers, pastoral counselors can make the changes necessary to do good work with this population.

Revision of Traditional Pastoral Care and Counseling Methods

Confidentiality. The purpose of the traditional emphasis on confidentiality within the churches is to provide safety for confession of sin to be addressed by the rituals of the church. Within the mental health field, confidentiality allows shame-based transference issues to emerge for therapeutic intervention. Without such confidentiality, little in-depth pastoral care or psychotherapy can be accomplished. This principle is true in work with male abusers, except that issues of safety for his victims must be paramount. In working with a man who is violent or abusive, it is crucial not to collude with the destructive and self-destructive impulses of the personality at the expense of those who are vulnerable. For violent men, manipulating such collusion is often their greatest interpersonal skill.

The limits of confidentiality must be clearly negotiated at the beginning of a pastoral counseling relationship. Whenever the pastoral counseling contract identifies violence against others as a focus, the pastoral counselor must cooperate with others to provide accountability for acts of violence. As a pastoral counselor, I agree to keep confidential any matters that do not involve the safety of others, to keep the man informed of any contact I have outside of therapy, and to openly discuss any concerns the man has about my commitment to his health and safety. Two situations periodically occur. Sometimes I hear from another professional that the man has been abusive or threatening to his partner or children, and I use the information to confront him. Sometimes the man himself gives me information during therapy that he is being abusive or threatening, and I warn the persons involved. In both these cases, information is being exchanged with persons outside the therapeutic relationship, which contradicts some expectations of confidentiality, that is, that confidentiality equals secret-keeping.

I believe these are legitimate limits on confidentiality when working with violent men. As a pastoral counselor, I have a moral commitment to protect the safety of those who are vulnerable. I also have a moral commitment to enjoin the healthy psychological development of the person and to refuse to collude with his violent impulses and behaviors. This means helping him face the consequences of his behaviors and maintaining, if possible, a therapeutic alliance at the same time. The ability to sustain a positive therapeutic relationship during episodes of violence in the man's life may itself be the healing moment.

There are some sacramental definitions of confidentiality that interfere with a pastor's ability to accept these suggested limits of confidentiality. There are two responses to this problem. One is to clearly distinguish general pastoral counseling from the sacrament of confession and absolution of sins. It may be possible to maintain the Roman and Lutheran sacrament of confession in limited use but not extend it to all pastoral conversations. In this case, pastoral care and counseling would not be covered by the secrecy of sacramental confession. Another response is to rethink the theology of the sacrament of confession itself. Does the safety of other people set any limits on the confidentiality of the confessional? I believe it does.[34]

Therapeutic neutrality. Among pastoral counselors using psychoanalytic and systems theories, neutrality is considered a high value. Certainly it is important for a pastoral counselor to seek to provide positive regard, empathy, and authenticity in every pastoral encounter, and to respect the process by which an individual seeks healing. It is also important that the pastoral counselor not be abusive or manipulative in seeking values and goals that are foreign to the person. But these legitimate forms of neutrality must not be confused with the lack of a moral context for pastoral care and counseling. Much research has been done on the moral horizon within which pastoral care and counseling is practiced.[35] But issues of violence challenge the definitions of what we usually mean by neutrality or fairness, because the consequences for vulnerable persons requires constant monitoring.

---

[34]Fortune and Poling, "Calling to Accountability," 460. Fortune, *Violence in the Family,* 230–31.

[35]Don Browning, *The Ethical Context of Pastoral Care* (Philadelphia: Westminster Press, 1976); James N. Poling, "Ethics in Pastoral Care and Counseling," in *Handbook of Basic Types of Pastoral Care and Counseling,* ed. Howard Stone and William Clements (Nashville: Abingdon Press, 1991), 56–69.

In entering the treatment relationship, the therapist promises to respect the patient's autonomy by remaining disinterested and neutral. "Disinterested" means that the therapist abstains from using her power over the patient to gratify her personal needs. "Neutral" means that the therapist does not take sides in the patient's inner conflicts or try to direct the patient's life decisions...The technical neutrality of the therapist is not the same as moral neutrality. Working with victimized people requires a committed moral stance. The therapist is called upon to bear witness to a crime. She must affirm a position of solidarity with the victim.[36]

In pastoral counseling of violent men, a pastoral counselor who takes a moral stance against violence in interpersonal, intimate relationships may be faced regularly with a person's attitudes and behaviors that are abusive and violent. The traditional "bracketing" of moral values for the sake of in-depth pastoral or therapeutic work is not appropriate because it represents a form of collusion against the best interests of the person. It risks forming a nontherapeutic alliance, what Robert Langs calls "lie therapy."[37] Learning how to bring clear moral principles of nonviolence into the therapeutic setting without being judgmental and moralistic is a test of therapeutic skill.

Couple and family counseling. Couple and family counseling in situations of family violence is not advisable. Why? Because anything the partner or child of a violent man might say could become an occasion for future violence. If a victim of violence discloses the family secret, there will likely be violent consequences for that person as the abuser reasserts his control of the family. Under the threat of such violence, many victims of violence will not disclose what is happening, thus misleading the pastoral counselor into misdiagnosis. "Safety for victims first" is always the motto in situations of interpersonal violence. This means in every situation where violence is disclosed or suspected, pastoral counselors must seek consultation and be prepared to file a report to the proper authorities that a crime has been committed. The victims of violence need an effective safety plan, and the

---

[36]Herman, 135.

[37]Robert Langs, *The Bipersonal Field* (New York: Jason Aronson, 1976).

abuser must make a full confession and accept responsibility for his behavior. Likely, the family members will need a program of rehabilitation.[38]

Consultation with victims and other family members. There is some difference of opinion about whether a counselor working with a man who batters should have direct contact with the victims and other family members. Some say yes, because it is the only way to know whether the man is a danger to his partner and children during therapy. Some say no, because asking the partner to disclose how she feels about him may further endanger her. The underlying principle seems to be that the counselor should never rely solely on the information received from a man who is violent, but must have other sources of information about his ongoing behaviors without further endangering family members.

Transference and countertransference. Intense emotions are generated in the helping relationship when the man has a history of violence. Such a man is used to having his way; is an expert at manipulating, coercing, outsmarting, and threatening others; and feels justified in controlling others. This means that effective limits on his behavior will often generate rage and resistance. On the other hand, such men are singularly inept at meeting their emotional needs through vulnerability and mutuality and thus can be hurt and shamed. Managing these transference issues is a challenge to any therapist.

One of the main countertransference issues for the pastoral counselor is fear. Violent men know how to frighten others and play on their fears. They may have sustained family terror for years for the gratification of power and control needs. This predictably generates fear in the pastoral counselor. It is crucial that the pastoral counselor be intimately familiar with her or his fear response and have resources for using fear as a signal anxiety of what is going on in the therapeutic relationship. When the pastoral counselor feels fear, there may be actual danger to women or children or to the therapist. Thus, fear must become a form of signal anxiety as a part of assessing the safety of other people. In some cases the pastoral counselor's fear means that the man also

---

[38]For a fuller discussion, see Adams, *Woman-Battering*, 56–58; and Gus Kaufman, "The Mysterious Disappearance of Battered Women in Family Therapists' Offices: Male Privilege Colluding with Male Violence," *Journal of Marital and Family Therapy* 18, no. 3 (July 1992): 233–44.

is afraid and is intimidating others in order to become more comfortable. It is important to ask why the man might be afraid at this moment, and why he is resorting to power and control.

Another countertransference issue is rage. One way the counselor can defend against feeling afraid is to go for power and control. Righteous anger can be tempting when in the presence of someone who is deserving of our anger. The public reaction to child molesters is instructive here: *Lock them up; castrate them; let them be raped and see how they like it.* When one feels personally affronted by the violence of another, rage gives the illusion of power and superiority. Yet fear and rage show the risk that the counselor can become very similar to the violent man. A violent man is the expert at using anger to frighten others, at controlling and manipulating others into submission, at the games of domination and terror. Although the counselor might have all these human feelings, pastoral counseling depends on the ability to contain such feelings within a larger context of compassionate strength. These countertransference issues must become the subject of regular supervision when dealing with violent men.[39]

Religious Issues of Male Violence [40]

Male violence against women and children raises many issues for theological reflection. Because the church and its theologians have been silent for so long about male violence, it is apparent that the church bears complicity with the extent of this problem. The following doctrines have been highlighted by the issues of male violence against women and children.

Salvation

It is remarkable to remember how many biblical stories focus on safety and freedom from violence. To be saved often means to

---

[39]James Poling, "Child Sexual Abuse: A Rich Context for Thinking about God, Community, and Ministry," *Journal of Pastoral Care* 42, no. 1 (Spring 1988): 58–61; James Poling, "Issues in the Psychotherapy of Child Molesters," *Journal of Pastoral Care* 43, no. 1 (Spring 1989): 25–32.

[40]For further discussion of religious issues, see Adams and Fortune, *Violence against Women and Children*; Joanne Carlson Brown and Carole R. Bohn, eds., *Christianity, Patriarchy and Abuse: A Feminist Critique* (New York: Pilgrim Press, 1989); Emilie M. Townes, ed., *A Troubling in My Soul: Womanist Perspectives on Evil and Suffering* (Maryknoll, N.Y.: Orbis Books, 1993); Elisabeth Schüssler Fiorenza and Mary Shawn Copeland, *Violence against Women,* Concilium Series I (Maryknoll, N.Y.: Orbis Books, 1994).

be rescued from death and destruction: God rescues Hagar and Ishmael from the desert and starvation; God rescues Joseph from the pit and sends him to Egypt; God leads the Israelites to freedom from slavery; God rescues Jeremiah from the cistern; God raises Jesus from the tomb; God frees Paul and Silas from prison and other dangers. Yet there is a tendency among settled, wealthy communities of Christians to spiritualize the meaning of salvation into some kind of psychological inner freedom from shame and guilt. Victims of interpersonal violence are recovering the meaning of salvation as safety and freedom from violence.

Salvation as safety and freedom from violence can also be a spiritual resource for men who are violent. Without overstating the case and minimizing the differences between perpetrators and victims of violence, it is possible to see violent behavior as a kind of prison also. One who has chosen to be interpersonally violent may feel powerful for the moment and may be puffed up by the experience of control over others. But ultimately, one who uses violence in interpersonal relationships is alone, in a prison of isolation from others and alienated from the self.

I have worked with violent men over years of pastoral psychotherapy and have felt their imprisonment. When they come to themselves, they realize that they have never been able to love themselves or others. The violence they have inflicted on others comes back on themselves. Salvation from this inner prison can be a commitment to safety and freedom from violence. It is not an exaggeration to say that some men have prayed: *Save me from my own violence.* Parallels to Paul's conversion after killing Christians and to King David's repentance for the violence he did to Bathsheba and Uriah are useful. Salvation can mean safety and freedom from violence for victims, and it can also mean safety and freedom from doing harm to others.

Confession, Repentance, Sanctification, and Restitution [41]

Some of the deepest cries of some violent men are: *Can I change? Will I ever be safe with my children and my partner again?* Fortunately, the Christian tradition strongly emphasizes the necessity and possibilities of human transformation. Jesus began

---

[41]See discussions in Heggen, 121–34; and Marie Fortune, *Sexual Violence: The Unmentionable Sin: An Ethical and Pastoral Perspective* (New York: Pilgrim Press, 1983), 211–15.

his ministry by calling his followers to repent. Paul was struck with the blinding light and asked by Christ, "Why are you persecuting me?" This moment changed his life and initiated a reexamination and transformation of his identity. He spent the rest of his ministry calling others to repentance.

Unfortunately, established churches tend to spiritualize the basic concept of repentance so that it becomes a cheaply bought absolution of unnamed sin and evil. Many abusers turn religion into another form of manipulation and control. Caught and threatened by the criminal justice system, some abusers manufacture a conversion. *Judge, I've found Jesus; I'm a new man, and I promise you this will never happen again.*[42] Sometimes religious leaders, lacking an adequate understanding of the deep roots of violence in some personalities, mistake this formulaic response for genuine transformation. As Marie Fortune says: "If it is a genuine experience, this conversion becomes an invaluable resource to the offender who faces incarceration and possibly months of treatment...If it is not genuine, the pastor is virtually the only person who has the authority to call the offender's bluff."[43]

Confession, repentance, sanctification, and restitution are biblical terms that could describe the long road to healing and personal change required of men who are violent. *Confession* means complete openness and honesty about multiple offenses, the consequences for others, and the attitudes and beliefs that lie behind behaviors that harmed others. It means an end to secrecy, deception, lying, rationalization, minimization, and avoidance of the consequences of one's behavior. Full confession itself can be a major undertaking for men who have relied on violence in their lives.

Repentance means turning one's life around and going in a new direction. It means rooting out all the old patterns that made violence an option, and seeking new values, beliefs, behaviors, and relationships. In many cases it means leaving one's subculture and circle of friends and seeking out peer groups, mentors, and spiritual directors who have the strength and skill to confront any laziness or self-deception.

---

[42]Marie Fortune, "Forgiveness: The Last Step," in Adams and Fortune, 204.
[43]Ibid., 204–5.

Sanctification means practicing the new patterns of behavior with such faithfulness that they become second nature. The old self has died, and a new self is born. It usually takes many years before the new self is reliable.

Restitution means providing resources to victims for the harm that one has caused. In many cases the damage will have been so severe that a man who has been violent must be restrained from direct contact with victims. In most cases, attempts by an abuser to pursue a relationship with a prior victim should be discouraged. The purpose of this principle is to give the victim/survivor the power to determine the nature of any future relationship. Pursuing an ongoing relationship is often experienced by the victim as additional harassment and is often terror-filled. Instead, restitution might take the form of providing resources to the victim for therapy, for education, and for beginning an independent life.

After child abuse or battering, a violent man has an incredible debt to that person that may last for many years. Part of confession, repentance, and restitution is the willingness to do whatever it takes to restore the balance of justice in these relationships. In other cases, when support of the victim is impossible, a man in recovery from violence can provide financial and other kinds of support for other victims who seek healing from their experiences of violence. Contributions could be made to a local women's shelter, to organizations that provide low-cost therapy services for children and adult survivors of sexual abuse, and to educational programs to change the attitudes and practices of institutions such as churches, schools, business, and law. If substantial numbers of violent men were to have such a change of heart and mind that they would be willing to dedicate their resources to the support of all women and children who suffer from violence, our society would begin to see a new day.

Forgiveness[44]

The meaning of forgiveness has been so cheapened by Christian churches that it is almost useless in terms of healing and reconciliation between people. Because forgiveness is automatically

---

[44]See Frederick W. Keene, "Structures of Forgiveness in the New Testament," in Adams and Fortune, 121–34; and Fortune, "Forgiveness," 201–6.

and unconditionally given to everyone without the work of repentance and restitution, this doctrine has become a part of the problem rather than part of the solution. For example, abusers have developed a reputation for going to their pastors after disclosure of their violence and asking for prayers and forgiveness. In too many cases, pastors are willing to engage in this empty ritual and send the abuser back to the family to continue his terror. As a result, many survivors have rejected forgiveness as an important part of their healing process. Rather than forgiveness as the restoration of a relationship with God, forgiveness has become a tool of abuse and stigma. Survivors who are angry are frequently told to stay out of the church until they are willing to forgive. Many survivors have left the church for their own spiritual health, while the men who abused them continue to serve in leadership positions, having interpreted the church's forgiveness as wiping clean all memories of the past.[45]

Yet in spite of this false theology of forgiveness, some survivors are offering a reinterpretation of the true meaning of forgiveness. Rejecting forgiveness as forgetting, as false reconciliation, as covering up the past, as an obligation laid on those who are vulnerable, some survivors are seeing forgiveness as one of the last steps in the healing process. After a former victim is safe from violence, after she has grieved the many losses caused by her experiences of violence, after she has reorganized her life the way she wants it to be, after she has gained inner strength and a relationship with God, then the work of forgiveness can be considered.

For the victim, forgiveness is letting go of the immediacy of the trauma, the memory of which continues to terrorize the victim and limit possibilities. Memory is the lens through which the world is viewed. Forgiving involves putting that lens aside but keeping it close at hand. It is the choice to no longer allow the memory of the abuse to continue to abuse. But this step of healing must be carried out according to the victim's timetable.[46]

In this context, forgiveness is redefined as an aspect of healing, not only inner healing of the spirituality of the survivor, but also

---

[45]Annie Imbens and Ineke Jonker, *Christianity and Incest* (Minneapolis: Fortress Press, 1992), 15.

[46]Fortune, "Forgiveness," 203.

healing of the relational web that includes other people. Violence rends God's web of relational love, which holds people together. Forgiveness as healing creates new webs of relational love through solidarity between victim/survivors and their advocates.[47] This reinterpretation of forgiveness moves beyond a naive desire for forgetting and overlooking that many offenders wish for but is often re-abusive for the survivor. In this context, forgiveness does not mean one-to-one reconciliation, but it means that the internalized hatred that resulted from the violence has been overcome in the loving spirit of the survivor. Healing has progressed to a spiritual depth where hatred of abusers is no longer the primary force in one's life.[48]

Theology of Power and Sexuality

Some of the distortions about male violence come because of the church's confusion about power and sexuality. Historically, rape has often been blamed on the seductive woman, battering on the rebellious woman, and even child abuse on the responsibility of parents to instill discipline and respect for authority. When children and women complain of abuse and violence, church leaders often refuse to believe their stories and side with the man, whom they perceive as having authority in the situation. The blessing of heterosexual relationships within the family without regard for issues of power and violence has created dangerous situations for women and children.

Fortunately, much good work has been done lately on issues of power and sexuality. Marie Fortune's *Sexual Violence*[49] was one of the first to identify this problem, and much other work has been done to revise the church's theology in this area.[50]

The Sin and Evil of Male Violence

Male violence against women and children must lead the church and its theologians to reconsider the questions of sin and

---

[47]The image of mending the relational web is nicely developed by Christine Smith, *Weaving the Sermon: Preaching in a Feminist Perspective* (Louisville: Westminster Press, 1989).

[48]I am indebted for these ideas to Karen Doudt, author of chapter 3 in Poling, *The Abuse of Power.*

[49]Marie Fortune, *Sexual Violence: The Unmentionable Sin: An Ethical and Pastoral Perspective* (New York: Pilgrim Press, 1983).

[50]See Poling, *The Abuse of Power,* and "Sexuality: A Crisis for the Church," in Pamela Couture and Rodney Hunter, eds., *Pastoral Care in a Society in Conflict* (Nashville: Abingdon Press, 1995).

evil.[51] A significant pastoral problem in working with violent men is that they don't know how to confront the reality that they have deliberately harmed someone they thought they loved. In spite of biblical passages about the slaughter of the firstborn sons of Egypt, the slaughter of people and animals in the time of the Judges, Herod's slaughter of all male infants in the region of Bethlehem, and the torture and murder of Jesus, the church has been virtually silent on the issue of male violence against women and children.

If more than 25 percent of Christians have experienced sexual and physical violence at the hands of men, what does this silence mean? It means that the church and its theologians have failed to address one of the most common experiences of evil among its own members. Violent men have a right to ask the church: *How could I be violent toward someone I love? How could the church allow me to engage in this behavior to the damnation of my soul and not confront me with God's judgment and grace?* Most men who have come to me for help are at a total loss to face these questions themselves. They have never heard sermons, Bible studies, prayers, or spiritual guidance on these questions. They have been left on their own to figure out the religious importance of their experience, and their thought process has led them in even more destructive directions.

I dream of a time when male violence against women and children becomes a part of the church's theology of sin and evil. What would it look like? It would be a theology that refused to ignore the danger of tyrannical power in interpersonal relationships, whether enforced by physical strength, sexual abuse, male dominance, or threat of violence. It would be a theology that was realistic about the spiritual dangers to one's soul of abusing power over those who are vulnerable. It would be a theology that squarely faced the evils of gender inequality, forced sexual abuse, male power and control, and exemption from accountability and consequences. The new theology of evil would acknowledge that the church perpetuates these dangers when it idolizes the family, when it idealizes parental authority, when it accedes to the male dominance of our culture, and when it contributes to the confusion of sexuality and power. I believe that facing the evil of male violence within the church requires a reinterpretation of much of the church's theology. The only way a massive evil such as this

---

[51]See Poling, *Deliver Us from Evil.*

could be overlooked is by the church allowing the evil of male dominance to cloud its vision of the gospel, and thus overlooking the presence of violent interpersonal relationships among Christians.

Jesus: Authority without Violence

Can the figure of Jesus be reconstructed as an image of authority without violence? In a culture where authority is patriarchal in structure, christology has often been problematic. Some liberal christologies project a docile Jesus who, though nonviolent, was hardly a figure of authority. Rather Jesus' virtues of submission, obedience, long-suffering, and meekness corresponded very closely to the nineteenth-century "cult of true womanhood" that included piety, purity, submissiveness, and domesticity.[52] It was thought that the Christian virtues of love were best preserved by women who stayed at home away from the brutality of the raging industrial economy. Conservative theologians have emphasized the imperial and victorious Jesus, the right hand of the Father-God, who wields power with terrible consequences for those who are lost. This Jesus bore the cross with full confidence in the victory afterward and has full authority to reign on behalf of the almighty, omnipotent God.

Neither of these christologies is helpful for men who want to recover from their violent patterns. They need a new christology that reveals an image of internal strength. Such inner strength takes responsibility for one's violent tendencies and accepts accountability to those whom one abused and controlled in the past. They need a new christology that reveals a different kind of authority, not only authority that is nonviolent, but one that also values mutuality, equality, and respect between all persons. Given the long history of patriarchal theology, a new christology will take many years to fully emerge. Fortunately, the women's movement has already started the process of theological transformation, and Christian men need to join in.[53]

---

[52]Hazel Carby, *Reconstructing Womanhood* (New York: Oxford University Press, 1987), 23.

[53]See Kelly Brown Douglas, *The Black Christ* (Maryknoll, N.Y.: Orbis Books, 1994); Jacquelyn Grant, *Black Women's Jesus and White Women's Christ* (Atlanta: Scholar's Press, 1989); Maryanne Stevens, ed., *Reconstructing the Christ Symbol: Essays in Feminist Christology* (New York: Paulist Press, 1993).

Conclusion

This chapter has summarized some of the pastoral care and counseling issues of a complex subject: male violence against women and children. Many women are coming to the church with complaints and lawsuits about male violence in Christian families and against Christian leaders. A few men are coming to the church and its pastors for guidance concerning their violent behaviors and attitudes. The church is not prepared to deal with the pastoral needs because they seem to be new, and because the church has not faced its complicity in this problem.

In this chapter, I have summarized some of the current literature about male violence and suggested some ways that pastoral care and counseling must be revised to respond to this pastoral issue. Finally, I have suggested some theological implications for the church's doctrine and practice. I hope that facing the issue of male violence against women and children will enable the church to fulfill its pastoral care responsibilities to all God's people whether they are victims and survivors of violence or recovering perpetrators who seek redemption for their lives.

2

Social and Ethical Issues of
Child Sexual Abuse[1]

*"It is time for the church to look squarely at the many forms of
child abuse, including child sexual abuse."*

This chapter is about a forbidden topic, a taboo. I did not even
see the problem at first. But then, of course, that is the nature of a
taboo.

In chapter 1, I provided an overview of some of the issues of
male violence against women and children and the appropriate
pastoral care responses by the church and its leadership. In this
chapter, we look more closely at child sexual abuse, one of the
forms of male violence against children. My own awakening to this
problem came slowly over several years of experience, first as a
pastor and later as a pastoral psychotherapist. I found that this
issue challenged my thinking about myself, my identity as a man,
my theology of ministry, and my understanding of basic doctrines
such as the nature of God. Here you see my beginning struggles as
I tried to make sense of a situation in which an adult or adolescent
male has taken advantage of the vulnerability of a child and
inflicted lifetime damage. What would it mean to see the child
molester as a mirror of a patriarchal society in which the more

---

[1]Original version published as "Social and Ethical Issues of Child Sexual Abuse,"
American Baptist Quarterly 8, no. 4 (1989): 257–67.

powerful are given immunity for their abuses of those who are less powerful?

I remember Stacey, an adult woman who had been molested by both her father and her grandfather. She was recovering from a suicide attempt and subsequent hospitalization. As her pastor, I couldn't understand what she was experiencing, but I could see the awful pain she was going through. I wanted to help, but I didn't know how.

I also remember Brenda, a fifteen-year-old girl, who came to me because her father was touching her breasts and saying he wanted to have sex with her. Even though her father was a Sunday school teacher, he didn't think he was doing anything wrong. But he agreed to stop when I confronted him.

As a seminary professor, I have listened to countless stories of young adults who grew up in the church. Gail's father was a deacon in the church, but at night he came into his daughter's bedroom and forced his penis into her mouth. Tom was "punished" by his father at age twelve by forced oral sex.

As a psychotherapist, I have been working with families in which there is criminal sexual abuse of children. These parents have done awful things to their children, but the patterns are only extremes of the same things I have seen as a pastor.

My ministry experience has led me to conclude that child sexual abuse in church and society is not unusual. A large percentage of children are significantly damaged by experiences of sexual abuse. These experiences have long-term consequences. Children who are sexually abused often suffer as adults from depression, alcohol and drug abuse, suicidal impulses, and other symptoms. They sometimes grow up to be adults who abuse their own children and have difficulty forming healthy adult relationships.

Slowly the reality of child sexual abuse began to break through the taboo in my mind. As I began to see, I wondered: If sexual abuse of children is so widespread and the consequences are so serious, why doesn't the church do more about it? Why is the church so silent?

I discovered some troubling answers. Child sexual abuse is only one form of fairly widespread mistreatment of children. As I became more aware of the suffering of children, I noticed forms of insensitivity toward my own children. As a parent of young children, "no" was often my favorite word when one of my children asked for something. And if they dared to challenge me, I had a temper that usually ended the conversation. My wife and I had frequent fights about whether I was "too hard on the children." I have learned the slow way that for most of their formative years I did not see my children as persons with needs different from mine. I usually thought of my need for order and control first and then rationalized my behavior as something that would be good for them.

When the awareness of my inadequacies as a parent reached a crisis for me, I began to understand the roots of the taboo. The families I saw when I was a pastor and the families I treated as a therapist are not significantly different from my own family. In order to talk about child abuse in the church, I must be able to talk about my own potential for abuse. But how can a Christian confess an act of child abuse? The church has its list of approved sins—using profanity, not going to church enough, watching a questionable movie. But confessing child abuse? I had never heard a Christian talk this way, and I wasn't volunteering to be the first.

So I understood a little more. Child abuse is a taboo topic in the church because we don't want to look at our own parenting deficiencies. Sometimes we complain about our children, but rarely do we talk about our mistakes and inadequacies. The taboo protects us from talking about a very painful area of our lives as parents.

But I suspect there is another reason why child abuse is a taboo subject. One of our unspoken rules is that we don't criticize our parents, reasoning that "They did the best they could." Saying anything else makes us ungrateful for the sacrifices our parents made. We don't want to face any anger toward our parents or have to deal with the pain from our own childhood. But how can we find healing for pain that we cannot acknowledge? If our parents made no mistakes, then we must carry the burden of our injuries in silence, and inadvertently we teach our children to do the same. The taboo is powerful because breaking it would unravel the silent agreement that nothing is wrong in our families or in ourselves.[2]

---

[2]This argument is well developed by Alice Miller, *For Your Own Good* (New York: Farrar, Strauss, Giroux, 1983).

It is time for the church to look squarely at the many forms of child abuse, including child sexual abuse. Even if the looking is painful and even if it challenges some of our sacred myths about families and sexuality, we cannot afford to protect ourselves anymore. This chapter attempts to expose some of the facts and myths about child sexual abuse.

The Ethical Issues of Child Sexual Abuse

There is a growing body of literature about child sexual abuse and its consequences.[3] According to a respected study:

- 12 out of 100 girls in most junior high schools have been sexually abused by a relative;

- 20 in 100 girls in junior high have been sexually abused by a non-relative;

- 38 in 100 girls in most high schools have had at least one experience of sexual abuse.[4]

Other studies indicate that 20 percent of boys may have been sexually victimized as children.[5] These studies indicate a massive problem of human suffering that is not receiving adequate attention. There are strong ethical implications in these data for church and society.

First, church and society have an ethical responsibility to protect children who are victims of child sexual abuse. Any time a child is sexually abused, there is potential traumatic injury to personality that can be long-lasting.[6] Intervention and protection are crucial. Injury to children from sexual abuse is severe for several reasons. Children are dependent on adults for protection, and sexual abuse means that the adult protection has failed (even if the failure is inadvertent and unavoidable), and the child feels helpless and

---

[3]For an excellent summary of the research on child sexual abuse, see Dante Cicchetti and Vicki Carlson, eds., *Child Maltreatment* (Cambridge, U.K.: Cambridge University Press, 1989), 95–128.

[4]Diana Russell, *The Secret Trauma: Incest in the Lives of Girls and Women* (New York: Basic Books, 1986).

[5]David Finkelhor, *Child Sexual Abuse* (New York: Free Press, 1984).

[6]For excellent discussions on the dynamics of child sexual abuse, see Ellen Bass and Laura Davis, *The Courage to Heal: A Guide for Women Survivors of Child Sexual Abuse* (New York: Harper and Row, 1988); and Mike Lew, *Victims No Longer: Men Recovering from Incest and Other Sexual Child Abuse* (New York: Nevraumont, 1988).

vulnerable. Often sexual abuse of a child involves betrayal by an adult who is trusted: a parent, other relative, friend, or community leader. Even if the abuse is by a stranger, the child feels betrayed by the adult world. Children are taught to respect and obey adults, and when adults injure them, their trust in the world they know is jeopardized.

Often part of the dynamic of sexual abuse is a threat of further injury if children tell anyone what happened. This dynamic of feeling helpless, betrayed, and threatened is one reason that many children keep their abuse a secret. Most children believe that the injury is their own fault and fear being punished again. This means that the response to the child if they disclose is terribly important. Many adults who were abused as children report that they did tell someone and yet nothing happened. Often the adult they told was afraid to do anything, and the feelings of betrayal and helplessness were compounded. Society must create an atmosphere in which children are clear that sexual abuse is wrong, they know that they should tell some adult whenever they feel an adult has touched them improperly, and they can count on the adult acting in their best interests. Rather than act shocked when we hear a child make such a report, we should know that 20 percent to 40 percent of all children have this experience. It happens frequently. It is serious when it happens.

A child who has been sexually victimized needs immediate protection to feel safe.[7] All children who have been sexually abused need therapy to deal with their anger, their fear, their loss of faith in the adult world, and their damaged self-esteem. We need to teach children about sexual abuse so they can be better protected and get help when they need it. Every instance of child sexual abuse that is known by an adult should be reported to authorities who have competence to evaluate the damage and protect that child and other children. We need programs of education, prevention, and aggressive intervention. Child welfare workers already know this, but the broader public has yet to embrace this.

---

[7]Suzanne M. Sgroi, *Handbook of Clinical Intervention in Child Sexual Abuse* (Lexington, Mass.: D.C. Health, 1982), has one of the best discussions of the important issues in effective intervention strategies. See also Mary D. Pellauer, Barbara Chester, and Jane A. Boyajian, eds., *Sexual Assault and Abuse: A Handbook for Clergy and Religions* (New York: Harper and Row, 1987).

Second, church and society have an ethical responsibility to provide aggressive programs of treatment for adults who were molested as children. (One frequently cited organization is Adults Molested As Children [AMAC].[8]) Child sexual abuse is a much more frequent childhood cause of adult dysfunction than previously thought. If 30 percent of women and 20 percent of men were molested as children, then child sexual abuse may be a contributing factor in many adult symptoms. Testimony from adults who are in therapy is showing that the major ways that children deal with the trauma of sexual abuse is denial and dissociation. These are common psychological defenses against overwhelming trauma. Denial is the total repression of the experience from conscious memory. Many therapy clients do not remember being molested until several years into treatment. The experience is so painful that the ego cannot tolerate the memory that it happened. As a consequence, many adults do not initially remember that they were molested.[9]

Dissociation is another common defense. In this case, the fact of the molestation is remembered, but the hurt and pain are dissociated from the experience. There simply is no feeling around the memory. It happened, but it has no conscious significance. This defense protects the ego from being overwhelmed by pain. Ironically, denial and dissociation are exactly the same defenses that society uses. Our society has a history of denying the existence of child sexual abuse or dissociating the fact from its significance. Freud believed that reports of molestation had little significance for adult pathology. We are gaining enough experience now to know that the quality of therapy is vastly increased when experiences of child sexual abuse are identified as a primary cause of adult symptoms. When therapists collude with clients by denying the existence or significance of this childhood trauma, then therapy becomes a continuation of the original trauma; its existence and significance are denied. There are many

---

[8]Euan Bear, *Adults Molested as Children: A Survivor's Manual for Women and Men* (Brandon, Vt.: Safer Society Press, 1988).

[9]The vivid testimony of adult victims/survivors is presented in collections of short testimonies and longer narratives. See the following: Charlotte Vale Allen, *Daddy's Girl* (New York: Berkeley Books, 1982); Maya Angelou, *I Know Why the Caged Bird Sings* (New York: Random House, 1970); Louise Armstrong, *Kiss Daddy Goodnight* (New York: Simon Schuster, 1978); Ellen Bass and Louise Thornton, eds., *I Never Told Anyone: Writings by Women Survivors of Child Sexual Abuse* (New York: Harper and Row, 1983); Katherine Brady, *Father's Days* (New York: Dell Books, 1979); Martha Janssen, *Silent Scream: I Am a Victim of Incest* (Philadelphia: Fortress Press, 1983).

adults in need of adequate treatment for the damage done by child sexual abuse.

Third, church and society have an ethical responsibility to understand and provide healing experiences for child molesters. One ethical issue is whether child molesters want, deserve, or can benefit from psychotherapeutic treatment. I do not raise this issue because child molesters should receive priority over children or adult victims. The first priority in this field is the protection of children, the prevention of child sexual abuse, and the treatment of children who have been sexually abused. The second priority is the treatment of adults who were molested as children. But we do need a spirited clinical debate about the etiology, diagnosis, prognosis, and appropriate treatment modalities for the various categories of child molesters.

I am concerned about the moral responsibility of society toward child molesters, namely, whether child molesters deserve opportunities for healing as human beings. Our society has not made an ethical commitment to helping child molesters. Child molesters are severely damaged human beings, often the victims of child abuse or deprivation themselves.[10] They continue the cycle of violence that is so widespread in our society in families, schools, the military, and the workplace. Society must be protected from this violence through the creation of adequate external structures to compensate for the lack of internal structure. But when there are firm limits on their violence and abuse, whether that involves probation, halfway houses, or jails, then clinicians should turn their attention to understanding and healing. What kind of inner pain can cause such destructive behavior toward others? How is such pain created (etiology)? What is the internal structure of such pain (diagnosis)? What are the likely symptoms of such pain (prognosis)? What is the appropriate treatment that gives some sense of hope for the person caught in such internal and external destructiveness (treatment goals)?[11]

---

[10]D. W. Winnicott has one of the best discussions about the relationship between antisocial behavior and intrapsychic pain in children and adults who were abused, in *Deprivation and Delinquency* (London: Tavistock Publishing, 1984).

[11]For an excellent summary of current assessment and treatment of child molesters, see George W. Barnard, et al., *The Child Molester: An Integrated Approach to Evaluation and Treatment* (New York: Brunne/Mazel, 1989).

Based on my experience as a pastoral psychotherapist with men who have abused children, I believe that child molesters are fragile and inadequate as human beings. Children are attractive to molesters because they are so full of life in contrast to the molesters' own emptiness. Children are small and vulnerable and thus give these inadequate adults a feeling of relative power. Molesters are dangerous because they act out primitive, destructive impulses in relation to children who are helpless to defend themselves. When an average person encounters the primitive unconscious material of a molester, they become frightened, and they often hide their fear behind hostility. As a result, child molesters are among the most harshly scapegoated persons in our society.

We do not have enough clinical knowledge and skill yet to treat successfully most child molesters. But we must understand the etiology of the rage that child molesters provoke in us and not project that rage on others to escape involvement. Child molesters evoke in others the same helplessness and rage that they live with constantly, and clinicians must be able to manage their own feelings in order to make good clinical judgments.

The Social Issues of Child Sexual Abuse

Child sexual abuse does not occur in a vacuum. It occurs in a society with its own confused and conflicting images of male and female, adult and child, intimacy and violence. Psychopathology is not just an individual phenomenon. There is also social pathology. Mental illness can be interpreted as a critique of social pathology. We can examine a deviancy such as child sexual abuse for its penetrating analysis of how a culture violates its own people.

There is a tradition of understanding mental illness as metaphor about the society in which it occurs. Freud studied hysteria, a disorder affecting women in a Victorian society that was sexually violent toward women and children. When Freud discovered the effects of sexual violence, he was so horrified that he attributed the cause to children's fantasies rather than to reality. But it turns out that hysteria was a predictable mental illness for women in a society where sexuality was repressed and sexual abuse was denied. In the midst of society's betrayal, women suffered. Another of Freud's discoveries was the obsessional neurosis, a form of rebellion against the rigid conformity demanded by an industrial society. According to this theory, obsessive symptoms arise out of rage at authority, which Freud traced to problems with the father, a predictable problem in a culture where many men are encouraged to be in control yet denied the right to feelings and personal power.[12] Both hysteria and obsessive disorders are as much a critique of society's symbols and political order as they are descriptions of individual pathology. Child sexual abuse is a metaphor for at least three forms of social pathology.

1. *Devaluation of women and children.* Our society does not want to face the injustice for women and the destructive images in our culture concerning women and children. The idealization and devaluation of women is so predominant in our culture that we take it for granted. In spite of a strong feminist movement for 140 years in this country, women are portrayed in advertising and movies primarily as sexual beings who find their identity in submission to men. In spite of social justice reforms, women still earn less than half what men earn in the job market. Some estimates say that as many as 30 percent of children live below the poverty level, mostly in single-parent homes headed by women. The inequality of women in our society is a part of the reason why violence against women in the forms of rape and physical abuse is so inadequately dealt with. And the sexual abuse of children is an extension of the attitudes of a society that overvalues men and cannot face the facts about how men treat women and children.[13]

2. *Ideology about the family.* Most child sexual abuse occurs within the family, especially the forms of abuse that go on for years without disclosure. In our society parents are responsible for the care of their children, and the larger society does not

---

[12]For a discussion of Freud's use of metaphor, see Don S. Browning, *Religious Thought and the Modern Psychologies* (Philadelphia: Fortress Press, 1987), especially chapter 3, "Metaphors, Models, and Morality in Freud," 32–60.

[13]For a summary of the feminist discussion, see Hester Eisenstein, *Contemporary Feminist Thought* (Boston: G. K. Hall, 1983), especially chapter 3, "Rape and the Male Protection Racket," 27–34, and chapter 12, "Sexual Politics Revisited: Pornography and Sadomasochism," 116–24.

interfere. In effect, parents have almost total control over their children as long as they do not bring themselves to the attention of the community. In addition, parents are allowed to maintain control of their children with force if necessary. Alice Miller has studied instructions dating back 100 years on how parents are encouraged to relate to their children.[14] The primary emphasis has been on the parent's responsibility to control the child's so-called natural tendency to act impulsively and to turn the child into a well-behaved citizen. Even with the more nurturing emphasis of Dr. Spock, there is still a strong ideology of parental "discipline" and encouragement for parents to use physical and other harsh punishments. The consequence of our ideology that parents have total authority over children and a social responsibility to make them behave means that children have no real social protection from abuse. Even though sexual abuse of children is illegal, society is hesitant to interfere with parents even if they are abusing their children. Parental rights have much stronger protection than children's rights. Often pedophiles who abuse children are treated harshly more because they violated the boundaries of the family than because they hurt a child, and often the children in these cases do not receive the therapy they need.[15]

3. *Confusion of sexuality and violence.* One of the reasons why child sexual abuse has never been squarely faced is that it has been seen as a sexual offense rather than a violent act. The sexual offenses of fathers, brothers, and uncles are often overlooked by male prosecutors and male judges who cannot imagine that men would actually hurt little children, or that the abuse is really that serious. One of the most troubling cases for me was a wealthy man who had charges of child sexual abuse dropped by the court partly because his pastor testified as a character witness. He was not convicted of any crime even though he admitted that he had engaged in sexual intercourse regularly over five years with two teenage daughters. Our system tends

---

[14]Miller, *For Your Own Good;* and *Thou Shalt Not Be Aware* (New York: Farrar, Strauss, Giroux, 1983).

[15]The discussion of religious family ideology is well summarized in Pellauer et al., especially chapter 8 by Marie Fortune and Judith Hertze, "A Commentary on Religious Issues in the Family," 67–83.

to see such behavior as a sexual problem rather than a crime of violence against the person of the child. If a responsible citizen has a slight sexual problem, where is the harm? In fact, men tend to protect one another because sexual problems of various kinds are not unusual in the male population. But if child sexual abuse and sexual violence against women are seen as the violent crimes they are, we will have to change our attitudes and policies. As long as we confuse sexuality and abuse, we will tend to underestimate the harm done by sexual violence.[16]

What would it mean to understand child sexual abuse as a cultural metaphor about violence? What is the social critique implicit in this? My limited experience with child molesters is that they are inadequate persons with primitive needs and defenses. They feel entitled to seize what they need without regard for its effect on others. They interpret any limits as persecution. They don't feel bound by the normal rules of social conduct. Yet they are fragile and easily fragment into helplessness, fear, and incompetence. I speculate that this configuration is a deep metaphor of masculinity in society today. One of the reasons child sexual abuse could not surface as an issue of public morality until recently is that it leads to a radical critique of the Euro-American male ideal. Freud could not tolerate the possibility that men were raping the governesses and children of his time. So he developed his theory of infantile sexuality to account for data he could not ignore, that is, the reports of sexual violence in the lives of his adult patients, mostly women.

The discovery of child sexual abuse is related to two developments. First, women are beginning to speak for themselves. Child sexual abuse was uncovered as an issue of public morality by women who began talking about their own experience. This is a direct result of feminism and the growing consciousness of all women that they can find their public voices and use their own experience as authority.[17] Second, some men are slowly listening to women and trying to attend to the depth of their

---

[16]For a good discussion about the confusion of sexuality and violence, see Marie Fortune, *Sexual Violence: The Unmentionable Sin: An Ethical and Pastoral Perspective* (New York: Pilgrim Press, 1983).
[17]See Eisenstein.

own experience also. Our culture's violence toward women, children, racial minorities, enemies, those in massive poverty, and the environment has got to be stopped. And men are discovering that the source of this violence is not just the system, or the symbols of our culture, but also our very psyches.[18] Here I must shift to the personal pronoun so I don't presume to speak for other men.

I have discovered the counterpart to the violence in our society in my own soul. In a sense, U.S. society and my soul are mirrors of each other. In both places I find a desire for power and a willingness to use power against others in narcissistic ways, that is, without taking into account the consequences for myself or others. In other words, I find myself and our society mirrored in the child molester who exploits others for his own consumption without a realistic perception of his own needs or the consequences of his behavior for others.

Several times people have asked me why I want to work with child molesters. That is always a difficult question for me because I have to resist telling my own long story of how I have struggled with my own violence and have acknowledged the potential child molester within me. I have a sense of identification with child molesters that is hard to talk about without dumping out my own unresolved unconscious material. But in one conversation I had an insight that surprised and comforted me. It is not only my identification with child molesters that draws me into this work, but my sense of wonder at the courage of some of the men I have known through treatment. Facing the reality and horror that one has molested a child is one of the most difficult things any man could ever do. It means facing the damage one has done to another, and facing the emptiness in oneself that led to such destructive behavior. I have seen men face themselves in this way and suffer the agony of the long road to healing. I find this inspiring. If child molesters can have the courage and hope to seek treatment in order to get better, then I can have hope in the world where violence seems out of control. If a child molester can face

---

[18]See James Nelson, *Embodiment: An Approach to Sexuality and Christian Theology* (Minneapolis: Augsburg, 1978); and *The Intimate Connection: Male Sexuality, Masculine Spirituality* (Philadelphia: Westminster, 1988).

his limits and learn to live within them without doing further damage, then I can face the violence in my life. And perhaps our U.S. society can rediscover its compassionate soul. If we can face our personal and social violence with the courage of a child molester in treatment, then perhaps there is hope for a world itself in jeopardy of extinction through uncontrolled violence.

3

Understanding Male Violence as an Ethical Problem[1]

Most Christians assume that rape is wrong, but until recently there has been little careful reflection about why rape is wrong, and why the church has been so silent on the prevalence of this form of evil. For if most people agree that rape is wrong, then why does it persist, and why is there not more effort expended to prevent it and discipline the evil-doers? As I explore in the following reflection, understanding male violence against women and children requires dialogue with various theological disciplines, including biblical, historical, systematic, and ethical theology. As I dialogue between my ministry practice and the debates in biblical and ethical theology, I become more clear about the ethical mandates of the scriptures and their implications for new ministry practices.

A Biblical Ethics Case

Second Samuel 13 is a story about David and three of his children: Amnon, the eldest; Absalom; and Tamar. Amnon becomes infatuated with Tamar; his half-sister; and arranges a situation where he rapes her. She protests but is overpowered, after which she makes her disgrace known in public. Absalom shelters her and then plots revenge, eventually murdering Amnon.

[1]Original version published as "An Ethical Framework for Pastoral Care," *Journal of Pastoral Care* 42, no. 4 (Winter 1988): 299–308.

Phyllis Trible has done a remarkable exegesis of this story in her book *Texts of Terror.*[2] After reading this story aloud, I ask the students two questions: What is wrong here? On what basis would you say it is wrong?

In order to answer these questions, we can look at the story in relation to the various characters. What does the text say? Amnon "fell sick with love for his half-sister...but he thought it an impossible thing to approach her since she was a virgin." He was filled with hatred afterward. Tamar courageously responds to his threat of violence by appealing to the ethical principles of the people of Israel: "Do not dishonor me...We do not do such things in Israel...Do not behave like a beast...Where could I go and hide my disgrace?...Why not speak to the King for me...He will not refuse you leave to marry me." Absalom says: "Has your brother Amnon been with you?...Keep this to yourself, he is your brother...Do not take it to heart." He hated Amnon, for having dishonored his sister Tamar. David was very angry. But he would not hurt Amnon because he was his eldest son and he loved him" (vv. 1–21, author's rendering).

What is wrong in this story? From the Christian tradition, several possibilities suggest themselves: rape, sexual violence, incest, loss of virginity, violation of the property rights of men, disruption of family unity, violation of community standards, violence against women, violation of universal law.

On what basis are any of these things wrong? There are at least four possible types of ethical arguments:

(1) Violation of God's law. The Ten Commandments and their restatement by Jesus are often accepted as universal ethical standards. Several laws are violated: You shall not covet; you shall not steal; honor your father and mother; you shall not commit adultery; you shall not murder; love God and love neighbor as self (Exodus 20, Matthew 5–7). This type of ethics argues that certain standards are given in the nature of things, the violation of which results in the destruction of the moral fabric of human community. Amnon's act violates these standards and destroys the structure of love within this family.

(2) Destructive Consequences. What is wrong in this story is that a destructive sequence of events was unleashed that increased

---

[2]Phyllis Trible, *Texts of Terror* (Philadelphia: Fortress Press, 1984), 37ff.

evil and decreased the possibility of good. The deceit of Amnon led to the rape of Tamar, which caused the revenge by Absalom, the murder of Amnon, and an ongoing system of family violence.[3]

(3) Violation of community character and narrative. The key statement is made by Tamar: "We do not do such things in Israel." This is an appeal to community character and virtues. The problem with her appeal is that such things *are* done in Israel. David abused Bathsheba and murdered Uriah. In some ways Amnon is following in his father's footsteps by abusing his sister, and Absalom is following his father's example by murdering Amnon. This event raises the key issue: What is character and virtue in Israel? What kind of people are we?

(4) Social injustice. A liberation ethic raises questions about the violation of power. If we start from the experience of the woman, Tamar, it is apparent that in spite of her ethical courage, she has no social power to actualize her moral vision. She is victimized by Amnon, ignored by David, and avenged by Absalom without her participation. Tamar is violated and then marginalized in a way that reveals the injustice she experiences as woman. Looking at the story from the perspective of the socially marginalized, one uncovers the distortion of power and morality of this story.

Types of Ethics

In this analysis we can see four different types of ethics:

(1) Ethic of intuition. We know the right by intuition, conscience, revelation, and reason, but not by experience. Morality is given by the structure of existence or God's revelation. The key question is, What principles should we follow?

(2) Ethic of purpose. We know the right by the consequences of human decisions, from the situation as it unfolds. The key

---

[3]The traditional ethical discussion focuses on rules about behavior based on principles or consequences or some combination of the two. The debate between deontology and teleology is whether we know what is right or wrong based on intuition, that is, the nature of things; or by purpose, that is, the consequences of human choices. William K. Frankena, *Ethics* (Englewood Cliffs, N.J.: Prentice-Hall, 1963).

question is whether the good is increased. What are the goals of our choices and the consequences that follow?

(3) Ethic of character. What is right depends on the story and vision of a particular community. "We do not do such things in Israel" is the key statement. What kind of persons and community do we become by our choices? What is our vision of who we are?[4]

(4) Ethic of liberation. We know the right through taking the perspective of those who are marginal in the community. This perspective reveals the distorted power relationships that determine the moral choices that are permitted. What are the power arrangements that determine and preclude the choices people can make and construct the context for doing ethics?[5]

---

[4]Stanley Hauerwas argues that abstract rules about behavior make no sense outside of some particular community. In this notion, universal rules should not be the center of the ethical discussion. In his book *A Community of Character,* he argues that every particular community has a narrative about its identity that defines its values and gives clues about the kind of person one should be. In order to answer a question about behavior, one must first ask about the particular community where this question arose. Even the definition of the ethical question will be shaped by the community context. Essentially, Hauerwas' position questions the usual definitions of authority. Traditional ethics always assumes some "universal experience" that can be asserted. This has the effect of assuming that the perspective of the one doing the ethics is normative for everyone. Hauerwas posits a radical pluralism in the world characterized by lack of consensus about values and virtues. This has the possibility of granting power to those whose voices are not usually heard in the ethical debates. Particular, deviant communities present their ethical vision by the way they live their loyalties and commitments. This view is consistent with James Fowler's definition of faith as the way one lives one's commitments and loyalties. Stanley Hauerwas, *A Community of Character: Toward a Constructive Christian Social Ethic* (Notre Dame, Ind.: University of Notre Dame Press, 1981).

[5]Liberation theology defines ethics in terms of social justice and liberation. In this perspective, traditional ethics is criticized because it does not attend carefully enough to the question of oppression in human relationships. Abuse of power is often the primary cause of human suffering and must be central to any debate about normative ethics. For example, in the African American experience, the meaning of behavior must be understood within the context of racism. The African American family historically has struggled to define its identity and values within a context of racial oppression. Therefore, ethics must take their witness into account. Similarly, feminist theology takes women's experience as the context for ethics. Its perspective criticizes traditional ethics for having a male bias that does not understand the inequality and injustice facing women. Liberation theology redefines ethics in relation to social critique. The ethical questions and ethical methods will be very different when seen from communities that are oppressed than when seen from the ideology of the dominant culture. The relation of suffering and power is the key to ethics. Archie Smith, Jr., *The Relational Self: Ethics and Therapy from a Black Church Perspective* (Nashville: Abingdon Press, 1982); Barbara Hilkert Andolsen, Christine E. Gudorf, and Mary D. Pellauer, eds., *Women's Consciousness, Women's Conscience: A Reader in Feminist Ethics* (San Francisco: Harper and Row, 1987).

Each of these four types of ethic has a contribution to make, and certain limitations.

(1) Some principles are virtually universal. "Do no injury to another." "Do not exploit social power and privilege." Immanuel Kant argued that in order for human society to be possible, there must be respect for oneself and the other as a center of freedom. Otherwise human life is impossible. A limit of this type of ethics is that it is very difficult to know what a principle means in a complex, concrete situation. What is respect when one is unsure what to do? For example, Phyllis Trible considers Absalom's revenge as less evil than Amnon's rape because it was motivated by support for Tamar. But in some ways Absalom's morality is as self-serving as anyone's, because he became the heir to the throne.

(2) Consequences are important. An act that starts in motion a pattern of destructive consequences is wrong. The story of the rape of Tamar is just one incident in a sequence of family violence: David's abuse of Bathsheba and murder of Uriah, Ammon's abuse of Tamar, Absalom's murder of Ammon, David's murder of Absalom. Any act that increases evil is immoral. We are obligated to live so that love is increased for others. A limit of this view is that we can never fully calculate the consequences of our behaviors and decisions. Our motives for our behaviors often distort our ability to see the consequences. Another limit is the lack of consensus over the moral good that should be increased. What is considered good by one subgroup is not valued by another subgroup.

(3) Good and evil are particular to community vision and character. We live in a world of plural visions and virtues. What is good in one context may not be good in another context. In twentieth-century America, we can see the abuse of power by the men in this story. But within the context of early Hebrew Scriptures, where the rights of men were often unquestioned, the ethical vision of Tamar and the support of his sister by Absalom may be remarkable. Yet Tamar was marginalized and forgotten as the story unfolds. This story focuses the relation of ethics to the vision of a particular community. It also reveals the limit of this view. How does one attend to particular community context without slipping into relativism? By what criteria do

communities resolve their different moral visions in order to live together peaceably?

(4) Injustice and oppression are relevant to ethics. What liberation thinkers have proved is that much of what passes for "objective, rational ethics" is really support for the unexamined dominant ideology that favors the privilege of those with power and does not attend to those who are marginalized. Traditional ethics assumes that there is such a thing as universal experience, whereas, in truth, experience is radically different for those with privilege and power in contrast to those who are marginal. Unjust power arrangements totally change both the method and content of ethics. When the story is told from Tamar's perspective, it is evident that because her choices were taken from her, after her rape, her future was tragically limited. In the same way, the child in an incestuous family is denied the social power to make known her suffering; and a black woman who is raped has to choose whether to turn the racist police loose in her community. These are choices based on a lack of social power, and thus, the ethical debate for the poor is vastly different from that of those with privilege. However, a limit of this view is that every analysis of power arrangements is also subject to distortion. Replacing the power of one subgroup with another does not necessarily result in an improved ethical vision.

An Ethical Method

In addition to identifying types of ethical thinking, we need a method for moving from ideas to decisions. How do we move from a metaphor such as "God is love," to a concrete answer to the question, "What sexual behaviors are permitted?" This involves the move from concrete to abstract and from abstract to concrete. Such a move involves three levels: (1) the level of an ethical system itself: story, metaphor, social context, norms, goals, consequences; (2) the level of middle axioms: rules based on an ethical system that provide concrete guidelines for behavior; (3) the level of decisions: actual choices in concrete situations.

If we put together the four types of ethical questions with the move from abstract to concrete through middle axioms, we develop a more complete ethical method. Moving from the most concrete to the most abstract, we have the following components.

This method can be conceived as a hierarchy of levels with movement up and down in a rhythm between practice and reflection.[6]   .

1. Decisions

2. Rules–middle axioms

3. Norms–intuition and purpose

4. Social analysis of oppression and power

5. Community story and vision

    a. Anthropology: What kind of persons?

    b. Ecclesiology: What kind of community?

    c. Doctrine of God: What kind of God?[7]

---

[6]For comparison, see my method for practical theology in James Poling and Donald E. Miller, eds., *Foundations for a Practical Theology of Ministry* (Nashville: Abingdon Press, 1985), 69ff.

[7]These ethical components can be compared with other attempts to develop an ethical method: James M. Gustafson (*Theology and Christian Ethics* [Philadelphia: United Church Press, 1974]) emphasizes the importance of the moral agent, or the human self as moral agent. Archie Smith (127) has five components to his ethical method: action, selfhood, reflection, praxis, and post-critical reflection. The last is an addition to the above list. As I understand him, he means reflection on the ethical methodology itself, which needs to be identified in order to account for the critique of marginalized groups that are excluded when the terms of the ethical discussion itself are established by those in power, those who represent the dominant ideology. June O'Connor (in Andolsen et al., 265ff.) has four levels: 0 = Ground level, experience itself. 1 = Reflection on daily experience: (a) collecting facts; (b) seeking wisdom–reason, history, feelings; (c) anticipating future implications (imagining alternatives); (d) decision, judging. 2 = Worldview, metaphysic, vision of life; whether we are free agents, extent of relationality, loyalty, and authority. 3 = Epistemology–How do I know what I know? What are your sources of knowledge and why do you trust them? Her emphasis on epistemology is similar to Smith's "postcritical reflection." I also like her organization into four levels with a simplified ethical method at level 1 that seems to correspond to most decision making that people actually do. When level 1 does not work, we examine assumptions; and when assumptions are inadequate, the issue of epistemology and authority becomes central. This is crucial again for marginalized groups who are excluded when the rules of the ethical conversation are limited to those in power. James Nelson (*Embodiment: An Approach to Sexuality and Christian Theology* [Minneapolis: Augsburg, 1978], 118–26) has seven categories: self as decision-maker; basic religious beliefs; styles of decision making (obedience, aspiration, response); method, motive, intention, nature of the act itself, consequences; facts and interpretation; norms, principles, rules; church as a moral community. Although there are similarities to what we have discussed so far, this list has several interesting suggestions. Facts and interpretation are important; motive and intention put things slightly differently; and church as moral community I like. Carol Robb (in Andolsen et al., 211ff.) has a list of nine: starting point for ethics (women's experience); historical situation; oppression; loyalties; theory of value; mode of decision making (deontology, teleology, situational); source of authority; presuppositions of ethical action; motives. I like her list and consider that it highlights several items that are only implicit in my list, such as loyalties, source of authority, motives, and starting point.

Ethical Reflection on the Case of Tamar

How does this method work in terms of the case of Tamar? The story begins as Amnon *decides* to do evil. The story is remarkable in terms of recording his decision-making process. Amnon follows his desire and ignores Tamar when she appeals to the ethical tradition of Israel. The rules of that society are revealed in Tamar's appeal to the practical problems she faces because of this abuse: Do not violate me; do not behave like a beast; how will I bear my disgrace? The norms Tamar cites are the implied codes about acting according to love rather than lust, being truthful in one's speech, being loyal in one's family. The *story and vision* of Israel is about a people who are trying to be faithful to God, yet are constantly falling short. Where is God in this story? In the honest integrity of Tamar who does not give in to gross evil? In the loyalty of Absalom who avenges his sister even though it may cost him the throne? The paradox of this story is that evil has real, destructive consequences, and that human courage cannot be totally destroyed by evil. God has created a world in which genuine evil exists (the desire and behavior of Amnon), yet God is one who acts with courage in the face of evil (the clear moral vision of Tamar), thus giving us courage to face the evil we have experienced.

This story reveals a *human nature* that is capable of great evil and great courage. Amnon was overcome by desire because he lacked the strength to face his deep loneliness and pain. Tamar knew her experience was evil and fought for her integrity. David was a coward. Absalom was loyal to Tamar but devious in terms of his other motives for power. The story is a tragedy on the individual level because the good in humans is mostly overcome by evil.

In this story we see a *faith community* that is unable to transcend its limitations. Their devalued view of women and overvalued view of men led to misperceptions of power and justice issues. Remarkably, the narrator preserves a thread of decency in Tamar and Absalom, but this thread is unable to win the day. A community that cannot face its own injustice and evil will be destroyed from the inside.

God is not particularly inspiring here. There is no clap of thunder and justice rolling down like water. Tamar is dropped from the story (though her memory is revived by Absalom's daughter). The big concern of the next chapter is whether Absalom will be allowed home after David has some time to forget Amnon's murder, and a female prophet enables David to welcome him home. But justice delayed is justice denied. Justice seems to be denied here. Where is God when justice needs to be done? There is a certain insensitivity in God according to this story, which all victims of injustice understand.

Liberationists say that the starting point for ethics should be the experience of the oppressed. To our generation, this story reveals how women are victimized by individual men and by a patriarchical society. The deceit that traps Tamar shows the evil of some men and the complicity of other men. And the story seems to shift from the abuse of a woman to a drama between men. The partial sensitivity in Absalom to women's experience is lost, and patriarchy is firmly reestablished, even for the narrator. Yet the community remembered the story for us.

Phyllis Trible calls this a text of terror because of the terror Tamar experienced on behalf of all women. Yet the story has been frequently repeated without the full terror being identified. How do we know evil? How do we know love? What evils in our midst are we ignorant of in our drive to prove our ideas correct? The knowledge of good and evil is a continual human problem. We must know the difference, or else evil patterns become systemic. But history reveals that the human effort to know good and evil is badly bungled. We must continually risk ourselves in commitment and trust, knowing that our best efforts will be ambiguous. We must listen to those who suffer for clues to the injustice of the distribution of social power. If Tamar had lived in a just society that was not naive about evil, she could have told her story and been protected and/or vindicated in public.

Ethics for pastoral care is about the relation of suffering and power. We who are pastoral care specialists have been called by God to minister to individuals and communities to alleviate suffering. But we are under constant pressure by our privileged social location to maintain the established systems of power and the suffering that is endorsed and hidden by these systems. Whether we can be liberated from our middle-class bondage depends on whether we become more self-critical and more sensitive to the deviant communities that protest current power arrangements. This means a critical examination of the moral horizon of our perceptions and our love. The sufferings of women, of blacks, of abused children, of the poor have been hidden for too long by both church and society. The ethical calling of the pastoral care movement is to attend to suffering as a critique of a social order that is unjust.

4

Pastoral Care with African American Victims and Survivors of Abuse[1]

written in collaboration with Toinette Eugene

"You are a beautiful child of God.
You don't deserve to be abused."

(The comforting words of a black pastor
to a victim of family violence.)

Pastoral caregivers must be aware of the many intercultural issues involved in sexual and domestic violence so they are prepared to respond to all persons in our churches and neighborhoods. I include this chapter on pastoral care with African American families to sensitize the readers to persons of African descent, and by extension, to help readers gain intercultural competence that will extend care to other cultural groups. Given the history of slavery and racism in the United States, there are persistent stereotypes that African Americans are more violent than other groups and that the church cannot effectively help African American victims and perpetrators. Such prejudices distort the reality that abuse exists in all cultural groups and that intercultural sensitivity is required to provide care in situations of violence. This chapter discusses many of the difficult

¹Original version published with Toinette Eugene as "Pastoral Interventions with Victims and Survivors of Abuse," in *Balm for Gilead: Pastoral Care for African American Families Experiencing Abuse* (Nashville: Abingdon Press, 1998).

59

issues regarding male violence in African American families and suggests strategies for effective interventions.

In the black community, pastors and other church leaders are more likely to know about family violence than other professionals, including doctors, teachers, social workers, and counselors. This means that the ability of the pastor to correctly understand and intervene in abusive families is important for the physical, emotional, and spiritual health of the black community. The goal of this chapter is to outline appropriate pastoral care that will provide support for victims of black family violence.

Pastoral Care with Victims and Survivors

Every situation of black family violence is complex and challenging for pastoral intervention. Providing protective space for a person who is being stalked and threatened with death is different from trying to help a child who has known physical or sexual violence his or her whole life. In this section, we cannot cover all the variables and complexities that a pastoral team might encounter in its pastoral care ministries to black families. We hope to provide some principles of assessment, referral, and ongoing support that could make the difference between life and death for some people.[2]

One of the obstacles to good pastoral care with black persons experiencing abuse is misdiagnosis. Persons seeking care often present with a problem other than abuse: an ill or bad child, a lack of parenting skills, a breakdown of couple communication, the effects of economic or other crises, alcohol and drug abuse, and so forth. Although these and other problems may well be present in black families, we are suggesting that, when violence is present, stopping the violence must take precedence over other problems as the primary diagnosis. This involves a shift in the way most religious leaders learned about pastoral care, because family violence has too often been ignored as a presenting problem.

---

[2]For further study on issues of family violence in African American families, see Robert H. Hampton, ed., *Violence in the Black Family: Correlates and Consequences* (Lexington, Mass.: Lexington Books, 1987); Evelyn C. White, ed., *The Black Women's Health Book: Speaking for Ourselves* (Seattle: Seal Press, 1994); Pearl Cleague, *Mad At Miles: A Blackwoman's Guide to Truth* (Southfield, Mich.: Cleague Group, 1989); White, *Chain, Chain, Change: For Black Women Dealing with Physical and Emotional Abuse* (Seattle: Seal Press, 1985).

After hearing the story and allowing the possibility of its truth, the next step to providing safety is to ask what must be done if the complaint is true. That is, what steps must be taken to ensure the safety of the victim and to begin a process of evaluation and referral? At this point, pastors and other religious leaders in the black community are usually confronted with their lack of skills and resources for providing the needed safety. Church leaders, including pastors, seldom have enough authority to intervene in the sanctity of the family. Laws and mores in the United States provide strong protection for families to engage in their private lives without interference from neighbors, friends, and institutions, including the government. It is not likely that a pastor would be able to remove a child or other vulnerable person from a family against that family's will, and it would usually not be proper to do so. Therefore, church leaders within the black community need to see themselves as part of a larger community network concerned for the health of children and all citizens in the community.[5]

When a child is in danger because of sexual or physical abuse, then a crime has been committed. More than just the church's interests are at stake, and the black church must work in cooperation with legal and social service authorities. At this point, the normal suspicion of the police, legal, and welfare systems come into play in the black community. This suspicion takes several forms: Will the child receive the protection she or he needs from the police? Will the police create another trauma in the child's life? Will the involvement of the legal system unfairly jeopardize the family and their ability to survive? Will the social service system treat the family with respect so they can deal with their problems? However well founded these suspicions are, religious leaders also need to ask another set of questions: What will happen to the child if the legal and social service systems are not alerted? What help will the family get if they are not forced by law to face their problems? The precarious life and health of a black child in a violent family should force pastoral leaders to figure out how to use the legal and social service systems in ways

---

[5]A good discussion of the need to use "emergency response agencies" in the black community is found in White, *Chain, Chain, Change,* 36–45.

that protect black children rather than asking the children to bear the brunt of society's racism.[6]

When the health or life of an adult is at risk because of family violence, the laws are often more ambiguous than with child abuse. In some cases, physical or sexual assault within the family is a crime that can be reported. New legislative initiatives in some states now mean that perpetrators of family violence can be arrested and tried without a decision to "press charges" by the victim. When fairly applied, such laws shift the burden of responsibility for confronting the perpetrator from the victim to the larger community where it belongs. However, many archaic laws continue to be based on the privacy of the family and the rights of adults to "discipline" their children, and, in some cases, for husbands to enforce their leadership and their so-called conjugal rights on their wives. Until such laws are changed, adult violence in the black family will be treated differently from street violence.

The legal system is usually a necessary but not sufficient resource for dealing with black family violence. Fortunately, other resources are available for pastoral leaders to use. Twenty-four-hour hotlines for the protection of battered women and rape victims are available in most communities. Pastoral leaders can call these numbers for advice on how to handle difficult situations, and victims themselves can be encouraged to call. During these calls, a trained person will listen, provide emotional support, offer alternative courses of action, and identify community resources for crisis intervention. Among other available resources are shelters for battered women. Shelters are safe houses with trained staff and security systems where women and children can go when their lives and health are at risk. In most cases the exact location of the shelter is secret, and in all cases, the shelter has a relationship with the police department for emergency help when needed. Pastoral leaders should know the hotline and shelter phone numbers and should invite shelter and other leaders to do workshops on black family violence for the congregation. Successful referral to a shelter by a pastoral leader depends on whether he or she knows the shelter staff and has confidence in its staff and program.

---

[6]See White, *Chain, Chain, Change,* especially chapter 6, "The Legal System: Blacks and the Legal System," 46–53.

Finding a shelter with expertise in intercultural and interclass issues is very important for most black families.[7]

In addition to the legal and social service systems, pastoral leaders need to know something about working with the health system. Often a pastoral leader will first learn about family violence because there is a health crisis. It may be a crisis of physical health that requires immediate attention by a family physician or in an emergency room. Whenever a pastoral leader suspects physical injury, he or she should request a detailed assessment of medical need. Often victims have been terrorized into hiding or minimizing their injuries for fear of further harm. For example, one perpetrator told his victim that if she sought medical help or talked to anyone, he would kill her. It is not unusual for battered women or children to have broken bones or serious internal organ damage and yet be afraid of going to see a doctor. Pastoral leaders must know the available health services in the community and which ones have skill and understanding of family violence issues.[8] Some studies have shown that 25 percent or more of emergency room visits by adult women are caused by family violence.[9]

Some child and adult victims present themselves to pastoral leaders in a mental health crisis. Symptoms such as panic, high anxiety, depression, paranoia, suicidal ideation, or fragmentation of the personality may be linked to family violence.[10] Pastoral leaders must be skilled in recognizing such psychological symptoms and be able to connect them to family violence in the present or the past. There is an unfortunate tradition within the black church of dismissing some symptoms as being "all in the head," self-pity, or irresponsibility. Religious resources such as prayer and Bible study can be important for ongoing pastoral care, but they must not be used as the only pastoral response in a severe mental health crisis. Rather, in addition to prayer, pastoral leaders must know how to make effective referrals to emergency rooms, psychiatrists, and community mental health centers. Although these institutions are not always sensitive to the needs of African

---

[7]See Fortune, *Violence in the Family.*

[8]White, *Black Woman's Health Book.*

[9]Surgeon General Antonia C. Novello, address to an American Medical Association press conference on violence, New York City, January 16, 1992.

[10]Herman, 33–50.

American families, pastoral leaders must investigate which places are reliable and learn how to get the help that people really need. If there are no good mental health resources in the community, this could become a long-term project for the black church. We must not deny black people the resources they need for safety and healing. Religion and mental health can be complementary forms of healing for people in black communities.

Sometimes victims of family violence present safety needs that are rooted in self-destructive behaviors in addition to, or years after, violent experiences. Judith Herman, a psychiatrist in Boston, shows how the long-term consequences of family violence affect the personality development of children and adults.[11] Violence, especially when it exists over many years, results in tearing down the personality. Children who grow up in violent homes where they have been beaten and/or sexually assaulted over and over again develop personalities with internalized violence. Many of the self-destructive symptoms in adults are the result of chronic family violence. Herman also suggests that adults who did not experience violence as children can be psychologically damaged if they are trapped in an intimate relationship that includes battering.[12] The results of a malformed or fragmented personality are frightening to see. Drug and alcohol addiction is a common form of self-abuse because these substances numb the psychological pain and create a sense of euphoria that hides the reality of one's suffering. Alcohol and violence can be a lethal combination in a black family. Some survivors of violence use alcohol and drugs to numb the painful memories and ongoing dysfunction of past abuse. Alcohol and drugs are self-destructive behaviors that tear down physical health, destroy one's ability to work, and often lead to encounters with police, hospitals, and work supervisors. Other forms of self-destructive behaviors include self-mutilation (cutting parts of one's body with knives and razors), suicide attempts, reckless driving, fascination with guns and knives, reckless endangerment of the self in a variety of dangerous activities, or criminal activity. Some of these behaviors have addictive qualities that serve the psychological function of distracting a person from his or her inner pain, providing an

---

[11]Ibid., 166–68.
[12]Ibid.

illusion of bravado and potency, and denying and dissociating from the inner suffering caused by past violence. Whenever a pastoral leader encounters symptoms that are destructive of self or others, she or he should ask about a history of violent family or other relationships.

When pastoral leaders focus on safety first for the victims of violence, all of the above issues need to be taken into account: legal issues, social service resources, physical and mental health, and self-destructive behaviors. How can pastoral leaders intervene in a person's life to enhance safety from further violence? It may mean calling the police or child abuse hotline to report an abused child because criminal abuse has occurred. It may mean calling a hotline or shelter to find immediate safe housing and other services for adults and children. It may mean encouraging the person to seek medical attention for a physical or mental health problem. Finally, it may mean dealing realistically with the danger of self-destructive behaviors that could lead to violence and/or death. All these considerations must be in the mind of pastoral leaders when they encounter a situation of black family violence.

A corollary principle follows from the principle of safety first: Respect the agency of the victim. By the time a pastoral leader learns of a situation of black family violence, it has probably been going on for some time already. Usually the pastoral leader will not hear of a violent incident the very first time it occurs. This means that the victim has already survived other situations of violence. An important principle of crisis counseling is mobilizing the resources of the person seeking help. It is not enough to identify the emergency needs of the person. One must also identify the strengths of the person who has survived many things before. Part of pastoral assessment is learning how the person has coped with past crises and how these inner resources can be used in the present crisis.[13] Enacting the principle of supporting the agency of a care-seeker prevents pastoral leaders from feeling totally helpless themselves. Even with all the resources of the community—police, hospitals, community mental health centers, shelters, hotlines, counselors—the victim has choices that must be exercised. For example, a pastoral leader may decide that a victim must go to the emergency room of the local hospital, and then

---

[13]David Switzer, *Pastoral Care Emergencies* (New York: Paulist Press, 1989).

may be frustrated and angry when the victim refuses to go. The refusal of the victim to comply with the advice of a pastoral leader causes much confusion for the pastoral leader about the nature of family violence. If the victim refuses the pastoral advice, then one must ask what this means to the victim.

Why would a person refuse to follow the advice of a pastoral leader?

• The perpetrator may have threatened further harm for this course of action, which means that realistic fear is behind the refusal. Pastoral leaders must understand the level of terror and fear that is a part of the lives of victims. From the chair of the helpful professional, such terror might be hard to comprehend. Just think for a moment of how your life would change if someone were actively trying to kill or otherwise harm you. Then translate this feeling into respect for the agency of the victim you are trying to help. Mobilizing the resources of the victim depends on having respect for the resources that the victim brings to her or his situation.

• The person may have already tried a particular resource and was mistreated or ignored. Some battered black women have already been to the emergency room many times, and they know what kind of treatment they will receive there. This means victims often know more than the pastoral leader about the relative value of the available agencies on issues of violence. A black child may have already talked to the school social worker many times and was patronized and blamed for his or her problems. Victims of black family violence are often treated differently than other patients or clients because of personal and institutional discrimination. The pastoral leader must be flexible in developing a plan of action that is sensitive to the needs and resources of a particular person or family.

• The person may not have the inner resources to do what the pastoral leader wants. Violence and the threat of violence work because they disempower and damage the agency of the victim. After years of captivity and violence, the inner spirit of the person may need time for recovery of her or his strength. This does not mean that the person is weak, because tremendous strength may have been required to survive to this point. The pastoral leader must have respect for the person's own evaluation of his or her readiness for particular actions. What would be possible for someone who has not been a victim of violence may not be right for a victim who is trying to change her or his life circumstances.

In summary, "safety first" is a more complicated pastoral intervention than first appearances might suggest. "Safety first" reverses the usual approaches to pastoral care that emphasize the abilities of the person to take charge of her or his life. Rather, this principle recognizes the presence of real external and internal dangers that must be addressed. Believing the story of the victim for the moment and asking what must be done if the story is true initiate a form of crisis counseling that emphasizes assessment of the violence and empowering the victim through use of community resources. Respecting the agency of the victim means consulting with the previous experience of the victim in designing and following through on a plan of action.

Mourning, Healing, and Reconnection[14]

For many victims of black family violence, both children and adults, safety is an ongoing issue. Some black families are dangerous, and pastoral leaders need to constantly monitor the relative danger for victims. There is no such thing as absolute safety for survivors of family violence. Rather, the internal and external struggle to live in safety continues for the rest of one's life. Having faith in God means learning to live in a world with only relative safety. But for victims and survivors of family violence, the trust needed for faith in God has been shattered. Learning how to live in a world of relative safety without inner confidence in the trustworthiness of the self and other people is a challenging task. It is important for a pastoral leader to remember the reality of life-shattering terror and fear that is a lifelong struggle for many black people, and to keep vigilant for dangers in real families and other intimate relationships. Pastoral leaders should not quickly interpret a survivor's fears as signs of weakness rather than pay attention to real danger.

---

[14]The ideas in this section are informed by the discussion of healing in Herman, 175ff.

When relative safety has been established, the second stage of pastoral care begins, a stage that Judith Herman calls a time of remembering, mourning, and reconnection. Pastoral leaders must continue to support and work in cooperation with other persons and agencies during this stage: with counselors, social workers, therapy groups, educational programs, and so forth. One must resist the temptation to see the black church as the total answer to the needs of victims and survivors after the initial crisis has passed. There is wisdom in the communities of survivors and professional caregivers that can complement the religious community for survivors.

After a child has been rescued from violence in a family, there remains much pastoral care to be done. It is not unusual for the child to continue to live with other family members, either with extended family, with a single parent without the perpetrator, or, in some cases, even in the same home with the perpetrator. Depending on what kind of intervention occurred, the perpetrator may be in jail, separated because of a non-contact court order, allowed supervised visitation with the child or children, or closely monitored while living in the home. The most dangerous situation for a child-victim of physical or sexual violence is unmonitored contact with the perpetrator. In such cases, the pastoral leader should attempt to maintain a regular relationship with the child in order to nurture the trust needed for the child to be able to tell again when violence occurs.

Assuming that one result of reporting abuse is a breakup or radical transformation of the black family, loss is one of the issues facing children. All children form strong emotional attachments with caregiving adults. Abused children are often forced to rely on the same persons who abuse them. Such attachments are necessarily very strong because they must incorporate the abuse as well as the caregiving. This means that the loss children experience when the family breaks up is actually exaggerated. They have learned to rely on an abusive parent and mistrust other adults who failed to protect them. One problem of pastoral leaders is misdiagnosis of this loss and a failure to appreciate the importance of the child's attachment-seeking behavior. It is hard for someone outside the black family to understand the strong attachments that hold abusive families together. When the pastoral leader distances from the perpetrator as a way of handling the horror of his or her crimes, it can be hard to accept the fact that the child is still attached to that person. In some cases, the primary attachment is not with the perpetrator, but with the non-abusing parent. The pastoral leader may also be angry at this parent for refusing to act on the available information and protect the child. Now that the perpetrator is gone, the pastoral leader may have trouble understanding the attachment of the child for the non-abusing parent. But one must remember that these were the only adults available in the child's life, and attachment to them was the difference between life and death. Children who cannot attach to some caregiving adult do not survive. So even if the available adult is less than ideal, the child has little choice but to become dependent on him or her for survival.

The result of loss of attachment figures is mourning–strong emotional reactions such as shock, numbness, dissociation, depression, shame, anger, and guilt. Such feelings in their acute stages can interfere with the normal tasks of childhood, such as paying attention in class, doing homework, forming friendships, engaging in free play. It is crucial for the recovery of children from experiences of black family abuse to have safe places to deal with these feelings. The typical peer group will withdraw from children who are so angry that they pick fights and arguments every day. Teachers in school become frustrated with children who are too depressed to understand history or math lessons and never do their homework. Parental caregivers at home often do not understand why children have nightmares, refuse to eat prepared meals, and would rather watch TV than play with friends. Experienced counselors who can engage in play therapy with younger children and talk in age-appropriate ways with adolescents are important resources for children who are mourning the loss of family and other things. Church leaders should support counseling for black children after they have suffered the trauma of abuse and loss of important relationships.

Similar principles also apply to black adult-survivors. Some adults remember the trauma of childhood abuse during a crisis in their lives, such as divorce, illness, loss of job, death of a parent or child, and so forth. The unresolved feelings from the past rise up and demand attention. Other adults are thrust into a process of mourning when they have been battered in marriage or other intimate relationships. In spite of the perspective of friends and family who are often ready for the person to reorganize and get on with their lives, survivors themselves are often caught in a period of mourning that takes precedence over everything else. When one has lost his or her self-image and important relationships, these losses trigger the stages of mourning that must be attended to. Some survivors, to comply with social pressure, try to ignore or abbreviate the period of mourning.

The wisdom of pastoral care has taught us that mourning delayed is mourning made complicated. Acute depression, shame, anger, and guilt turn into dissociation, low self-esteem, chronic rage, and self-blame, which, when they become life patterns, are difficult to change. Good pastoral caregivers can provide safe space and resources for mourning. For most survivors, this mourning requires periods of moratorium from normal social responsibilities. Survivors in acute grieving may need respite from parenting responsibilities, from regular work, from leadership tasks. Some may need extended retreats or intensive residential treatment to deal with the accumulated and delayed reaction to the traumas caused by violence.

The biblical image of the black church as a sanctuary from violence describes the safe space needed for many children and adult survivors of family violence. In times of war, soldiers could escape death by going to the sanctuary of a church, where they were protected from their political enemies. We need to recapture this idea for survivors of family violence. When a person has been physically and emotionally damaged by physical or sexual violence in a family, that person should be able to find safety in the church. After relative safety has been secured, the church should be a safe place to mourn the losses that occurred because of family violence and begin to make a plan for a new life. Pastoral leaders, in cooperation with community resources, can make a big difference in the lives of people with such a theology of sanctuary. Rather than breaking up families, the black church would be leading the way in providing a foundation for sound families in black communities.

Healing and reconnection are closely related to mourning. Healing is a result of good mourning as a person acknowledges the losses of the past, accepts the reality of a broken present, and begins to hope for a new future. Healing means understanding and accepting the traumas of the past and their consequences. Past trauma from family violence means that the persons who were trusted and loved in the past betrayed and tried to destroy the person. Giving up the attachments and idealizations about these people is one part of mourning. Healing means understanding and accepting one's own helplessness to change things in the past, and giving oneself credit for the forms of resistance, whether they were effective or not. Healing means acknowledging the ways in which the family violence was internalized and became a self-destructive pattern of attitudes and behaviors. Healing means letting go of the idealized illusions one had about life and relationships with others and accepting a realistic future without these illusions. There are many excellent books written by survivors and therapists about these processes of healing.[15] Some persons with much experience estimate that the mourning and healing stages after prolonged and/or severe family violence require five to seven years of fairly constant work in group and individual therapy. Understanding the importance and requirements of this process would change the way pastoral leaders see their pastoral care within the context of the black family. In a society that expects instant solutions to complex problems, the church must be a significant and reliable force that provides safe and stable space and time for persons who are healing from family violence. Such a witness would give all of us the time and space we need to be the sometimes fragile and yet resilient children of God that we are.

Reconnection refers to the process of forming a new network of interpersonal and familial relationships that do not include violence.[16] For some black children and adults who have known nothing but violence in their families, this process is a constant discovery of new possibilities that could not even be imagined before. For others who experienced traumatic violence in spite of their best efforts to avoid it–for example, a woman from a nonviolent home who becomes the victim of a batterer in marriage–the process of reconnection means recovering hope in a previous world that has been shattered by threats of injury and death.

---

[15]Ellen Bass and Laura Davis, *The Courage to Heal: A Guide for Women Survivors of Child Sexual Abuse* (New York: Harper and Row, 1988).

[16]For a good discussion of reconnection in African American families, see Nancy Boyd-Franklin, *Black Families in Therapy: A Multisystems Approach* (New York: Guilford, 1989).

One of the biggest losses from family violence is the ability to trust. Babies are born into the world with an ability to trust. They accept whatever love, food, and comfort they receive from their adult caregivers. If the accompanying price of receiving these necessary resources for life is violence, babies and young children adapt however they must to survive. Babies in violent homes who are not resilient enough to survive violence from their caregivers die. Every child in a violent home who survives deserves respect and care. But the ability to trust is damaged in the process. Even adults who experience violence much later in life go through extreme trauma. No matter how much self-esteem and self-respect one has, the threat of death, injury, and/or sexual assault undermines one's trust in other people and in the world. Many people who have been victims of various kinds of violence will never be able to recover the sense of God-given trust they had when they entered for the first time into the world. Lack of trust because of violence is one of the leading causes of self-destructive and antisocial behavior as well as general unhappiness in the world. This means that recovering a sense of trust is one of the most important and most difficult aspects of healing for survivors.[17]

How does a survivor of black family violence learn to trust again? Although there are many techniques for learning to trust, the principle of pastoral care is simple: Trust is learned in relationships with people who are trustworthy. When one's world has been shattered by the betrayal of trust by family members, such as parents and intimate partners, trust in people is difficult to establish. Trust is built up again slowly, in small step after small step, by interacting with persons who are trustworthy. Time after time, survivors have reported to us that their trust in people was built up, not just when everything was going well, but when someone they were beginning to trust handled a conflict or difficult incident with empathy and honesty.

Judith Herman summarizes the wisdom of the survivor movements when she says that therapy and support groups are often crucial components of the tasks of reconnection. Some of the

---

[17]For good discussions of helping individuals and families recover trust, see the work of Edward Wimberly, *African American Pastoral Care* (Nashville: Abingdon Press, 1991). See also by Wimberly, *Pastoral Care in the Black Church* (Chicago: University of Chicago Press, 1978); *Pastoral Counseling and Spiritual Values: A Black Point of View* (Nashville: Abingdon Press, 1982); *Using Scripture in Pastoral Counseling* (Nashville: Abingdon Press, 1994).

most intense and private moments in healing are best done in the safety of one-to-one therapeutic relationships. Some are best done in groups of survivors who can learn from one another and work out their trust issues with others who understand only too well what healing from family violence involves.[18]

What is the role of the black church during the stage of reconnection and recovering trust? This leads us to revise the above principle of pastoral care: Trust is learned when the black church community is trustworthy. This principle suggests two things: first, that the black church has often not been trustworthy with victims and survivors of family violence; second, that the black church should become a trustworthy community for victims and survivors of family violence.

First, the black church has often not been trustworthy with victims and survivors of family violence. In fact, the church bears some moral responsibility for the widespread prevalence of family violence in our communities. As teachers and pastors of the church, we have heard many horror stories about the inappropriate and damaging things pastoral leaders have said to children and adults who are caught in violent families.[19]

One mistake many pastoral leaders have made is refusing to believe the victim and defending the perpetrator. Pastors have said such things as the following: *Are you sure he really meant to hurt you? What makes you think your child is telling the truth? I know Deacon Jones; he would never do the things you have accused him of.* According to many survivors of family violence, such responses often prevent the truth from coming out. If a victim has been beaten or sexually assaulted by a member of the family, and then the pastor says it couldn't have happened, where does a victim go? Many survivors have returned to the family in silence for years and decades after such an event. Such a response undermines trust.

Another mistake made by pastoral leaders is to blame the victim and sympathize with the perpetrator. Pastors have said such things as the following: *What did you do to make him mad? That child*

---

[18]Herman, especially chapter 11, "Commonality." She includes sections on groups for safety, groups for remembrance and mourning, and groups for reconnection, 214–36.

[19]For further discussion of the typical mistakes pastors make with victims and survivors of abuse, see Marie Fortune and James Poling, "Calling to Accountability: The Church's Response to Abusers," in *Violence against Women and Children: A Christian Theological Sourcebook,* ed. Carol Adams and Marie Fortune (New York: Continuum, 1995), especially 452.

has always been seductive. No wonder she got her father into this trouble. What do you think will happen to your mother if this story gets out? Don't you think she has enough trouble already? The tendency to blame the person who is complaining and feel sorry for the perpetrator undermines the sense of trust. Some survivors report that it is very hurtful when the perpetrator of their violence is still a respected leader in the church years after disclosure, while the victim had to leave the church to get the support she needed.[20]

Another mistake some churches have made is rushing to talk about forgiveness and reconciliation for the perpetrator without dealing with issues of truth and justice for the survivor. Even at the point of first disclosure of violence, some pastors have encouraged a victim of family violence to forgive, to pray harder, and to make things right at home. Years after family violence has been known to others, some churches still withhold fellowship from the survivor because she is angry and unforgiving. What is missing is the willingness of the people to empathize with the victim/survivor in her struggle for healing and justice, and to understand the harm that was done. The double tragedy in many black churches is that other survivors are listening to these conversations and choosing to stay in dangerous situations in order to please the members of the church.[21]

These are some of the ways that church leaders are untrustworthy in their relationships with black victims and survivors of family violence. The good news is that our congregations and pastoral leaders can learn to do better. The Christian gospel is not a timid gospel about cheap forgiveness and the reign of the powerful. Rather, the gospel is about Jesus' love for the common people who were oppressed by the economic and political structures of his day, about his compassion for their illnesses and struggles with demons, and about his commitment unto death for the sake of justice and love. Family violence is a frightening reality in our lives, but we follow a Leader who had to suffer in his day, and we count as ancestors the slaves who suffered but found comfort in Jesus as Lord and Savior. The gospel has the

---

[20] Annie Imbens and Ineke Jonker, *Christianity and Incest* (Minneapolis: Fortress Press, 1992).

[21] See Marie Fortune, "Forgiveness: The Last Step," in Adams and Fortune, 201–6.

resources to help us understand and respond with empathy and trustworthiness to the victims and survivors of family violence.

How Can the Church Become a Trustworthy Community for Victims and Survivors of Family Violence?

(a) The church can respond with truth-telling about black family violence. The church has heard the stories of family violence for many decades. Domestic and sexual abuse are not new. It is time to tell the truth about what is happening. Telling the truth is one form of being trustworthy. Truth-telling allows the victims of violence to speak up in church and tell their stories. The shame of family violence should not be on the heads of the victims and survivors. The shame should be on the perpetrators and on the silent community who has known the truth but has protected those who abuse others. The church needs to reverse the power relationships so the most vulnerable can be free to tell the truth about their lives and have their stories believed.

(b) The church can respond with confession about its complicity with family violence. The church has often refused to listen to its children tell about how they are beaten and sexually assaulted. The church has refused to listen to teenagers who are beaten and raped when they participate in the dating rituals in our schools and communities. The church has refused to hear black women who have been beaten by their husbands. The church has refused to listen to older black adults complain about being mistreated by caregivers and relatives when they are too weak to protect themselves. The church bears a share of the guilt for the prevalence of black family violence, and our guilt is relieved by confession and repentance.

(c) The church can educate itself about the issues of black family violence in order to have a context for understanding the stories of victims and survivors. Religious leaders who do not know the facts about family violence make inappropriate pastoral responses to victims and survivors of violence. Parents do not beat children because the children are bad. Adults do not molest children because the children are seductive. Men do not batter women because women are rebellious. These are myths that serve to protect the perpetrators and blame the victims of violence.

Pastoral leaders must educate themselves about the rationalizations perpetrators use to justify their behaviors. This would go a long way toward earning the trust of victims and survivors and making the church into a trustworthy community.

In summary, pastoral interventions with victims and survivors of family violence are complex and challenging. "Safety first" must be the motto whenever vulnerable people are threatened with violence. This means learning how to do crisis counseling, empowering victims, mobilizing resources, and dealing with the long-term changes in our churches that survivors deserve. Mourning, healing, and reconnection describe the various stages of recovery from the consequences of violence. We have suggested attitudes, knowledge, and skills that pastoral leaders need to respond with compassion and justice to the pastoral care needs of those who suffer family violence.

5

Male Violence in Central America[1]

Written in collaboration with Brenda Consuelo Ruiz

Intercultural research on male violence against women and children is a complex issue because every culture has its own particular ways of organizing power according to gender, race, and class. Men and women in intimate relationships relate quite differently to one another from culture to culture. Parents understand the tasks of nurture and socialization according to the norms of their religion and the history of their families. Culture shapes the normative ideas of sexuality, aggression, hierarchy, and religion in ways that are partly unique. In my search for intercultural understanding, I have made studies of African American and Latino(a) cultures through participant observation and careful consultation.

The following chapter follows a somewhat different format than all the other chapters in this volume because I am trying to report accurately on my experience in Nicaragua without overreaching my level of understanding. This means that my subjectivity is much more apparent, and my observations are much more tentative. However, I believe that this way of proceeding preserves the respect I have gained for the complexity of issues of male violence in Nicaragua. I share these thoughts and feelings with my readers to provide a bridge into another culture.[2]

---

[1]Original version published as "Family Violence in Nicaragua," *The Journal of Pastoral Care* 49, no. 4 (Winter 1995): 417–22.

[2]My further reflections about male violence in Nicaragua are written in *Render Unto God: Economic Vulnerability, Family Violence, and Pastoral Theology* (St. Louis: Chalice Press, 2002).

In August 1994, I made my fourth trip to Nicaragua to do intercultural research on family and gender violence in a situation of postwar trauma and extreme poverty. The following is an edited version of my personal journal during the trip. I share it to encourage our solidarity with the suffering and hope of Christians in Central America and to understand the intercultural context for male violence against women.

> *Saturday, Aug. 6, Managua.* I am sitting in the living room of our apartment at Seminario Teologico Bautista (STB, the Baptist Seminary)[3] after a restless first night of attempted sleep. In front of me on the table is a basket of fresh fruit that greeted my son and me on our arrival–a pineapple, bananas, mangoes, and a large papaya–a beautiful sight. My host is Brenda Consuelo Ruiz, a Nicaraguan pastoral counselor who teaches part-time at STB.
>
> Jenny Atlee and her five-year-old daughter, Carmen, met us last night. She works as a volunteer for the Quakers and helped plan a conference for former prisoners and leaders of the police on "Alternatives to Violence." She said the first crops planted in May have totally failed. The people are hungry and there is no food they can afford.
>
> *Monday, Aug. 8, Acahualinca, Managua.* This morning we joined a CEPAD tour of Barrio Acahualinca. (CEPAD is the Protestant Council of Churches.)[4] About one thousand families live by the city dump, where they sort through the garbage for anything that can be used or resold. From our bus we saw several hundred people going through the new trash. There is a whole system of shoulder bags and carts for the purpose, and we saw children sitting by carts waiting for their parents to return. Brenda said there is bribery and prostitution as drivers further exploit the people. There is frequently violence and even murder over "valuable trash." It was one of the most awful sights I have ever seen. The people are surviving the only way they can.

---

[3]The Baptist Seminary (Seminario Teologico Bautista), Apartado 2555, Managua, Nicaragua, Deborah Garcia, president.

[4]CEPAD (Nicaragua Council of Churches, Consejo de Iglesias Evangelicas Pro-Alianza Denominacional), Apartado 3091, Del Puente Leon, 11/2 cuadra arriba, Managua, Nicaragua.

On the bus, a woman from Palestine asked me, "You are a theologian. Where is God in this?" I said, "I can't see God either. God must be in the will of the people to survive this evil."

Some of the women leaders told us about their school and a feeding program. The government has provided some land, but the parents are forced to pay for teachers and textbooks. We visited the children, who were being served lunch. About seventy children were gathered under a shelter with five women cooking; six older girls were supervising the children. The children were very orderly and were singing and clapping as they waited for the food. It was a beautiful, sad sight. Lunch was rice, beans, squash, a little beef, and an enriched drink. CEPAD supplies the food, but volunteers run the program and do the cooking. I was impressed with the energy and drive for life in the children. They have as much right to live as any other human being, yet they lack the resources they need to thrive/survive.

We visited a reforestation project. The community is trying to plant trees to save a lagoon near the dump, and they are making progress. Actually, the dump is part of Lake Managua, though it is now raised dozens of feet above the lake. The mayor of Managua said that as the dump expands, he will not protect the lagoon. The reforestation project is an act of hope in the midst of evil. The whole visit was very moving–seeing the energy and activity of the people in the most horrible of situations trying to create community in the absence of resources. The sadness in the eyes of the women and the children shows both suffering and hope.

Aug. 8, Managua. In the afternoon I returned to STB to meet with President Don Carlos Vallagra. I presented gifts, discussed finances, and asked about the seminary. Apparently, they have survived a serious financial crisis for this year and are trying to pay off an $8,000 deficit from last year. They graduated eleven students from the bachelor's program last year. Many students want to attend but have no money. The churches support the seminary but have no money because of the economic crisis in the country. I agreed to write a testimonial letter that STB can use in fundraising with United States seminaries and thirty other agencies.

Aug. 9, Managua, Seminario Teologico Bautista. I spoke in chapel today, and Luther Miguel, a student from the Atlantic Coast, translated. The text was Matthew 18:1–7 on children. I made a few comments on family violence and asked for responses. A male student said he has never run into this problem. A female student said there is lots of violence in Nicaragua, but the church is silent. Professor Ruben Pak asked about the relationship of violence in the family to the structural violence in the society. One student criticized the seminary for refusing to include several books on sexuality in the library. Brenda thought the discussion went well. At least there was a discussion, even though some of the men were defensive.

After speaking in chapel, I met with about ten students and pastors over lunch. I asked them to continue the discussion of chapel: (1) How does the church discuss the discipline of children and distinguish it from violence? (2) Are men more likely to engage in extreme violence than women? (3) At what age is a young woman considered an adult if she becomes pregnant? (4) What is the relationship between alcohol and violence? (5) What should the church do about family and gender violence?

Two women pastors were strong in saying that there is much violence in families and that the church does nothing about it. One sister told of a young boy who ran away from home with wounds on his back from beatings by his stepfather. He was gone for several days, and the whole family looked for him. When they found him, the stepfather beat him, the uncle beat him, and the mother beat him. In another case a man molested three daughters and got the youngest one pregnant. In another case a drunken father made his son climb a tree to get a coconut, and he fell and broke his arm. The church has no programs for these families. Some pastors use the biblical writings of Paul to teach the subordination of women, which contributes to violence.

Brenda asked me what a pastor should do if a wealthy member of the church is violent in the family. I said that dealing with violence always involves risk, but that some pastors must have courage to act so that things will change. I also talked about the sadness in situations where effective action cannot be taken because of family secrecy and lack of congregational support. One brother said that he excluded a deacon from all leadership activities because he mistreated his children. I said that he was courageous. Then I said that not acting also has consequences because the congregation is watching. If the pastor tolerates violence, it has a negative effect on the faith of the congregation. One sister said that pastors sometimes abuse their children because they are expected to be model children. It was a painful but good discussion, and Brenda was happy because these were all former students of hers.

Aug. 9, Managua. Discussion with AEDAF (The Evangelical Center for Family Pastoral Counseling) leaders, Brenda Ruiz, Madlyn West, and Mirna Rocha. We had a good, wide-ranging discussion on issues of gender and violence and pastoral counseling. They are feminist and aware of issues of family and gender violence and have been working for many years on these issues. The most common complaints from families are issues of parenting, especially with adolescents, and marital problems. Women have most of the responsibility for relationships and are most likely to seek counseling. Men are more likely to ask about work or unemployment. It is difficult to get men to come for family counseling because they consider this an area of privacy, and they have guilt and shame about their behaviors. Part of the problem is the lack of support in the culture for counseling, especially for men. Most counseling is brief and crisis-oriented. A lot of issues can be raised in brief counseling, but issues of family violence are not likely to be adequately addressed. They clearly see the issues of power and gender in family violence, but have inadequate models for long-term treatment of families with violence.

We talked some about doing education in the churches, encouraging pastors to mention violence from the pulpit in prayers and sermons and in Bible studies.

Madlyn said that much of the church's message is spiritualized and unrelated to the real problems of the people. We also talked about male and female pastors— male pastors are more likely to blame women for the violence of men, and there are too few female pastors to make a difference.

We talked some about a relationship between AEDAF and American Association of Pastoral Counselors. Brenda had an article published in *The Journal of Pastoral Care.*[5] They would like opportunities for support and collegiality from North America. I hope that their center can become affiliated with AAPC and that we can engage in a mutual exchange of training and support.

Aug. 15, 6:00 a.m., Achuapa. (About three hours from Managua, Achuapa is a small town in the mountains populated by farmers and peasants.) So much has happened that there hasn't been time to write anything. We arrived about 1:00 p.m. on Friday. Jenny had to clean the cabin because no one had been here for a while. Florentina de Maria, a local healer, came, and we walked around town. We stopped at an office where Flo made a call on the only telephone in town. The line was out because of rain, and we probably waited an hour until Flo was finished. We visited the *tienda campesina,* a store that is part of a regional cooperative. Then we went to Flo's house. In one room she has a row of five to six beds for patients. Five of us had diagnostic exams. She uses herbal teas, acupuncture, and encouragement to help people survive their illnesses. Her goal is to help the people become less dependent on North American medicine because it is expensive and undermines the integrity of the community.

Flo came over in the morning and told me her story. She told about having severe arthritis, being treated by the Japanese doctors and getting well, getting trained in Leon, being abandoned by her husband, and finally starting her practice of acupuncture and herbal medicine. I asked her

[5]Brenda Consuelo Ruiz, "Pastoral Counseling of Women in a Context of Intense Oppression," *The Journal of Pastoral Care* 48 (1994)163–68.

questions about family problems and violence against women. At first she said that violence was not a problem here, but after some discussion she gave many examples. She said she would like to have additional training in counseling because many people talk to her. I said I would try to return to talk with her again. Maybe I could bring the AEDAF staff next time to do a women's workshop.

Flo's life was transformed by her participation in the literacy campaign during the Sandinista Revolution. She didn't have a chance for an education before then. In some ways her life parallels the story of Nicaragua–the bright hopes of the revolution, the sickness of war and blockade, a personal experience of healing, and an ongoing ministry of healing others based on natural methods that are independent of the United States. She even seems to understand herself this way.

About 10:30 a.m. we went to Lagartillo. Much of the day we hung out at the home of Tina Perez. She prepared a lunch of rice, beans, tortillas, and hot tea. Sergio, a twenty-four-year-old man from Scotland, has come to give some money from people in Europe. He will spend about six weeks trying to decide how best to use the money. In the late afternoon, we went to a nearby mountain peak and talked for an hour. During the United States Contra War, Tina remembers planes bombing the mountains below us where the guerrillas were hiding. I asked Tina about her feelings about the future. She said she saw no signs of hope, especially since the people in Nicaragua are so divided and the economic oppression from the United States is so overwhelming. I said that perhaps it was a time of waiting. She said it is a time of sadness. The difference is whether there is a basis for external hope. I felt she was talking about a worldwide phenomenon.

Tina said she lost a son at age five and dreamed about him a lot, but then she felt he was OK, and she stopped dreaming of him. But she still dreams about her husband and fourteen-year-old daughter who were killed in a Contra attack on December 31, 1984. We visited the memorial on the spot where her daughter was killed by a mortar explosion. Tina said that they have a service every year on the anniversary. On the way back, a silver shower fell on us from a small cloud. The sun was brightly shining, and the rain was bright silver. We got wet. Tina said it was a holy rain.

Aug. 14, Sunday morning, in Achuapa. Jenny and I planned a workshop on family and sexual violence. Thirty Nicaraguans were there. I made a speech and several comments, but Jenny did most of the talking because of my language limitations.

The workshop was incredible. Jenny led with competence, and the discussion went well. The young men did most of the talking, with occasional contributions by one of the grandmothers, some of the women, and Amancio Perez, a leader in the Base Christian community. One of my goals was to see whether they could apply revolutionary principles about rich and poor and power to gender and the family. They had no trouble at all and were able to see that women and children are vulnerable in the family and should be protected by law and custom. I could find no ambivalence in the men about the need to stop male violence against women, which is very unusual in my experience.

We had planned two sociodramas to dramatize some of the actual situations in their context. Sociodramas, a series of dramatic role-plays that illustrate a local problem, were an important part of the literacy campaign during the 1980s and became a powerful tool for local education and action. The groups chose to illustrate two family problems. In the first, a husband was instructing his wife to do her work and stay at home while he was gone for several days. After he left, a health promoter from the Bloque came to get the family to attend a meeting. The husband returned and promised the health promoter he would be there. But after he left, he was emotionally abusive toward his wife, accused her of being interested in other men, threatened her with violence if she showed any such interest, and told her not to go to the meeting. The actors were trying to illustrate how many people are cooperative in public but abusive and uncooperative in private.

In the second sociodrama, the husband was drinking. He came home and let his son go out without supervision, but forced his daughter to stay home and work. After he left, the daughter ran away from home. When the husband came back and found the daughter gone, he beat his wife and blamed her for not controlling the children the way he wanted. Both sociodramas were clear examples of male power and control enforced by violence. Flo said later that the sociodramas were excellent ways to communicate the ideas discussed in the workshop. At the end Amancio gave a moving speech about a recent teenage suicide in the community and how parents should be more open to their children when they have problems. It was a moving conclusion to the workshop. We ended by singing *Nicaragua, Nicaraguita* and songs from the *Campesino Mass.*

I want to come back to visit Flo, Tina, and Amancio, to do additional interviews about their lives and their vision of the future, and to facilitate training about families and women's justice issues. My main goal is my own spiritual growth and enlightenment, but I also feel that I can contribute something. Perhaps something between a U.S. delegation and the AEDAF leaders. Jenny liked the idea and suggested that the topic could be "Alternatives to Violence," focusing on communal and familial levels.

Aug. 16, Managua. My last hours in Managua. This afternoon has been a form of decompression. For several hours I talked intensely and personally with my son Nathan, and then we gradually fell silent. Tom Louden stopped by to drop off letters and tell us about sesame seeds and other hopes for miracle plants. Then we were quiet—the transition back has begun. We are both talked out and homesick. We have been converted again by Nicaragua and can't do any more about it. We have dinner tonight with Brenda and Ivan, her husband, and then leave STB at 5:00 a.m. It is nearly dark, and we will be at the airport when the sun rises again.

Aug. 18, Rochester, N.Y. I remember listening to the singing of seventy children in a compound under posts and a tin roof in Acahualinca, which is often called the poorest barrio in Managua. Four women prepared a meal of beans, squash, meat, and a fruit drink with oatmeal, the only daily meal for most of the children. Most of their parents were at work, combing through the recent garbage at the city dump for any retrievable items. They risk infection, assault, pollution, and heat stroke to provide for their children.

These are the poorest of the poor in the two-thirds world.

How can we hope less than the children do?

6

Stories of Recovering Perpetrators[1]

In this volume of essays, I strive to understand the complex issues of male violence against women and children, especially in families and intimate relationships. I find the most difficult aspect of this goal to write about the treatment issues for male abusers, often called perpetrators. Many church leaders cannot conceive of an individual they know personally engaging in such acts of abuse and evil. They consider such violence unbelievable. Therefore, they minimize and ignore the cries of victims and let the perpetrators go free. However, this response is dangerous because it leaves victims at the mercy of ongoing abuse and leaves survivors in recovery isolated from the resources they need for healing.

In this chapter, I write frankly about my own experience with perpetrators of violence as a pastoral counselor. I do not advocate that pastoral caregivers engage in such pastoral counseling without extensive training and supervision. Rather, pastoral caregivers need to understand the many difficult issues facing male abusers if they want to be healed from their sin. Without such understanding, the church alternates between passivity and vindictiveness; either they do nothing, or they banish the abuser from the community. Male violence against women and children is not the behavior of just a few isolated men. Rather, it is a pattern of male behavior that is quite common in U.S. society, including

---

[1]Originally published as "Stories of Recovering Perpetrators," in *The Abuse of Power: A Theological Problem* (Nashville: Abingdon Press, 1991), 49–73.

the church. Male abusers need clear limits on their behaviors and rehabilitation programs that confront them with the requirements of transformation. The church needs to face its responsibility to protect those who are vulnerable and provide resources for men who seek transformation. This process requires extensive rethinking and reorganization of priorities by the church.

My Personal Story

Several years ago I began working as a psychotherapist with incestuous families.[2] In the agency where I practiced I was one of only three men on a staff of fifteen. I was assigned to a perpetrator's group and worked with child molesters in individual and group psychotherapy. When I moved to a new city later, I continued with the same population.[3]

It was a shock to hear the stories of molesters and to be in the presence of such disturbed and dangerous men. As a therapist I had to be clear about limits both inside and outside therapy. The ethical responsibility of the therapist is high and remains a constant issue. A therapist must work in partnership with other professionals in social work and legal professions to provide for the safety of women and children. It is difficult to set up adequate accountability for perpetrators of sexual violence so that the abuse does not continue during treatment. Anyone who works with this population needs to be alert to the extreme danger and receive information from other family members about safety issues. Denial and minimization are common defenses by perpetrators, which makes the truth nearly impossible to discern. All perpetrators lie to avoid the consequences of their crimes. Male

---

[2]My previous research in child sexual abuse has been published in several articles: "Child Sexual Abuse: A Rich Context for Thinking about the God, Community, and Ministry," *Journal of Pastoral Care* 42, no. 1 (Spring 1988): 58–61; "Issues in the Psychotherapy of Child Molesters," *Journal of Pastoral Care* 43, no. 1 (Spring 1989): 25–32; "Social and Ethical Issues of Child Sexual Abuse," *American Baptist Quarterly* 8, no. 4 (December 1989): 257–67, now chapter 2 in this book.

[3]I also engaged in systematic study of the literature about child molesters. Some helpful books include A. Nicholas Groth, *Men Who Rape* (New York: Plenum Press, 1979); David Finkelhor, *Child Sexual Abuse* (New York: Free Press, 1984); Mary H. Lystad, ed., *Violence in the Home: Interdisciplinary Perspectives* (New York: Brunner/Mazel, 1986); Richard Gelles and Murray Straus, *Intimate Violence* (New York: Simon and Schuster, 1988); George Barnard et al., *The Child Molester: An Integrated Approach to Evaluation and Treatment* (New York: Brunner/Mazel, 1989); Mike Lew, *Victims No Longer: Men Recovering from Incest and Other Sexual Child Abuse* (New York: Nevraumont, 1988); Mic Hunter, *Abused Boys: The Neglected Victims of Sexual Abuse* (New York: Lexington, 1990).

therapists need to understand that they are not adequately sensitive to abuse by men and therefore need feedback and accountability to female therapists.

When legal and therapeutic limits are put in place to discourage further abuse, and when educational efforts are organized to challenge the cognitive distortions, the nature of therapy includes listening to and interpreting the pain from these men. They are out of touch with the emptiness and isolation of their own lives, and they externalize their problems by blaming others. They feel entitled to emotional control of the women and children in their families and resent any interference from child protective agencies, courts, and therapists. In order to work with this population, one must be firm about violation of limits and patiently wait for the fragile development of trust in the midst of manipulation and rationalizations. These factors make clinical work with perpetrators difficult and challenging.

I have never been able to give a good answer about why I work with child molesters. I wonder if it is not because I grew up in a traditional middle-class culture in the United States in which emotional pain was denied. My parents had survived sad childhoods of their own, and they were determined to make things better for their children. The culture of the fifties encouraged conformity and offered prosperity for those who were the most socialized. I was the oldest child and most anxious to please. So I grew up as an achiever with many strong feelings that had to be repressed. I have struggled in my own psychotherapy to mend my childhood woundedness.

There is something about working with molesters that keeps me in touch with my own primitive feelings, with impulses that have been repressed. On the other hand, it seems that there is something about me that is a calming influence for perpetrators. I give them hope that their impulses can be controlled so they do not continue to hurt children and destroy themselves.

Another motive for my work with molesters is as a critique of culture. The culture of the fifties when I was a child was controlling and numbing. Individuals were taught to sacrifice their own impulses in exchange for social respectability and success. The cost for individuals is not only the loss of feeling and integrity, but also a blindness to social injustice. American culture depends on the uncritical cooperation of its people. Working with child molesters breaks through my anesthesia toward the injustice of culture.

A convicted child molester is a frightening example of how culture can fail to hold the powerful accountable for their abuses. To the extent that men are protected from the consequences of their crimes against those who are vulnerable, the culture bears responsibility for the violations of women and children. Many molesters are confused by the consequences that follow arrest and conviction because they have exerted the control that men are expected to have in the family. Society looks very different for victims than it does for perpetrators who are excused. I have been able to see through some of the lies that protect the powerful at the expense of the vulnerable. My gain is an awareness of society's wrongs that breaks through my own numbness about social evil.

Working with molesters has also challenged and transformed my theology. As a follower of process theology, I have a radical empirical view of the relation of God and the world. I believe that God is present in every moment of experience, working to increase intensity and harmony. Perhaps I accepted this view of reality because of my own feeling of distance from God. I want to believe that God is present in a personal way, even though I often cannot feel it.

In working with child molesters, however, the problem of evil cannot be ignored. In the presence of such human destructiveness, it is impossible to have a naive doctrine of the goodness of God. Evil is so apparent in child sexual abuse that it challenges any easy conception that God's grace is available to all. Where is God's justice in the life of a man who has raped a child? Within child molesters, within their families, and within a society that ignores the extent of child abuse, evil is organized and powerful. Other examples of extreme evil such as the Holocaust and U.S. slavery may have similar patterns to sexual violence. There seems to be no limit to evil when the conditions are right. The tragedy of human suffering when evil is in control is enormous. The relation of evil and goodness in God is a puzzle that is not easily solved when we face the full implications of sexual violence.

Where is the hope in a God of love and power when one has perpetrated evil? Here, recovering perpetrators have been my teachers. For those men who choose the arduous road to healing and want to make a radical change in their lives, there is still a resilient hope that has not completely died. This courage of the human spirit in the face of the internal power of evil is remarkable. If hope is still present in some of these men, then perhaps hope is still possible in a society that invented modern slavery and nuclear weapons.

Where is the hope? One recovering perpetrator suffered severe sexual abuse as a teenager and was arrested just as he was making the transition to abusing others. One of his counselors told him that he had one chance in a thousand to recover. He said, "I do not plan to be a statistic." The resiliency of his spirit cannot be explained by any theory. A few molesters have not given up hope for themselves and have a determination to face the evil in their own lives. This may be validation of faith in a God who is resilient in the presence of evil.

Finding the Stories of Perpetrators

In order to understand how abuse of power is organized, we need to hear the voices and testimonies of those who know sexual violence firsthand. We have listened to survivors who have the courage to speak about their suffering even though there is great risk of being abused again. Survivors are too often blamed for their own suffering and are silenced again.

There are very few child molesters who are willing to give public witness to their suffering and their complicity with evil. We need to hear the truth about sexual violence from those few men who are trying to recover from their addiction to power and are willing to be vulnerable with their inner psychic processes. In the midst of their distorted cries for help are clues about how all men need to change their basic perceptions about power. By listening for the truth in the midst of evil, perhaps we can begin to see the patterns of abuse in all men that require radical transformation.

Because I have been unable to coauthor a chapter with a child molester, I have made a second choice—to report my general perceptions about perpetrators. In addition to my clinical work with molesters, I have been immersed in reading and have discussed the dynamics of incestuous families with other therapists in workshops and conferences. I have heard hundreds of stories about the various issues that arise out of this population. From my total experience I have created stories of fictional characters, stories that describe some of the pain and rage I have heard. I have tried to discern general patterns that seem to be true and filled them with fictitious content. This way I have been true to my oath of confidentiality, yet I have been able to share some of my general perceptions about child abusers. Nothing I say is the exact story of any person who has shared with me.

One additional caution about the following story. I have been working as a psychotherapist with individuals and families for seventeen years after training in several intensive programs. I have been working under supervision for five years with perpetrators of sexual abuse. It is important that pastors and other untrained counselors not underestimate the difficult clinical issues of this population. This story is meant to serve as an educational tool, not as a guide for clinicians.

There Is No Typical Story

The fictional story of Sam that follows represents one of the more optimistic case studies to show that the issues are difficult to face and resolve even under optimal conditions. This composite case presentation does not give an accurate picture of the group of child molesters in several ways:

First, Sam's story gives a distorted view because most molesters do not acknowledge the truth of what they have done, and most never seek or take the opportunity of therapy. Most who do begin therapy do not respond positively to treatment. Even when they have been confronted by the victim after years of therapy, most molesters still maintain denial about the significance of their behaviors. Denial is the typical defense against accountability for sexual violence and is the most serious problem blocking molesters from seeking the treatment they need. Sam is unusual because he gradually began to face the truth about his life and stayed in treatment over a long period of time in spite of his pain and depression.

Second, Sam's story gives a distorted picture because more girls are victims than boys. There are fathers who molest their daughters over a period of eight years or more. There are also molesters who behave abusively with girls within the extended family. Women report that brothers, uncles, grandfathers, and other men in the family are often the perpetrators of sexual abuse.

This means that girls are in more danger than boys, and women are more vulnerable than men. Sam was sexually abused as a boy, but this still does not explain why he abused his own son. Almost none of the many women who are sexually abused become molesters of other children. We need much more research about sexually abused boys.[4]

Third, this story does not explore adequately the question of why child sexual abuse is primarily perpetrated by men rather than women. There are clearly differences in the way men and women are socialized as children and in the expectations for male and female behavior in the adult culture. Men are socialized to be dominant in interpersonal relationships and are excused for their abusive behaviors. Women are often victimized in early life, and their oppression continues in their subordinate positions in the adult world. Men abuse children because they are not held accountable for their actions and because they choose to inflict suffering on others.

Fourth, Sam represents only one of many types of molesters. There have been several attempts to categorize the types of molesters.[5] One could think of molesters as a group along a continuum. At one end are those men like Sam who molest less frequently, usually under stress, and for whom the prognosis is only fair even under optimal treatment conditions. Some in this group receive help under other diagnoses, such as alcoholism, depression, or suicidal ideation, without ever revealing their history of sexual violence. At the other end of the continuum are those violent molesters who rape and/or kill children they do not know and for whom there is no known treatment.

In between these extremes there are molesters with every diagnosis and many different patterns. There is no correlation between the symptom of child sexual abuse and any particular psychological pathology. There is also no correlation between child sexual abuse and social class except to the extent that stress increases the risk for children. The population of child molesters is much larger and more complex than the public understands. In

---

[4]See footnotes 2 and 3 in this chapter for some resources on sexually abused boys.

[5]See the summary of this discussion in Finkelhor, 33ff; Diana Russell, *The Secret Trauma: Incest in the Lives of Girls and Women* (New York: Basic Books, 1986), 215ff; and Groth, 151.

order to understand why child sexual abuse is so widespread, we must listen to the testimonies of survivors as they describe the consequences of growing up in such terror. Hearing the voices of survivors will give us an understanding of the phenomenon we are trying to understand and treat. In addition, we must hear the destructive images and inner pain of the molesters themselves. Until we can begin to identify the individual and social causes of sexual violence, we will not be able to prevent the widespread prevalence of this evil.

Sam: A Recovering Perpetrator

Sam grew up pretty much on his own with few attachments that he could count on. His father left home before he started school, and he does not remember any positive contact with him. As an adult he learned that his father died of alcoholism in his early fifties. Because Sam's mother could not manage the four children after the departure of Sam's father, Sam and his siblings spent several years in foster care. It was here that he first remembers being mistreated. He was beaten for minor offenses and has a vague recollection of being molested by the older children in the family, but he is not sure. Sam's early life was characterized by family instability and unreliable adult relationships.

Sam was greatly relieved when his mother remarried and collected the children. Things were better for a short time—at least there was greater financial stability. When Sam turned eleven, his stepfather promised him what seemed a significant sum of money if he would "give him a blow job." He felt forced by the situation to comply because he did not know how to protect himself. This incident was repeated several times before his stepfather stopped. Extreme distance characterized their relationship after that. Later he was also molested by his mother's brother, who forced Sam to masturbate him to orgasm. Sam was terrified by these experiences and unable to talk to his mother because his relationship to her was fragile and she always sided with adults against him.[6]

---

[6]I don't mean to leave the impression that all perpetrators have been victims of child sexual abuse. The issue of the relation between being a victim of sexual abuse and becoming a perpetrator of sexual abuse is a complex one. According to Finkelhor, there are increased rates of child sexual abuse among the population of child molesters who have been studied. But there are many molesters who have not been sexually abused (Finkelhor, 47). Studies of child molesters are incomplete because of the secrecy and denial about these problems within the male population.

These incidents of sexual abuse led to increasing depression and isolation from peers and adults. He had difficulty concentrating on his schoolwork and frequently was in trouble with teachers at school. He made one friend in fifth grade who moved away at Christmas, and Sam never saw him again. When he was fifteen, Sam began abusing alcohol as a form of relief from the daily pain and loneliness. When he used alcohol, he became enraged and got into fights, which occasionally got him into trouble with the police. He spent several nights in jail and spent several months in the local detention center for boys. At age seventeen he had his first sexual encounter with a girl in an abandoned car at the back of her father's lot, an experience that had very little meaning for him.

After high school Sam worked in a factory on the assembly line, where he met Peggy, an equally immature woman his own age. They started dating and decided to get married when she became pregnant. Their second child, a girl, died of a heart defect when she was one year old. Sam was devastated because he identified so strongly with this frail child who reminded him of his own lost self. Soon after her death, Sam lost his job, and the family lived on unemployment for a year.

When he could not find work and Peggy went to work as a waitress, Sam was alone with his five-year-old son, Johnny. Sam had no understanding of the deep crisis he was in. This was the year he first touched his son sexually. At first it was rough play and tickling, but later Sam was touching Johnny's genitals and masturbating in front of him.

In Sam's mind, his son seemed to enjoy the attention and did not mind the touching. The sense of power and excitement for Sam was intoxicating. Here seemed to be the admiration and physical contact that he had always longed for but had never experienced before. One day while they were playing, he forced his penis into his son's mouth. It seemed good for a moment, but then Sam remembered with horror his own experience with his father. He stopped, cried, and promised his son that he would never do anything like this again. In his preoccupation with his own shame, he did not notice the devastating effect of this event on his son, who began to have nightmares, physical symptoms, and phobias at school and home.

The next week while he was playing with Johnny, Sam abused his son again. This time he was frightened that he would get into trouble. He cried and forced his son to promise that he would never tell anyone what happened. His son was terrified and promised he would never tell.

It was several months before Sam played with his son again. But when he thought the danger was over, he began touching his son again. Once the pattern started, Sam did not stop. He began abusing his son on a weekly basis. Sam started drinking again to try to deal with his pain and escape the horror his life was becoming.

One day when he was at the tavern, two policemen arrested him and took him to the station. They said there had been a report from the nursery school teacher that he was molesting his son. At first Sam denied everything and blamed his son for being a liar. But later that night he confessed everything.

He was arrested and kept in jail for several days while child protective services worked out an arrangement for the family. They decided that Sam could be released on the condition that he have no contact with his son, that he find his own apartment, and that he participate regularly in the program of a sexual abuse treatment agency.

The next day Sam was interviewed at the agency, placed in an orientation group with Peggy and other couples from incestuous families, and assigned to me as his therapist. I saw him about three weeks later. He was very cooperative in the first session, relieved to be out of jail, glad to have a chance to keep his family together, and relieved to not be molesting his son anymore. He felt mistreated by the police, the courts, and the guards at the jail. He was angry, scared, and willing to do anything our agency wanted him to do. He told a lot about his life, including detailed descriptions of molesting his son, as well as detailed stories about his own sad childhood. At one level he wanted help. He was desperate, and he hoped that our agency would be able to fix his life. Several months later there was a family therapy session in which Sam apologized to his son and to Peggy and took responsibility for his misconduct. This was a first, tentative step to help his son avoid self-blame that would require much follow-up later. Peggy was devastated that the man she loved had become so destructive. She was given support, her own therapist, and other resources for trying to cope with this crisis in her life.

After a few weeks, Sam was impatient. He heard from other men in the therapy group that the separation from the family often lasted twelve to eighteen months, and that not infrequently there was a divorce. When he shared his perception that his son enjoyed the touching and playing, the counselors confronted him with his rationalization and confusion about his son's real needs. Peggy vacillated in her feelings for him. One day she never wanted to see him again; the next day she helplessly called him and pleaded with him to come over even though it would violate the court order. He did not know whether he wanted to stay married to her or not. He did miss his son terribly and could not understand why his counselors said it was best not to see him for now.

The limitations set by the courts, the county child protection agency, and the treatment center rules infuriated him. He felt he was being treated like a child rather than an adult. His feelings of helplessness often turned to rage, though he was careful not to let his counselors see him angry. The "system" had disrupted his position of dominance and taken away "his" family that he abused to compensate for the deficiencies of his empty self.

This phase of resistance and avoidance of responsibility lasted many months. He made few comments in therapy group and talked, in individual therapy, about how lonely he was without his family. His possessive feelings toward his family were a part of his pattern that provided the context for abuse. He also talked about being unemployed, about his concern over finances, about his in-laws. In fact, he discussed many things except the sexual abuse of his son and his other abusive patterns. The initial euphoria about the opportunity to get well gave way to depression.

One day he came to therapy group after he had been drinking. The counselors took him aside and said that if he came to therapy group again after drinking, he would not be able to continue. He would have to make up his mind whether he wanted to be in the program.

In individual counseling, Sam complained about how the therapy group counselors were unfair, how they did not really care about him, and how they did not understand how hard it was for him. I listened and asked him to tell me how bad he really felt. He broke down and cried in a different way than he had cried before. This time he seemed to be crying not only out of fear and desperation, but also out of a deeper sense of despair about his whole life. Four months into treatment he finally was beginning to feel something and find a few words to express himself. He became more active in therapy group and asked for time to discuss his situation.

In the meantime Sam had found a job as a carpenter's assistant with a small contractor who built porches and remodeled rooms. At the end of two months' work Sam had not yet been paid. His boss owed him two thousand dollars and was not sure when he could pay up. Sam came to a session one night and told me he was planning to assault his boss because he believed he would never be paid. He was enraged that someone would do this to him. What he did not see was his own inability to make sound judgments for himself. He could not see that he should have quit after two weeks when it became apparent that he was not going to be paid on time, or that he should have seen the signs of mismanagement much sooner. He also did not see that controlling his impulses was one of his therapeutic issues and that losing control could not be blamed on external circumstances. Being in a situation where he felt humiliated and abused was too close to his own inner pathology, and he responded with fantasies of violence.

Explanations did not help. He seemed to be a potential danger to his boss. After thinking about this situation and talking it over with my supervisor, I decided to tell Sam that I needed to call his boss to tell him about the potential danger. I explained that this would serve two purposes: It might protect his boss from physical harm, and it might help Sam to contain his rage in this situation. An assault charge would jeopardize his probation, his marriage, and his treatment. I said I was willing to provide support as he tried to work out this conflict, but that I needed to take action to protect others and to help him in a situation fraught with danger. It is crucial for therapists to know the limits of confidentiality, especially when the health and safety of others is at risk.

I called his boss to warn him that Sam was telling me he was in danger of assaulting him. The next day Sam confronted his boss with his feelings of being mistreated. They worked out a compromise that involved getting paid part of the money right away and the rest a week later. When Sam came back to the following session, he was feeling much better about himself. A situation that would have led to the kind of fighting he indulged in as a teenager was averted. Sam was beginning to learn new ways of behaving. He started taking more assertive action in therapy group around a number of topics.

After about a year of treatment without serious incidents, Sam began to get restless about living alone in an apartment. He felt that he had cooperated with treatment, had not violated his court orders, and yet was not moving toward being reunited with his family. There had been occasional family sessions, and he was getting weekly supervised visits with his son. Sam's assertiveness toward the counselors and courts had a different feel from the complaining of many months ago. This time he was asking for help, and he was willing to compromise. It was the policy of our agency that recommendations to the court about reuniting incestuous families be made by the staff in consultation with all counselors, social workers, and probation officers.

Of first priority was the victim and his counselor. Johnny was now six years old and attending first grade. There had been gradual improvement in his ability to play in therapy, and he had made the transition to school without serious incident. But he remained a fragile, easily discouraged, and depressed little boy. The sexual abuse had severely interrupted his development, and he had major deficits in impulse control, peer skills, and ability to concentrate on goals. He was afraid of adults and had a negative view of himself and the world around him. The counselor thought that the father-son relationship might still be salvaged, but was skeptical about reuniting the family. Much more work needed to be done in family therapy before Johnny could tolerate his father's presence on a full-time basis.

Peggy's counselor was also skeptical. She had seen small progress in this inadequate and fragile woman who often fell into helplessness in a crisis. She had also grown up in a dysfunctional family where she was alternatively neglected and abused, and she was depressed about the death of her daughter and the terror of discovering that her husband had sexually abused their son. She did not yet have the strength to oppose her husband directly. In the few family sessions, the counselors could see that Sam remained dominant in the family and that he was still unable to see his wife and son as separate people with needs different from his. However, all the counselors agreed that some interpersonal work could be added to individual and group therapy. Regular marital and family sessions were added.

The increased emotional load was difficult for Sam and Peggy. Sam could tolerate very little confrontation about his abusive behaviors. Peggy was still terrified and felt unsafe with him. They had few skills for expressing their feelings to each other and for resolving conflicts between them. The gains they had made in talking with their counselors did not easily translate into effective marital communication. One week Sam missed all his therapy sessions with no explanation. Peggy had not heard from him, and he had not contacted his counselors. It was two weeks before Sam showed up at his counseling session, red-eyed, unshaven. He had driven fifty miles to a nearby town, had slept several nights in his car, then stayed with a friend from work. He said he had been "thinking"—about whether he wanted to be married to Peggy and whether he could live with himself as a father who had molested his son. He had not been able to answer either question, but he realized that he really had nothing else to do. Running away was appealing, but it did not solve anything. He missed seeing his counselors and visiting his son. His attachments helped him through a most difficult time.

Peggy was enraged at Sam's absence. Just as she was beginning to trust him a little and to make a few demands, he let her down. Now he was the helpless one who could not stand any confrontation. This crisis began to shift some of the power dynamics of their relationship. Peggy began to see that she was stronger than she thought and that Sam had his weaknesses. These insights contributed to their marital therapy.

A crucial issue in the treatment of an incestuous family is whether the non-abusing parent is strong enough to protect the children. Child molesters cannot be trusted fully to put the child's interest ahead of their own, even after years of treatment. This makes the role of the mother critically important. This image of family life is very far from a healthy functioning family unit where the adults are partners in the nurture of their children. Until now, it appeared that Peggy was unable to oppose Sam in any important conflict. But Peggy's counselors helped her to see that she had survived as a single parent for over a year now and had enforced limits on Sam's behavior. Now she had survived his absence and kept functioning. This provided a basis for strengthening her role in the family in the future.

It took about six more months of therapy before the counselors felt there was enough change to warrant the risk of reuniting the family. Certain rules had to be negotiated first, including a rule that Sam would not be alone with his son until it was approved by the counselors. This meant that Johnny had to stay with his grandmother whenever Peggy was at work. Regular progress was made over the next two years until the end of court probation. After probation, Sam and Peggy decided to remain in therapy on a somewhat reduced schedule. They faced many difficult problems that were hidden from them during the first eighteen months of crisis. Now they had to face the problems of every family—developing patience with each other in the midst of the stress of modern life, making adjustments to the changing developmental needs of their children, negotiating satisfactory times of intimacy and enjoyable activities, resolving conflicts of values and priorities. They discovered that life was more difficult and more interesting than they earlier thought. As far as I know, there was no repetition of Sam's molesting behavior over the three years of treatment. No one knows the long-term prognosis of child molesters.

The Organization of Abuse of Power in Child Molesters

The process by which a man develops into a perpetrator of sexual violence against women and children is the next topic we need to consider. Sam's story gives only a bare outline of his life and does not explain the processes by which he became a perpetrator of sexual violence against his son. In this chapter we begin a preliminary analysis of themes in the lives of men who have sexually abused women and children. There is no one-to-one correlation for men between childhood experiences of abuse and becoming an adult perpetrator. Some men who have been victims of sexual violence do not become perpetrators.[7] They become survivors with personal pain. They may have self-destructive symptoms that continue the effects of the abusive patterns of their childhood trauma, such as substance abuse, but they do not

---

[7]Finkelhor, 47: "[M]ost children who are molested do not go on to become molesters themselves. This is particularly true among women, who whether victimized or not rarely become offenders. Obviously, if victimization is a causal factor it interacts with some other factors."

engage in the extreme abuse of power that we know as child sexual abuse. As sexual violence is identified as a problem that can be treated, more men who have been victims will self-identify and seek help. This will provide research for understanding how men overcome victimization without becoming abusers.

Some men who have not been victims of sexual violence become perpetrators of sexual violence on others. This means that there are factors at work in sexually violent behaviors that cannot be attributed only to individual pathology. Further research on the relation of sexual violence to gender issues is necessary.[8]

Some men like Sam who have been victims of sexual violence develop into abusers who act out their trauma on those who cannot protect themselves. One of the questions of our research is why some victims become perpetrators while others do not.

More men than women become perpetrators. Some estimates are that 80 to 95 percent of sexual violence is perpetrated by men.[9] Whenever we uncover a gender difference this extreme, we must try to account for the difference. We need to ask why men are more likely to become perpetrators of sexual violence than women.

These questions cannot be fully answered here. There are many theories about why some men become perpetrators and why more men than women are sexually violent. David Finkelhor has developed a four-factor analysis that will inform later discussions. He suggests that there are four "preconditions that needed to be met before sexual abuse could occur."

1. A potential offender needed to have some motivation to abuse a child sexually.

2. The potential offender had to overcome internal inhibitions against acting on that motivation.

3. The potential offender had to overcome external impediments to committing sexual abuse.

4. The potential offender or some other factor had to undermine or overcome a child's possible resistance to the sexual abuse.[10]

---

[8]Ibid. Finkelhor's summary of other studies suggests that as many as two-thirds of child molesters were not molested as children.
[9]Ibid., 12.
[10]Ibid., 54.

The importance of Finkelhor's theory is that it shows the possibility of any man engaging in sexual violence regardless of individual history or previous abuse if there is inadequate accountability in society.

A conviction of this study is that the analysis of causes for sexual violence by men must be done at three levels: individual and intrapsychic; social institutions and ideologies; and religious. The following section is organized around four intrapsychic themes from my research that seem to be present to some extent in the population of men who become perpetrators of sexual violence.

- sexualized dependency

- destructive aggression

- the grandiose self

- inability to respect limits

These themes begin to help us understand the process by which some men become perpetrators of sexual violence and the connection of this process with the stereotypes of what it means to be male and female in U.S. culture.

We also need to know if there is any hope that the abuse of power in sexual violence can be understood and justice can be found for the thousands of victims. We need to know if there is any hope of transformation for men for whom abuse of power through sexual violence has become a way of living.

Sexualized Dependency

One way to understand a man who has molested children is that he has a dependency disorder.[11] Something is wrong internally with his ability to meet his needs for love and nurture with other adults. He sexualizes his emotional needs and projects them onto children. He feels that he is justified in meeting these needs by abusing persons who are vulnerable, and he is confident that he will not be held accountable for his crimes.

---

[11]Gertrude and Rubin Blanck, *Ego Psychology II: Psychoanalytic Developmental Psychology* (New York: Columbia University Press, 1979), 31ff.

There are two reasons why children may be likely targets of such projections. First, children are vulnerable unless protected by adults. Many children are unprotected and thus are defenseless against adults who want to use them for inappropriate needs. Second, because of their youth and innocence children seem, for some men, symbolically closer to the source of life. To an adult whose inner life is empty, the spontaneity and energy of children is mistakenly interpreted as the fullness of life.[12]

In terms of childhood history, many molesters grew up in situations where basic dependency needs were unmet. Robert grew up in a home where his parents and grandparents were active alcoholics. One of his earliest memories was trying to separate his mother and grandmother from physical fights. The men in the family were usually gone, and he felt responsible for trying to keep the two women from killing each other.

When he was eight or nine, his uncle used to take him on fishing trips and camping together in the mountains. He loved his uncle because he felt included in the male subculture. Unfortunately, his uncle also molested him, leading to a lifetime of confusion about intimacy and sexuality. Sexual abuse became something that he had to tolerate in order to be accepted by men.

When he was ten, Robert was sent to a foster home along with his younger brother. In this home, Robert became enthralled with his foster father and his brothers. They treated him like a little man, included him in their activities, and gave him a sense of positive worth. Unfortunately, his foster mother would give the two boys long baths in which she would spend many minutes painfully cleaning their genital areas. Robert hated these baths and the confusion and pain he experienced. In his child's mind, he thought that sexual abuse was something that went along with normal family life.

Robert's story illustrates a phenomenon that occurs in the childhood of some child molesters. The most important relationships in his life included sexual abuse. He internalized sexual abuse as a part of nurturing and acceptance.[13] In his mind, sexual abuse became identified with love. This led to confusion in his psychic life between love, sexuality, and abuse.

---

[12]Finkelhor, 39ff; Alice Miller, *Thou Shalt Not Be Aware* (New York: Farrar, Strauss, Giroux, 1983).

[13]Finkelhor, 47; Miller.

As an adult, he was seriously injured in an industrial accident and spent eighteen months in recovery, without his usual preoccupation with work to distract him from his inner pain. He lacked the inner strength to cope with his crisis and turned to the form of nurture he knew as a child himself—molesting. He raped his eleven-year-old stepdaughter. In his distorted mind, sexual contact with a child met his need for someone who was totally accepting and nonthreatening. It seemed like the love he had known as a child.

Although he felt some fear after each incident of abuse, his need for closeness with someone was so distorted, and his inability to connect with other adults was so severely limited, that it seemed to him the only way he could survive. Through threats and secrecy, he was able to continue the abuse for three years until his wife found out and confronted him.

While there is nothing in this story that explains why Robert molested a child, there are certain themes that can be identified as contributing factors. For Robert, becoming a perpetrator became a "repetition compulsion"[14] for meeting dependency needs that had become sexualized in his childhood. Because important attachment figures in his childhood molested him, Robert internalized abuse as a distorted form of interpersonal closeness. He molested a girl because she was defenseless against his power in a society that ignores child abuse and because he could fantasize that the relationship to her was real.

One reason men are more likely to become child molesters than women is because sexualized dependency is more consonant with dominant images of what it means to be male. Some scholars have suggested that growing up in a patriarchal society means that men and women learn very different ways of expressing dependency needs and sexuality.[15] It is much more acceptable for a women to be vulnerable, to allow herself to be taken care of by another person. Women are encouraged to share feelings and touch with others without fear of loss of identity.

Being loved like a child often feels contradictory for men who think they are supposed to be strong and autonomous. Denial of dependency needs in some men takes an aggressive sexual

---

[14]Alice Miller, *For Your Own Good* (New York: Farrar, Strauss, Giroux, 1983), 229.

[15]Nancy Chodorow, *The Reproduction of Mothering* (Berkeley, Calif.: University of California Press, 1978), 173ff.

direction. The paradigm of rape in which the man is in complete control of the other is a more comfortable way of being physically close for someone who is incapable of intimacy.[16] The need for touch is met without the terrifying possibility of vulnerability to another. A "real man" must be dominant in every relationship.

We can see this confusion in Robert's story. As a child, he became attached to a man who expressed his affection through sexual abuse, and Robert needed this affection so much that, in his young mind, affection and sexual touching became synonymous, especially in a society that confuses intimacy and sexuality. When he was an adult in crisis and depression, he sought intimacy with a child who was defenseless against his initiative. He felt as if he could talk and be himself with this eleven-year-old girl in a more complete way than with any adult he knew. Raping a child as a way of expressing intimacy is a caricature of what it means to be male in U.S. society.

Destructive Rage

Another way to understand the child molester is to recognize that he has an aggressive disorder.[17] Something is wrong in his ability to protect the self or pursue a goal without hurting another person. He has difficulty understanding that he is acting in destructive ways toward others and does not understand the consequences of his aggression on others, especially in a society where there is so little accountability for such crimes.

John was sexually abused by a neighbor. Through severe threats and bribes of money, alcohol, and drugs, this man was able to keep John entrapped for many years. The relationship with the molester became the center of John's life. It was a clear case of "identification with the aggressor."[18] Because of his own impoverished relationships and his psychic immaturity, John was helpless to get out of this destructive relationship. He survived by internalizing the abuse at the core of his personality.[19]

---

[16]Larry Baron and Murray Straus, *Four Theories of Rape in American Society* (New Haven, Conn.: Yale University Press, 1989).

[17]Heinz Kohut, *The Restoration of the Self* (New York: International Universities Press, 1977), 111ff; D. W. Winnicott, *Deprivation and Delinquency* (London: Tavistock, 1984), 81ff.

[18]Blanck and Blanck, 43ff. "Identification with the aggressor" is a term introduced by Anna Freud and elaborated by Rene Spitz.

[19]Ruth F. Lax, Sheldon Bach, and J. Alexis Burland, eds., *Rapprochement: The Critical Subphase of Separation-Individuation* (New York: Jason Aronson, 1980), 439–56.

One of the major characteristics of his abuse was the constant threat of violence and death. The molester was sadistic in his treatment, verbally explicit in his threats, and backed up his threats by keeping loaded guns lying around the house. John was terrified and identified with his molester as the only way he knew how to survive.

As an adult, John adapted the same personal style. He molested a child while under the power of his molester, and was a danger to children because of his history of sexual abuse and drug addiction. Whenever John was frightened or unbalanced for any reason, he became threatening toward others. His inappropriate verbal aggression was a sign that he was losing his internal balance. He became enraged and nearly out of control whenever he was afraid. Because of his fragile state, every situation was fraught with great danger. Because his rage was his best defense, he lashed out at authority whenever he felt threatened.

This is a common characteristic of many child molesters. When he was frightened, John tended to be outwardly aggressive. Some perpetrators are deferential with authority figures but sadistic when they are with someone they judge as less powerful. Rage is dangerous whenever the molester is with an unprotected child.

The sexual abuse of a child is always a violent act. In order to sexually abuse a child, the adult has to override all the signals from the child that this behavior does not correspond to her or his needs. No matter how damaged a child is, or how starved she or he is for adult affection and acceptance, any truly sensitive adult can see that the child needs something else besides sexual contact.[20]

> Sexual violence is first and foremost an act of violence, hatred, and aggression. Whether it is viewed clinically or legally, objectively or subjectively, violence is the common denominator. Like other acts of violence (assault and battery, murder, nuclear war), there is a violation and injury to victims. The injuries may be psychological or physical. In acts of sexual violence, usually the injuries are both.[21]

---

[20]Alice Miller, *Thou Shalt Not Be Aware.*

[21]Marie Fortune, *Sexual Violence: The Unmentionable Sin: An Ethical and Pastoral Perspective* (New York: Pilgrim Press, 1983), 5.

The child molester has a problem because he cannot see the child as separate from himself. He lacks empathy. If he wants something, he distorts his perception until he thinks it is something the child wants also. His aggression is unneutralized,[22] and he treats the child as an extension of his needs. If he wants something, he feels he should have it, especially if the other is unprotected and can put up no effective defense.

One reason more men than women become perpetrators of sexual violence is because expression of destructive rage is more consonant with the dominant images of what it means to be male in U.S. culture. The image of a man who gets what he wants without regard for the other is a stereotype of male insensitivity. The "real man" is one who does not tolerate resistance to meeting his needs. If he meets resistance, he turns to threats and violence. Any resistance is an attack on his masculinity and must be destroyed.

Some child molesters imitate this super macho image in their social behavior. They boast of their power and their lack of tolerance for any opposition. Their macho demeanor is actually in direct contrast to their symptoms of abusing children. They deliberately choose the most helpless, defenseless persons in society on which to dump their rage. They are far from being macho men who are not afraid of anything. Their disordered aggression is hidden and secret. They are macho in their own eyes when in the presence of children.

One of the reasons for the aggressive demeanor of molesters is to protect them against the societal rage they would receive if the public knew who they really were. Acting super macho serves as an aggressive outlet, and it also protects them against society's suspicion of child molesters.

Other molesters are not super macho in their presentation of self; some, in fact, are very deferential. But such good behavior is not to be trusted. They are frightened around anyone with authority and may act respectfully. But outside the eyes of authority and in the presence of someone who is vulnerable, they become tyrannical and controlling, expressing the deep rage that they carry hidden all the time.

---

[22]Blanck and Blanck, 31ff.

The Grandiose Self

Another way to understand child molesters is that they have a narcissistic disorder.[23] Something is wrong in their ability to accurately evaluate self and other. According to Heinz Kohut, one of the biggest challenges facing any person is maintaining narcissistic equilibrium or balance between self and other. Any imbalance tends to lead to devaluation of either self or other and an inability to foster accurate perceptions of both self and other and their interrelationship.

When an abused person experiences narcissistic imbalance, there is a regression to infantile images of the grandiose self and the omnipotent object. The grandiose self is the self who is never wrong and is entitled to whatever privilege and pleasure is available in an interaction. The omnipotent object is the demanding, all-powerful other against whom there is no defense. In the state of imbalance, there is a battle between self and other that is life and death. The grandiose self who is not satisfied can become enraged and destroy the other. The omnipotent object who is not obeyed can annihilate the self.

Bob's life was organized around fear of the omnipotent object. He was extremely deferential in therapy, with his counselors, and with his bosses at work. He tended to present himself as worthless. In his childhood, he was treated in a mean and cruel way. He has memories of playing outside beside the railroad track right up to the last minute of curfew. Then he hoped to sneak up to his room without attracting his father's attention. Frequently, his father heard him come in and would call him into the living room for extended sessions of humiliation and abuse. His father would tear him down in every conceivable way.

Afterward, Bob would go to his room alone and fantasize about being on the train whose whistle he could hear in the background. As an adult he became a train buff because these fantasies were his solace in childhood. His childhood was characterized by the omnipotent object and the worthless self.

Bob married a woman who was abusive like his father. She would frequently humiliate Bob, but she eventually tired of him and divorced him. It was during weekend visits with his nine-year-old

---

[23]Ibid., 176ff; Otto Kernberg, *Internal World and External Reality* (Northvale, N.J.: Jason Aronson, 1980); 135ff; Kohut, 63ff.

son that Bob repeated his own childhood trauma. Even though he had not been molested himself, on several camping trips, he raped his son during the night. It was his attempt to turn the tables and humiliate someone else the same way he had been humiliated. It is often puzzling that a person who has suffered the humiliation and injury of abuse would perpetuate the same experience on another victim. Many women and men take care never to abuse anyone because they remember the pain of their own experience. But many men and some women pass their trauma on to others in a cycle of violence that seems unending.

Bob showed signs of some progress in therapy when he began to act more assertively toward his supervisors at work. As he improved, he was no longer content to tolerate abuse from persons in authority. He was beginning to make internal connections between his sense of self and the possibility that the other was actually interested in his welfare.

Other molesters have had similar experiences of childhood humiliation. They defended against abusive situations by identifying with the grandiose self. They felt that their family was wrong to mistreat them, and they felt justified in hating them and their arrogance. In a sense they identified with the grandiosity of their abusers and incorporated extreme narcissism into their self-presentation.

In their adult life, some molesters give the impression of total fearlessness about the consequences of their actions. They are ready and willing to abuse anyone who stands between them and the goals they set. They despise the devalued object from the perspective of the grandiose self.

This tendency to see life as a competitive life-and-death battle between self and other is a stereotypically male way of organizing the world. In this perceptual world, whenever two persons are interacting, one must be dominant and the other subordinate. If a person finds himself in the subordinate position, he must be deferential to avoid harm or challenge very carefully. If a person is in the dominant position, he can do whatever he wants to the other without consequences. The possibility that persons could work together in a cooperative way without one or the other being destroyed seems impossible. Violence becomes a way of enforcing power. Either they become the victim of abuse of power, or else they victimize others. There is no other alternative. Ann Wilson

Shaef calls this the "either-or syndrome," which she says is characteristic of the white male system.[24]

Inability to Respect Limits

One of the most troublesome areas in working with molesters is setting limits and establishing appropriate boundaries.[25] It is obvious that a man who molests a child does not know how to set limits on his own destructive behaviors and does not respect the boundaries that other persons need in order to survive. Therapy with molesters is often a tug-of-war over who is responsible for what. The molester will blame the therapist for cooperating with authorities and creating more damage than the molester did in the first place. Keeping limits and boundaries confused is one of the skills of molesters.

An example of this is Paul, who after many months of therapy said to his wife, "Cindy was running around with only a towel on, giving me the eye, you know the way she does. I'm not the only one to blame for what happened." His wife responded, "But Cindy was only seven years old!"

After many months of therapy, Paul still felt that he was not responsible for molesting his stepdaughter. His ability to set limits on his own behaviors and respect the boundaries of others was still defective. His perspective was informed by five years of involvement in sibling incest with an older brother and a younger sister when he was ten to fifteen years old. The values of his home life were so distorted in terms of sexual attitudes and behaviors and exposure to pornography that he was unable to understand the full extent of his guilt for what he did.

Establishing realistic objectives for one's life is also difficult for molesters. In ten years Paul worked at a job no longer than six months. Part of the motive for molesting his stepdaughter was to compensate for the feeling of failure in the rest of his life. Yet he is unable to set and accomplish realistic goals that are fulfilling.

Male abuse of power in our culture means that many men have trouble setting appropriate limits when they are in a dominant position. Hierarchically organized business and

---

[24] Anne Wilson Schaef, *Women's Reality* (New York: Harper and Row, 1981), 149.

[25] Heinz Kohut, *How Does Analysis Cure?* (Chicago: University of Chicago Press, 1984), 192ff.

education means that the power at each level is checked by accountability to the power at the next level. But within the limits of the job, each power level is able to do what it needs to do to get the job done. This means that whenever there is a power differential, there is danger that someone will be controlled or damaged as long as it does not threaten the assigned task.

Women complain of serious sexual harassment in the workplace. Because such abuse is misunderstood as the sexual play between men and women rather than intimidation, harassment is often not considered a serious problem. Paul did not consider his sexual abuse of Cindy to be a serious problem because, in his mind, she wanted it as much as he did and because it did not interfere with anything else in the family. He was enraged that outside authorities would interfere in his life and limit his access to Cindy. The male sense of entitlement to abuse of power, especially in relation to women and children, is a widespread social problem.

In summary, although acknowledging the vast differences between molesters, we have explored four themes that seem to characterize many child molesters: sexualized dependency, destructive rage, grandiose self, and inability to respect limits. These themes help us to understand how experiences of being the victim of sexual violence sometimes lead to becoming a perpetrator.

These themes correspond to stereotypical images of what it means to be masculine in U.S. culture. This chapter is a phenomenological description of human personality in its social context.

Where Is the Hope?

Given the above description of individual and social pathology of sexual violence directed against children, is there any hope that sexual violence can be stopped and that perpetrators can be held accountable for their crimes? So far our society has not shown the kind of determination that is required for understanding and responding adequately to this problem.

The courage of survivors who are breaking the silence and speaking about their suffering and healing gives hope. They are already changing the context in which we all understand this problem. Stories of survivors need to be told in many settings until the public begins to understand the scope and tragedy of sexual violence.

The community of therapists and health care workers who are willing to work with victims and perpetrators in order to find answers gives hope. This book is only one of many that have been written in the last ten years to try to respond to issues of sexual violence. Many persons are dedicated to changing our society concerning the issue of sexual violence.

Some recovering perpetrators who show unusual courage in facing their own pathology give hope. We continue our search for hope by hearing some stories that represent some hope within the group of molesters themselves.

One group for whom there seems to be hope is adolescent molesters.[26] Young men aged twelve to twenty-one who are just beginning to make the transition to being perpetrators may be amenable to treatment before their abusive patterns become deeply entrenched. Most adolescent molesters have been victims of sexual violence who didn't get help when they most needed it, that is, when they were first molested as children. Someone should have provided treatment at that time so the confusion could be sorted out and they could discover that adults really cared about their pain and would protect them, not abuse them. But perhaps they can get help before they have firmly established a pattern of hurting others through sexual violence. Often they are anxious to talk with someone about what has happened to them and try to sort out identity questions.

One of the most difficult clinical issues with this group is autonomy. That is such a distorted issue in trying to become a man in U.S. society. Young men of this age are very protective of their autonomy, and their right to make their own decisions has to be encouraged in therapy or it will fail. This can be hard because some of their ideas about the meaning of autonomy are immature and underdeveloped. In spite of its difficulty, there is a possibility that, with proper help, these young men can temper their abusive behaviors in the future.

There is also some basis for hope in some molesters who are forced into treatment by the threat of prison. Often there is a desire to become whole in some molesters when counselors are

---

[26]Barnard, et al., 43ff.

available within a controlled environment. Once structures to prevent further abuse are in place, some molesters are relieved to be able to talk about their lifelong agony and their fears of hurting children in the future. We need further research about the combination of safeguards and therapy that will work with this group.

Issues for Counselors

My work with molesters has changed me in significant ways. It has helped me to understand how fragile we all are. One of the reasons molesters are feared in our society is because they evoke feelings of helplessness and rage in others. Some molesters have been poorly treated as children. Their stories of terror are heart-rending. We don't want to believe that such human evil is actually possible right in our own communities and churches! These molesters are enraged about their own victimization, and they act out their rage on helpless children. This destructiveness triggers our rage, and we feel like killing anyone who would do such destructive things. The victims have become the perpetrators. They have lived both sides of the secret horror facing many children in our communities. We don't want to deal with molesters because we don't want to deal with our own feelings about these things. Yet by not facing the evil in our molesting neighbors, we trivialize and support their crimes.

Another way in which I have been changed in my work with molesters is through an increasing awareness of the oppression of classism. Take a fictional but typical character named Bob, a molester who has been arrested and is serving probation. Bob was a single parent who had been convicted of child sexual abuse, who was barely holding on to a factory job, and who, if anything drastic went wrong, could be unemployed, homeless, and poor, without health insurance and perhaps without friends. He was one step away from being excluded from the protection of the social system.

Given his fragile situation, his relationship with me was highly symbolic. On the one hand I was a symbol to him of social respectability: I have the education, the economic support, the normative family situation, and so forth, that makes it likely that the society will reward me for promoting its values.

On the other hand I represent the social class that was a source of his oppression. It was in contrast to men like me that he was judged inadequate and expendable in society. When I decided to make a moral issue out of his child abuse, I was being selective about the range of ethical issues that impinge on this life. Perhaps his situation needs additional resources such as a better job, better housing, better economic support, and a community of love and caring.

From a distance, I was horrified to hear that a father had sexually abused his son. But the closer I got to the actual father, the more I discovered my own complicity. My horror at his sin was the reaction of one who lives in the protection of social respectability. My indignation about him was a direct expression of the sin of a society that needs an oppressed minority in order to justify its values. It was in contrast to this father that I understand myself as "good" in a moral sense. And my silence about his social situation and its consequences for him and his son contributed to the context in which such abuse occurs. Social oppression and class issues do not explain sexual violence, but they become part of the context for some molesters.

I shared in responsibility for the social situation that circumscribed his life. I was among the silent respectable leaders who have ignored children when they were abused by their parents. The suffering of these children and these parents labeled me as "righteous" because I didn't have to face this particular sin. I had never been arrested for child abuse, and I didn't have to deal with the harshness of a society toward those who are outside its protection.

If I shared moral complicity, then my moral response required personal involvement. Although this father was the one who sexually abused his child and lived with the intrapsychic and social consequences of his action, I shared the same theological condition of sin. My rage could find other outlets than severe child abuse. I could express my rage through my prejudices toward those in poverty, those who were socially marginalized because of gender, sexual orientation, social class, or ethnic heritage. Society gave me socially acceptable outlets for my needs for power and control, so I did not need to abuse my children as badly as he did. Bob's otherness confirmed my righteousness. It was only when I could identify with the same propensity toward sin as I found in Bob that I could reintegrate the projections that protected my fragile defenses. I was horrified in his presence because I was secretly horrified at my own sin.

So where is the hope? On the surface, hope is hard to find when it comes to sexual violence. Thousands of persons live in hell every day because they are victims of sexual violence. We live in a society that is only beginning to examine this horror and its widespread prevalence. The church has been silent about this evil and has much work to do before it will begin to realize its severity.

Yet there are glimmers of hope that are inspiring when one begins to look closely. There is a growing community of survivors and their counselors who are understanding more and more about the causes and consequences of sexual violence. And there is a small group of molesters and their counselors who are exploring a frontier that could change the face of modern society.

7

Freud, Women, and Male Dominance:
The Case of Freud and Dora[1]

To understand male violence against women and children, one must confront the work of Sigmund Freud. In his earliest work, Freud adopted a trauma theory to explain adult symptoms of mental illness that he believed were caused by childhood experiences of abuse. Later, Freud changed his mind and attributed his patients' memories of abuse to fantasies about their parents. He adopted the doctrines of penis envy and Oedipus complex to explain the motive for inventing such fantasies.

One of the extended case studies that gives insight into Freud's transition from trauma to fantasy theory is the case of Dora. At first Freud supported Dora in her charges against her father and Herr K. But gradually he seemed to blame Dora for exaggerating the events because she was unwilling to face her own complicity in the abusive events of her adolescent years. In this chapter, I explore some of the complexities of Freud's case study and raise critical questions about why we should both retrieve and subvert his theories today. Understanding male violence against women and children raises many countertransference issues for pastoral counselors, issues of sexuality and attraction, power and vulnerability, and rage and destructive behaviors. This study of Freud confronts all of us with our complicity in male violence in a

---

[1]Original version published as "Women and Male Dominance: The Case of Freud and Dora," in *Deliver Us from Evil: Resisting Racial and Gender Oppression* (Minneapolis: Fortress Press, 1996).

patriarchal society. Although more technical than some other chapters, this study will help to explore some of the complexities of gender and class issues that contribute to male violence.

When she was eighteen years old, Dora's father, concerned over a suicide note and a loss of consciousness during a family argument, sent Dora to see Sigmund Freud for psychoanalysis. Freud had first seen her two years earlier, when she was sixteen, for medical treatment of a cough and hoarseness. Once again her father handed her over to Freud, requesting that he get to the root of her physical complaints and learn why she was unhappy. Very quickly Freud discovered reasons for her problems. The family drama revolved around Dora's relationships to her father and mother (who were unhappily married) and two family friends– Herr K. and Frau K. When younger, she had become attached to Frau K. while helping with her children. Furthermore, Frau K. had nursed Dora's father back to health, a relationship that led to an affair.

During her adolescence, two traumatic events changed Dora's life. At age fourteen, Herr K. kissed her while they were alone at his place of business. Dora, who was disgusted and fled for safety, told no one what had happened. Two years later, when she was sixteen, Herr K. proposed a sexual relationship to Dora during a walk by the lake. She slapped him, ran away, and left town with her father. Several days later she told her parents what had happened. Freud describes Herr K.'s response.

Herr K. had been called to account by Dora's father and uncle on the next occasion of their meeting, but he had denied in the most emphatic terms having on his side made any advances that could have been open to such a construction. He had then proceeded to throw suspicion on the girl, saying that he had heard from Frau K. that she took no interest in anything but sexual matters and that she used to read Mantegazza's *Physiology of Love* and books of that sort in their house on the lake. It was most likely, he had added, that she had been overexcited by such reading and had merely "fancied" the whole scene she had described.[2]

Dora's father, accepting Herr K.'s version of the story, told Freud, "I myself believe that Dora's tale of the man's immoral

---

    [2]Sigmund Freud, *Dora: An Analysis of a Case of Hysteria* (New York: Collier Books, 1963), 41.

suggestions is a phantasy that has forced its way into her mind...Please try and bring her to reason."[3] But Freud, who had a commitment to his patients, resolved "from the first to suspend my judgment of the true state of affairs till I had heard the other side as well."[4] When he heard Dora's story, Freud accepted her version, including her perception "that she had been handed over to Herr K. as the price of his tolerating the relations between her father and his wife."[5] These experiences of betrayal and sexual harassment provide Freud's focus for the case:

> The experience with Herr K.–his making love to her and the insult to her honour that was involved–seems to provide Dora's case the psychic trauma which Breuer and I declared long ago to be the indispensable prerequisite for the production of a hysterical disorder.[6]

However, even though Freud accepted Dora's version of the family drama, he focused on her sexual desires rather than the family dynamics. At this point the case becomes complicated for most readers, because Freud seems to blame Dora for what happened. "[Dora] had made herself an accomplice in the affair, and had dismissed from her mind every sign which tended to show its true character."[7] Why did Freud focus on Dora's complicity rather than the family pathology? Freud's apparent motive for this exploration was his scientific interest in the disease of hysteria, that is, the symptoms and cures of frigidity and physical ailments in women. Commenting on the time when Herr K. kissed her in his office, Freud said, "I should without question consider a person hysterical in whom an occasion for sexual excitement elicited feelings that were preponderantly or exclusively unpleasurable."[8] In a footnote on this section, Freud also said, "I happen to know Herr K., for he was the same person who had visited me with the patient's father, and he was still quite young and of prepossessing appearance."[9] Freud apparently thought that Herr K. was an appropriate suitor for Dora in spite of

---

[3] Ibid., 42.
[4] Ibid.
[5] Ibid., 50.
[6] Ibid., 42.
[7] Ibid., 51.
[8] Ibid., 44.
[9] Ibid.

her age, his friendship with her father, and the multiple betrayals of fidelity within the family.[10] Freud decided that the therapeutic goal was to help Dora see that her illness was caused by an inner conflict, namely, sexual desire for Herr K., and fear of her sexual feelings.

Freud organized his therapeutic work by exploring Dora's sexual conflict and uncovering her love for Herr K. He decided that her physical symptoms were responses to her love for Herr K. She was sick when he was gone and well when he was present. She rejected a governess/maid who tried to expose her father's affair with Frau K. Freud worked on the assumption that Dora must acknowledge her love for Herr K. in order to get well; that is, she must see that saying no to Herr K. actually meant that she loved him.[11]

> If this "No," instead of being regarded as the expression of an impartial judgement (of which, indeed, the patient is incapable), is ignored, and if work is continued, the first evidence soon begins to appear that in such a case "No" signifies the desired "Yes"...There is no such thing at all as an unconscious "No."[12]

In his attempts to show that Dora actually loved Herr K., Freud explores his insistence that her no means yes through many detours about Dora's sexual fantasies about men and women, about masturbation and bed-wetting, about oral sex and homosexuality. He even defends himself against charges that he was sexualizing Dora through this process.[13]

---

[10]"A glance back at her history will remind us that her family had exposed her to multiple sexual *infidelities,* while all concerned—father and mother, Mr. K. and Mrs. K.— tried to compensate for their pervading *perfidy* by making Dora their *confidante,* each burdening her (not without her perverse provocation, to be sure) with half-truths that were clearly unmanageable for an adolescent," Erik Erikson in Charles Bernheimer and Claire Kahane, eds., *In Dora's Case: Freud, Hysteria, Feminism* (New York: Columbia University Press, 1985), 51–52.

[11]For a good discussion of how patriarchy turns a woman's no into yes, see Marie M. Fortune, *Love Does No Harm: Sexual Ethics for the Rest of Us* (New York: Continuum, 1995).

[12]Freud, 76, 75. This view of Freud's is an infamous example of the hidden influence of psychoanalytic theory on U.S. society. This clever statement denies the possibility of consent in a patriarchal society. If there is no such thing as an unconscious no, how does a woman withhold consent from an abusive sexual assault?

[13]"It is possible for a man to talk to girls and women upon sexual matters of every kind without doing them harm and without bringing suspicion upon himself," ibid., 65.

In the case study, Freud focuses on two dreams. In the first, Dora dreamed that she was rescued from a burning house by her father:

> A house was on fire. My father was standing beside my bed and woke me up. I dressed myself quickly. Mother wanted to stop and save her jewel-case; but Father said, "I refuse to let myself and my two children be burnt for the sake of your jewel-case." We hurried downstairs, and as soon as I was outside I woke up.[14]

Dora had first dreamed this dream just after Herr K.'s kiss by the lake, and Freud interpreted it as a wish that her father would protect her from Herr K. The jewel-case represented her virginity and drew on her memories of her father waking her as a young child when she had a problem with bed-wetting. Freud interpreted this as a defensive reaction against the underlying love she had for Herr K.

> The dream confirms once more what I had already told you before you dreamed it—that you are summoning up your old love for your father in order to protect yourself against your love for Herr K. But what do all these efforts show? Not only that you are afraid of Herr K., but that you are still more afraid of yourself, and of the temptation you feel to yield to him. In short, these efforts prove once more how deeply you loved him.[15]

Then Freud wrote, "Naturally Dora would not follow me in this part of the interpretation."[16] However, he maintained his theory of dream interpretation with its emphasis on early childhood experiences of bed-wetting and masturbation and continued his belief that Dora was in love with Herr K.[17]

In the second dream, Dora was informed by her mother that her father was dead. She had trouble finding her way home, and

---

[14]Ibid., 81.

[15]Ibid., 88.

[16]Ibid.

[17]In fairness, we must acknowledge that this case study may be Freud's earliest reference to transference. Thus, he does not have the advantage of the research and development of this idea. "He was, in fact, just beginning to learn about this therapeutic phenomenon, and the present passage is the first really important one about it to have been written," Steven Marcus in Bernheimer and Kahane, 89.

when she finally got there, "The maidservant opened the door to me and replied that Mother and the others were already at the cemetery."[18] Again Freud explored a sexual interpretation that led back to Herr K.

Two sessions later, Dora announced that this was her last session. Freud concludes in the same place where he starts: "The fact is, I am beginning to suspect that you took the affair with Herr K. much more seriously than you have been willing to admit so far."[19]

At the end of the case, Freud tried to explain why Dora terminated prematurely. Perhaps her father lost interest because Freud did not "bring Dora to reason." Perhaps Freud had not shown enough "warm personal interest in her."[20] Maybe Dora decided to return to her symptoms rather than get well. ("Incapacity for meeting a real erotic demand is one of the most essential features of a neurosis."[21]) Perhaps, "I did not succeed in mastering the transference in good time."[22] Perhaps he had underestimated Dora's attachment to Frau K. ("I failed to discover in time and to inform the patient that her homosexual [gynaecophilic] love for Frau K. was the strongest unconscious current in her mental life."[23])

Fifteen months later, Dora returned to tell Freud that she had confronted Herr and Frau K. with their lies.

> To the wife she said: "I know you have an affair with my father"; and the other did not deny it. From the husband she drew an admission of the scene by the lake which he had disputed, and brought the news of her vindication home to her father. Since then she had not resumed her relations with the family.[24]

Freud tried to disguise his disappointment that Dora terminated therapy before he was finished with her. "I do not know what kind of help she wanted from me, but I promised to forgive her for having deprived me of the satisfaction of affording her a far more

---

[18]Freud, 114.
[19]Ibid., 129.
[20]Ibid., 131.
[21]Ibid., 132.
[22]Ibid., 140.
[23]Ibid., 142.
[24]Ibid., 143.

radical cure for her troubles."[25] The day after he finished writing up this case, Freud wrote to a friend that this was "the subtlest thing I have written so far."[26] His judgment that this case would turn out to be an important part of his life work was correct because it has become one of the most widely read clinical cases in the history of modern psychology.[27]

Dora's Resistance

Freud's case study about Dora belongs in a study of male violence because of its importance in contemporary debates about gender and sexuality, and because it provides accessibility to psychoanalytic methods. Though we have no access to anything written by Dora about her experience, Freud's account offers clues about her resistance to patriarchy and to him.

Dora seems to have resisted in silence for many years. In spite of Freud's attempt to manipulate her into revealing her own desires, at the end of the case he confessed that he had underestimated her attachment to Frau K. Dora was silent about her plans to terminate therapy after only three months. Freud could not complete his analysis because she resisted him through silence. At the last session, where Freud revealed his own view that Dora wanted to marry Herr K., he reports that Dora responded with polite silence: "Dora had listened to me without any of her usual contradictions. She seemed to be moved; she said good-bye to me very warmly, with the heartiest wishes for the New Year, and—came no more."[28]

Sometimes Dora resisted through language. During sessions, Freud became more aggressive in trying to convince her that her unhappiness and physical symptoms were caused by her repressed love for Herr K., even though she consistently denied that it was true.

> I did not find it easy, however, to direct the patient's attention to her relations with Herr K. She declared that she had none with him...

---

[25] Ibid., 144.

[26] Ibid., 7.

[27] "Dora is thus no longer read as merely a case history or a fragment of an analysis of hysteria but as an urtext in the history of woman, a fragment of an increasingly heightened critical debate about the meaning of sexual difference and its effects on the representations of feminine desire," Bernheimer and Kahane, 31.

[28] Freud, 130.

My expectations were by no means disappointed when this explanation of mine was met by Dora with a most emphatic negative...

Naturally Dora would not follow me in this part of the interpretation...

[Dora] "Why, has anything so very remarkable come out?"[29]

After many hours of psychoanalysis, Dora had the audacity to tell Freud that his interpretation did not impress her very much. Freud seemed confused by this comment, and he ruminated often in the future over his inability to convince Dora of his own brilliance.

Dora resisted through action. She ran away from Herr K. in the first incident of sexual harassment, and slapped him in the face the second time. She told Freud the family secrets, fully expecting him to side with her just claims. But her final victory came when she announced her termination.

She opened the third sitting with these words: "Do you know that I am here for the last time to-day?"–"How can I know, as you have said nothing to me about it?"–"Yes, I made up my mind to put up with it till the New Year. But I shall wait no longer than that to be cured."[30]

Thus, Dora acted out her resistance to Freud's mistreatment and abuse.

The Nature of Male Dominance

In this case study of Freud and Dora, we can see some of the outlines of the structures of power behind male violence against women and children, namely, male dominance within a patriarchal system. Through this discussion, we can begin to understand the system of power and dominance that has its effects on the church and that begins to explain our silence about such abuses of power.

The "matrix of domination" is a "system of attitudes, behaviors and assumptions that objectifies human persons

---

[29]Ibid., 47, 76, 88, 126.
[30]Ibid., 126.

on the basis of [socially constructed categories such as race, gender, class, etc.], and that has the power to deny autonomy, access to resources and self-determination to those persons, while maintaining the values of the dominant society as the norm by which all else will be measured."[31]

1. The matrix of domination is "a system of attitudes, behaviors and assumptions that objectifies human persons on the basis of [socially constructed categories such as race, gender, class, etc.]."

What are the clues that Freud had a system of attitudes, behaviors, and assumptions that objectified Dora on the basis of gender? If we rely on Freud's report of Dora's resistance, it appears that she first came to him under pressure from her father. Perhaps she stayed awhile because Freud believed her story about the family infidelities. Through her hope that someone would believe her story, she resisted by disclosing family secrets. Her first sign of resistance was trying to enlist Freud to take her side and the side of justice. Even after Freud pressured her to accept his fantasy of her love for Herr K., she rejected this interpretation in hopes that he would believe her again. "She had all these years been in love with Herr K. When I informed her of this conclusion she did not assent to it."[32] When it became apparent that Freud would not change his attitudes and behaviors, she terminated her analysis.

If we follow this line of thinking into Freud's mind, then we begin to find other attitudes, behaviors, and assumptions that objectified Dora on the basis of gender. For example, in the introduction Freud says "that the causes of hysterical disorders are to be found in the intimacies of the patient's psycho-sexual life, and that hysterical symptoms are the expression of their most secret and repressed wishes."[33] Freud decided that Dora must be repressing her sexual attraction for Herr K., because only an abnormal person would respond to "an occasion for sexual excitement" with "feelings that were preponderantly or

---

[31]The phrase "matrix of domination" is appropriated from Patricia Hill Collins, *Black Feminist Thought* (New York: Routledge, 1990), 225. The rest of the definition is appropriated from The Cornwall Collective, *Your Daughters Shall Prophesy* (New York: Pilgrim Press, 1980), 39.

[32]Freud, 53.

[33]Ibid., 22.

exclusively unpleasurable."[34] Based on our knowledge of Freud's other theories of sexuality and gender, we can see that, by objectifying Dora so that she would conform to his idea of a "true womanhood,"[35] he himself became her abuser.

Much of the debate about this case focuses on countertransference. Herr K. held a position of authority, allowing him to engage in a crude seduction and attempted rape, while Freud depended on overpowering Dora with words. One wonders what might have happened if Dora had been even more vulnerable and had accepted Freud's pressure to believe she was in love with Herr K. Perhaps then the voyeuristic exploitation of Dora would have been more severe, like the contemporary sexual abuse by therapists and clergy. Freud's power and his interest in her being attracted to Herr K. were a dangerous combination for Dora, but fortunately she resisted.

2. Domination "has the power to deny autonomy, access to resources and self-determination to those persons."

Although Freud's social power over Dora was not absolute, his social status allowed him to be an oppressor. Not only did he write and publish, therefore setting the terms for future public discussion of Dora's personal life, but he was male, middle-aged, established as a physician, upper-class, a published scientific writer, and relatively wealthy. Dora too came from a wealthy family, which gave her social class, but she was an adolescent, female, and symptomatic. Freud's profession as a physician rested on his responsibility to provide access to resources, in this case, insight into the psychological motives of one's life, and education in an emerging scientific anthropology. Many of Freud's students and clients went on to become leaders in the new field of psychoanalytic psychology, gaining personal and social power.

Ida Bauer (Dora's real name) was a gifted woman, with the potential for personal achievement. Whereas her brother became a leading intellectual leader of European socialism, she, based on the witness of Felix Deutsch many years later, did not reach her potential.[36] One can speculate that a more therapeutic and less abusive analysis might have provided her the resolution she needed to make a larger contribution. Instead, she suffered a form

[34]Ibid., 44.

[35]Hazel Carby, *Reconstructing Womanhood* (New York: Oxford University Press, 1987), 23.

[36]Bernheimer and Kahane, 35ff.

of gender oppression that reinforced her subordinate status in her family and in society. Freud went on to become the most famous psychologist of the century without penalty for his mistakes, whereas Ida Bauer paid for his mistakes with a damaged psyche and spirit.

3. Domination "maintains the values of the dominant society as the norm by which all else will be measured."

Many of Freud's followers and critics consider the case study of Dora important for constructing contemporary gender power relations. Freud has maintained his power and prestige in spite of being both loved and hated. Although his view of women as deficient and deformed persons continues, many feminists count Dora among their heroes because she employed silence, language, and action to resist Freud. Freud's case study exemplifies the manner in which the dominant society maintains norms. Freud's construction of the Oedipus complex as the basic definition of gender and sexuality has bolstered patriarchy for almost a century in spite of the resistance of Dora and other women witnesses to evil's creativity and persistence.

Why Study Freud?

There are many reasons not to study Freud. His ideas have been discredited in the minds of many people because of his patriarchal attitudes toward women, because of his individualistic theories that ignore familial and socioeconomic realities, because of his obsession with sexuality as the central drive in human life, and because of his negative evaluation of religious faith and practice. For these reasons many have rejected Freud and gone on to other theories such as behaviorism, cognitive development, family therapy, and humanistic psychology.

However, I believe that Freud is important for understanding the modern psychological age, and especially for understanding issues of race and gender as ideologies of oppression.

First, in his attitudes about gender, Freud was typical of the European men of his time. Because Freud's theories reflect gender inequality and the oppression of women, understanding how Freud's values and ideas were patriarchal gives us insight into how this evil is created and perpetuated.

Feminists have been quick to point out that the reason for Freud's failure are clearly sexist: Freud is authoritarian, a willing participant in the male power game conducted between Dora's father and Herr K., and at no time turns to consider Dora's own experience of the events. That Freud's analysis fails because of its inherent sexism is the common feminist conclusion.[37]

Second, Freud has been identified by some feminist scholars as an important dialogue partner because he placed sexuality and gender politics at the heart of his theory and thus created the possibility of making gender thematic for other critical theories.

> I would like to look at this case once again with feminist eyes...I will argue...that Freud's analysis is only partly true...because it is structured around a fantasy of femininity and female sexuality that remains misunderstood, unconscious if you will...[P]sychoanalysis is not simply the theory of the formation of gender identity and sexuality in patriarchal society but is profoundly ideological as well.[38]

Third, Freud is important because a study of his critical methods can unmask forms of patriarchy of the nineteenth and twentieth centuries. Certain scholars have argued that it is possible to use Freud against Freud, that is, to adopt his methods in a way that explodes the metapsychology reinforcing patriarchy.

> There is a difference between Freud's metapsychology and his methodology. Freud's metapsychology includes such powerful constructs as the Oedipus complex, ego–id–superego, and eros-thanatos. His methodology includes such potent analytic concepts as transference, resistance, anxiety, countertransference, counterresistance, and counteranxiety...I accept the judgment that, practically, in the therapeutic situation, it is the analysis of phenomena using methodological concepts that is primary and that allows change while the metapsychological constructs

---

[37]Toril Moi in Bernheimer and Kahane, 182.

[38]Maria Ramas in Bernheimer and Kahane, 150. See Juliet Mitchell, *Psychoanalysis and Feminism* (New York: Pantheon, 1974). Mitchell's important contribution to feminist theory was her insight that classical psychoanalysis, which has as one objective the study of formation of gender identity and sexuality in patriarchal culture, is a useful tool for feminism. "The critical task is to separate those aspects of the theory that are ideological from those that are insightful and useful–if incomplete," footnote 2, 177.

provide supplementary, multidimensional structures of interpretive insight.[39]

Interpretations of Freud

Freud published his "Fragment of an Analysis of a Case of Hysteria" in 1905, based on three months of therapy with Ida Bauer in late 1900. He originally wrote the case in 1901, one year after *The Interpretation of Dreams* and four years before *Three Essays on Sexuality.* "[I]t is caught quite literally between...the theory of the unconscious and the theory of sexuality...*Dora* would then mark the transition between these two theories."[40] It has become known as "Dora's Case" because of the pseudonym Freud gave the client to protect her privacy. Her true identity was revealed when Felix Deutsch wrote in 1957 that he had seen Ida Bauer for consultation in New York City in 1922. He published her name after he heard she had died in 1945.

The following discussion analyzes Freud's interpretation of the case of Dora in three ways: as an example of patriarchal distortion, as a flawed critical theory of gender and sexuality, and as a method to unmask patriarchy.

Dora as a Frigid Hysteric

Until recently, many interpreters of Freud followed his view that Dora represents a classic hysteric personality whose fear of sexuality led to frigidity.

> "Fragment of an Analysis"...is considered a classic analysis of the structure and genesis of hysteria and has the first or last word in almost every psychoanalytic discussion of hysteria. Although some have written addenda to Freud's case study, following up on one or another of Dora's multiple identifications or reconsidering the case from the point of view of ego psychology, or from that of technique, or transference, the essential meaning of the analysis remains unchallenged. Dora's frigidity, so haunting to Freud and to us, is still considered a cornerstone of hysteria and its most profound symptom. And the meaning Freud

---

[39]David R. Blumenthal, *Facing the Abusing God: A Theology of Protest* (Louisville: Westminster Press, 1993), 12–13.

[40]Rose, 130; Moi in Bernheimer and Kahane, 184.

attributed to it is still considered to be "truth" by psychoanalytic theory and by popular culture.[41]

The case study of Dora defines and illustrates several basic ideas in classical psychoanalytic theory: (1) Hysteria is the repression of sexual desire (frigidity); (2) dream interpretation confirms unconscious dynamics; (3) sexuality is formed through Oedipal conflict; and (4) transference is a basic technique of psychoanalysis.

However, classical interpretations also criticize Freud for misunderstanding Dora. Philip Rieff, a translator of Freud, summarizes this viewpoint:

> Of course, Freud knew that the girl was right. He had to admire Dora's insight into this intricate and sad affair-within-an-affair. Yet he fought back with his own intricate insights into the tangle of her own motives; that was his error; there is the point at which the complexity of Freudian analysis must reach out, beyond the individual patient, to the entire tangle of motives of all the bad actors—father, mistress, would-be lover, stupid mother. Only then would the analysis have been complete, true and adequately pedagogic.[42]

Dora as a Feminist Hero

Feminists studying Freud's case of Dora have pointed out that, far from representing the typical hysteric whose frigidity is an illness, Dora actually engaged in revolt against the control and oppression of patriarchy. In spite of Dora's being surrounded by men who disrespected her (her father), abused her (Herr K.), and manipulated her in therapy (Freud), she stood against them all and exposed their games. In the end she told the truth about her

---

[41]Ramas in Bernheimer and Kahane, 150. For other authors who address the importance of this case for the development of Freud's theory of hysteria, see Mark Kanzer and Jules Glenn, eds., *Freud and His Patients* (New York: Jason Aronson, 1980); Samuel Slipp, "Interpersonal Factors in Hysteria: Freud's Seduction Theory and the Case of Dora," *Journal of the American Academy of Psychoanalysis* 5 (1977); Jean Laplanche, "Panel on 'Hysteria Today,'" *International Journal of Psycho-Analysis* 55 (1974); Hyman Muslin and Merton Gill, "Transference in the Dora Case," *Journal of the American Psychoanalytic Association* 26 (1978).

[42]Philip Rieff in Freud, 17.

father's affair, forced a confession of abuse from Herr K., and rejected Freud's interpretation of her sexual desire. Thus, Dora becomes a hero who rejects male dominance in her life and a model for the resistance of all women to patriarchal oppression.

Maria Ramas gives one of the most forceful presentations of this argument:

> I will argue that at the deepest level of meaning, Ida Bauer's hysteria was exactly what it appeared to be–a repudiation of the meaning of heterosexuality...It was an attempt to deny patriarchal sexuality, and it was a protest against postoedipal femininity.[43]

Ramas uses Dora's real name, Ida Bauer, as a way of challenging Freud's control of the patient he wrote about. She also questions Freud's preoccupation with Ida's frigidity, so important to his theory of hysteria. As we saw in the previous section, psychoanalytic theory actually created the category of the frigid hysteric, the woman who fears her unconscious sexual desire and must be forced to acknowledge this desire in order to avoid illness. In other words, marriage and an active sex life could cure hysteria.

These problems, of course, arise out of the theory of psychoanalysis itself, especially the Oedipal complex. Because a girl's first erotic attachment is usually with her mother, she must transform this attachment to become heterosexual. Accepting heterosexuality as the goal of normative development, within a theory that assumes a primitive human bisexuality, is an internal contradiction of psychoanalysis, and one that is at the root of Freud's treatment of Ida Bauer.

Ramas' interpretation notes the absence of the mother in Freud's study. Freud called Kathe Bauer a neurotic housewife, that is, a woman with an obsessive need for order and cleanliness. Ramas suggests that, having contracted a venereal disease from her husband, Kathe Bauer's resulting fear of contamination may have contributed to her daughter's negative views of sexuality. Ramas suggests that, given her mother's experience, Ida's disgust with sexuality was a realistic response. Yet "Freud indeed argues here that Ida Bauer was hysterical because she was disgusted by

---

[43]Ramas in Bernheimer and Kahane, 151–52.

Herr K.'s kiss when she should have felt aroused."[44] So Ramas asks:

> In the face of such consistent behavior, why should we follow Freud in his assertion that Ida Bauer's attitude toward Herr K. was not what it appeared to be? That her symptoms revealed reversal of affect? Why should we be convinced that her behavior and her desire were at odds?[45]

However, Ida Bauer's forms of resistance were limited. As a child, she had no choice about being a member of this family, with its illnesses and immoralities; but she did have the choice, as she became old enough, to expose the infidelities. By rejecting Herr K.'s advances, Ida threatened the whole structure of adult liaisons.

> When Herr K. demanded that Ida's romantic fantasies succumb to his sexual desire, she blew the whistle, so to speak, on everyone's fantasy, including her own...In a sense, Ida Bauer was an outlaw. As Freud noted, Frau K. was the one person whom Ida spared, while she pursued the others with an almost malignant vindictiveness. In sparing Frau K. Ida spared herself. In this way she denied both her love for Frau K. as well as its futility.[46]

Ida Bauer is a feminist hero because she exposed the sexual abuse in the family even at the expense of jeopardizing her own security.

Dora as Freud's Fantasy

A third interpretation of Freud's case study focuses less on Dora as a patient and a woman, and more on Freud as narrator, therapist, and man. In this reading, the case study is less about Dora as a real person and more about Dora as Freud's fantasy.

Freud ended his case study with two astounding acknowledgements: first, that he did not adequately interpret Dora's transference to Freud of her feelings about Herr K.; second, that he failed to understand Dora's homosexual attachment for Frau K. These issues form the basis for much of the feminist debate about Freud.

---

[44]Ibid., 161.
[45]Ibid., 162.
[46]Ibid., 165.

First, Freud said he misunderstood the significance of Dora's transference. When he interpreted the first dream, Freud said that leaving the burning house meant "you have decided to give up the treatment—to which, after all, it is only your father who makes you come."[47] Later he suggested that Dora connected him with Herr K. because they were both smokers, and wondered whether "the idea had probably occurred to her one day during a sitting that she would like to have a kiss from me."[48] He refers to the transference again when she hid a letter: "I believe that Dora only wanted to play 'secrets' with me, and to hint that she was on the point of allowing her secret to be torn from her by the physician."[49] Later he comments that the first dream might be about termination: "The dream-thoughts behind it included a reference to my treatment, and it corresponded to a renewal of the old resolution to withdraw from danger."[50] However, Freud did not see that Dora might run from the danger of therapy the same way she ran from the abuse by Herr K.

In the postscript, Freud struggles with Dora's transference to him and wonders about its significance.

> I did not succeed in mastering the transference in good time...At the beginning it was clear that I was replacing her father in her imagination...But when the first dream came, in which she gave herself the warning that she had better leave my treatment just as she had formerly left Herr K's house, I ought to have listened to the warning myself. "Now," I ought to have said to her, "it is from Herr K. that you have made a transference on to me. Have you noticed anything that leads you to suspect me of evil intentions similar (whether openly or in some sublimated form) to Herr K.'s? Or have you been struck by anything about me or got to know anything about me which has caught your fancy, as happened previously with Herr K?"...In this way the transference took me unawares, and, because of the unknown quantity in me which reminded Dora of Herr K., she took her revenge on me as she wanted to take her

---

[47]Freud, 88.
[48]Ibid., 92.
[49]Ibid., 96.
[50]Ibid., 113.

revenge on him, and deserted me as she believed herself to have been deceived and deserted by him. Thus she *acted* an essential part of her recollections and phantasies instead of reproducing them in the treatment.[51]

Freud's post-facto question to Dora about whether he, Freud, had "any evil intentions similar to Herr K.'s" or whether there is "anything about me which has caught your fancy, as happened previously with Herr K." is fruitful because it raises the issue of countertransference—that is, not just why Freud was connected with Herr K. in Dora's imagination, but also what Dora meant in Freud's imagination.

Second, Freud failed to understand Dora's homosexual attachment for Frau K. At least five figures appear at various times for Dora's erotic and emotional identification: her mother, her father, Herr K., Frau K., and the governess/maid. At various times, Freud considered each of these figures as Dora's primary identification.

Freud considered and rejected the mother as a figure of identification by saying: "The relations between the girl and her mother had been unfriendly for years. The daughter looked down on her mother and used to criticize her mercilessly, and she had withdrawn completely from her influence."[52] Freud's rejection of the mother is ironic considering that the mother appeared in a central role in both of the dreams, and that psychoanalytic theory itself has always insisted that the mother is the most likely central figure in the object world of patients.

As we have clearly seen, Freud believed that Dora's primary identification figure was Herr K. because of her repressed love for him, and that behind this was her identification with her father. Based on the first dream in which her father rescued her from the fire, Freud decided that the father was an important attachment figure because of her "wish that her father might take the place of the man who was her tempter."[53] This interpretation began to fail when Dora killed off her father in the second dream and Freud was left to scramble for who was left.

---

[51]Ibid., 140–41.
[52]Ibid., 35.
[53]Ibid., 107.

Dora's father was dead, and the others had already gone to the cemetery. She might calmly read whatever she chose. Did not this mean that one of her motives for revenge as a revolt against her parents' constraint? If her father was dead she could read or love as she pleased.[54]

But whom did she want to love in her freedom? Freud tried to return to her love for Herr K: "'So you see that your love for Herr K. did not come to an end with the scene, but that (as I maintained) it has persisted down to the present day–though it is true that you are unconscious of it.'"[55] The presence of the governess/maid at the end of the dream proves to be very important in some feminist interpretations, as we shall see below.

At the next session when Dora announced that this was her last, Freud tried to put her in the role of the governess because she had decided two weeks earlier to terminate (the usual notice for governesses). Then, in perhaps the most bizarre episode of the whole case, he suggested that she wanted to marry Herr K. "'I know now–and this is what you do not want to be reminded of–that you did fancy that Herr K.'s proposals were serious, and that he would not leave off until you had married him.'"[56] In the footnotes Freud acknowledges that he missed the importance of Frau K. "Behind the almost limitless series of displacements which were thus brought to light, it was possible to divine the operation of a single simple factor–Dora's deep-rooted homosexual love for Frau K."[57]

Freud's Betrayal of Dora

My thesis in this chapter is that Freud refused to respect and support Dora's resistance to the evil of patriarchy, and thus he betrayed her trust in him as a healer. In this section I will examine Freud's complicity in patriarchy as a leader of the intellectual debates about gender in Europe and the United States.[58]

---

[54]Ibid., 121.
[55]Ibid., 125.
[56]Ibid., 130.
[57]Ibid., 126.
[58]For discussion about the importance of Freud in the intellectual debates within the United States, see Ann Douglas, *Terrible Honesty* (New York: Farrar, Strauss, and Giroux, 1995).

Several issues in this case study reveal Freud's complicity with patriarchy. Why did it take so long for Freud to recognize the importance of Frau K. in Dora's desire? Why did Freud refuse to consider Dora's mother even though she was prominent in her dreams? Why did the governess/maid became a symbolic figure for Freud at the last session?

Two conclusions about this case are especially relevant to our discussion of the relation of male dominance and evil.

First, Freud did not see the abusive behaviors of the other men in this story because he failed to understand his mistreatment of Dora. Freud did not adequately interpret Dora's transference from Herr K. and her father because he would have seen that his own abuse of Dora was similar to Herr K.'s.

Second, Freud's patriarchal worldview prevented him from identifying with Dora's vulnerability and understanding her resistance as a form of active agency. Freud could not see her attachment to Frau K., her mother, and the governess because he did not see women as active agents in their own lives.

Freud and Male Violence

Freud did not see the violence of the other men in this story because he failed to understand his own abusive behaviors against Dora. For many readers, Freud's insistence that Dora's sexual desire was directed to Herr K. is the most shocking part of the case study. Ignoring the interpersonal and family issues, Freud focused on Dora's so-called frigidity.

In the beginning Freud seemed to support Dora's protest against the sexual abuse from Herr K. and agreed that it was inappropriate for her father not to protect her. He even called Dora's experience a "sexual trauma."[59] Because he initially seemed to understand her terror and support her wish for safety, Dora may have thought that Freud was different from the other men in her life. Later she must have been confused to discover that he was more interested in her sexual fantasies than in her safety. True, Dora's fantasies seem to have been sexualized because of the family pathology, but Freud betrayed her trust when he attributed these fantasies to her desire rather than to her best efforts to cope with the family craziness.

---

[59]Freud, 43.

In the first dream, we can now see that the burning house may have represented Dora's unconscious awareness of the danger of therapy with Freud. Dora was endangered with Freud just as she was with Herr K. Freud himself acknowledged this when he wrote, "But when the first dream came...she gave herself the warning that she had better leave my treatment just as she had formerly left Herr K's house..."[60] Freud's focus on Dora's sexuality was endangering her sexual life (her jewel case).

In spite of his own insight, Freud continued to focus on Dora's sexual desire for Herr K., which led to the second dream, in which Dora killed off her father so she could be free to "read or love as she pleased."[61] In the second dream Dora indirectly communicated to Freud that she wanted him dead so she could be free to go on with her life. When he was unable to hear her communication, she terminated therapy, thus killing him off as a continuing influence in her life. Dora's implicit commentary on Freud's mistreatment was a communication he did not hear.

Why did Freud identify with Dora's father and Herr K. and insist that Dora focus on her sexual desire for these men? Why did Freud fail to see that he was acting toward Dora in the same way as her father and Herr K.? The reason is that male sexual violence against women was built into his theories and into relationships between women and men in nineteenth-century Vienna. Freud's developing theories of gender and sexuality included the Oedipus complex, castration anxiety, and the primal scene. At the heart of the Oedipus complex is the idea that, because women are the primary parents, both boys and girls are originally erotically attached to their mothers. Women are their first sexual objects. When boys become aware that the father has a sexual claim on the mother, their first impulse is to hate their fathers. But because they fear being castrated by the father's overwhelming power, they repress their desire for Mother, identify with Father, and transfer their sexual feelings to other women. Unfortunately, men also internalize the right of men to possess and dominate women.

However, the theory of the Oedipal complex does not work with girls because it requires that they comply with the heterosexual norm by denying their sexual feelings for their

---

[60]Ibid., 140.
[61]Ibid., 121.

mother and developing sexual feelings for men. According to Maria Ramas, psychoanalytic theory offers two solutions to this contradiction for women. In the first solution, the girl hates her mother when she discovers that her mother is already castrated and transforms her wish for a penis into a wish for a baby. This wish brings her into heterosexual compliance with society. In the second solution, the girl seeks a relationship with her father as a way of freeing herself from the omnipotent mother. Thus, the search for a penis is a form of individuation from the mother.

Ramas rejects both these theories because of their devaluation of the mother (women and femininity), and because they fail to acknowledge the ambivalence toward the father (men and masculinity).

> Neither theory seriously considers the possibility of an essential ambivalence toward the phallus itself... Psychoanalytic formulations present the phallus alternatively as signifier of desire, as symbolizing protection, invulnerability, potency, or freedom from an all-engulfing, preoedipal mother. The fantasies of castration and of the Father-as-castrator force us to posit other meanings: violence, destruction, sadism. The primal fantasy of castration depends, on the one hand, upon the equation of femininity, masochism, and annihilation and, on the other, upon the sadistic meaning of the phallus/Father.[62]

The Oedipus complex fails as a theory for girls because it cannot explain how the essentially negative attributes of sadism provide adequate energy for heterosexual desire. Identifying with the annihilating mother does not create a positive construction of feminine sexual identity; and idealizing the sadistic, violent image of the father/phallus does not lead to female heterosexual desire.

Sexuality and violence are also related in psychoanalytic theory through the primal scene, that is, through the trauma involved when the child witnesses sexual intercourse between her or his parents. Freud believed that most children interpret sexual intercourse as a scene of violence and degradation because they first experience it during the anal-sadistic stage of their own development.

---

[62]Ramas in Bernheimer and Kahane, 156.

Psychoanalytic theory argues that the fantasy of the "primal scene" is in fact a misinterpretation on the child's part...In contrast, I believe it is an accurate perception of the dominant patriarchal sexual fantasy...Embedded most definitively in pornography, the "scene" is one of dominance and submission, and these are its essential erotic components...[and] the fantasy is heterosexual; it is a "scene" between a man and a woman. Even when those acting out the fantasy are of the same sex, the "scene" depicts the submission and degradation of whoever is in the feminine position. That is to say, ultimately and always, a woman is being degraded. The fantasy may be mild in content, or it may reach to the extreme other end of the continuum to express a sadomasochistic desire that seeks ultimate satisfaction in the total annihilation of the woman–the feminine.[63]

Freud's attempt to explain sexual violence by locating sadistic sexual desires in the small child is contradicted by recent research about the prevalence of sexual violence in Western society.[64] However, his emphasis on the violence of the "primal scene" accurately describes much adult male sexual fantasy in a patriarchal culture. Because psychoanalytic theory incorporates the violence of the primal scene as central to its theory of sexuality, Freud misinterpreted the sexually abusive behaviors of Herr K. as legitimate sexual overtures. Because he believed that it was essential for an adolescent girl to become heterosexual, and he also believed that sexual development was always plagued with fears of violence and castration, he was unable to see Dora's legitimate fears of the violation in Herr K.'s proposals. In Freud's fantasies, Herr K. was merely acting as any man would around an attractive woman, and her frigidity in response was a sign of her illness. Therefore, instead of focusing on Herr K.'s violence toward Dora, he chose awakening her sexual desire for Herr K. as his therapeutic goal in order to help her become a healthy woman.

Freud failed to see that his obsession with her sexual desire replicated Herr K.'s abuse. Because psychoanalytic theory

---

[63]Freud, 157.
[64]Judith Herman, *Trauma and Recovery* (New York: Basic Books, 1992).

presupposes that gaining a mature sexual identity depends on sexual conflict that is usually sadistic, he was blind to the male violence that Dora experienced.

Sexual violence is not only a feature of family relationships, it was built into the economic conditions of nineteenth-century Victorian society.

> During the latter half of the nineteenth century, domestic service became an almost exclusively female profession. Increasingly, domestic servants, who were predominantly young and unmarried, took over tasks involving manual labor and the routine aspects of child care from bourgeois wives...But gender and class, femininity and service, were at the same time conflated—insofar as the question posed was sexuality. Bourgeois sexual fantasy did not distinguish between classes of women...[Ida Bauer's identification with the governess] reveals...that femininity was linked with service specifically with regard to sexuality. That is, what lies at the heart of these identifications is a particular fantasy of heterosexuality as service due men, and one explicitly based on submission and degradation.[65]

Therefore, we can see that the presence of the governesses/maids in Freud's story was not accidental. All the maids were presented by Freud as sexualized figures who fell in love with the master of the house or actually had affairs with him. Freud feared that Dora might identify too closely with the maids.

> As Cixous points out, the Dora case is punctuated by women being declared "nothing." Both Herr K. and Dora's father say that of their wives. What is true of the wives (mothers) is even more explicit for the two governesses. Dora "sees a massacre of women executed to make space for her. But she knows that she will in turn be massacred." Neither Dora, the hysteric, nor Freud, the governess, can tolerate the position allotted them by the system of exchanges. Neither Dora nor Freud can tolerate identification with the seduced and abandoned governess.[66]

---

[65]Ramas in Bernheimer and Kahane, 174.
[66]Jane Gallop in Bernheimer and Kahane, 216.

When class is added to gender within a social system that defines human life, the expendability of working-class women and all women becomes clear. Freud could not afford to see the violence of the men, including himself, toward Dora, because he could not afford to see male violence against the governesses who were raped and expelled from the Victorian families of the time. Sexual violence was not a fantasy of children from the anal stage of development, but was an ongoing structure of patriarchal power in which men of status exploited women from the family and from the "lower" classes. Had Freud seen the violence of Dora's father and Herr K., he might have been confronted with the violence of all high-status men in his society. Finally, he would have been confronted with the male dominance of his own theories and practices, which focused on the sexuality of women and ignored the sexual violence of men.

Freud and Women's Agency

Freud's patriarchal worldview prevented him from identifying with Dora's vulnerability and understanding her resistance as a form of active agency. His inability to see Dora, her mother, Frau K., and the governesses as active agents in their own lives, as full human beings, is a common patriarchal attitude.

In a footnote, Freud admitted his failure to understand the importance of Dora's attachment to Frau K. As we have seen from looking at the two dreams, he also missed the importance of Dora's relationship with her mother. Freud no doubt mishandled the case because his theories did not construct roles for women as full human beings and because the economic conditions of his society fostered the subordination of women to men.

Freud's theories of sexuality and gender prevented him from seeing Dora's vulnerability and resistance. As we have seen, his Oedipal theory required that the little boy aggressively leave his mother and identify with his father in order to escape castration, but the little girl must identify with her mother and accept a passive role in relationship to her father and other men. This developmental difference creates a hierarchy of power that corresponds to the dominance of men in the economic and political order. Furthermore, men find it difficult to identify with women without fearing passive homosexuality and becoming victims of sexual violence.

Freud...systematically refuses to consider female sexuality as an active, independent drive. Again and again he exhorts Dora to accept herself as an object for Herr K. Every time Dora reveals active sexual desires, Freud interprets them away...His position is self-contradictory: he is one of the first to acknowledge the existence of sexual desire in women, and at the same time he renders himself incapable of seeing it as more than the impulse to become passive recipients for male desire...[Freud] fails to see that Dora is caught up in an ambivalent relationship to her mother and an idealizing and identifying relationship to Frau K., the other mother-figure in this text. Freud's patriarchal prejudices force him to ignore relationships between women and instead center all his attention on relationships with men.[67]

Freud's theory and his social status as an educated white male in a patriarchal society encouraged him not to identify with Dora or any woman. He could "help" Dora by reminding her of her passive role in relationships with men, but he could not join her in her object world and side with her desire. A man in his position could not be a passive nurturer of the desire of another, especially of a woman, and yet a psychoanalytic principle requires just this kind of identification with the person who comes for treatment. The therapist is a paid helper who offers insights and skills for the needs of the other. To avoid this ethical logic of the deep structure of psychoanalysis, Freud engaged in competition with and domination and abuse of Dora.

Since Dora is a woman, and a rather formidable one at that, a young lady who hitherto has had only scorn for the incompetent (and surely, impotent) doctors who have treated her so far, she becomes a threatening rival for Freud. If he does not win the fight for knowledge, he will also be revealed as incompetent/impotent, his compelling powers will be reduced to nothing, he will be castrated. If Dora wins the knowledge game, her model for knowledge will emerge victorious, and Freud's own model will be destroyed. Freud here finds himself between Scylla and

---

[67]Moi in Bernheimer and Kahane, 191, 194.

Charybdis: if he identifies with Dora in the search for knowledge, he becomes a woman, that is to say, castrated; but if he chooses to cast her as his rival, he must win out, or the punishment will be castration.[68]

Being a man in a patriarchal society and being a therapist whose skills are available for the healing of an "other" are logically contradictory. In order to be a man, Freud must be dominant and win any competition for control. In order to be a therapist, he must engage in a process of mutual transformation with another person. Thus, Freud discloses the contradictions of therapy between men and women in a patriarchal society, and a reason why violence and abuse by male therapists is so prevalent. A male therapist such as Freud must maintain dominance in order to fulfill the hierarchy of men and women, but he is thus prevented from fulfilling the purpose of his therapeutic vocation. To see Dora as an active moral agent would confront Freud with the violence in his own theories and social location.

Jane Gallop describes Freud's inability to identify with Dora through an analogy to the economic status of the governess/maid. Freud cannot identify with Dora, her mother, or Frau K. because they are women, and he can even less identify with the two governesses of a different social class who are sexually abused and rejected.

What shows in the Dora case that neither Dora nor Freud wanted to see is that Frau K. and Dora's mother are in the same position as the maid. In feminist or symbolic or economic terms, the mother/wife is in a position of substitutability and economic inferiority.[69]

It is this inability to see the interlocking hierarchies of gender and class that prevented therapeutic identification. Freud's inability to identify with Dora, who represented the less-than-human gender, and his inability to identify with the governess, who represented the less-than-human social class, limited his ability to be a healer of the psyche.

At the end of the second dream, just before Dora terminates her therapy, Freud narrates: "The maidservant opened the door to

---

[68]Ibid., 195.

[69]Gallop in Bernheimer and Kahane, 217.

me and replied that Mother and the others were already at the cemetery."[70] Later, Dora produces "a piece of the dream which had been forgotten: 'she went calmly to her room, and began reading a big book that lay on her writing-table.'"[71] In this observation we see Dora's agency. Yet Freud insisted to the last session that Dora would only be fulfilled if she admitted her love for and wish to marry Herr K.[72] He could not imagine other possibilities—that Dora had desires that he would never understand, that men (her father, Herr K., Freud) were not the source of meaning and power for her, that she could find fulfillment in the company of other women (mother, Frau K., governesses), that her revolt against patriarchy provided meaning in her life even if it did not lead to happiness.

In this case, Freud betrayed his therapeutic contract with Dora. Instead of understanding her suffering and the structure of her unconscious life, he imposed his patriarchal theories and practices on her, and thus betrayed his commitment to be a healing agent in her life. Paradoxically, feminist analysis of Freud provides a source of hope that patriarchy can be understood and dismantled as both men and women seek to exercise a moral agency that does not need the approval of ideologies and authorities.

In this chapter we have explored the issues of resistance and domination in an important nineteenth-century case study by Sigmund Freud and have uncovered some of the ways that gender evil is maintained. In the next section we look at the social context in which the same dynamics of resistance and domination between groups and social classes is played out.

---

[70]Freud, 114.
[71]Ibid., 120.
[72]Ibid., 130.

8

Resisting Violence in the Name of Jesus[1]

Re-imagining Jesus as the Christ is sometimes challenging for those who have experienced physical and sexual abuse at the hands of Christian fathers, Christian relatives, and Christian clergy. In recent research I have focused my attention on the poetry and other writings of survivors of various forms of abuse in Christian homes and churches. When the Christian scriptures and stories about Jesus are used to justify and perpetuate the terror and violence of abuse, how do survivors reconstruct positive images of God and Christ for their healing? This chapter is an initial, tentative exploration of some of the ways survivors of child abuse resist violence in the name of Jesus.

We live in a time when God is speaking with new power through the people of God. As usual, God often does not speak through the most well-known leaders—that is, the loudest voices of politicians, entertainers, and even religious leaders we hear on television, film, and read about in newspapers and magazines. In the past God spoke through Hagar when she cried to save her son Ishmael (Gen. 21:8–21); God spoke through Rahab, who risked her life to save Israel's spies (Josh. 2:1–24); God spoke through the woman with the flow of blood (Lk. 8:43–48); God spoke through Mary Magdalene when she told the disciples that Jesus had risen from the dead (Jn. 20:1–2). In the same way, God is raising up

---

[1]Original version published as "Resisting Violence in the Name of Jesus," *Journal of Pastoral Theology* 7 (Summer 1997): 15–22.

prophets and saints today in unexpected places and with new images.

Psalm 30:1–3 is one of the psalms that speaks to the experiences of many people today.

> I will extol you, O LORD, for you have drawn me up,
>   and did not let my foes rejoice over me.
> O LORD my God, I cried to you for help,
>   and you have healed me.
> O LORD, you brought up my soul from Sheol,
>   restored me to life from among those gone down to
>   the Pit.

This psalm is a favorite of a new community of theologians in the church, theologians who have not been fully recognized for the new revelations of God they have received, namely, survivors of physical and sexual abuse. The following psalm, written by Karen Doudt, was recently republished in *Alive Magazine,* a United Methodist publication.

> My God, my God
> Why have you forsaken me?
> My body cries out.
> My hands are in knots
> My neck is pained with tension
> My chest is tight, breathing is labored
> My stomach groans with unrest
> My mouth is dry
> My eyes will not close with sleep
> My ears ring
> My mind is pregnant with unrest
> My legs are curled, the muscles crying with tightness
> My heart beats on while pain abounds
> Oh God, my God
> Where are you now?

> My spirit longs for thee
> for the peace that comes with rest
> for the peace that arrives on the footsteps of truth
> for the peace that comes with the healing of brokenness
> for the peace that comes with the release of the
> pained soul from bondage

for the peace that creeps in when I can share the
depths of my pain with trusted ones.

Oh God, my God
release the wells of my eyes
break down the remaining walls of my defense
destroy the fear that enfolds my being
awaken the courage to continue to reach out, to
unfold

 Grant me patience, Lord, to endure
−the time required for healing
−the pain of the width and depth of my emotion
−the pain of aloneness
−the search for truth and understanding
−the search for meaning

O God. I feel like the abandoned child, hardening myself
to survive because I feel so alone. I cry out again−please
enfold me in your arms and wrap me with care. Melt my
defenses. Help me to surrender to complete trust in
significant others so my story can be told and I can find the
things that make for peace. I pray that through this death
I may find life.[2]

By resisting the violence in their lives, Karen and other
survivors are bringing a new religious witness about the love and
power of God in our day. Issues of family and gender violence
require significant changes in the church, in our practices of
pastoral care, and in our theology. As survivors have so vividly
shown, ideas such as the sanctity of marriage and the submission
of women and children to husbands and parents provide the
context that allows abuse and violence.[3] One way for church
leaders to think about these issues is to ask how our preaching,
teaching, and pastoral care would have to change if the entire
congregation understood and responded to the religious witness of
survivors of violence. How do some of our traditional ideas affect

---

[2]Originally published by Karen Doudt in James Poling, *The Abuse of Power: A
Theological Problem* (Nashville: Abingdon Press, 1991), 37–38. See *Alive Now* (Nashville:
Upper Room, 1995).

[3]Annie Imbens and Ineke Jonker, *Christianity and Incest* (Minneapolis: Fortress Press,
1992); Poling, *Abuse of Power.*

persons who are trying to survive in a violent situation or are seeking healing from past abuse or violence in their lives? Annie Imbens and Ineke Jonker summarize their research on the religious life of survivors of incest in *Christianity and Incest.*[4] They suggest that uncritical appropriation of traditional theology creates problems in three areas: (1) images of women, (2) images of God, and (3) images of faith and practice. Women survivors of incest are especially sensitive to the mixed messages aimed at Christian women, messages that say they are supposed to be pure and spotless like Mary or else they will become seductive and evil like Eve. The fact that their fathers sexualized them as children creates enormous guilt and shame and often blocks access to the divine. A God who is presented as an all-powerful father increases their fear of their father's power rather than creating an alternative faith. Some survivors find comfort in the compassionate Jesus, but are confused by his command to obey the father-God. Finally, religion often mandates forgiveness, humility, servanthood, and sacrifice rather than rebellion and resistance against their oppression. Women survivors are calling for revisions in such basic doctrines as God, christology, and the Christian life.

The following psalm poem was written by Valerie J. Bridgeman Davis to hear into speech African American women who suffer from various forms of violence. Listen for the echoes of John 5:2–9.

Do You Wanna Be Whole

She lay on a bed of pain
holding her head, the throbbing pounding to the
rhythm of insanity, out of mindful distance of
Reason:
He had beat her again—and told her
she had asked for it.
Laying there, she tried to recall
when she had made the request.
The couch could have been her coffin
so paralyzed she.
But the Prophet inside her soul cried out:
Do you wanna be whole?

---

[4]Imbens and Jonker.

The furlong back to Reason is Infinity.
No one but the Prophet knows the way back.
But the beaten brow knew
the Journey began with an Eternal No More.[5]

Here, the vivid images of Jesus' compassion for the man at the pool of Bethesda provided the inspiration for one woman to say no to continued violence and find the strength to get off her couch and live. She did not turn to the verses about women being silent in church or women submitting to their husbands. Rather, she identified with the person who had waited so long for healing and needed Jesus' loving confrontation to choose to live.

The following psalm and litany was written by Christian women in Nicaragua to speak of the unspeakable and multiple forms of violence against the bodies of women and children. The destruction of peasant life caused by the United States' Contra War against the Nicaraguan people has continued in the postwar period as the society, local communities, and family life have deteriorated under the crushing poverty and oppression.

Remembrances

God,
We remember the bleeding woman
whose blood converted her into an outcast.
We remember all the unnamed women
who exhausted themselves working the camps
until they bled from their hands and feet.
We remember our slave grandmothers,
beaten and violated by their masters.
We remember our mothers, whose blood
nourished us in the womb.
We remember our sisters, who died
without being given the opportunity to see
a priest or pastor in the church they loved.
We remember the healers, our friends,
our holy mothers who gave us the ancestral
secrets.
We remember the bloody wounds of the women

---

[5]Valerie J. Bridgeman Davis, in Linda H. Hollies, ed., *WomanistCare: How to Tend the Souls of Women,* vol. 1 (Joliet, Ill.: Woman to Woman Ministries, Inc. Publications, 1991).

who work in manufacturing and prostitution.
We remember all our sisters widowed
or without children because of the violence of the
war and the invasions.
We remember all our sisters and daughters
whose blood was stained by AIDS.
We remember the women, our mothers,
our sisters and their daughters, mangled
and bloodied in their houses due to the evil
treatment inflicted on them by husbands and
lovers.

We remember that these bloody women were moved
profoundly by Jesus. We also
are moved by the blood of the woman. Jesus
accepted this woman, gave her life and risked
himself to become near when
she was alone, dirty and marginalized.

God, we trust that you remember all these women. That
you remember all our names and all the histories of our
lives. That our tears have moved you. We trust also that
you know us and for that we are not alone. We trust that
you are always present, although we do not always
understand where and how. For this we wish to ask you:
Bless us and be always for us. Amen.[6]

This litany by and for women in Nicaragua recalls Jesus'
compassion for the woman with the flow of blood (Lk. 8:43–48).
Outcast and despondent, she reached out to Jesus for a miracle,
and touching him revealed a faith that healed her of her physical
condition and her social stigma. Likewise, this story can empower
the thousands of women whose flow of blood is brought on by
violence, rape, poverty, malnutrition, and disease. Their image is
not about twelve men alone in an upper room with Jesus, or the
imperial Jesus in heaven with men on his right and left hands.
Rather, their image is Jesus among the people, one of the people,

---

[6]Adapted from a sermon in Network in Liturgy, Council of Latin American Churches. Received from Brenda Consuelo Ruiz, pastoral counselor with AEDAF (Asociacion Evangelica de Asesoramiento Familiar–The Protestant Association for Family Therapy) in Managua, Nicaragua. Translated from Spanish by James Poling.

raised up by God from the people. This Jesus understands the injustice and violence imposed on women in double doses whatever their social class or economic status. Jesus knows and loves these women as his mothers, sisters, and daughters and supports their resistance to the evil they experience.

In a recent book, Catherine J. Foote gives her witness about her own suffering as a survivor of child sexual abuse and connects it to the violent abuse suffered by Jesus.

> A scar is a scar. It doesn't go away.
> The broken bone may be set, but in the healing,
> traces of the injury remain.
> There it is.
> I was abused. I was hurt. And a scar is a scar.
>
> People around me say, "Forgive."
> Those who know nothing about brokenness and healing
> say to me, "Move on."
> Those who fear the pain say, "Don't look back."
> I insist on acknowledging this pain.
> I insist on recognizing the scar.
> I insist on remembering why there is this jagged, thin
> line.
> I insist on being here with me, on holding me, on
> saying,
> "That was wrong."
>
> Jesus, I know that you remember your pain.
> You still carry those scars that Thomas touched
> with his doubting.
> You insist that there was a real cost when you were
> hurt.
> Stand with me in this place of remembering.
> Stand with me as I clarify: Real injury means real
> pain.
> Stand with me in this truth: A scar is a scar.
>
> Amen.[7]

---

[7]Catherine J. Foote, *Survivor Prayers: Talking with God about Childhood Sexual Abuse* (Louisville: Westminster/John Knox Press, 1994), 71.

By exposing his scars after his torture and crucifixion (Jn. 20:24–30), Jesus responded with truth and compassion to the doubt of Thomas. Likewise, Catherine Foote has responded to the doubts of the church about the reality and consequences of child abuse. Because Jesus was wounded and scarred, she does not have to submit to the conspiracy of silence about her pain. Rather, her scars can become a symbol of her faith in the God of Jesus Christ whose wounds are visible for all to see in the crucifixes and stories in Christian places of worship.

The psalms by Karen Doudt, Valerie Bridgeman Davis, the Nicaraguan women, and Catherine Foote follow the great tradition of biblical psalms and New Testament stories in their honesty and ability to trust God with all of their feelings. They bring their experiences with evil and violence and call their enemies to accountability just like the psalmist. I present these psalms and stories in order to provide a window into the faith of persons who have been abused by family members and by the church. I present these psalms and stories because of the new religious witness that God is giving in our generation. Their raw suffering and hope reveal the power and love of God who cannot be controlled by the official theologies and practices of the churches.

Some of the best minds of our day are hard at work on translating the insights of these religious witnesses into systematic theology.[8] White feminist theologians have been working for 150 years, and womanist theologians are drawing on the resilient faith of black women lasting more than three centuries. They are not asking orthodox questions that have easy answers. They ask questions like Job did when he rejected the politically correct advice from his friends and settled for nothing less than an audience with God. The church must be open to these voices, even if a sacred doctrine is criticized. Reimaging Jesus from the

---

[8]Fortunately, an excellent foundation has been laid for this ongoing work of reimaging Jesus. See Kelly Brown Douglas, *The Black Christ* (Maryknoll, N.Y.: Orbis Books, 1994); Jacquelyn Grant, *White Women's Christ and Black Women's Jesus: Feminist Christology and Womanist Response* (Atlanta: Scholars Press, 1989); Joanne Carlson Brown and Carole R. Bohn, eds., *Christianity, Patriarchy and Abuse: A Feminist Critique* (Cleveland: Pilgrim Press, 1989); Elisabeth Schüssler Fiorenza and Mary Shawn Copeland, eds., *Violence Against Women,* Concilium Series 1 (Maryknoll, N.Y.: Orbis Books, 1994); Maryanne Stevens, ed., *Reconstructing the Christ Symbol: Essays in Feminist Christology* (New York: Paulist Press, 1993); Carol J. Adams and Marie M. Fortune, eds., *Violence against Women and Children: A Christian Theological Sourcebook* (New York: Continuum, 1995).

perspective of abused women and children is a task for this generation of Christian believers.

In my work as a pastoral theologian, I confess a renewed understanding of Jesus as one who resists evil and violence in the world. I believe that Jesus' resistance to evil discloses that resistance to evil is a fundamental attribute of God and human life.[9] Jesus' resistance to evil is a manifestation of God and humanity. One reason why Jesus' spirit has not been fully destroyed by evil systems is because resistance to evil is a fundamental characteristic of God and because Jesus' spirit lives on through those who resist evil. Thus, resistance is not just a human response to life's difficulties, but is a part of the human and divine life. In the crucifixion of Jesus, which was a failure by most human standards, God's commitment to resistance was disclosed. Theologian Ellen Wondra says:

> The meaning of Jesus' life is confirmed in his death and vindicated in his resurrection. Jesus' own suffering and death are the outcome of a just life lived in resistance to an unjust world...Jesus remained faithful to the marginalized in whose company he lived and taught, and to his prophetic and iconoclastic vision of God's reign. In suffering an ignominious and agonizing death, Jesus maintained his solidarity with the suffering and with victims of domination.[10]

This is how much Jesus identifies with the victims and survivors of violence: Jesus loves them enough to die in solidarity with them, and his spirit accompanies all who resist the violence and oppression of our age.

I suggest that pastoral caregivers develop a special sensitivity to the religious thoughts of survivors of male violence. Starting with the published materials, we can become familiar with the growing witness that is emerging. In our accompaniment with survivors, we can encourage private journaling, writing poetry, rewriting psalms and other scriptures, and then begin to

---

[9]The christological perspective in this section is developed more fully in James N. Poling, *Deliver Us from Evil: Resisting Racial and Gender Oppression* (Minneapolis: Fortress Press, 1996).

[10]Ellen K. Wondra, *Humanity Has Been a Holy Thing: Toward a Contemporary Feminist Christology* (Lanham, Md.: University Press of America, 1994), 333.

incorporate those testimonies of faith into public prayers and worship. Such a practice fulfills our vocation of providing deep caring for all God's people and empowering those in our communities who are most vulnerable.

The work of re-imagining Jesus as a salvific figure for those who have experienced violence in personal relationships has just begun. But, thanks be to God, it has begun. I end with praise to the God of love and power who is the head of my life, and to Jesus Christ, from whom nothing can separate us, not interpersonal violence, not society's exploitation of women and children, not even the pronouncements of the church. God is doing a new thing for our generation. Blessed are we if we believe and act with power and compassion.

9

Hearing the Silenced Voices:
The Work of Justice in Pastoral Theology[1]

Research shows that "the combined conviction rate for [perpetrators of] child sexual abuse is 1 percent."[2] When estimates of unreported cases are added, the accountability of men for their crimes of sexual violence is even more shocking. In *The Abuse of Power,* I told some of my own stories about work with child molesters.[3] This chapter provides theological reflection on my ministry experience with survivors and perpetrators of sexual abuse, particularly reflecting on this ministry as a work of justice.[4]

Because pastoral theology is rooted in ministry experience, I want to shift attention to theological method with a focus on epistemology. What can we know and how can we know it? I have three basic questions:

---

[1]Original version published as "Hearing the Silenced Voices: The Work of Justice in Pastoral Theology," *Journal of Pastoral Theology* 1 (Summer 1991): 6–27, based on research in *The Abuse of Power: A Theological Problem* (Nashville: Abingdon Press, 1991).

[2]Diana Russell, *The Secret Trauma: Incest in the Lives of Girls and Women* (Basic Books, 1986), 86.

[3]These stories are now in chapter 6 of this book.

[4]For summaries of basic research in the sexual abuse of women and children, see Russell's book and the following: David Finkelhor, *Child Sexual Abuse* (Free Press, 1984); Ellen Bass and Laura Davis, *The Courage to Heal* (Harper and Row, 1988). See also Marie Fortune, *Sexual Violence: The Unmentionable Sin: Ethical and Pastoral Perspective* (Pilgrim Press, 1983); Marie Fortune, *Is Nothing Sacred: When Sex Invades the Pastoral Relationship* (Harper and Row, 1989); Mary Pellauer et al., eds., *Sexual Assault and Abuse: A Handbook for Clergy and Religious Professionals* (Harper and Row, 1987).

- First, if experience is the base of all knowledge, what is the nature of experience, and how do we describe it?

- Second, what kind of critical theories do we need to sort out truth and distortion in persons, families, and society?

- Third, what theological assumptions about God and the world shape our perceptions and actions?

For over a year I corresponded with Karen about her experiences of sexual abuse as a child and as an adult. She has been a compelling witness for me about the power of evil and the resilience of hope. I will use her testimony to illustrate my convictions in response to the above questions and to guide our understanding about the consequences of sexual abuse, which is perpetrated mainly by men.

First, how can we know anything about the contrast of evil and hope in human experience?[5]

Part of Karen's story is published as the article "I Promised Not To Tell."[6] In fact, her promise was so complete that she had almost no memory of being molested by her father, an experience not uncommon for survivors. As a young adult after college she took a job as a consultant with a friend of the family. On a business trip he manipulated her into a hotel room and raped her. Because of her past pattern she again decided not to tell. She entered graduate school, completed a Ph.D. in education, and obtained an appointment as a college professor. At one point she did talk to her pastor about her rape experience, but he made sexual advances toward her in the session. Finally, she became physically ill, and in the course of her treatment she confided in a doctor. Later she talked to a pastor who was professional and empathic and who referred her to a competent therapist.

It was in therapy that she remembered the incest. Her father had visited her bedroom from before she could remember, perhaps as young as age three. These nighttime visits continued until she was a teenager. She was so traumatized that she could find no way out. Her entrapment was reinforced by the family,

---

[5] I am indebted to Rob van Kessel for insight into the dynamic tension of suffering and hope. See *Zes Kruiken Water: Enkele Theologische Bijdragen Voor Kerkopbouw* (Netherlands: Gool and Stricht, 1989).

[6] "I Promised Not To Tell," *Messenger* (November 1989): 20–21.

who thought she was such a nice girl, and by the school, which reinforced her academic achievements but ignored her headaches and other physical symptoms. Even the church taught her that her parents were good, that children must be obedient, and that God was a good father.

With the help of her therapist, a support group for women, and a widening circle of others, Karen has found the courage to face her pain and become a survivor rather than a victim.

Several weeks ago she went to worship at her local church. One Sunday her father was serving communion. Another Sunday the minister who had sexually approached her during a counseling session was leading worship. She told me in a letter this week that she has decided to stop attending church.

I am reporting Karen's experience to illustrate principles of research in pastoral theology. There are thousands of stories like Karen's, and many ministers and counselors have listened to similar ones. The suffering and injustice of such testimonies is overwhelming and infuriating. Fortunately, many people are listening in a new way, and society itself is beginning to change. All of us are touched by stories of suffering. But suffering in itself is not what makes Karen's story compelling. Her story is compelling because of the resilient hope in her spirit, which stands in such contrast to her suffering, and this contrast is the key to understanding experience itself.

As long as Karen's life was characterized by private suffering, there was a lack of depth to her experience. But when she acted on the latent hope in her spirit by talking to someone about her suffering, her life was changed. I am enraged at the pastor who violated his call from God by abusing Karen again. I thank God for the doctor, the second pastor, and the therapist who gave reality to her suffering and gave her connections for her hope.

In my accompaniment with survivors, it is not primarily the evil and suffering that are compelling, but the contrast of their pain with a resilient hope that will not die. I believe this contrast begins to unlock the depth levels of experience for our participation and research. Then all the tools of our trade from psychology and theology become available for analysis and reflection.

My first epistemological principle is that the depth of human experience is the data for pastoral theology, and that experience is unlocked by seeking the contrast between human suffering and experiences of hope.

Description of individual experience is not enough in itself, because experience as shaped by language and culture contains many distortions. The confusion of truth and distortion must be sorted out through critical theories[7] that are adequate to examine the personal and social horizons of meaning and power. The three theories that have most influenced me are psychoanalytic theory as reinterpreted by postmodern analysis, feminist theory, and black theology. In this section I use psychoanalytic and feminist theory.

Karen's life has been controlled by secrecy, by distortions about the truth of her life. Her search for the truth of her life has spanned four decades, and still today, her family and local congregation are unable to face the truth about their own lives. How can we know the truth in a situation of secrecy and suppression?

The resilient human spirit seeks in each moment to mend and repair the web of relationships within which their identity is defined. Sometimes evil wins out in the subjectivity of a person or a society, such as the antisocial personality or a society based on slavery or genocide. But the relational web itself seems to strive for an increase in value.[8]

I believe there is a *search for self* of integrity and justice in the human spirit. I have found such courage and hope in the most unlikely places, among the survivors and perpetrators of child sexual abuse. If hope can be found there, perhaps it exists in other places where evil seems predominant.[9]

One of the places where Karen's hope found expression was in somatic symptoms. In elementary school, she sought help through severe headaches. She was tested medically at the school's request and was told that nothing was wrong. This increased the suppression in her life. Later, she broke through her own denial

---

[7]See David Tracy, "Practical Theology in a Situation of Global Pluralism," in *Formation and Reflection: The Promise of Practical Theology,* ed. James Poling and Lewis Mudge (Philadelphia: Fortress Press, 1987), 144ff.

[8]See Bernard Loomer, "The Free and Relational Self," in W. Widick Schroeder and Gibson Winter, *Belief and Ethics: Essays in Ethics, the Human Sciences and Ministry in Honor of W. Alvin Pitcher* (Chicago: Center for the Scientific Study of Religion, 1978), 80ff; William Dean and Larry E. Axel, *The Size of God: The Theology of Bernard Loomer in Context* (Macon, Ga.: Mercer University Press, 1987), 42.

[9]My theory of the self is largely dependent on psychoanalytic theory. See Althea Horner, *Object Relations and the Developing Ego in Therapy* (New York: Jason Aronson, 1984), for a good summary.

again through physical illness, and a physician helped her make the connection between her illness and her abuse. The truth of Karen's life was remembered by her physical body for many years when her conscious mind had forgotten. I believe this illustrates Freud's conviction that the unconscious is essentially truthful and that it is often more closely related to the physical body than to the conscious mind.[10] The search for an integrated self is resilient and can be a source for attachments that move toward redemption.

The search for self has an essentially interpersonal dimension. The self is relational; that is, the intrapsychic experience of the self is formed by internalization of others, through emotional cathexis.[11] The distinction between self and other is a theoretical one that does not accurately reflect the structure of the self. The self is its relationships. For Karen, evil entered her life through the internalization of her family relationships. She was damaged by her family, by the nightly visits from her father, and by the denial and secrecy of her family. Through her identification with her family, Karen suffered the consequences of the family sickness.[12]

But it was also through relationships that Karen's hope for herself was actualized. In her healing process, Karen reached out to others who could stand the truth and maintain a supportive relationship with her. Karen continues to struggle to maintain a benevolent web of relationships and to limit the continuing threats of assault on her self.

There is a *search for community* in the human spirit. This is more than the face-to-face interpersonal relationships that are so emotionally important to all of us. Rather, community includes institutions of power and ideologies that shape and control the very context of our lives.

---

[10]Freud believed that truth from the unconscious demands to be expressed. "He that has eyes to see and ears to hear may convince himself that no mortal can keep a secret. If his lips are silent, he chatters with his fingertips; betrayal oozes out of him at every pore. And thus the task of making conscious the most hidden recesses of the mind is one which is quite possible to accomplish," in *Dora: An Analysis of a Case of Hysteria* (New York: Collier Books, 1963), 96.

[11]For a discussion of the process of internalization according to object relations theory, see W. W. Meissner, *Internalization in Psychoanalysis* (New York: International Universities Press, 1981); Heinz Kohut, *The Restoration of the Self* (New York: International Universities Press, 1977).

[12]For an excellent discussion of how unconscious processes are passed from parents to children, see Alice Miller, *For Your Own Good: Hidden Cruelty in Child-rearing and the Roots of Violence* (New York: Farrar, Strauss, and Giroux, 1983).

Institutions are centers of power that determine the rules by which we live.[13] For Karen, one of the main institutions besides her family was the school. In school she learned to be a good girl who obeyed her parents and other authority figures. She learned to be silent about the pain in her life. She learned to sit still, to answer questions when spoken to, to look pretty, and not to complain. This training served her well when she responded to the crisis of her rape by entering graduate school. She was the ideal Ph.D. student. Institutional conformity reinforced the family rules and her intrapsychic defenses. She survived as a well-adjusted and well-socialized achiever. This conformity also prevented the truth from being known. Paradoxically, the same institutions were a source of hope for her. Her survival was closely related to her academic success in school.

The search for community also includes an ideological dimension. Ideology is the normative horizon of language and the implicit assumptions that govern perception and identity.[14] Karen grew up in a society where male privilege was dominant. She faithfully lived out the submissive role of the good girl and good woman as long as she could, and she was rewarded by social respectability and success. The collapse of her physical health was a signal of the increasing tension between her experiences of evil and her resilient hope for herself and her future. As her life collapsed internally, she began to question the impact of ideologies about what it means to be a woman in a patriarchal society. The ideology of patriarchy gave men the permission to abuse her and protected them from accountability.[15] She has borne the brunt of her healing without justice for the crimes done against her.

Karen's resilient hope for community appears dramatically in her initiative to form a countercommunity for herself. With

---

[13]I am indebted to the following sources among others for my understanding of institutional power: George Herbert Mead, *Mind, Self and Society* (Chicago: University of Chicago Press, 1936); Walter Wink, *Unmasking the Powers: The Invisible Forces that Determine Human Existence* (Philadelphia: Fortress Press, 1986).

[14]David Tracy, *Plurality and Ambiguity* (New York: Harper and Row, 1987). "Ideologies are unconscious, but systematically functioning attitudes, values and beliefs produced by and in the material conditions of all uses of language, all analyses of truth, and all claims to knowledge. More than any others, feminist thinkers have demonstrated that language was never innocent—especially the phallocentric language of the 'man of reason,'" 77.

[15]For summaries of how feminist theory defines and understands patriarchy, see Hester Eisenstein, *Contemporary Feminist Thought* (Boston: G. K. Hall, 1983).

support from her physician, her pastor, and her therapist, she carefully selected a group of women and asked them to be a special community for her during her healing. With the help of this group she has gradually widened the circle of her community through people who know the truth and have a commitment to stand with her against the institutions and ideologies that continue their abuse of her.

Third, the resilient human spirit continues its *search for God* of love and justice in spite of the dominance of evil. The images of God, community, and human nature that are predominant in a culture establish the ideals and limits of human potential at its deepest level.[16]

For Karen, there was a deep mythological connection between the privilege of her father, the privilege of her rapist, the privilege of all men, and the privilege of God the father. In church she was taught that God was a loving father just like her own father, and that her role was to be a submissive, grateful, obedient child. The men who abused and raped her still represent the image of God the father in a church that refuses to acknowledge their sin. In some contemporary feminist writing, this same theme has been carried further into the examination of theories of atonement. Theories of atonement seem to be based on God the Father's wrath at human sin, which could only be satisfied by the abuse and death of the innocent child, Jesus. Even in its more liberal forms, the willingness of Jesus to suffer and die for the salvation of others teaches us to suffer silently in obedience to an all-loving father who always knows what is best for us.[17] Karen knows this kind of God well because she has been taught the line of authority from her father to all male authority to the authority of a male God. She has had great difficulty finding a relationship with a God who is characterized by justice and love and who is available for a real relationship with her. She has found a small community of persons

---

[16]Bernard Meland summarizes the basic ideas of process theology in *Faith and Culture* (Carbondale, Ill.: Southern Illinois University Press, 1953). "The faith, understood as an accumulative consensus of sensitivity and valuation, giving quality and range to the psychical thrust of the culture, determines the dimension of depth in feeling and conception within the culture. Thus the range and depth of perception and of imaginative power in any given period is proportionate to this persisting, elemental source of qualitative meaning," 12.

[17]Joanne Carlson Brown and Carole R. Bohn, eds., *Christianity, Patriarchy and Abuse: A Feminist Critique* (Cleveland: Pilgrim Press, 1989). See also Ronald Goetz, "God's Plan to Kill Jesus," *Christian Century* (April 11, 1990): 363.

who have surrounded her with acceptance during her healing, which may provide new symbols of God for her. The impact of the feminist discovery of sexual abuse of women provides the hopeful context for Karen's growing courage to speak openly about her suffering.

One of Karen's reasons for corresponding with me is to find images of God that support her inner search for truth and hope in her life. Her ability to find a religious faith of integrity depends on whether she can find a Christian community that is willing to reconstruct its basic ideas about God.

In this section I have tried to describe and illustrate the use of critical theories in the epistemological search for knowledge. Because persons and societies distort truth so badly, we must have critical theories that attempt to unmask the systematic distortions that keep the truth suppressed. Liberating truth is available for those with eyes to see. A task of pastoral theology is to hear the silenced voices of truth so that justice and mercy are available for all creation.

One goal of pastoral theology is constructing statements about God's relation to human experience that lead to strategies of liberating action. This illustrates my theological method. One starts with the contrast of evil and suffering with experiences of hope. This leads to the analysis of experience and culture through the use of critical theories. Eventually there is the moment of constructive religious interpretation.[18] Given our research into truth, what generalizations can we make? What is our confession about the nature of truth, that is, the nature of God?

I am aware that the following statements have a double character. In some ways they are based on empirical research into the depth of human experience, generalizations from experience to confession. In other ways these statements are restatements of assumptions I started with. I think there is no way to avoid both things being true. Our research leads us full circle to reaffirm some of the convictions about which we have always felt deeply. Here are my current theological affirmations about the nature of truth.

First, *truth has a narrative structure.* Alfred North Whitehead said that experience is initially made up of the accumulated causal

---

[18]For a summary of this method, see James Poling and Donald Miller, *Foundations for a Practical Theology of Ministry* (Nashville: Abingdon Press, 1985).

efficacy of the past actual world. Our identity is largely given to us by the past.[19] Our prehension of the past is the raw material out of which we construct our future. This means that memory is central to identity and freedom. We are free to the extent that we can remember the past in its fullest sense. Whatever is suppressed and unconscious from our past remains causally efficacious, but with little chance for reconstruction.[20]

Karen's identity was formed by experiences of incest and rape. But her freedom as a person was severely limited until she could remember her trauma and seek healing through new relationships and new communities. She was trapped by her past until it became available to her. In other language, the official narrative of her life was false as long as she thought of herself as coming from a stable, healthy, middle-class family, and as long as she played the role of a well-adjusted adult. This narrative had to be deconstructed by acknowledging the truth of her accumulated past, including its lies and distortions. When the false narrative was demythologized and hope was intensified, Karen was free to begin construction of a more adequate narrative.

Every person and group forms its identity through story. But stories themselves tend to give only an official version of the past. Stories partially distort identity in favor of the ideological restrictions of those who are dominant. Persons cannot report the latent structure in most cases. This is one reason why the voice of oppressed groups must be heard. They are often the carriers of the suppressed stories that must be heard for the full identity of a community to be known.

Research in pastoral theology is based on a process of deconstructing and reconstructing narratives. A narrative is an interpretation of how the cumulative efficacy of the past has structured the present immediacy. An inadequate story distorts the structure of the present and affects perception and freedom of response. An example is the difference between doing a history during intake and reconstructing the history after several years of psychotherapy. The structure of the internal object world does not emerge through self-report, but through analysis of the

---

[19]See Alfred North Whitehead, *Process and Reality* (New York: Free Press, 1978).
[20]For a discussion of memory and healing, see Daniel Day Williams, "Suffering and Being in Empirical Theology," in *The Future of Empirical Theology,* ed. Bernard Meland (Chicago: University of Chicago Press, 1969), 185.

transference. The narrative that gives a more true picture of the object world is the more true narrative.[21]

In theological terms, *God is the story.* There are deeper narratives of which we are all a part, and to which our stories relate. The human soul hopes that its own self-conscious stories will be congruent with the great stories of divine life. We want our stories to be true rather than false. But we fear that the deeper truth of our lives will destroy the pseudo-stories we have created in order to defend ourselves against non-being. One way to understand God is to reflect on our individual and collective stories.

Second, *truth is a relational web.* The discovery of the radical interdependence of all things is a basic paradigm shift from the Cartesian world of the imperial self and the isolated object. In the old paradigm, internal relationships are problematic. But according to Whitehead, experience itself is relational and social.[22] Everything exists in a web of interdependence. Our experience is experience of the web of reality, and our individual response to the web is our contribution to its quality in the future.[23]

The web includes the interpersonal world of persons we interact with on a daily basis, with special importance to those with whom we have deep emotional attachments. The web includes institutions of power that set limits on behavior and action. The web includes the structure of language and the structured ideologies that determine perception and identity. *God is the relational web,*[24] that is, the totality of everything that exists at a particular time. To the extent that we are in the web and the web is in us, our experience is the very incarnation of God, along with everything else that exists in the actual world.

How do we study the web of relationships? How do we understand the complexity of internal relations? How do we articulate the full scope of the context in which life occurs? The

---

[21]For a discussion of narrative in pastoral theology, see Charles Gerkin, *The Living Human Document* (Nashville: Abingdon Press, 1984); Gerkin, *Widening the Horizons* (Philadelphia: Westminster Press, 1986).

[22]See Whitehead.

[23]One of the best discussions of the relational nature of being is by Bernard Loomer; see Dean and Axel, eds., *The Size of God,* 31ff.

[24]Ibid., 20. "In terms of this analysis, God as a wholeness is to be identified with the concrete, interconnected totality of this struggling, imperfect, unfinished and evolving societal web," 41.

principle of empiricism[25] means attending to the web that is God. The web is preconscious in its influence. When we become conscious, we become conscious of the web.

The web of relationships includes the possibilities and limitations of the ideologies of gender, class, racial, and sexual issues. Unless these ideologies are critically examined, they have major influence on the normative horizon of theology without awareness of theologians. The "container" of research is politically constructed with certain normative assumptions about the nature of human life and relationships. Distortions of reality are evil and are homeostatic unless critically examined and transformed. But the relational web is also the source of hope. In our interdependence and the implicit values that make us compassionate toward one another emerges the hope that makes us free. One way to understand God is to reflect on the relationships within which our lives are embedded.

Third, *truth is a process of immediacy.* Whitehead called his view "process philosophy" to distinguish it from the substantive views of human experience and nature. We are still trying to understand the revolution this creates in our consciousness. Bernard Meland refers to the movement of process as the "vital immediacy."[26] Clinical practice involves attending to the details of the unconscious process and providing true and timely interpretations of what is immediately happening, with special attention to the therapeutic relationship. The process of immediacy can only be known through analysis of relationship, what we know in clinical terms as transference and countertransference. Analysis of the process of immediacy means attending to the movement of God in the moment. The creative urge of the human soul is a divine urge. There is a flow of energy from entity to entity, from event to event. Every event is interconnected with others by this flow of energy, and it passes its life on to the future. There is a moment of freedom, of novelty in the center of the process that determines how the process moves.

Because of the trauma of her past, Karen was unable to attend to the vital immediacy of her life at first. She needed the secure

---

[25]See James Poling, "Empirical Theology" in *Dictionary of Pastoral Care and Counseling* (Nashville: Abingdon Press, 1990), 356–58.

[26]Meland, *Future of Empirical Theology,* 13, 297.

and compassionate presence of other souls with her. As she trusted these relationships, she gained in her strength to trust the flow of her own experience. She has had a remarkable impact on me through our conversations. She has taught me to be much more alert to the presence of truth in our relationships.

God is the process of vital immediacy. Within the internal movement of our own spiritual experiences, our memories of the past, and our interactions with other persons and communities, God is present. This is a form of incarnational theology.

How do we attend to the flow of the process in the immediacy of events?[27] What kind of attention is needed? How do we attend to the process when it is preconscious and unconscious? Robert Langs speaks of "lie therapy" in which therapist and client conspire to construct a relationship based on untruth. "Truth therapy" is based on a commitment to interpret the flow of the process in its immediacy. Empathy and accurate interpretation of the process is the basis of every form of healing.[28] One way to know God is to reflect on the vital immediacy of our experience.

In summary, my pastoral theology is based on three basic assumptions about the nature of human experience and our relationship to God: Truth is a narrative; truth is a relational web; truth is a process of immediacy. This illustrates the third epistemological principle, namely, that research in pastoral theology requires awareness of one's basic assumptions about God and the world.

I believe that pastoral theology is based on an empirical and personal epistemology. We know the truth by attending to the depth of experience empirically and by honestly reflecting on our personal relationship to truth within the relational web. I have shared some aspects of my clinical ministry. Trying to function as a therapist with victims and perpetrators of sexual abuse has radically revised my own theology. I have encountered the resilience of hope in experiences of extreme suffering and evil. My own tendencies toward social conformity and anesthesia of feeling have been partly overcome. I feel more deeply and am more radically critical of church and society than ever before.

---

[27]Bernard Meland, "Can Empirical Theology Learn from Phenomenology?" in *The Future of Empirical Theology*. See his discussion of "appreciative consciousness," 296. He also says, "Immediacy and ultimacy traffic together," 297.

[28]Robert Langs, *Psychotherapy: A Basic Text* (New York: Jason Aronson, 1983), 718–19, 731.

My own life is being transformed as I witness the resilient hope of those whose lives have been more evil than good. I have found glimpses of faith in a God of love and power. This God is so completely identified with the world that our normal distinctions about good and evil do not apply to such a God. Whatever is evil is as much a part of God as whatever is good. Yet in the midst of such radical ambiguity there is a resilient hope, a restlessness toward beauty that cannot be completely suppressed. In the midst of the worst evil, God's resilient hope is ceaselessly at work. That is why the witness of slaves, Holocaust survivors, and victims of child abuse is so important. They know the truth about good and evil. They know whether there is a hope at the center of reality that cannot be destroyed by evil. Those of us with social privilege who are oversocialized and anesthesized against our own evil and suffering discover such hope only with great difficulty. We must attach ourselves to those who have been to the bottom and have found there the source of good itself. The task of pastoral theology is to hear the silenced voices of truth. The voices of truth must be heard against the destructive force of ideology and religion. This is the work of justice in pastoral theology. This is the knowledge we seek.

10

Telling the Truth: Preaching about Sexual and Domestic Violence[1]

This chapter begins a section on the liturgical aspects of pastoral care in situations of male violence against women and children. Here I deal with the theological hermeneutics of preaching, use of scriptures, and some of the theological and ethical issues that emerge when male violence is taken seriously. In chapter 8, I discussed some of the recent religious poetry written by survivors that has liturgical significance and can provide resources for private and public worship. In chapter 11, I present a sample sermon on forgiveness that illustrates a practical way that male violence can be addressed from the pulpit. In chapter 12, a local pastor struggles with the issue of how to construct a healing service for male abusers. Although these chapters only begin the discussion of the worship life of a church, it is important to begin thinking carefully about how these reforms can be implemented.

When George was arrested for sexually abusing his teenage daughter, he was remorseful and wanted to be forgiven by God and by his church. When I asked him what he thought this meant, he didn't know. As a faithful church member all his adult life, he had heard sermons about sin and forgiveness, and he had engaged in confession before the eucharist. But he had never heard a

[1]Original version published as "Preaching to Perpetrators of Violence," in *Telling the Truth: Preaching about Sexual and Domestic Violence,* ed. John S. McClure and Nancy J. Ramsay (Cleveland: United Church Press, 1999), 71–82.

sermon that named sexual and domestic violence in the family as a sin that could be brought to God for redemption. After he was arrested, he was shunned by friends and members of his church. He felt rejected and alone, and he didn't know whether there were spiritual resources to help him through this crisis in his life. On the one hand, he wanted to avoid all consequences for his own evil by being restored to the fellowship of the church without accountability. On the other hand, he needed to hear genuine words of judgment and grace that pointed the way toward spiritual renewal.

Encountering people such as George points to a problem—preachers of the gospel have been preaching sermons as if there are no survivors and perpetrators of violence in the congregation. So persons in families experiencing violence have not been getting the sermons they need. Survivors and perpetrators are not hearing clear ethical guidelines against family violence—as a problem that includes church members. In order to correct this problem, we need to realize that every congregation includes survivors and perpetrators of family violence who need to hear that God hates violence, so that vulnerable persons are protected. But neither are survivors and perpetrators hearing about the redemptive value of confession, repentance, and the possibilities for new life after safety is established and the violence ceases. So families hide their problems and hope everyone else will ignore them also. Yet it is crucial that survivors and perpetrators know what it takes to repent of their sins and how to find their way back into the honest and full fellowship of the church.

Principles for Sermons for Perpetrators of Violence

The principles for developing sermons on sexual and domestic violence are simple:

1. Protect the vulnerable from further abuse (hospitality).

2. Call the abuser to accountability (confrontation, confession, repentance).

3. Restore the relationship (between victim and abuser) *if possible.* Often this restoration is not possible. The harm is too great, the damage too deep, the resistance of the abuser to change too formidable. *If not possible,* then mourn the loss of that

relationship and work to restore the individuals (comfort to the grieving).[2]

The practice of preaching about family violence is complicated because of the church's long history of silence and complicity on these issues. In the balance of this chapter, I will review some of the challenges facing preachers who want to preach the whole gospel to the whole people of God, including survivors and perpetrators of violence. First I will discuss some of the historical issues that have created this problem. Then I will review several hermeneutical principles and look at some New Testament texts that need reinterpretation in our increasing awareness of the presence of perpetrators in our congregations.

A History of Preaching Domination

In order to preach about family violence, we must ask, Why do some people perpetrate violence against others, and what are the consequences for those who must suffer this violence? My research has led me to conclude that the answer is complex. According to Victor Lewis in the video *Broken Vows*,[3] many men feel entitled to own and control women; in addition, many parents assume absolute control over children, and such adults are willing to use violence to enforce their power. This sense of entitlement has very old roots. Scholars such as Patricia Hill Collins have convinced me that, especially in the United States, the ownership of other people and enforcement of that right by violence is rooted in three hundred years of slavery and oppression of women.[4] I have been especially interested in the role of religion in helping to construct the arguments that ownership of other persons was legitimate, as well as whatever violence was necessary to enforce that ownership.[5] We know that U.S. slavery not only included physical violence but also sexual violence against women and

---

[2]Carol J. Adams and Marie M. Fortune, eds., *Violence against Women and Children: A Christian Theological Sourcebook* (New York: Continuum, 1995), 458.

[3]*Broken Vows,* a video on prevention of domestic violence (Seattle: Center for the Prevention of Sexual and Domestic Violence, 1995).

[4]Patricia Hill Collins, *Black Feminist Thought: Knowledge, Consciousness, and the Politics of Empowerment* (New York: Routledge, 1990).

[5]For further discussion of the issues of this section, see James Newton Poling, *Deliver Us from Evil: Resisting Racial and Gender Oppression* (Minneapolis: Fortress Press, 1996), 136–48.

children who were slaves. We live in a country that for three hundred years officially promoted the ownership and abuse of people, a country in which even religious leaders and theologians supported these policies and practices.

Kelly Brown Douglas in *The Black Christ* asks how ownership of persons was justified religiously. Her answer: by spiritualizing the meaning of Jesus. "Evangelists were able to spiritualize the themes of Christian freedom and equality...Jesus' salvation had nothing to do with historical freedom."[6] For example, the following question was asked of many slaves at the time of baptism:

> You declare in the presence of God and this congregation that you do not ask for Holy Baptism out of any design to free yourselves from the Duty and Obedience you owe to your Master while you live, but merely for the good of your Soul and to partake of the Graces and Blessings promised to the members of the Church of Jesus Christ.[7]

By imposing this vow as a requirement for baptism into Jesus Christ, pastors justified the physical and sexual violence necessary to enforce enslavement and ownership of other Christians. They said that Christian freedom was a state of grace that would take effect only in the next life and had nothing to do with freedom from violence in this life. This spiritualization of the gospel helped perpetuate three hundred years of violence in support of slavery in the United States.

According to Riggins Earl, the miracle of God's action in history is that Jesus' spirit of compassion for all people has lived on in spite of the evil of those who justified slavery. How could the slave community in resistance confess Jesus in the midst of profound evil? Through trusting their own religious experience of Jesus' presence and rejecting the lies that created their captivity, converted slaves resisted evil and confessed the love and power of God in Jesus Christ. In the process, they found a precious interior spiritual space of freedom from domination, a sanctuary from evil.[8]

---

[6]Kelly Brown Douglas, *The Black Christ* (Maryknoll, N.Y.: Orbis Books, 1994), 15.
[7]Ibid., 17.
[8]Riggins Earl, Jr., *Dark Symbols, Obscure Signs: God, Self and Community in the Slave Mind* (Maryknoll, N.Y.: Orbis Books, 1993), 52.

Jacquelyn Grant and Delores Williams and other womanist and feminist theologians articulate the long history of African American resistance to slavery, racism, and violence. Jacquelyn Grant says we have to rethink our use of servanthood language because of the history of slavery and the domestic servitude of black women.[9] Delores Williams says we have to rethink our theories of atonement based on surrogacy because of the enforced surrogacy of black women in the United States.[10]

There is a parallel story about the oppression of European American women. The Victorian-era "cult of true womanhood" emphasized the importance of piety, purity, submissiveness, and domesticity—all of which justified the property rights of men.[11] Christian theologians were in the forefront of this debate in the nineteenth century to justify the subordination of women to men and the violence required to enforce this oppression. The Women's Rights Act of 1848 protested the fact that women could not vote, own property, have custody of their children, or protect themselves from drunken husbands. Rita Nakashima Brock questions our doctrines of innocence, such as the cult of true womanhood, which we project on Jesus to protect ourselves from the disclosure of actual evil.[12]

These brief references remind us of the longer history of theological justification for the idea that certain people can be owned as property and that ownership of persons can be enforced by violence. As Gerda Lerner says, we are trying to overturn a very long tradition.[13] I think it is fair to say that the liberal view of individual human rights has not changed the underlying ideologies of white supremacy and male dominance in the United States. As so many writers have emphasized, the struggle has to go much deeper.

---

[9]Jacquelyn Grant, in *Reconstructing the Christ Symbol: Essays in Feminist Christology*, ed. Maryanne Stevens, (New York: Paulist Press, 1993). See also Jacquelyn Grant, *White Women's Christ and Black Women's Jesus: Feminist Christology and Womanist Response* (Atlanta: Scholars Press, 1989).

[10]Delores Williams, *Sisters in the Wilderness: The Challenge of Womanist God-Talk* (Maryknoll, N.Y.: Orbis Books, 1993), 164.

[11]Hazel Carby, *Reconstructing Womanhood* (New York: Oxford University Press, 1987). 25.

[12]Rita Nakashima Brock, in Stevens, *Reconstructing*. See also Rita Nakashima Brock, *Journeys By Heart: A Christology of Erotic Power* (New York: Crossroad, 1988).

[13]Gerda Lerner, *The Creation of Feminist Consciousness: From the Middle Ages to 1870* (New York: Oxford University Press, 1993).

From my work with survivors and perpetrators, I know that we pastors have much work to do. In the immediate future, we must support the justice work of shelters and the legal system to protect women by stringent consequences. In the long run, our work to reconstruct Christian theology and thus change our preaching is crucial.[14]

A Hermeneutics of Suspicion and Confession [15]

In terms of hermeneutical method, I start with the premise that human beings do not have access to a pure gospel undistorted by history and social location. Although attempts to recover "the historical Jesus" can be helpful by showing that descriptions of the first-century peasant are not identical to the debates about Christ throughout history,[16] the results of this research do not resolve the conflicts between contemporary religious groups. Even conservative religious creeds teach that the scriptures must be "rightly explained" (2 Tim. 2:15) and interpreted by the Holy Spirit.[17] Historical research is crucial because it forces the church to uncover the layers of distortion starting in the oral traditions and continuing through every version of the Bible and its interpretations.[18] Searching for the truth is a crucial aspect of deconstructing any lies about Jesus. Therefore, we must have a *hermeneutics of suspicion* of attempts of Christian groups to misuse the gospel for their own privilege and power.

My method is also based on a *hermeneutics of confession* that Jesus as a spiritual power continues to empower those who are faithful to God. The love and power of Jesus lives in people's struggles for survival and freedom in the face of massive evil and injustice. Church leaders are called to become attuned to Jesus'

---

[14]See James Newton Poling, *The Abuse of Power: A Theological Problem* (Nashville: Abingdon Press, 1991).

[15]See Poling, *Deliver Us from Evil,* 148–55.

[16]John Dominic Crossan, *Jesus: A Revolutionary Biography* (San Francisco: HarperSanFrancisco, 1994); Burton L. Mack, *The Lost Gospel: The Book of Q and Christian Origins* (San Francisco: HarperSanFrancisco, 1993); William Herzog II, *Parables as Subversive Speech: Jesus as Pedagogue of the Oppressed* (Louisville: Westminster Press, 1994).

[17]The Westminster Confession of Faith (1647), *The Book of Confessions* (Louisville: Presbyterian Church USA), 6.010.

[18]Itumeleng T Mosala, *Biblical Hermeneutics and Black Theology in South Africa* (Grand Rapids, Mich.: Eerdmans, 1989); Cain Hope Felder, ed., *Stony the Road We Trod: African American Biblical Interpretation* (Minneapolis: Fortress Press, 1991); Elizabeth Schüssler Fiorenza, *Bread Not Stone: The Challenge of Feminist Biblical Interpretation* (Boston: Beacon, 1984).

spirit in the scriptures and to bring voice to the gospel. Jesus lived and died and was resurrected in the past, and Jesus lives, dies, and is resurrected every day when violence against the vulnerable is resisted. Learning to see Jesus in the present is a way of remaining faithful to the Jesus the Bible proclaims as fellow-sufferer.

In practice, the hermeneutics of suspicion and confession work together to define the method for interpreting the scriptures. We must be suspicious of every individual and group who calls on the name of Jesus in such a way that their claims to power create systems of domination and evil. "Not everyone who says to me 'Lord, Lord' will enter the kingdom of heaven, but only the one who does the will of [God]" (Mt. 7:21). We must also hear the confessions of those for whom Jesus has been a liberating and empowering figure of religious piety. Finding a healthy balance between suspicion and confession is a challenging task.

Clarice Martin, a womanist New Testament scholar, describes this tension when she distinguishes between hermeneutics of truth and hermeneutics of effects.

> "[H]ermeneutics" is not simply a cognitive process wherein one seeks to determine the "correct meaning" of a passage or text. Neither are questions of penultimate truth and universality solely determinative of meaning. Also of essential importance in the interpretive task are such matters as the nature of the interpreter's goals, the effects of a given interpretation on a community of people who have an interest in the text being interpreted, and questions of cultural value, social relevance, and ethics.[19]

Martin continues by quoting from *The Responsibility of Hermeneutics*: "What is at stake in hermeneutics is not only the 'truth' of one's interpretation, but also the effects interpretation and interpretive strategies have on the ways in which human beings shape their goals and their actions."[20] This form of hermeneutics involves a rhythm or dynamic interplay between biblical texts from the canon and the lived faith and experience of communities of

---

[19]Clarice J. Martin, "Black Theodicy and Black Women's Spiritual Autobiography," in *A Troubling in My Soul: Womanist Perspectives on Evil and Suffering,* ed. Emilie M. Townes (Maryknoll, N.Y.: Orbis Books, 1993), 25.

[20]Martin here quotes from Roger Lunden, Anthony Thistleton, and Clarence Walhout, *The Responsibility of Hermeneutics* (Grand Rapids, Mich.: Eerdmans, 1985), x, xi.

resistance. An interpreter cannot understand Jesus by studying the Bible in isolation, but must also be immersed in a community of resistance that lives out faith in Jesus today. Without participation in resistance today, one cannot comprehend the spirit of Jesus' resistance in the past. The truth of Jesus in scripture is revealed in the ongoing resistance in the name of Jesus.

Another version of the hermeneutic circle can be described as a dialectic of preaching and pastoral care. The preacher preaches the gospel as the truth of the Bible. The people speak back to the preacher through the problems they bring in pastoral care. This relationship could be visualized as a circle, in which the practice of Christian life results in problems of pastoral care, which in turn yield questions for preaching; these questions call for Bible study, which in turn influences the practice of Christian life. The questions the people bring to the pastor in pastoral care represent the problems and questions that arise when the people try to live the gospel the preacher preaches within a particular historical and social context.

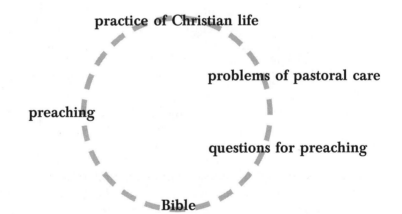

Some of these problems are a critique of the culture Christians live in—for example, individualism, hedonism, materialism. When members of a Christian community try to live according to love, justice, and the Holy Spirit, they come into conflict with the culture, and the people need pastoral care to sort out their confusion and strengthen their resolve to live according to the gospel. Some of these pastoral care problems are a critique of the gospel that is preached. That is, every preached gospel is only a partial description of the triune God who created the universe. Whatever accommodations the church and its preachers make to the world will create problems when the people try to live out the gospel. For example, when the people forgive perpetrators too quickly and endanger children and other family members, the preacher creates problems for the survivors. In this case, preaching distorts the real gospel in favor of the ways of the world. Therefore, a preacher/pastor must be able to hear both critiques–of culture and of the preached gospel (as distinguished from the whole gospel).

Sexual and domestic violence, including child abuse, is a new pastoral care issue, though not a new behavior, because of the denial and silence of church leaders. In what way is sexual and domestic violence a critique of the culture of the United States? In what way is family and interpersonal violence a critique of the preached (not the whole) gospel? We can see many examples of the way that such violence is a critique of the culture–sexism, racism, distorted sexuality, idealized marriage and family. I believe sexual and domestic violence is also a critique of the gospel that has been preached for many years. If we listen to the information we are getting from pastoral care, we hear distorted theological messages about male headship, nuclear families, parental authority, obedience to authority, suffering and forgiveness, and the nature of salvation.

In our preaching we have to pay attention to both the hermeneutics of truth (the relationship of preaching to Bible) and the hermeneutic of effects (the lived experience of the body of Christ). In terms of hermeneutical principles, we must ask whether a sermon is true as an interpretation of biblical texts, and also whether it is true when practiced in a particular historical and social context.

The Practice of Preaching the Bible to Perpetrators of Violence

In this section I make some practical suggestions about preaching the Bible when there are survivors and perpetrators of violence in the congregation.

1. *Pastoral Care as Worship.* As preachers and pastors, we should mention victims and survivors in our pastoral prayers and in sermon illustrations: abused children, teenagers facing dating

violence, battered women, adult survivors of child abuse, abused elders. In addition we should pray that the perpetrators of violence will see the sin in their lives and come to the church for accountability and repentance for their destructive behaviors. This is the extension of the loving care of God for all persons in all circumstances. When we bring such prayers and examples, religious leaders must be prepared with referral resources when members disclose their experiences with violence. All congregations must know the names and phone numbers of shelters for battered women, child abuse hotlines, elder abuse services, and rape counseling centers, so they are ready to respond to the pastoral care needs of their members.[21]

2. *Ethical Sermons on Family Violence.* As preachers and pastors, we need to take clear ethical positions about family violence and its root causes. The following are ethical positions recommended by the Center for the Prevention of Sexual and Domestic Violence.

(a) Violence and abuse have no place in the family. There is no legitimate justification for striking or otherwise abusing a family member. "People are not for hitting under any circumstances" is one way to express this value. Hitting or abusing another person is a violation of that person's very self. Violence sets up and enforces an imbalance of power based on physical strength. It minimizes the potential for trust, openness, and intimacy in the family. This includes a critical examination of corporal punishment of children which often serves as a justification for child abuse...

(b) A strong, vocal public stance against violence in the family is needed. Traditionally, violence committed against persons by strangers has been righteously condemned as a social evil that threatens our community. All too often, however, violence in the family has been

---

[21]For reading on responses to sexual and domestic violence, see the following: Carole Warshaw and Anne L. Ganley, *Improving the Health Care Response to Domestic Violence: A Resource Manual for Health Care Providers* (San Francisco: The Family Violence Prevention Fund, 1995); Carol J. Adams, *Woman-Battering* (Minneapolis: Fortress Press, 1994); Michael Paymar, *Violent No More: Helping Men End Domestic Violence* (Alameda, Calif.: Hunter House, 1993); Jeffrey L. Edleson and Richard M. Tolman, *Intervention for Men Who Batter: An Ecological Approach* (Newbury Park: Sage, 1992).

silently condoned and seen as no one else's business. Rarely has anyone publicly asserted that family life should not be violent and abusive...

(c) Families are [an] important social unit in our communities. Families, which come in many different forms, are the groupings from which we receive nurture and caring, through which we learn to share intimacy and trust. Many families do not fulfill these expectations. These families are in trouble. Many are literally being destroyed by violence and abuse...

(d) The problem of violence in the family is a social problem, not an isolated, individual problem. Personal incidents of violence in the family take place in a larger societal context...

(e) Preventing violence in the family means addressing the root causes of the problem...

(f) Education is a primary means of changing the destructive patterns of violence in the family...

(g) Sexuality is a very important dimension of every person's life...

(h) Intervention from the outside into families where abuse occurs is often needed to stop the abuse...

(i) Religious resources can be indispensable for family members who come from a religious background...

(j) Ultimately, violence in the family is about power and control...

(k) The sum of all efforts to address violence in the family in religious communities must be justice making.[22]

3. *Reevaluation of Certain Traditional Doctrines.* We need to listen to our own sermons, prayers, hymns, litanies, and all worship materials for how they will be heard by persons who are experiencing violence in their families, by persons who are in

---

[22]Marie Fortune, *Violence in the Family: A Workshop Curriculum for Clergy and Other Helpers* (Cleveland: Pilgrim Press, 1992), 18–22.

crisis right now because of violence, by adult survivors who are recovering from the effects of violence in their past, and by perpetrators of violence. The "least of these" principle of solidarity with the most vulnerable is crucial when preaching to perpetrators of violence.

A. Subordination of Women, Dominance of Men

Certain scriptures have a long history of being used to promote the subordination of women, and these texts are among the most frequent rationalizations by male abusers to promote violent domination of their partners.

> Wives, be subject to your husbands as you are to the Lord. For the husband is the head of the wife just as Christ is the head of the church, the body of which he is the Savior. Just as the church is subject to Christ, so also wives ought to be, in everything, to their husbands. (Eph. 5:22–24)

Thousands of sermons on this text have made the idea of male domination a part of the general religious piety of U.S. society. Male children have been socialized into this dominance throughout their lives in many ways. When men become husbands, they feel entitled to dominance and control, and when they feel threatened, they often feel justified to use violence to maintain their control. Fortunately, there is a spirited feminist discussion about the "household codes" that seem to contradict other scriptures that call for equality and freedom between women and men.[23] Other scriptures, for example, promote a view of gender equality between women and men.

> [F]or in Christ Jesus you are all children of God through faith. As many of you as were baptized into Christ have clothed yourselves with Christ. There is no longer Jew or Greek, there is no longer slave or free, there is no longer male and female; for all of you are one in Christ Jesus. And if you belong to Christ, then you are Abraham's offspring, heirs according to the promise. (Gal. 3:26–29)

---

[23]See Catherine Clark Kroeger in Adams and Fortune, 135–40.

Preaching equality and freedom in Jesus Christ for women and men will make a big difference for some couples, and eventually will begin to change the traditional themes of male dominance that have caused so much violence.

B. Subordination of Children in the Family

Certain scriptures have been used to promote absolute parental authority over children so that children have no ethical claim on adults for safety and protection. In *The Abuse of Power*, Karen gives witness to the effect of hearing the commandment to honor her parents, which kept her silent about the incest she experienced from her father.[24] Scriptures such as the following need to be carefully interpreted so that parents realize there are ethical limits to their authority. Parents cannot use violence to injure or sexually assault their children with permission of the Decalogue and the New Testament.

> Children, obey your parents in the Lord, for this is right. "Honor your father and mother"—this is the first commandment with a promise: "so that it may be well with you and you may live long on the earth." "And, fathers, do not provoke your children to anger, but bring them up in the discipline and instruction of the Lord. (Eph. 6:1–4)

The end of this scripture provides a soft guideline for parents, but it is not sufficient to counter the authority given to parents in the first lines. Perhaps such scriptures need to be set in contrast to Jesus' words about protecting the children because they are messengers from God.

> At that time the disciples came to Jesus and asked, "Who is the greatest in the kingdom of heaven?" He called a child, whom he put among them, and said, "Truly I tell you, unless you change and become like children, you will never enter the kingdom of heaven. Whoever becomes humble like this child is the greatest in the kingdom of heaven. Whoever welcomes one such child in my name welcomes me. If any of you put a stumbling block before

---

[24]Poling, *The Abuse of Power*, 35–48.

one of these little ones who believe in me, it would be better for you if a great millstone were fastened around your neck and you were drowned in the depth of the sea. Woe to the world because of stumbling blocks! Occasions for stumbling are bound to come, but woe to the one by whom the stumbling block comes! (Mt. 18:1–7)

C. Doctrines of Forgiveness and Reconciliation

Scriptures about forgiveness and reconciliation are frequently used by perpetrators to avoid the consequences of their violence and to coerce others to remain under their authority. Not infrequently, a perpetrator of violence goes to his pastor immediately after being arrested and asks for forgiveness. Because he appears remorseful and seems to be following the prescribed formula to activate God's grace, many pastors utter the words of assurance: "You are forgiven." Then the perpetrator pleads with the pastor to mediate reconciliation in order to "preserve the family." Counselors who work in shelters often say that the only time they see a pastor is when he or she follows the perpetrator to the shelter and asks the vulnerable woman and her children to return home for the sake of reconciliation. I have been in the presence of a perpetrator when he pressured his wife and child to forgive him as the Bible said they must. Scriptures such as the following, when interpreted outside a doctrine of sin and redemption, endanger vulnerable family members and support the denial and continued control of the perpetrator.

> For if you forgive others their tresspasses, your heavenly Father will also forgive you; but if you do not forgive others, neither will your Father forgive your trespasses. (Mt. 6:14–15)

Preaching on Matthew 18:15–20 and Luke 17:3–4 has also encouraged perpetrators to believe they can demand forgiveness. Fortunately, there is significant work being done on forgiveness and reconciliation that provides much needed reinterpretation of the history and intent of these scriptures. Perpetrators need help from good interpretations of the Bible to stop their sinful acts. A pastor in the video *Broken Vows* said to a perpetrator: "My job is not to tell your wife to come back to you to preserve the family, but to tell you that you have destroyed your marriage through violence. You have committed sin in the eyes of God, and you must repent to be saved. My responsibility is to tell her to seek life, not death." Perpetrators of violence need to be confronted and instructed that forgiveness for violence is a process of repentance and sanctification that will take many years within a disciplined fellowship of Christians.[25]

D. Doctrines of Obedience, Servanthood, and Suffering

Other scriptures that cause problems for perpetrators of violence are the texts that seem to identify being Christian with obedience, servanthood, and suffering. Unfortunately, perpetrators do not apply these scriptures to themselves, but they do try to enforce such behavior in those over whom they have power. Parents often expect children to obey them without question, to run errands and do chores for the parent's benefit, and to accept the suffering that comes with punishment and abuse. Men often expect to be head of the marriage and the house, to make decisions their partners have to obey, and they see nothing wrong with requiring service from women and often minimize any suffering that is caused by their violence. Scriptures such as the following can be misinterpreted by perpetrators to justify their violent behavior.

> For to this you have been called, because Christ also suffered for you, leaving you an example, so that you should follow in his steps. "He committed no sin, and no deceit was found in his mouth." When he was abused, he did not return abuse; when he suffered, he did not threaten; but he entrusted himself to the one who judges justly. He himself bore our sins in his body on the cross, so that, free from sins, we might live for righteousness; by his wounds you have been healed. For you were going astray like sheep, but now you have returned to the shepherd and guardian of your souls. (1 Pet. 2:21–25; see also Jn. 13:12–17; 14:15, 21; Mt. 20:24–28; 2 Cor. 1:5–7; Rom. 5:1–5; 1 Cor. 12:26; Jas. 2:15–17)

---

[25]See chapters by Frederick W. Keene and Marie Fortune in Adams and Fortune, 121–34, 201–6.

A perpetrator who thinks of himself as the "shepherd and guardian of...souls" could use this scripture to justify his power and control. He would also have support from a history of interpretation of such passages. The nineteenth-century cult of true womanhood specifically connected the suffering and obedience of Jesus to the preservation of Christian values by women who stayed home during the beginning years of industrialization. Women who remained undefiled, who loved and obeyed their husbands, and who endured suffering for the sake of the family were the repositories of Christian civilization. Although this language has been challenged by women's rights movements, the rhetoric is alive and well in many Christian homes and is explicitly supported by some evangelical preaching. Preachers need to be careful when preaching about Jesus' obedience and suffering that it does not support the violence and domination of parents over children and husbands over wives and children. Fortunately, much good work on resistance to violence is being developed by liberation theologians as an extension of the stories about Jesus.[26]

E. Doctrines of Surrogacy and Crucifixion

> But God proves his love for us in that while we were sinners Christ died for us. Much more surely then, now that we have been justified by his blood, will we be saved through him from the wrath of God. For if while we were enemies, we were reconciled to God through the death of his Son, much more surely, having been reconciled, will we be saved by his life. But more than that, we even boast in God through our Lord Jesus Christ, through whom we have now received reconciliation. (Rom. 5:8–11; see also 1 Tim. 2:5–6, Mt. 4:17)

Not infrequently, sexual and domestic violence results in permanent physical injury and sometimes death. More than 30 percent of the women who were murdered in the United States in 1995 were murdered by their intimate partners: husbands, ex-husbands, boyfriends, ex-boyfriends. Two thousand children every

---

[26]See Joanne Carlson Brown and Rebecca Parker, Emilie Townes, Rita Nakashima Brock and Marie Fortune in Adams and Fortune, 36–91.

year are murdered by their parents or other caregivers.[27] With so much violence in families, preachers must be careful how we talk about the crucifixion and about images of surrogacy, that is, the necessity of someone dying for someone else. The idea that persons in authority have the right of life and death over subordinates unfortunately appeals to the sadistic impulses of some perpetrators. Batterers who murder are often heard to say, "If I can't have her, no one else will." Abusive parents sometimes say to their children, "I will kill you if that is what it takes to make you listen."

This leads us to a difficult theological discussion of the purpose of Jesus' death and the theories of atonement. Did Jesus die as a sacrifice to accomplish the victory over evil, to satisfy the wrath of God, to demonstrate the cost of sacrificial love? In our theories of the crucifixion, are we encouraging victims and survivors to identify with Jesus, who died as a sacrifice for the sins of others? The gospel of Jesus, as I understand it, does not allow us to answer yes to these questions. Jesus came to seek and save the vulnerable, the lost, the abandoned; Jesus did not come to justify further abuse of those already abused. But given that preaching is sometimes used to justify evil and that some perpetrators are listening in order to justify their abuse of power, preachers of the gospel must courageously address these questions.[28]

Are survivors and perpetrators of family violence getting the sermons they need? In many cases, I think not. In this chapter we have reviewed some of the issues that arise when preachers are confronted with the presence of survivors and perpetrators of violence in their congregations. As preachers, we must assume that men and women in our congregations have engaged in violence within marriage, against children, and against elders and other family members. Our research suggests that 25 percent to 50 percent of the members of any congregation have experienced significant interpersonal violence in their lives and are struggling to survive this trauma. As we preach a God of love and power who cares for all people in all circumstances, we need to address this

---

[27]Dawn Bradley Berry, *The Domestic Violence Sourcebook* (Chicago: Contemporary Books, 1995). See also statistics collected by the Center for the Prevention of Sexual and Domestic Violence, Seattle, Wash.

[28]See Williams.

violence. The silence of the church is not an expression of the whole gospel of Jesus Christ.

We need to understand our history within the United States of ownership of persons, which developed to justify slavery of African Americans and was applied to women and children within families. We have abolished slavery and have voted for gender equality, but we have not yet purged our theologies of the ideas of domination and submission. This is a crucial theological and historical task as we try to reduce the violence in our families and in our society.

We need hermeneutical principles for interpreting certain biblical texts that mislead perpetrators into feeling justified in their violence. They rationalize their violent acts through submission of women and children in the family; through demands for forgiveness and reconciliation; through appeal to doctrines of obedience, servanthood, and suffering; and through misinterpretation of biblical emphasis on surrogacy and crucifixion. Fortunately, significant theological work is being done on these biblical texts and doctrines in light of what we are discovering about violence in our society.

The most important principle for preaching to survivors and perpetrators of violence is to listen to the witness of victims and survivors of violence. They have the authority of their experience as victims of violence, and they have the witness of their own religious experience. As preachers listen carefully in their pastoral care, we can begin a new dialogue about the meaning of the gospel for our time. And through such pastoral work, the saving stories of Jesus' life, death, and resurrection become real for another generation. In this work, God is glorified and the church becomes the body of Christ.

11

Is It Time to Forgive Yet?
A Sermon on Forgiveness

The following is a sermon that I wrote for a corporate worship experience. I explore the issue of forgiveness from the perspective of the gospel in dialogue with survivors of abuse. Although there are many questions that survivors raise, forgiveness is one of the most critical because they are often pressured to reconcile with their abusers when it is too dangerous to engage in such activities. Many Christians believe that forgiveness is the central meaning of the gospel, even though it is unevenly applied to those who are powerful and those who are vulnerable. The vulnerable are expected to forgive to make the community feel better, but the powerful are protected from accountability. This understanding of forgiveness endangers those who are vulnerable and makes the church complicit in male violence. In chapter 10 I discussed some of the hermeneutical issues involved in preaching about male violence. In this chapter, I give an example of how a preacher might address the issue of forgiveness with knowledge that survivors and perpetrators are present.

Luke 23:33–34 "When they came to the place that is called The Skull, they crucified Jesus there with the criminals, one on his right and one on his left. Then Jesus said, 'God, forgive them; for they do not know what they are doing.'"

It has been five years since Michael was sexually abused by his scout leader. Is it time for Michael to forgive him yet?

It has been twenty-five years since Michelle was incested by her father. Is it time for her to forgive her father yet?

It has been fifty years since the Holocaust in Germany. Is it time for the survivors to forgive the war criminals yet?

Recently I was asked to teach an adult forum at a local congregation on "The Language of Lent." The first word they gave me to discuss was forgiveness. This assignment forced me to do some study and soul-searching I had not planned to do.

For most of my life, forgiveness has been a background idea, one that was always there, but one I had not thought carefully about. Most Sundays we Christians begin worship by confessing our sins before God and receiving the assurance of God's love and forgiveness. Forgiveness is something I have asked for and received many times in my life. I believe, with Jeremiah, that when God made my life new, God forgave my iniquity and remembered my sin no more (Jer. 31:34).

I always assumed that I knew what forgiveness meant. Because we are all sinners before the righteousness of God, we cannot come before God without confessing our sins (Isa. 6:5). Unless God forgives our sin, how can we worship? As the Psalmist said, "God does not deal with us according to our sins, nor repay us according to our iniquities" (Ps. 103:10). Again the Psalmist said: "If you, O LORD, should mark iniquities, Lord, who could stand? But there is forgiveness with you, so that you may be revered" (Ps. 130:3–4). For all my Christian life, my faith in God has been rooted in the knowledge of God's forgiveness of my sins. Because God forgives me every day, I can forgive myself and dedicate my life in faithfulness to Jesus Christ.

But in recent years I have been troubled by stories that seemed to involve abuse of the doctrine of forgiveness. Some pastors advised their parishioners to forgive in ways that put them in danger. About five years ago a former student told me her story. Five days after she had broken off a five-year sexual relationship with a pastor who had abused her, Fran went to the pastor of her new church. Before she had even had a chance to make sense of what had happened to her, her pastor was talking to her about forgiving her abuser. In their very first conversation, she gave Fran a book called *Learning to Forgive*,[1] which listed ten things that happen to people when they don't forgive. The list included such

---

[1]Doris Donnelly, *Learning to Forgive* (Nashville: Abingdon Press, 1979).

things as: "They keep a controlling grasp on situations and people. They are pressured by lives of tension and stress. They probably shorten their lives. Their relationship with God is weakened." In other words, failure to forgive someone who has abused you is a sin with severe consequences for the self. Fortunately, Fran did not read the book and postponed forgiveness until "the later stages of her healing."[2] Her first responsibility was her own spiritual healing, not taking care of others by forgiving her abuser.

In an important study conducted in The Netherlands, forgiveness emerged as one of the most dangerous ideas for survivors. Annie Imbens and Ineke Jonker report the stories they heard: "Charlotte said that a pastor told her that it was extremely important that she maintain a good relationship with her uncle, after she had told him that her uncle had abused her, and how this had affected her life. Ellen was repeatedly told that she must stop ignoring her grandfather and should go to family gatherings in which he was included. When Mary Beth told her mother what her brother had done to her, [her mother] said, 'Will you forgive him? Please work things out between the two of you. I'll pray that it all works out.'"[3] I have heard such stories repeatedly.

Listening to stories of how pastors urged premature forgiveness in situations of abuse created a tension in my theology. Until recently my faith was based on the undeserved and unconditional forgiveness of God for my sins. Yet I was horrified to hear this doctrine used to minimize the consequences of incest in the family and sexual abuse by clergy. This dilemma forced me to think more deeply about this issue.

I am helped in my dilemma by some of the recent work in hermeneutics. I am thinking especially of the discussion about the relationship between the truth and effects of religious ideas. Lunden, Thistleton, and Walhout, in *The Responsibility of Hermeneutics,* say: "What is at stake in hermeneutics is not only the 'truth' of one's interpretation, but also the effects interpretation and interpretive strategies have on the ways in which human beings shape their goals and their actions."[4] In other words, those

---

[2]Marie Fortune, "Forgiveness: The Last Step," in *Violence against Women and Children: A Christian Theological Sourcebook,* ed. Carol Adams and Marie Fortune (New York: Continuum, 1995), 201–6.

[3]Annie Imbens and Ineke Jonker, *Christianity and Incest* (Minneapolis: Fortress Press, 1992), 235.

[4]Roger Lunden, Anthony Thistleton, and Clarence Walhout, *The Responsibility of Hermeneutics* (Grand Rapids, Mich.: Eerdmans, 1985), x, xi.

of us who preach are responsible not only for our exegesis of the scriptures but also for what the people hear and how it affects their daily lives. Sometimes I define pastoral theology as "the study of the beliefs and practices of the church to see whether they are liberating or oppressive in the everyday lives of believers and congregations." This kind of hermeneutics assumes that even the most precious doctrines of the church can be used for good or evil purposes. Part of the pastor's vocation is to listen to the Bible with one ear and to the people with the other (to paraphrase Karl Barth). Every sermon should ask two questions: What does the Bible say? and, What practical difference do ideas such as forgiveness actually make in the everyday lives of the people?

When I ask such questions about forgiveness, I realize that my theology of forgiveness has been part of the problem. When I seek God's forgiveness, I assume the perspective of the sinner who receives God's forgiveness as a result of grace freely given to me. When I hear Jesus' words from the cross, I listen as one of the soldiers who nailed Jesus to the cross. I do not consider the possibility that forgiveness can be used as a weapon against someone who is vulnerable. But hearing a demand that a child forgive her father after incest, or hearing a demand for premature forgiveness in response to the Oklahoma bombing or the Holocaust—that is turning forgiveness into a form of further abuse.

In thinking about forgiveness, I have come to two ideas that have helped me. First, because forgiveness can be turned into a new law, the church must be careful with its words and actions. When we pray the Lord's Prayer, "Forgive us our debts, as we also have forgiven our debtors" (Mt. 6:12), we should be praying for the grace of forgiveness from God so that we can be gracious to others in our life. How far from the spirit of this prayer we are if we demand forgiveness from others we have hurt. What a clever way to shift the responsibility for our sin to the shoulders of those we have hurt. This is not the grace and love of God, but the spirit of iniquity we had just asked God to forgive. In the parable of the unforgiving servant, the king was furious when he found out that the servant had not been gracious toward his servants after his own debt had been forgiven (Mt. 18:23–35). In the same way, demanding forgiveness from someone we have injured shows an absence of the forgiving spirit that God has offered us. On a practical level, this means that pastors must stop advising that their parishioners "learn to forgive" when they should be seeking justice instead. My first idea is that we should not make forgiveness a new law that oppresses by demanding it from those who are vulnerable.

My second idea is that the church must not make forgiveness just the responsibility of an individual. Rather, it should be a corporate process for the whole body of Christ.[5] We misuse the doctrine of forgiveness when we place the burden of responsibility solely on the individual who has been injured. One of the findings of the study *Christianity and Incest* is that many survivors of incest left the church because they were criticized for bringing up unpleasant subjects and were rejected because they were angry rather than forgiving toward their abusers. I believe this is a misuse of the doctrine of forgiveness. As the scriptures say, an injury to one member is an injury to the whole body of Christ. "If one member suffers, all suffer together with it" (1 Cor. 12:26, see also Rom. 12:15). I am struck by the corporate words of the Lord's Prayer—"Forgive *us our* debts, as *we* also have forgiven *our* debtors" (Mt. 6:12). This prayer about God's love should not increase the isolation and burden on individuals who have been hurt. Rather, the church as the body of Christ must bear the responsibility for justice and forgiveness in solidarity with those who have been hurt by sin and evil.

These two ideas help me: that forgiveness is not a law but grace from God; that forgiveness is the responsibility of the whole body of Christ, not primarily of individuals who have been injured.

So what are we to do? How do we maintain the focus on forgiveness as an expression of God's love as revealed in Jesus Christ, and also guard against its misuse against those who are vulnerable? Frederick W. Keene, in a recent article on forgiveness,[6] draws attention to the fact that Jesus himself does not forgive the soldiers who crucify him. He says: "God, *you* forgive them, for they do not know what they are doing." It is not Jesus' time to forgive yet. He is the victim of violence and not in a position to forgive. In the midst of his suffering, Jesus prays for God to be God and be

---

[5]This idea of corporate responsibility for forgiveness has been helpfully explored by David Livingston, *Healing Violent Men* (Minneapolis: Fortress Press, 2001).

[6]Frederick W. Keene, "Structures of Forgiveness in the New Testament," in Adams and Fortune, 121–34.

merciful to those who are committing violence. The prayer itself implies that in God's forgiveness, Jesus will be liberated from his suffering and raised into new life beyond the crucifixion.

This reading gives us a way to answer the question, "Is it time to forgive yet?" There is a time for justice and healing, and there is a time for forgiveness. At the right time God's love brings healing and justice, and at the right time God's love enables us to forgive. We all carry hurts and wounds from violation and violence from the past. When it is time to forgive, God will give us the grace and comfort of the Holy Spirit. In the meantime, when we know in our hearts that forgiveness is not yet possible, we can use Jesus' prayer in our own words.

> *O God of mercy and love. You know that it is not possible for me to forgive right now. I have a lot of healing and growing ahead of me before I can understand the fullness of your love for all people. But I pray that you have mercy on the soul of my abuser. For whatever is true, whatever is just, whatever is loving, I pray, that all violence on earth will cease, in the name of Jesus Christ. Amen.*

12

Beginning Thoughts on Rituals for Male Abusers

Hahnshik Min[1]

"Do the perpetrators of male violence deserve to worship God? Are they worthy of God's love?" These questions have haunted me since I started studying the issue of male violence against women and children. My encounter with them through books and articles has encouraged me to look at myself honestly and find my own tendency to be violent and abusive in my personal relationships. My study has also forced me to examine critically the male-centered religion and culture that makes male violence happen easily.[2]

Based on my research, I must assume that significant numbers of victims and perpetrators are worshiping in the congregation where I am serving now and will serve in the future, even though I do not know who most of them are. What is the proper pastoral

---

[1] Hahnshik Min is pastor of the Lamoine River Parish of the United Methodist Church and Macomb Korean Fellowship, and lives in Blandinsville, Illinois. He served as a research assistant in the office of James Poling during the 2000–2001 academic year. This paper was written for a class in healing liturgies taught by Ruth Duck at Garrett-Evangelical Theological Seminary.

[2] I do not have any professional relationship with abusers as a pastor. It is very likely, however, that I have met them in my life as the fathers of my friends, cousins, and children that I teach at church. The lack of firsthand experience with the perpetrators is the limitation of my thinking about worship with abusers. Even with this limitation, I hope to find God's healing presence with them, with myself, and with male-centered society, as we work to be nonviolent toward women partners. Another hope for this project is to make myself ready to deal with the issue of male violence in my future ministry.

response to this reality of male violence? How do I engage in general church planning and worship leadership with this newly acquired knowledge? Based on readings and personal observation, it is not unfair to say that the church has done little more than keep silent and blame the victims. Most church leaders have treated the topic of male violence as a taboo, unwilling to admit that it is happening in the church. Many of our church leaders have tended to believe stories from men and have ignored the voices of women, which has led to blaming women for being seductive.[3]

Another troubling response of the church to male violence is the misuse of the doctrine of forgiveness. In the previous chapter, James Poling explains how easily church leaders declare forgiveness to the perpetrators of violence and demand forgiveness from the vulnerable wives and children who were abused.[4] Most of the time, this is done without the process of confession and repentance on the part of the perpetrators. As a result, these inappropriate responses have covered and even promoted violence rather than providing healing for victims/survivors. It is sad to see the reality of a church where "survivors who are angry are frequently told to stay out of the church until they are willing to forgive. Many survivors have left the church for their own spiritual health, while men who abused them continue to serve in leadership positions."[5]

How can church leaders respond adequately to violent men in worship? What is the appropriate form of worship for them? In the last section of this chapter, I have designed a healing service for the perpetrators of male violence. In order to respond to this challenge, I have written the service for a select group of perpetrators who have been through significant experiences in

---

[3]In the case of Dora, who was sexually abused by an adult, Freud refused to see the violence of men. Instead, he concluded that Dora had sexual desire toward the men who abused her. His patriarchal attitude of Dora's case still seems to have a powerful and dangerous influence on present society and church. See James Poling, "Women and Male Dominance: The Case of Freud and Dora," in *Deliver Us from Evil: Resisting Racial and Gender Oppression* (Minneapolis: Fortress Press, 1996), 20–40, now chapter 7 of this book. A similar interpretation is found in Rosemary Ruether, *Women-Church: Theology and Practice of Feminist Liturgical Communities* (San Francisco: Harper & Row, 1985), 151.

[4]James Poling, "Preaching to Perpetrators of Violence," in *Telling the Truth: Preaching about Sexual and Domestic Violence,* ed. John S. McClure and Nancy J. Ramsay (Cleveland: United Church Press, 1999), 80, now chapter 10 of this book.

[5]James Poling, "Male Violence against Women and Children," in *The Care of Men,* ed. James Poling and Christie Neuger (Nashville: Abingdon Press, 1997), 158, now chapter 1 of this book.

accountability groups and are no longer in denial about the harm they have done to others and to themselves. This worship is a healing ritual that could take place toward the end of the treatment process. Assuming perpetrators' acceptance of the necessary stages of confession, repentance, accountability, and restitution, this service is designed to provide religious resources for their continued healing. To enhance the atmosphere of accountability, the envisioned worship will take place in a counseling center where follow-up work with them can be done. My lack of expertise on the issue of male violence makes it difficult for me to imagine an effective worship service for perpetrators in a regular church setting.

In consultation with James Poling, I have developed three principles for a healing service for perpetrators. First, the voice of victims/survivors must be present and predominant. The service intentionally gives power to the voice of victims/survivors so that they can serve as the context of accountability for their abusers. An immediate problem is that the church is not safe enough for survivors to be open and forthright about their experiences. Rather, they tend to be misunderstood, blamed for their own experience of abuse, and marginalized as emotionally unstable. The church must critically examine its treatment of victims/survivors and change the attitudes and behaviors that marginalize them instead of abusers. In worship services on domestic violence, the voices of survivors are given presence through their stories, songs, prayers, and poems. Such a process of planning requires an interdisciplinary team of feminist pastors and therapists who are committed to the domestic violence movement and know the literature so they can make the important decisions about what is appropriate for such a service. Chapter 10 lists several resources that could be used for this purpose.

Second, the ritual of confession and forgiveness of sins needs to be conditional. The worship must focus on the eschatological dimension, rather than present and completed declarations of healing and forgiveness. For example, the words, "you are forgiven," found in many traditional liturgies, must not be used, because they ignore the fact that forgiveness for abusers is a process of healing and accountability over time. Because of the church's notorious cheapening of forgiveness, it is important to emphasize the need for continued repentance for abusers and a commitment to be nonviolent. Fortunately, there are many biblical verses that emphasize the conditional nature of forgiveness. For example, Luke 17:3: "If another disciple sins, you must rebuke the offender, and *if there is repentance,* you must forgive." See chapter 11 for further discussion of forgiveness.

The third principle is the accountability of male worship leaders. The healing worship cannot be done only by males without input from the victims/survivors and their advocates. Before and after the actual worship, male leaders have to be open to correction from the standpoint of victims/survivors. This can be done through feedback sessions from female pastors and therapists who work regularly with victims/survivors. Organizing such accountability structures for worship leaders is one of the challenges of planning such a service because most male pastors are accustomed to being in charge without accountability to those who are marginalized.

Christian Healing Worship for Perpetrators

Christian healing has many faces, from highly dramatic services on TV to quiet and liturgical services of healing prayers. The diversity in Christian healing may be due to different ideas regarding what healing is. Tilda Norberg and Robert Webber explain that healing is neither magic nor the prediction of what God will do. It is neither a spiritual thrill nor a proof of faith or holiness, either for healer or persons who seek healing. Healing is the "process that involves the totality of our being—body, mind, emotion, spirit, and our social context—and that directs us toward becoming the person God is calling us to be at every stage of living and our dying."[6]

The United Methodist Book of Worship reminds us that in Greek the word *healing* shares the same root with *salvation* and *wholeness.*[7] The ministry of healing that Jesus entrusted to the church helps people be saved from the bondages that prevent them from becoming whole persons.

Ruth Duck explains that healing is the transformation that occurs when humans encounter God at the place of grief, pain,

---

[6]Tilda Norberg and Robert Webber, *Stretch Out Your Hand: Exploring Healing Prayer* (Nashville: Upper Room Books, 1998), 26–27.

[7]*The United Methodist Book of Worship* (Nashville: United Methodist Publishing House, 1992), 613.

suffering, and sickness, including such dimensions as physical healing, coming to peace about hurt and grief in life, changing attitudes, and prophetically challenging the community's attitudes and behaviors.[8]

The following healing worship liturgy for the perpetrators of male violence is based on these understandings of Christian healing. The healing service for the perpetrators is not intended to be magic or a prediction of what God will do in their lives. Instead, it is intended to help them confess and repent of their sins of violence, find God's loving presence in their effort to be nonviolent, and become the persons God created them to be. It is also intended to affirm their courage to admit and face their own violence, which many violent men want to avoid. In this way, we hope that they will be freed from their need to be violent and abusive, and eventually be whole persons. There is also hope for the transformation of male-centered church and society in their attitudes and behavior.

Order of a Healing Service for Perpetrators of Male Violence

Greeting

> I greet you in the name of Jesus Christ who gives us hope of healing.

> Jesus once said, "Those who are well have no need of a physician, but those who are sick; I have come to call not the righteous but sinners to repentance." (Lk. 5:31–32)

> By his healing ministry, Jesus brought wholeness to the persons who were once broken, blamed, and separated. With this hope in mind, let us open our hearts to the work of the Holy Spirit as we come before the presence of God in Jesus Christ.

> Hymn number 468, *United Methodist Hymnal,* "Dear Jesus, in Whose Life I See."

---

[8]Ruth Duck, handout in Christian Public Worship class, Dec. 5, 2000, 48.

Opening Prayer

Loving and tender God,
you have created us in your image to love one another.
Breathe into us your breath of life,
that we may become the people you dream us to be
in our relationship with our loved ones,
through Jesus Christ our Healer. Amen.

Poem

A poem written by a woman who has been sexually assaulted
by a man will be read.

O God,
through the image of a woman
crucified on the cross
I understand at last.
For over half of my life
I have been ashamed
of the scars I bear.
These scars tell an ugly story,
a common story,
about a girl who is the victim
when a man acts out his fantasies.
In the warmth, peace and sunlight
 of your presence
I was able to uncurl the tightly
clenched fists.
For the first time
I felt your suffering presence with me
in the event.
I have known you as a vulnerable baby,
as a brother, and as a father.
Now I know you as a woman.
You were there with me
as a violated girl
cut in helpless suffering.
The chains of shame and fear
no longer bind my heart and body.
A slow fire of compassion and forgiveness
is kindled.

My tears fall now
for man as well as woman.

....

You were not ashamed of your wounds.
You showed them to Thomas
as marks of your ordeal and death.
I will no longer hide these wounds of mine.
I will bear them gracefully.
They tell a resurrection story.[9]

Scripture

Acts 9:1–9

This is the story of Paul's conversion, which can perhaps serve as inspiration for those who want to repent of violence, experience conversion, and be transformed by God into a faithful disciple of Jesus Christ.

Sermon

Paul was a violent man who persecuted the Christians and contributed to their death. Acts 8:1 says that Paul approved of the mob action that martyred Stephen, and Acts 9:1 says that he breathed threats and murder against the disciples. Acts 9 is the story of his conversion. He did not see his own violence as a problem until a light from heaven struck him down. It may be similar to the experience of being arrested and exposed for one's violent behaviors against a vulnerable person. Some of us need to be struck down before we are able to see the harm we are causing to other people and to the new community of Jesus Christ. Before, Paul could see only the benefits of violence, but afterward he saw a new way. He changed from one way of life to a completely different way. Repentance means turning completely around and going in a different direction, which is what is required of violent perpetrators.

It took Paul some time before he could integrate his conversion into a new ministry. He spent many days in Damascus with a mentor, Ananias. Before they met, Ananias was afraid and said to the Lord, "I have heard from many about this man, how

---

[9]This poem is taken from Carrie Doering, *Taking Care: Monitoring Power Dynamic and Relational Boundaries in Pastoral Care and Counseling* (Nashville: Abingdon Press, 1995), 11.

much evil he has done." Ananias also mentioned Paul's authority to persecute the disciples of Jesus. But the Lord responded: "I myself will show him how much he must suffer for the sake of my name." After a process of introspection and reorganization of his life, Paul advocated the way of love rather than violence.

There are dangers in this scripture that have to be clearly pointed out. For many Christians, Acts 9 has been a model of instant conversion and new insight. At one moment Paul was acting against God through violence, and the next moment he was a new man. This is probably a misinterpretation of Acts 9. In any case, the conversion process for perpetrators of violence is long and hard. It requires confession, repentance, restitution, and accountability to the larger community. Even if God did convert Paul in an instant, it is not a good model for the rest of us, who need many years of reeducation and accountability. The gospel, or "good news," in this story is that conversion is possible, that even perpetrators can seek and find new life free from violence toward others.

The sermon will relate the story in the scripture to the situation of the perpetrators attending the worship. The sermon will help them reflect on their violent behaviors that harmed others, the social consequences of being arrested and held accountable, their resistance to being nonviolent, the promise of healing, and the hope of participating in Jesus' ministry in the future. As mentioned above, however, it is important to emphasize in the sermon that their healing is not complete at the present moment, but that they face a long process of reeducation and healing in order to stop being violent. They will hear the good news that Jesus' healing presence will be with them in their fight against their violent attitude and behavior.

I want to affirm their courage to face their destructive behavior and seek treatment. Poling writes, "Facing the reality and horror that one has molested a child is one of the most difficult things any man can ever do. It means facing the damage one has done to another, and facing the emptiness in oneself that led to such destructive behavior...I find it inspiring. If child molesters can have the courage and hope to seek treatment in order to get better, then I can have hope in the world where violence seems out of control."[10] For this reason, the courage of perpetrators of violence needs to be affirmed.

The sermon must also mention the responsibility of recovering perpetrators to prophetically challenge the larger society that tolerates high levels of violence against women and children. Like Paul, part of their calling to new life must include helping to make society safer for all people and confronting the continuing acts of violence of other men.

Witness

A confessional witness will be prepared by one or two of the perpetrators attending the worship. A man who has experienced an accountability group for batterers or sexual offenders over an extended period of time will be able to talk about the incidents of abuse that created the crisis in his life and the importance of commitment to a long healing process. The personal witness can include his religious experience of confession, repentance, accountability, and restitution.

Prayer of Confession

One: Most loving God, she has been severely wounded,
   All: It was we who wounded her.
One: Hurt beyond words with the betrayal of trust,
   All: It was we who hurt her.
One: With physical violence and abuse, and the absence of love.
   All: We were abusive and violent.
One: Bless her with the abundance of your love,
   All: As we repent our sins.
One: Restore love and trust in her,
   All: As we decide not to be violent any more.
One: And forgive us our sins,
   All: So that we may find hope to be better persons, through Jesus Christ. Amen.[11]
(Moment of silence for personal prayer.)

---

[10]James Poling, "Social and Ethical Issues of Child Sexual Abuse," *American Baptist Quarterly* 8, no. 4 (1989): 264, now chapter 2 in this book.

[11]This responsive prayer of confession is adapted with some changes from "Prayer for a Child Who Has Been Molested," in Vienna Anderson, *Prayers of Our Hearts: In Word and Action* (New York: Crossroad, 1991), 33.

Word of Hope

One: Hear the good news.

"Violence shall no more be heard in your land,
devastation or destruction within your borders...
[F]or the LORD will be your everlasting light,
and your days of mourning shall be ended."
(Isa. 60:18, 20)

All: Thanks be to God for the message of hope!

Laying on of Hands

Let us pray.

O God, as we come to be touched by your healing
hands, help us open our hearts to the work of the
Holy Spirit.

Bless the hands that gently touch our bodies, that we
may feel your touch through them.

Bless all of us, that we may find strength to be
nonviolent in Jesus' love. Amen.

*(Worship leader and others in worship will surround each
person and lay hands on him. The worship leader will say
the following)*

[Name], we lay our hands on you in the name of the
Creator God, Jesus Christ, and the Holy Spirit.

May the Holy Spirit breathe on you the breath of new
life, that you may be the person God created you to
be. Amen.

Sharing Peace

Hymn number 501, *Chalice Hymnal,* "There Is a Balm in Gilead"
(stanzas 1 and 2)

Sending Forth with Blessing and Hope

May God, who created you in God's image, continue to
shape you.

May Jesus Christ, who healed the sick, bring you
wholeness.

May Holy Spirit, the breath of life, give you new life.

With this hope and promise of God in your heart, go in
peace.

INDEX

205